DEATH'S LAW

'I've heard tell you're a demon, a Duaiteoiri.' Nevin
looked up from his hands, which had finally
stopped shaking, and stared directly at the bard.
The figure was as he remembered him; tall, thin,
with sharp, harsh features, and high cheek-bones.
Only his eyes had changed. They had once been
black, but were now the indeterminate colour of
metal – and like metal, mirror-like and reflective.
The metallic eyes robbed his face of all expression,
all traces of humanity.

Paedur smiled with what seemed to be genuine
amusement.

'So I've heard. And before you're much older
you'll hear me called a god, a butcher, a devil, a
myth, and even Death himself.'

'And what are you?' Aeal asked suddenly, his
voice cold.

Death's Law

Tales of the Bard
Volume Three

Michael Scott

SPHERE BOOKS LIMITED

SPHERE BOOKS LTD

Published by the Penguin Group
27 Wrights Lane, London W8 5TZ, England
Viking Penguin Inc., 40 West 23rd Street, New York, New York 10010, USA
Penguin Books Australia Ltd, Ringwood, Victoria, Australia
Penguin Books Canada Ltd, 2801 John Street, Markham, Ontario, Canada L3R 1B4
Penguin Books (NZ) Ltd, 182–190 Wairau Road, Auckland 10, New Zealand

Penguin Books Ltd, Registered Offices: Harmondsworth, Middlesex, England

First published in Great Britain by Sphere Books Ltd, 1989

Printed and bound in Great Britain by
Richard Clay Ltd, Bungay, Suffolk
Filmset in 10½/12 Monophoto Times

For Siobhan and John
without whose help . . .

List of the Gods

PANTHEON OF THE OLD FAITH

Lady Adur   Goddess of Nature; sister of Quilida
Alile   The Judge Impartial; Judger of Souls
Bainte   Winged messengers of Death, servants of Mannam
Baistigh   Lord of Thunder
Buiva   God of War and Warriors, the Warrior
Cam   God of Bridges
C'lte, Qua'lte and Sa'lte   The Triad of Life
Coulide Dream-Maker   God of Dreams
Lady Dannu   Prime female deity
Ectoraige   God of Learning and Knowledge
Faurm   Sea God; brother of Faurug
Faurug   The Nightwind
Feitigh   The Windlord, father of Faurm and Faurug
Fiarle   The Little God of Icy Spaces
Hanor and Hara   The first Great Gods
Huide   The Little God of Summer Rain
Luid   Fire Sprite
Lady Lussa   Goddess of the Moon
Maker and User   The Early Gods
Mannam of the Silent Wood   The Lord of the Dead
Maurug   The Destroyer
Nameless God   God of Madness and Delusion
Nusas   The Sun God
Ochrann   God of Medicine and Healing
Oigne and Uide   Gods of Cities
Quilida   Goddess of Growth
Shoan   The Smith

Sleed   The Maker of Mountains
Snaitle   The Cold God
The Stormlord   Unnamed God of Storms
Taisce   The Dewspreader
Tatocci   God of Fools
Uimfe   The Lord of Night
Visslea   The Spirit of the Mists

GODS OF THE NEW RELIGION

Aiaida   Lord of the Sea Wind
Hercosis   The Dreamlord; one of the twelve Trialdone
Hirwas   God of Far Seeing; one of the twelve Trialdone
Sheesarak   The Destroyer; one of the twelve Trialdone
Lady Asherat   The Taker of Souls; one of the twelve Trialdone
Ghede   Lord of the Beasts; one of the twelve Trialdone
Kishar Stormbrother   God of Storms
Kloor   God of War
Libellius   God of Death
Quatatal   Bronze Sun God
Tixs   Bat God; a minor godling
Trialos   The New God

OTHER GODS

Aonteketi
   Six great birds that were once Gods of the Pantheon
   1 Scmall: The Spirit of the Clouds
   2 Kloca: Lord of Stone and Rock
   3 Aistigh: Lord of Subtle Harmonies; brother of Danta
   4 Danta: Lord of Verse
   5 Dore: Lord of Smiths (silver and goldsmiths)
   6 Fifhe: Lady of Beasts; daughter of Lady Adur
Bor   The Man God
Chriocht the Carpenter   Halfling carpenter of the Gods of the
Pantheon; brother of Toriocht

Lutann   Demon God

Quisleedor   Life Child of Sleed, the Maker of Mountains (*see* Pantheon of the Old Faith)

Sinn   Mist Demon, Sun God

Toriocht the Smith   Halfling smith to the Gods of the Pantheon

PRIMAL SPIRITS

Chrystallis   The wind that blew through the soul of the One; the Soulwind

The One   The first being

The Three Cords   Disruption, Annihilation and Chaos

Duaite   Collective name for evil spirits; Duaiteoiri (singular)

Auithe   Collective name for good spirits; Auitheoiri (singular)

Death's Law

Tales of the Bard

Prologue

Call him Kingmaker . . .

So Paedur the Bard took a bandit prince and made him an Emperor against all the odds, helping to found the famous and ultimately the infamous line of Kutor.

There have been many accounts of that time and the bard's role in the uprising that followed and, as is usual with partisan histories, they all differ. For history, like truth, is a matter of perspective, politics and religion. What is agreed upon is that the new ruler's early days were not happy ones. Many did not accept the overthrow of the old order, especially the noble houses – the Twelve Families – who rightly felt threatened by the appearance of the Renegade and his rebel army.

To compound the new ruler's troubles, Geillard had escaped and there were rumours of his appearance everywhere, and the most persistent rumour – that he was raising a huge army to overthrow the Usurper – grew in the telling, as did the deposed Emperor's reputation, making him into something of a tragic hero.

Even the very elements – which had been thrown into turmoil by the Cataclysm – seemed to conspire against the new Emperor's rule. After a blistering summer and mild, mellow autumn, the Cold Months were bitter, and famine and disease walked hand-in-hand with their master, Death. Refugees made their way from all across the devastated nations to the capital, stretching already strained and limited resources to their limits. Stories of rebellion and uprising abounded, and Geillard's followers fomented trouble for their own ends.

Karfondal was a powder-keg awaiting a spark.

There are accounts too which show that the very Planes of Existence were in turmoil. The armies of Faith and Religion had gathered, facing each other across the chequered fields of Ab-Apsalom, awaiting the final call to war. But, mindful of the destruction of previous conflicts, representatives of the two beliefs had met and resolved to set in motion the Death's Law, wherein it is stated that men are but the playthings of the gods, pieces to be moved at will.

And so the Gods looked to their agents and followers, and this was a battle without rules, without codes of conduct or chivalry. But the Gods of the New Religion were fighting for their very existence, and in their last-ditch attempt to secure the belief of Man – and hence increase their strength before the coming battle – they had promised and delivered miracles. And the tide of belief, which had swung back towards the Old Faith with the appearance of Kutor and the bard, Paedur, was now swinging to the Religion once again. A tangible religion, with real gods, promising succour, found belief far more quickly than the Old Faith, with its mysterious and sometimes fickle Pantheon.

And the bard, the one person who could possibly swing that balance back to the Pantheon, had disappeared.

Life of Paedur, the Bard

1 Chopt Moon

They are the beasts that walk like man; they are the men that act like beasts; their food of preference is human flesh. They are the Chopt . . .
Lilis' Geographica

The beast bared its fangs, threw its shaggy head back and turned large round eyes to the clear night sky. The moon was full, the Lady Lussa riding the heavens in all her glory, while the Nightstars wove their arcane patterns around her. The silver light sparkled on the snow-covered ground, turning the night into a semblance of day, but deepening the shadows beneath the trees to pitch.

In the distance, a dog howled, a single cry of absolute loneliness. It was taken up almost immediately by a second and then a third dog, baying their hunger and chill to the bitter night.

The beast beneath the tree moved, its tongue clacking against its teeth in command, and then it was as if every shadow took life as dozens of the huge creatures moved out from the darkness. The moonlight shone on matted hair and rusted mail, torn leathers and scraps of armour culled from a score of lands and a century of years. Only the weapons, the huge swords, the clubs, and tridents and heavy broad-bladed knives were new and clean.

Without command, without sound, the creatures loped down towards a long snaking black line that cut through the snow-locked countryside, north to south, the Mion River. Throughout the day the guards from the nearby castle had painstakingly kept it unfrozen, clearing the ice with bonfires and axes, but the bitter night and Snaitle, the Cold God, were claiming it once again.

. The creatures paused on the edge of the sluggish river, watching it, gauging the thickness of the ice, and then looking up at the Lady Lussa, judging the time. And then they lay down on the iron-hard ground and rolled in the snow, covering their shaggy pelts and scraps of clothing with snow, becoming one with the ground. Even from a short distance, they were invisible. Deep yellow eyes moved from the river to the moon, watched the Lady Lussa move sedately across the heavens, moving towards the dawn.

But there was time aplenty and they could wait.

Thomas yawned hugely, stretching his arms wide away from his body, feeling his stiffened muscles crack. He glanced into the sky, gauging the time from the moon. Awhile longer and the Lady Lussa would dip low in the heavens; a little later and the Grey Lights, the precursors of the dawn, would ride across the heavens, and morning would follow.

The slender young man pulled off his thick mittens and dug the heels of his hands into his eyes, rubbing away the grittiness. He had been at his post since midnight and the glare from the moonlight on snow had set his head pounding and he felt vaguely nauseous. He shifted his pike, looking into the polished metal head; his eyes were bloodshot and raw. Well, at least he could report to the physician when he came off duty, and he would be sure to be excused. White-blindness took more warriors in the Northlands than any Chopt blade or bandit arrow. If he was excused sentry duty he would probably be placed on a river watch, ensuring the ice didn't freeze the Mion solid, making a bridge for the beasts to come across.

Thomas shivered in his furs; the night was bitterly cold, and like as not the river had already frozen over. He stamped his feet and poked his head over the edge of the merlons, looking down on the Mion River – and a broad-bladed knife neatly severed his throat . . .

Solan the Gateman looked up, head tilted to one side, hands automatically reaching for his pike; something had cracked beyond the gates. And Solan, who had watched the gates of Castle Nevin for nearly fifteen cold winters, knew all the sounds of the night. He sat in his tiny hut just inside the gate with a fire going all the year round – and that fire was his companion, his comfort. He needed no-one else, wanted no-one, was content

4

with his tiny scrap of flame. He controlled the gate, admitting –
or refusing – those who had come after sunset. And in the Northlands, especially in the Cold Months, the castle was always sealed
tight as the distant mountains burned red with the last rays of
the dying Nusas. And to be locked out meant death.

He heard it again, a click, a crack, a creak; something strange,
an odd sound; something he couldn't identify. Reason told him
it could be ice falling from the gate, or freezing in the hinges. It
could have been a stone shattering with the ice, or the river
freezing over, and then breaking again as an undercurrent pulled
away the ice-skin . . . but Solan knew all the sounds of the night
and the ice – and this was none of them.

The Gateman shuffled out of his tiny gatehouse and leaned
against the tall wooden gates, careful not to touch it with his
bare flesh. He heard nothing. Standing well back and using the
butt of his pike, he slid back the rectangular viewing slot cut into
the right-hand door. He could see nothing. Frowning, Solan
shuffled forward, his feet making hardly any sound in the snow-
covered courtyard; he should be able to see . . .

Suddenly the viewing slot was clear, and he realised – too late
– that someone had been standing up against it. He opened his
mouth to scream – and a slender spear punched through the slot
and took him through the mouth . . .

Count Nevin of Castle Nevin pushed the ornate chart across the
polished table towards Aeal, his Captain of Bowmen. The bulky,
grey-haired count tapped the vellum with a stubby finger.

'I say we raise an army and carry the fight to them before it's
too late. The beasts are becoming bolder, losing what respect
and fear we fought so hard to instil. We've had no word out of
Thusal for nearly two moons now, and we can only assume that
either it is held or the roads are held.'

'The roads more like', Aeal said softly. He was a tall slender
southerner from Talaria, his pale hair and eyes almost exactly
the same colour. He turned the chart of the Northlands with his
calloused fingers and touched the hieroglyph for Thusal, the
northernmost town of the Seven Nations. 'It is a walled town,

5

moated, with its own wells, plentiful supplies of food and grain, with physicians, mages and priests, as well as one legion of the Northern Guard.' He smiled, showing small square teeth, 'it cannot be taken.'

Count Nevin touched the patch covering his left eye and grinned fiercely. 'Of course it can be taken. Every town, every castle can be taken.'

Aeal nodded briefly. 'But we would have heard, or our mage would have picked up the signs.' He chewed on a thumbnail, looking at the chart. 'What we need is a Chopt base, a town, a village, caves, whatever . . . if we had that then I would consider an assault. But without that information . . .' He shrugged. They both knew what would happen. The weather would claim too many of the men and then the Chopt would complete the decimation. It would be suicide leading an army into the Northlands on a scouting foray.

Count Nevin rested his hands flat on the golden wood of the table, drawing strength from the antique. It had been in his family since Nevin Ironhand had commissioned it on the occasion of his handfasting to Maggan, the daughter of Thurle of the Two Forests. Chriocht the Carpenter, one of the mythical Crinnfaoich, had created the table from a single piece of wood, and invested it with a little of the Old High Magic – which Nevin had learned of only recently. And now, when he was troubled, he drew some consolation – and indeed, seemed to find the strength he sought – from the ancient table. 'Have there been more sightings?' he asked.

Aeal nodded. 'We sent out three men,' he said quietly, 'two returned. They both had sighted Chopts, sometimes singly, but also in groups of twos and threes. And you know the saying, "For every one you see . . ."'

Nevin nodded bitterly. For every one you saw there were a dozen you didn't.

'All the outlying farms that are still inhabited reported losses of livestock,' Aeal continued slowly, moving his hands slowly across the cracked vellum of the old map, 'and there have been some killings.' He looked across at the old count. 'Without any shadow of a doubt, they are massing for an attack . . .'

Nevin leaned forward on the polished wood of the table, his face contorted in anger . . . and then suddenly yelped in pain. He lifted his hands, looking at the palms; both were bright red, as if they had been burned!

Aeal touched the ancient wooden table; the wood felt smooth and cool to his fingers. But when he looked back at the count, he saw sudden panicked comprehension in the old man's single eye. 'We're being attacked! The castle is under attack!'

Uncomprehending, Aeal stared at him.

'The castle is under attack,' Nevin insisted, 'the magic in the wood reacts when the dwelling containing the table is threatened.'

Without waiting for anything further, Aeal grabbed his bow, which was propped against a chair, and ran for the door, the count behind him. As they raced out into the corridors, the booming gong of the alarm sounded – only to be abruptly silenced almost immediately.

They looked at one another and then, realising what had happened, they separated, their priorities altered. Their worst fears had been realised – the Chopts were within the castle!

Nevin raced down the deserted corridors, suddenly feeling more frightened now than he had been at any time in his life. The Chopts frightened him – they frightened any normal man – but doing battle with them in the snow-covered ice-fields was one thing, fighting a bloody hand-to-hand in the corridors of his own castle was quite another.

He rounded a corner – and ran straight into one of the creatures!

The Chopt was huge. It stood a head and shoulders taller than the count and was broad in proportion. Its face was flat and brutish, with a low sloping forehead and a weak, receding chin. Its nose was flat, with wide flaring nostrils and its canines were pronounced. Its eyes were deep set and a deep bilious yellow. And it stank.

Nevin hit out on instinct, his left hand slamming into the creature's throat, and as it fell forward and down, he brought his clenched fists down on the base of its neck. The snap of its spine was distinct.

Nevin grabbed the broad-bladed knife from its body and raced for his own chambers. Dimly now he could hear the growing sounds of battle, and then, rising above the din, the terrifying, nerve-shattering battle-howl of a Chopt. It was taken up and repeated again and again until it was a sustained wail of absolute viciousness. The castle walls took the sound and bounced it, until it sounded as if the very stones themselves were crying.

And then rising above the wall came another sound, a sound which twisted the old man's lips into a thin smile: the sound of screamers – broad-headed arrows, grooved and slit so that they whistled as they flew. At a hundred paces they could punch an armoured knight clean from the saddle, and he could only guess what effect they would have on the lightly armoured beasts in the confines of the castle.

The iron-studded door of his chambers was locked. He rattled the handle and called his wife's name softly, unwilling to draw attention to himself. 'Nessa . . .? Nessa . . .?'

There was no sound from within.

'Nessa . . .?'

Somewhere further down the corridor he heard a sound that could only be the click of claws on stone.

Nevin rattled the lock. 'Nessa!' He knew if he was caught here in the open, he was dead.

'Nessa!'

A Chopt rounded the corner, and stopped, looking at him, its yellow eyes gleaming. It was almost naked, although its matted body hair hid most of its flesh. It carried a wood and bone trident, the tips of which were barbed and were ominously dark stained. Poisoned, Nevin guessed, although that would be unusual, for poison would taint the meat and the beasts preferred their meat fresh. The creature bared its fangs, and a long, sickly red tongue appeared. The Chopt's mouth worked, tendrils of saliva appearing to run down its chin, and then it mouthed a single word. 'Nevin!'

'Nessa!' The count pounded on the door. 'Nessa, for Faith's sake!'

The Chopt moved the trident in its hand and then slowly, almost deliberately, it moved down the corridor, its mouth twisting, its thick lips moving back from its yellowed teeth in a rictus that might have passed for a smile.

Nevin put his back to the door and lifted the Chopt knife in his hand, weighing it for balance. But against the creature's longer reach and the trident, he had no chance.

And the door opened!

The old man fell through to sprawl on the floor and the door slammed, the bolts ramming home. And from the corridor there was a scream of rage, a solid thump and then the barbed tips of the trident broke through the solid wood.

Nevin scrambled to his feet, grabbed his wife, and pulled her towards the canopied bed. 'Use the Hole, quickly. Stay there, whatever happens,' he warned ominously. The door shook in its frame as the beast launched itself against it. He took her small face in his hands, brushing the strands of pale red hair from her eyes and kissed her lips gently. 'Please,' he said, 'do this for me.' And then he struck the wooden panelling beside the bed with the flat of his hand. Without a sound it swung open, revealing a tall, rectangular-shaped room. Nevin shoved his wife unceremoniously into the opening and then closed the panel silently, listening carefully for the click of the lock.

The door shook again and then a long crack appeared in the wood, running top-to-bottom. Another blow and the door would split. With no time to pull on his armour, the count grabbed his metal gauntlets, and lifted a morningstar off its clips on the wall. Then from beneath the bed he pulled a cocked and loaded crossbow. He smiled, remembering how his wife had always derided him for his stupidity and foolishness; well, that same stupidity might just save their lives.

The Chopt launched itself aganst the door again, its calloused feet striking dead centre where it had cracked, all its weight behind it. The door split and was simultaneously ripped from its hinges, catapulting the beast into the room . . . and Nevin nailed it to the floor with a broad-headed bolt.

'Stay where you are,' Nevin called to Nessa and then, grabbing

9

a quiver of bolts, he hurried from the room, wondering how the battle went.

Aeal had fought his way out of the confines of the castle and into the courtyard where he, with a trio of his bowmen at his back were slowly but steadily forcing the Chopts back towards the walls. The beasts had no defence against the archers, and without bows, arbalests or catapults of their own, they couldn't return fire.

But the archers were low – very low – on arrows.

Aeal paused to take stock. A decade of arrows between the four of them, and there were fifteen – no, sixteen – of the beasts left. So, even if they managed to make every arrow count, they were still left with six of the Chopts to face. And the archers were only armed with knives! Aeal drew an arrow, nocked, pulled and fired all in one smooth movement. It struck a Chopt high in the chest, lifting him off the ground, pushing him backwards into the slushy, crimson snow. He pulled another arrow, concentrating solely on choosing a target, holding and firing; he didn't want to think what would happen when they ran out of arrows.

The corridors were like a butcher's slaughtering house, red with blood and meat. A battle-weariness the count had not felt in many years settled over him as he kept stumbling across dead and mutilated servants and old retainers. There was a bitter satisfaction when he occasionally came across a slain Chopt, but these were too few compared with those he had lost.

But where were the guards? Surely he hadn't lost a full century to the creatures?

There was a shouted command and he heard the whine of screamers, the noise surprisingly brief, indicating that the enemy was close. Nevin, following the noise of the screamers, raced down the stairs from the upper floor and out into the courtyard in time to see Aeal draw his last arrow, pull and release in one smooth movement, dropping another of the creatures with a shot through the eye. Their arrows spent, the archers then threw down their useless bows and drew their knives, forming a simple wedge, with Aeal at the point, awaiting the attack.

With an exultant scream, the six remaining Chopts charged.

Nevin dropped one with a crossbow bolt, but he knew he wouldn't have time to reload before the creatures reached the archers. With a battle cry he hadn't used in a quarter of a century, he raced towards his men . . .

. . . And the Lady Lussa disappeared behind the thickening clouds that heralded the dawn, plunging the courtyard into a gritty vague darkness . . .

There was movement at the rear of the enemy; a shape, black with a thread of silver, darker, more solid than the surrounding night. It appeared briefly behind a Chopt, the silver thread moved blurringly fast to and fro, and then it moved to another – again the silver rose and fell. The shape had moved on to the third creature before the first actually fell to the ground, its spine laid open to the bone. The second fell, a similarly destructive wound opening its back. Another Chopt turned, the shadow shifted, the silver flashed in the wan light, and the creature fell back, its chest opened in a huge x-shaped wound. The two remaining Chopts turned to the shadow maker – and the silver thread rose, moved left to right, and then to the left and right again. The creatures fell, both their chests opened in a huge gaping wound, from waist to shoulder.

In the long silence that followed, the only sound was the trickling of the beast's blood, hissing slightly on the bloody slush.

And then Nevin cranked the crossbow and loaded a quarrel. He pointed it at the vague shadow shape. 'Who are you?' he demanded, unable to disguise the tremor in his voice.

Aeal pulled a guttering torch from its bracket and swung it to bring it to blazing life. He lifted it high, throwing milk-yellow light across the courtyard and the bodies.

The shadow shifted and then the silver thread moved again, but slowly this time, a gleaming half-moon of silver appearing, light dancing from the runes etched into it, and before the figure stepped into the light and pushed back the hood of its long travelling cloak, Nevin and Aeal had said the name and title.

'Paedur . . .'

'. . . the Bard.'

2 Threat

The circle turned. Once again the bard quit the security of the Imperial Court and took to the roads . . .

Life of Paedur, the Bard

'I've heard tell you're a demon, a Duaiteoiri.' Nevin looked up from his hands, which had finally stopped shaking, and stared directly at the bard. The figure was as he remembered him; tall, thin, with sharp, harsh features, and high cheek-bones. Only his eyes had changed. They had once been black, but were now the indeterminate colour of metal – and, like metal, mirror-like and reflective. The metallic eyes robbed his face of all expression, all traces of humanity. He had taken off his long furred cloak, and now wore a vest of fine link-mail over a shirt of purple cotton that had seen much wear. His leggings of deep brown were scuffed and stained almost black, and he wore an ancient pair of high black boots. He looked like any other road-weary traveller, but one had only to look at his face to realise that this was no ordinary tramping bard.

Paedur smiled with what seemed to be genuine amusement. 'So I've heard. And before you're much older, you'll hear me called a god, a butcher, a devil, a myth, and even Death himself.'

'And what are you?' Aeal asked suddenly, his voice cold. The archer was terrified of the bard and what he represented. He almost preferred the Chopts to this creature; at least he knew them, knew they bled if they were cut, died if the wound were serious enough. He wasn't so sure about the bard.

The bard turned to look at Aeal, sitting across from Nevin, and the smile faded from his thin lips. His eyes – flat and reflective, like polished metal – took the light from the candles and blazed warm gold. 'I am a man,' he said simply.

Aeal brushed strands of pale hair from his eyes. 'No man

could have done what you did earlier this day,' he remarked, watching the bard's face, but avoiding the mirrored eyes.

'I didn't say I was just a man.' The bard tilted his head slightly, considering. 'More than a man yes . . . but less than human,' he added, sounding vaguely wistful.

'Aye, well, whatever,' Nevin said, becoming uncomfortable with the way the conversation had turned, 'we were bloody lucky you came when you did. The beasts very nearly fed well this day.' He rubbed his sweating palms on the smooth golden wood of the ancient wooden table, abruptly remembering the previous occasion the bard had been in Castle Nevin – in this very room too. It had been the night of his daughter's handfasting to Adare, the son of Count Adare, their nearest neighbour. Nevin's daughter had taken to the study of the occult and he had prevailed upon the bard to tell his daughter a tale that might frighten her away from her sinister studies. The bard had recounted the ancient tale of Gered and Leal, the Doomed Lovers, but it had had no effect, or if it did, then it was opposite to what Nevin had hoped, and may in fact have driven Suila more deeply into her occult studies. And Adare, her betrothed, never actually became her husband; he was slain – supposedly by the Chopts – while on a hunting expedition in the Northlands. There were, however, those who noticed that Suila was not unduly upset by his death, nor was she seen to use any of her powers to avenge him. She herself had died mysteriously on a night of fire and storm as she practised her craft.

The old man looked up to find the bard's mirrored eyes resting on him; they had now taken the glow from the wooden table and were softer, sympathetic almost. And Nevin instinctively knew that the bard knew.

'Have you lost many?' Paedur asked.

'Not as many as I initially thought,' Nevin said, grateful to be back on a subject he could speak about. 'When I saw how few guards were about, I thought they had all been slaughtered in their beds, but Aeal found them this morning, safe, still snoring in their bunks . . .'

Paedur looked at Aeal, his face expressionless.

'Drugged,' the Captain of Bowmen continued. 'As far as I can determine, their wine last night had been drugged. It was a new shipment; it arrived only yesterday,' he added, anticipating the bard's question.

'The supplier would bear investigation,' Paedur said softly.

Aeal nodded with a grim smile. Both the supplier and the agent who had arranged for the sale of the wine were in chains in Nevin's cellars. They were admitting nothing, but several cases of drugged wine and rofion had been found in the wine merchant's cellars, packed and ready for distribution to some of the other border castles. In all likelihood, the men would be hanged in the next day or two.

'What were your losses?' Paedur asked.

Nevin looked at the bard. 'We lost nearly forty people last night; twelve of those were guards, the rest palace staff. But, bard, the beasts have never attacked a castle like this before; when faced with a force of any size they have always elected to fight in the snow-fields, but their targets are isolated farmhouses or small groups of travellers. It's probably significant that we've had no word from Thusal for too long . . .' he added quietly, his fingers nervously picking at the leather eye-patch. 'And now we find the beasts attacking one of the Seven Bastions,' he murmured, almost to himself. 'But surely the two events cannot be unrelated?'

Paedur nodded. He had turned to face the fire and the warm light had washed his pale features a saffron colour, and his reflective eyes danced with the flames. He lifted his left arm and rested the hook, that took the place of his left hand, down on the wooden table. Both Nevin and Aeal clearly heard the snap of power and a pale blue spark leapt from the ancient table and crackled on the rune-incised half circle.

'What is going on in the ice-fields?' Nevin demanded. 'Do you know?'

Paedur paused a moment before replying, and then he turned his head slightly, looking at the two men. 'You've heard of the recent events in the Southlands, in and around the capital?' he asked, seemingly ignoring the question.

Nevin glanced at Aeal before turning back to the bard. 'We've heard rumours of course. But a change at court has no effect upon us in any way. Our task is to keep the Chopts from the Southlands.'

The bard nodded briefly. 'But you do know that Geillard is no longer Emperor?'

The two men nodded. 'We heard you deposed him,' Aeal muttered.

'People and rumour have a habit of ascribing victory – or defeat – to one person or thing,' Paedur said, with a ghost of a smile. 'With some little assistance from those who had elected to follow him, and the help of the Pantheon, I put Kutor on the throne,' he continued, studying their faces carefully, wondering how they would react. Even with his god-enhanced senses, he sometimes found it difficult to gauge a person's snap judgement or reaction.

'It doesn't sit well with me to acknowledge a bandit my Emperor,' Nevin grumbled.

'There is royal blood in him,' Paedur said, 'albeit on the wrong side of the blanket.'

'The Gods of the Pantheon approve this choice?' Nevin asked.

'They do. He is a good man. Honest after a fashion, strong, not so easily led, but willing to follow advice, and loyal to the Faith. Because he was a Wasteland bandit, he realised the danger of the beast-folk, so one of his first acts was to begin preparations for the building of a series of defensive forts on the far side of the Mion River in the blind-spots between the Seven Bastions on this side.'

'I've been advising that for years,' Nevin grunted.

'Well, it will happen soon.'

'Is that why you're here?' Aeal asked.

Paedur shook his head, but said nothing.

When the silence had lengthened, Nevin asked quietly, 'Well, why are you here? Who sent you?'

'No-one knows I'm here, and that is the way I would like it kept.' The bard turned back to the fire and settled into his chair, suddenly – foolishly – wishing he could sleep again. The Gods of the Pantheon had granted him many gifts – immortality, almost complete invulnerability, the ability to divine men's thoughts, to perceive the aura of all living things, to call down Power – but the cost had been high, and he had lost much of his humanity. The bard was seldom seen to eat, neither did he drink anything except water, and he was never known to sleep. He regretted that loss most of all. 'What I tell you now is no great secret, but equally, it is not common knowledge. So perhaps it would be better if you were not to discuss it with others, even with the other holders of the Bastions.' He looked quickly at the two men. 'Well?'

'Yes . . .'

'Of course . . .'

Paedur looked back to the fire, staring deep into the flames, his eyes flickering in unison with their movements. 'Kutor's great victory at Karfondal was not as decisive as perhaps it should have been, and certainly not as decisive as he would have wanted. It was practically bloodless for a start, and whilst that was no bad thing, there can be no denial that blood is an excellent purge; it allows demons to be exorcised, old angers, ancient enmities to be washed away, and when the killing is done, there is a sense of relief that it is over, and a resolution that it must never happen again. Much can be achieved in such an atmosphere.' He lifted his left arm, allowing his hook to ring off the table. 'But that didn't happen.

'And of course, Geillard escaped.

'But his private circle of counsellors had been destroyed. Salier had been slain, as was Barthus the Hierophant, although because his corpse wasn't found, it has been assumed that he fled with the Emperor, and Fodla shifted her allegiance over to the new ruler. Their position has now been taken by Owen, the infamous Weapon Master, and Keshian, formerly Kutor's Commander but now the new Emperor's Chief Counsellor. Fodla has retained her position as Commander of the Emperor Legion and the Imperial Army, but her reputation has suffered somewhat because she shifted sides just before the decisive moment.

'Kutor left the old ruling clans – the Twelve Families – of

Karfondal intact; it would have been suicidal to attempt to oust them now, and indeed he has left everything much as it was except that he has installed the Old Faith as the official belief in the Nations.' Paedur shrugged. 'I had insisted on it; it was part of the price of my aid. However, Geillard was a convert to the Religion, and the New Religion had gained many converts during the deposed Emperor's reign and the Hierophant's excellent missionary work. The Religion is a belief which appeals to the wealthy and those in power, and nearly all the ruling families in the capital follow the Religion; naturally, these people were reluctant to accept a new ruler – especially a new ruler who followed the Faith.

'And lest you think that all of this had left the Gods unscathed and untouched, both the Faith and the Religion had lost their Deathgods!' Paedur smiled grimly; both 'deaths' – if the figure of Death could truly 'die' – were attributable to him. 'But Kutor's accession to the throne made the Religion step up its campaign to win converts. Miracle cures, sudden growth in desolate places, unseasonal flowering and fruiting of trees and bushes have drawn many to the New Religion. Of course the Old Gods retaliated, but slowly, slowly, and even now the battle rages.' He paused and added softly, 'And then of course the rumours began.'

'What rumours?' Nevin interrupted.

Paedur seemed almost startled by the man's abrupt question. 'Why, that Geillard is plotting to overthrow the Usurper from a base in the Northlands, with a Chopt army at his back.'

Nevin grunted derisively, but stopped suddenly. 'It might explain the beasts' sudden activity and boldness,' he said, almost to himself.

'How much credence do you put in that rumour?' Aeal asked the bard.

'Enough to come into the Northlands looking for him,' he said, turning back to the fire and closing his eyes, terminating the conversation. What he didn't tell them was that the rumour had been confirmed by an impeccable source.

Death had come for the bard in the last muggy days of summer.

Paedur had been deep in the bowels of the Imperial Library at

Karfondal, sitting in a darkened corner with his back against the cool stone, reading a slab of waxed wood which had been inscribed with the fine curling script of the Susurun. It told the legend of the Lady Esanne who had loved one of the dark ancient folk and who had borne the only known child of mixed blood, the Magus Narre.

The bard turned the tablet of wood and placed it face down in its cloth-lined protective box and was reaching for the fourteenth and final slab of wood when he experienced the unmistakable tingle of power along the curve of his hook. The curling runes sparkled briefly and then died, drawing into themselves all traces of the power that still lingered in the long darkened room. Paedur rested his head against the stone wall and allowed his consciousness to expand and his enhanced senses to come to the fore, questing the darkness and his surroundings. He was alone on this, the deepest of the library's four basement floors. On the floor above him was the librarian, an old man who had seen three – now four – Emperors take the throne, and he had watched them come without interest or even care. But he had never been so frightened in all his life as on the day the bard had descended on the library like some Duaiteoiri, and proceeded to scour the shelves, delving deep into portions of the great library that had remained untouched in centuries. Even now, Paedur could sense his fear and vague resentment of the strange unhuman creature in his domain. On the floor above the librarian were two scholars, monks of the Order of Ectoraige, the God of Learning and Knowledge, and they were deep in their studies, one reading Cambris' *Heraldic Genealogies*, the other – Paedur suppressed a smile – making notes on the *Life of Paedur, the Bard*. Other than these the library was empty, the cramped, book- scroll- chart- ledger- wood- stone- and skin-filled rooms proving too hot and uncomfortable in the oppressively humid weather.

But what had fired his hook? Paedur touched the incised metal with his fingertips; it was now cool to his touch, which usually indicated that no danger threatened.

Usually.

Paedur stood, coming fluidly and silently to his feet, but he didn't step out of the niche holding the Susurun writings. He looked out across the floor. This portion of the library had originally been a wine cellar, and it showed in the construction and layout of the floor. A series of arched niches ran along both walls, and whereas they had once contained wines of different vintages, times and origins, they now held writings from different eras, schools of thought or writers. Down the centre of the floor ran a series of low chart-chests, holding sea-charts and maps not only of this place but of most of the Planes of Existence. The only entrance to the cellar was by the stairs at the far end of the long room; there were no windows, and no light. The bard had been reading in total darkness.

Paedur looked from niche to niche, his enhanced sight bringing the room to a dull amber, speckled with shifting, twisting lines and spots of brighter, harder colours. When the colour obscured the object, he interpreted the shifting patterns of colour as books or scrolls, manuscripts or rune-etched wood or stone, the natural materials still retaining a little of their original auras. But all these niches seemed to be empty.

Perhaps he had been imagining it. Shaking his head, he turned away, about to return to his reading when a hand reached out and touched his face just below the eye!

Abruptly terrified – both by the presence and the failure of his powers – he reacted instinctively, his left arm snapping up, the curve of his hook aiming to take the person low in the body and then rip upwards, opening a huge wound from stomach to chest.

His arm struck stone – unnatural stone too, for his blade was capable of sundering stone. The shock sent him reeling, his arm and chest instantly, totally numb. He staggered back, crashing into the piles of ancient wooden tablets, scattering them to the ground.

Death stepped into the niche. 'Slow and hasty bard, if that is not a contradiction.'

Paedur looked up into the night-black face of Churon, once the infamous Onelord and now the Deathgod of the Old Faith. The god's bright blue eyes were sparkling with humour. The bard sat up, rubbing his aching shoulder, moving his elbow, loosening the stiffness, and then he examined his hook. He had struck Death's cloak; although it was as supple as cloth, it was actually made of stone from the Silent Wood, the domain of the Dead. The bard's own furred cloak had similar properties. His hook seemed to be undamaged, the magical blade surprisingly unmarked, unchipped.

'You've grown strong,' Paedur grunted, coming to his feet, 'or perhaps I'm losing my powers. Usually I can detect the presence of a god . . . indeed, magical forces of any kind.'

Churon smiled broadly, his teeth startlingly white against his ebon skin, matching in colour his closely-cropped hair. 'You've become over familiar with my presence,' Death said. 'And then again, perhaps I have come into my full powers. My predecessor, for all his bluster, was content to use barely a fraction of the position's full authority. Of course, he may have been unaware of the forces Death can command.'

Paedur brushed past Churon, his hook blazing cold blue light with the proximity to the god, and stepped out into the cellar. He strode over to a map-case and then turned to look back at the god. 'What do you want with me now? I've given the Pantheon what they wanted; I put a follower of the Faith on the throne.'

Churon grinned, but without humour. 'And now I'm afraid you must work to keep him there.'

'My part is done,' Paedur said firmly.

'You are still the Champion of the Faith,' Churon reminded him, a chill note entering his voice, his smile now nothing more than a twisting of his thin lips. 'You knew that was something you could not leave off when you were tired of it, like a worn cloak.'

The bard nodded, almost wearily. 'I know. But there seems to be no end to it.'

'There will never be an end to it – not while we have two prime religious systems vying for the belief of a limited number of followers.' Churon moved over to the bard, his footsteps sounding vaguely gritty although the floor was clean, almost as if he were walking on gravel. Paedur was briefly reminded of the time he had walked Death's Domain, the Silent Wood: it too was covered in a fine gritty gravel. Death stooped and pulled a long linen chart from beneath the table. Moving the bard gently to one side, he rolled open the chart, Paedur automatically holding down one edge with the flat of his hook.

It was the Scalae map – an original – and the most perfect representation of the geography of the Seven Nations, from Thusaland in the north to Lostrice in the south, and even showed the fabled Southern Continent in outline. It back dated before the Cataclysm which had changed the face of the entire Plane of Existence, especially along the coast.

Churon tapped the top left-hand corner of the map, in the trackless white ice-fields beyond Thusal, the northernmost town. 'Geillard is in the Northlands in one of the hidden Chopt towns, probably in the capital. He has a score of Gallowglas mercenaries by his side, as well as some of the Torc Allta, the Boar-Folk, a dozen priests of the New Religion, about two hundred of his own followers, those who either fled with him or went to him later . . . plus nearly three thousand Chopts.'

'I didn't think there were three thousand in the whole of the Northlands,' Paedur murmured.

'They are usually a solitary people, but they have been brought together by the presence of Geillard, who has made many promises, especially of land and title in the Southlands. More importantly, though, they have been drawn together by the twelve priests of the Religion: they have promised – and delivered – miracles. The Chopts now worship the gods of the New Religion, and when they kill, they kill in their name!'

'Blood sacrifice!'

Churon nodded. 'Blood sacrifice of the most powerful kind. Whatever victory we gained when Kutor took the throne has been negated – possibly we are even worse off than before. Our plan, successful though it seemed, has actually worked against us. Is there a lesson in that for us, I wonder?' he asked. 'Those whose allegiance to the Religion was never firm, have suddenly become fanatical, and the followers of the Faith have become . . . well, shall we say lazy in their devotions? The Faith has become complacent, while the Religion has been forced to work all the harder for converts – and they are reaping that reward now.'

Paedur looked at the chart, remembering the last time he had walked the King Road to the North. That had been . . . how long ago now? It would have been shortly – no, immediately – after he had been gifted by C'lte the Yellow God . . . and that had been the beginning of it all. On that road he had met the Weapon Master, Tien tZo, Keshian . . . and Kutor. He shivered suddenly; had the wheel turned? 'What do you want me to do?' he asked tiredly.

'Go north,' Death said decisively, 'as swiftly and as secretly as you can. Go north . . . and destroy this conspiracy!'

'You mean kill Geillard?' Paedur asked cynically.

'Kill Geillard, the priests of the Religion and whatever leaders hold the Chopt clans together. Without them, the Chopt army will disintegrate into individual warring clans, and the threat will be negated.' Churon shrugged.

'And if I fail?' Paedur wondered.

'Then the Chopts will come streaming out of the Northlands, and in the resultant butchery – and every death a sacrifice to the Religion, remember – their gods will grow too powerful for the Pantheon to contend with. They will destroy us, and you of course. Yes, they will have something special in mind for you.'

Paedur smiled humourlessly. 'Is that supposed to frighten me?'

Churon showed his teeth in a mirthless smile. 'Bard, if the Gods of Faith and Religion go to war, then the resultant destruction will wipe the myriad planes of life clean of all life, possibly for ever.'

'And I must do it alone, I suppose?'

'Do it whatever way you can, bard, but do it soon,' Death said, and merged back into the stone walls, and was gone.

3 The Assassin

And in the early days there were several attempts on the Emperor's life
...

from . . . The Warrior, the Life of Owen, Weapon Master

In a matter of moons, the price on Kutor's head doubled and then
redoubled . . .

Tien tZo

The assassin was small and slight and female.

She had boldly walked in with the evening staff as they were
coming on duty. She carried a coloured chip which proclaimed
her a rooms-maid, the irregular edge of which matched a similar
chip in the guard's possession. There was no admittance without
the chip. The assassin made her way through the servants' quarters and up various back stairs and servants' corridors, taking to
the palace corridors only when absolutely necessary and then
moving swiftly and in absolute silence. She was challenged only
once, and the guard had been more curious than alarmed at
finding a small young-looking woman marching boldly down the
centre of the corridor. When he called her, she had turned, smiled,
and walked up to him without hesitation. She was still smiling
as she drove the slim poisoned spike up through his eye into his
brain, and the same smile only wavered slightly as his blood
spattered across her patterned rust-coloured gown. But it mattered little; when the blood dried it would fade into the pattern
and become indistinguishable.

Two floors further up the assassin stopped to orientate herself,
vividly recalling the plans her employers had provided. The corridor here divided and divided again, each one leading to the
office of one of the many Imperial functionaries. Her decision
made, she took off down an insignificant side corridor, moving

23

swiftly now, keeping to the wall, a slender handleless throwing dagger resting lightly in her cupped palm. She would not be so lucky to be challenged on this floor. Standing orders called for an intruder to be slain without question, without hesitation. There had been a previous attempt on the Emperor's life, and it had been a close enough thing, she had heard.

The young woman stopped at the second door from the end of the corridor, her every sense tingling. There was no light coming from beneath the door and she gently pressed her sensitive fingers against the wood, listening with them, but there were no vibrations, no sounds from within. She moved her hand, pressing just above the lock, and pushed, but the door didn't move. Removing a flat finger-length piece of metal from her sleeve, she slid it into the jamb of the door and pushed upwards, lifting the simple bar, and she was in.

She had been provided plans of this room also, charts which her employers had drawn from memory and she hoped that memory hadn't been playing them false. Moving slowly and in complete darkness, she made her way across to the bed which was against the left hand wall. She reached out and up with her right hand and touched heavy, hanging cloth, and then slowly, infinitely slowly, she pulled the curtain back to admit a wan night light. It was enough for her to make out the vague shape of someone sleeping in the bed beside her. Taking the covers between forefinger and thumb she carefully peeled them back, ensuring that it was the person she wanted. Lying curled up in a ball on the bed was a naked female. Satisfied, the assassin killed her swiftly and noiselessly with a blow to the throat.

Turning back to the window, she pulled the heavy curtains fully open and looked out. Beyond and below her Karfondal lay spread out in all its capital splendour, but the assassin had no eyes for it. She had been raised in the tenements of the Lower City: she knew its every sight and smell; she knew the rot that lurked beneath the paint; she knew the unmarked but clearly demarcated line that separated the Lower from the Upper City. Karfondal might be the capital, but two wildly differing cities existed within the boundary walls.

24

Shaking her head slightly, she turned away from the vista and looked up: she was pleased to find that there was no light from the room above. The man she had come to kill, the Emperor Kutor, had obviously retired for the night.

The assassin moved back into the room and pulled off her rust-red gown. Beneath she was wearing a simple leather jerkin over leather breeks, and strapped around her waist were two knives, one broad and heavy, the other a slim stiletto. Around her wrist, secured by studded leather bands, were a dozen throwing spikes, and there were two matched throwing knives strapped low on her calves. Pulling on a pair of fingerless leather gloves, she touched her weapons, checking them, and then moved back to the window. She pulled herself up easily and without apparent effort so that she was standing on the window-ledge. Her fingers sought – and found – holds and she levered herself out of the room and up onto the wall.

The climb up the wall proved to be surprisingly easy. The palace was one of the oldest buildings in an already ancient city. It had originally been built by the Culai, the First Race, but had been added onto by successive generations. The walls were pitted by time and the elements; at one time a tenacious creeping vine had covered most of the wall, and although a drought had taken it, it had left the wall scarred in a score of places.

The assassin continued climbing until she was level with the balcony of the room above and then she waited; clinging to the wall, her every sense alert, listening, watching, even smelling, but there were no noises, no signs or sounds of movement from the room within – and the only smell was the bitter-sweet smell of a quenched candle.

Satisfied, the assassin moved over onto the balcony and dropped down, and once again she waited patiently. She had nearly two hundred kills to her credit, and she owed them all to the extraordinary degree of care and planning she undertook before their execution and then the caution she used while actually making the kills. An assassin usually only made one mistake – and that was the fatal one. She stilled her breathing and waited until her pounding heartbeat had slowed, listening, listening all

25

the time. And only when she was completely satisfied that there was no-one awake within, did she draw her heavy-bladed knife and enter through the open shutters.

With her eyes now fully adjusted to the light, she spotted the Emperor's bed immediately. The gods were with her; he slept alone tonight, although he occasionally took one of the females to his bed with him, and while she had no compunction about killing the Emperor and his bed-partner, she was only being paid for one. Well, this was going to be easier than she had thought. Where was the Emperor's much vaunted security? Where were the dreaded Emperor Legion, each one sworn to give her life for his?

The assassin moved over to the edge of the bed and raised her knife, adopting a two-handed chopping hold. Using the weight of the blade, she was going to remove his head.

Ice-cold steel touched her throat. 'Move and I will cripple you!'

And then the light hit her like a blow.

When her eyes had cleared and she could see again, she found that the room had filled with people, and all of them were armed and armoured. She had either been expected or she had tripped an alarm along the way. She recognised some of the people in the room. Facing her was Fodla, the Weapon's Maid, Commander of the Emperor Legion, formerly Geillard's personal bodyguard and now providing the new ruler with the same service. She was a tall, broad woman with flaming red hair and green eyes that had much the same glitter as broken glass. There was a savage grin on her face, and her teeth were bared in something that could never have been mistaken for a smile.

Beside her stood the legendary Weapon Master, Owen. He was as tall as Fodla, although not so broad, and his rough handsome features bore the scars of a lifetime of campaigning. His close-cropped hair, recently iron-grey, was now turning white. Owen's face was stone and completely expressionless.

The assassin moved her head slightly, drawing blood where the curved sword scraped the flesh of her throat, but she confirmed her suspicion: the Shemmat, Tien tZo, stood behind her.

In the long silence that followed no-one spoke, no-one even moved, until there was a noise in the hallway beyond and then Kutor, once bandit, now Emperor, followed by the short, stout figure of Keshian, strode into the room.

He stepped up until he was almost touching her, and the assassin was surprised to find that they were of a height, and somehow that robbed him of his dignity. 'Well, an assassin.' The Emperor's voice was surprisingly neutral, but his broad features were set in ugly lines. 'I have two dead people below, a guard and a serving girl. The girl, I presume, was killed because her room lay directly below mine.'

The assassin remained silent. She was assessing her chances of making a break for the window; if she could throw herself out . . . catch the balcony below . . .

'You are a professional,' Kutor said suddenly, startling her, 'a paid killer. I will double whatever price is on me and allow you to go free if you give me the names of your employers.'

The woman continued to look at him. There was a curious tone in his voice, one almost of pleading. She looked closely at his face for the first time, and found it softer than she had expected, the wrinkles around his eyes and mouth making it seem vaguely feminine, but it only confirmed the rumours she had heard that he was indeed a puppet, and that his spectacular campaign through the Outlands and on into the Nations had been little of his doing. She decided he was a weak man – and weak men were usually squeamish, and easily manipulated. And here he was offering to double her payment for information she would freely give. She was not paid to endure torture; she felt no obligation to her employers.

Kutor – who had watched greed in men's eyes for too long – recognised the change in her expression, and knew what her answer would be. But for good measure, he added smoothly, 'If you do not feel like selling me the names,' he continued, 'I will walk out of this room and leave you to these people. You know Fodla; you are aware of her reputation. And perhaps the Weapon Master's reputation is known to you also. However, you will not be so familiar with the Shemmat, Tien tZo. He is reputed to be able to extract information from a stone. He enjoys it.' Kutor's lips curled in a thin, cruel smile. 'Why, I remember the last person . . . he cut them up, but slowly, slowly, keeping them alive and in their senses and then he ate their flesh before their eyes – while they still had eyes, that is. How would you like to see the Shemmat consume you piece by piece?'

'I have no loyalty to my employers,' the assassin said suddenly.

'I didn't think you would have,' Kutor observed.

'But I don't know their names,' the assassin continued quickly. 'I only met their representative.'

'Where?' Fodla growled.

'A tavern in the Lower City. I don't know its name, I'm not even sure it has one, but it's off Shop Street, close to the spice merchant's. I've lived there all my life and yet I've never known the name of that tavern; it has a blue door . . .'

Fodla nodded. 'I know it.'

'A man called Stinger is their agent. He contacted the Guild of Assassins, asking for me particularly. I met him in the tavern where he outlined the mission, giving me to understand that he had backing from those closest to the throne. When we agreed the price he provided me with the plans of the palace defences and the room layouts which he had obtained from his employers . . .'

'What am I worth?' Kutor asked with a slight smile.

The assassin smiled, but it lent her pinched, sharp face no humanity. 'The highest price on the market at the moment is a standing reward offered by the New Religion for the bard Paedur – a thousand thousand pieces of fist-weight gold.'

Kutor gasped. A thousand pieces of fist-weight gold would keep a whole kingdom in grain and fuels for a year. A thousand thousand pieces was an incredible price; why, when he had been running in the Outlands as a bandit, the highest price on his head was around one hundred silver pieces, or the equivalent of ten gold pieces.

'But there is a price of one thousand pieces on your head,' the assassin continued.

'A king's ransom indeed,' Owen said softly.

'And you have promised me twice that,' the assassin reminded the Emperor.

'I haven't forgotten. But tell me more about this Stinger and the people he represents.'

'I know very little about him,' she said, attempting to shake her head, and then remembering the blade at her throat. 'He is well known in the Lower City as an arranger, a fixer. He deals in whatever will yield a profit: contraband, weapons, slaves, information. He has contacts at court and in the church and he often arranges assassinations or abductions for them. I don't know who he is working for, but that shouldn't be difficult for you to discover. You made many enemies when you took the throne from Geillard.'

Kutor grinned broadly. 'The Twelve Families have made their feelings clear.'

'It is common knowledge that they wish to overthrow you, and return Geillard to the throne. Even now an army is supposed to be gathering in the north which will sweep down to oust you and restore the old order. You must have heard the rumours.'

'I've heard them.'

'That is all I know,' the assassin finished. 'Now you must pay me.'

Kutor nodded slowly. He looked into the woman's hard, dead eyes, and smiled. 'Could I pay you to kill this Stinger for me?'

She nodded quickly. This would be a profitable night. She had already received half the payment due on Kutor's death, which was five hundred pieces . . . and she had been promised double the full price . . . two thousand pieces . . . and now a quick and easy kill . . . and possibly the man Stinger would be carrying the second half of the payment on him. It was time she retired anyway . . . headed south, made for the islands . . . and with two and a half or three thousand fist-weight pieces of gold to spend, she could live out the rest of her days in absolute luxury.

'How much?' Kutor asked.

'One hundred gold pieces, fist-weight.'

Kutor began to nod and then stopped and seemed to be

considering. 'But if I pay you, how do I know you will not betray me as you have betrayed your present employers?'

The assassin frowned, unsure what he meant . . .

Kutor turned away. 'Kill her.'

'You promised!' she screamed, and then Tien tZo snapped her neck with a single blow of his fist.

Fodla stood looking down at the body, her huge hands on her hips. 'Sometimes,' she said to no-one in particular, 'I forget that he was a bandit before he became Emperor.'

'Do you place so much faith in his word, then?' Owen asked quietly.

'But he promised her money and freedom, and if he breaks his promise to her, what will he do to us when the time comes, eh?' she demanded fiercely.

Owen shook his head. 'I've never trusted him. "Beware the word of a prince or a god,"' he quoted and turned away.

Keshian followed the Emperor into the tiny room he was now using as a bed chamber, and had been since he had first taken the throne; the Imperial bed-chamber was nothing more than a carefully laid trap. Keshian was now the closest person Kutor had to a friend, and one of the very few he actually trusted.

He came straight to the point. 'I suggest we move on this inn, take this Stinger and extract the names of his employers. If we don't stop this now . . . well, the gods alone only know where it may end.'

Kutor turned up the oil lamp; the room had no windows, no skylights and only one door, and that had been magically keyed to Kutor's touch alone – only he could open it. The room itself was tiny, and had once been used as a storage cupboard. It held a bed, an old wooden table and two chairs, and there was a large wooden chest at the foot of the bed. Propped up against one wall was a crossbow and a sword. The room was a cell – but at least Kutor could sleep secure at night. 'What do we do if this man doesn't know the names of his employers?' The pale yellow light from the lamp washed his features, deepening the shadows under his eyes, ageing him.

'He had to have a contact; we'll find that contact and work back from that . . .'

Kutor nodded wearily, pulling off his sword belt, tossing it onto the table and then dropping down onto his bed still fully clothed. 'It was easier when I was a bandit,' he said, looking at the high ceiling. 'You knew who your friends were; you knew who to trust . . .'

The short stout man nodded. Recalling his own days as a battle-captain with one of the minor lords, he could sympathise; it had been easier then, much easier than his present position as the Commander of the Imperial Army.

'Do what you have to do,' Kutor said finally. 'Find this Stinger, and discover what he knows. And then I want you to take this city apart, find those who oppose me, and exterminate them. We'll stop this now. You're right: if it continues, it'll start a rot that will threaten everything the bard has worked for, and I think I owe him enough to make some attempts to protect it.'

'There's no word,' Keshian said quickly, anticipating the Emperor's next question. 'We have news of him heading north, and then he vanishes. Perhaps he has moved on to one of the other Planes of Existence; perhaps he has gone back to the Silent Wood again, or to the Lands of Life Eternal – we just don't know.' He paused and added quietly, 'Oh, and Katani has disappeared also.'

The Emperor sat up quickly. 'Where? When?'

'It was only confirmed earlier this evening, but she has not been seen since early morning, and she didn't appear for her meals all day. So I sent a guard to her rooms just before twilight, but he found the door open and the room empty. If you want my opinion, she's headed north after the bard.'

'There is a spot in that iron-hard killer's heart of hers for him,' Kutor grinned.

'You think so? I think she'd have a better chance with a Chopt than with the bard; whatever was human in him is long gone now.'

The Emperor nodded. 'Aye; we all lost something when we took this road, eh, Keshian? But the bard, I fancy, lost most of all.'

The man called Stinger sat in a corner in the nameless tavern on Shop Street, his eyes on the shadow thrown by the rising sun that was slowly shifting across his much-scarred table. It was well past dawn and the assassin should have been here by now. What in the name of all the gods was keeping her?

He was a tall, thin hard-faced man, whose pale grey eyes betrayed something of his furtive character: they were constantly moving, never resting long enough on anyone or anything. His clothing was nondescript and of poor quality, and he could have passed unnoticed in any crowd – which was exactly what he intended.

Although not usually a nervous man, he found his palms were sweating this morning, but he put it down to the five hundred pieces of fist-weight gold around his waist – it was as heavy as a suit of full battle-armour. He would give her another few moments and then he would go; there was an alternative meeting place they had arranged for noon, but he knew if he hadn't heard from her by noon, then she was dead and the mission failed. In fact, he had half a suspicion that something was badly wrong – the woman had never failed before. The only thing which kept him in his seat was that he had heard nothing from his sources at the palace, and surely if an attempt had been made on the Emperor's life he would have heard something . . . unless . . . unless of course the Emperor was already dead and the palace had been sealed! If that was so, then the palace would be in an uproar while Kutor's friends frantically attempted to regain control, perhaps even arranging to place a figurehead on the throne . . . Then again, if the Emperor was dead, perhaps they were gathering their belongings and as much coin, metal or precious stones as they could carry. In any case they would seal the palace tight. Of course, that must be it! In better spirits now, he raised his arm to order another drink . . .

. . . and a pike burst through the thin shell window beside him, the barbed head touching the soft flesh just beneath his ear!

Simultaneously, doors to two of the rooms upstairs burst open and archers appeared, the weapons levelled at his chest. A crossbow man appeared in the kitchen doorway, followed by two pikemen.

Finally the inn door opened and Fodla tramped in. The Commander of the Legion was wearing full armour and the colours of the Emperor Legion, and in that moment, Stinger realised he was a dead man. The huge woman crossed the floor in two long strides, hooked her foot into a chair and spun it around towards her. Then she sat and stared at the terrified man for what seemed like an eternity.

Stinger's thin face was ashen, his slightly protruding eyes bulbous and darting. He kept licking his thin lips.

Finally Fodla spoke. 'An employee of yours gave us your name before she met with a fatal accident.'

For a brief moment Stinger thought about denying it, but as his eyes drifted across Fodla's face, he realised the Commander would just as likely kill him out of hand if he made some excuse.

'You have some information which is of interest to me,' the woman continued, her huge hands resting lightly on the wooden table between them. Stinger looked at the hands, immediately recalling the story about the time an island wildcat had come ashore from a boat in the harbour. The creature had killed three men and badly mauled two others, before Fodla had grabbed the creature in her huge hands and snapped its spine across her knee. His darting eyes moved across her face again, and he realized she would kill or cripple him with just as much compassion.

Stinger swallowed hard. 'How can I help?'

'Names.' Fodla looked around. 'Drinks here, innkeeper . . . rofion.' She looked back at the shivering man. 'Now, you can give me the name of the person or persons who contacted you and arranged for you to organise an assassination, and you can give me these names here or we can go to the palace and talk there. But I'm afraid the Emperor is not in good humour at the moment, and I think your reception would be anything but pleasant.'

'I know noth . . .' Stinger began.

'And if you were to say that you knew nothing, then I'm afraid all this will have been wasted, and if you are of no further use, then I'll just have to kill you.'

Stinger nodded. 'I'll tell you.' His face took on a slightly shifty, cunning look, and his eyes settled on her face. 'But would I be recompensed for this information?'

Fodla's urbane mask vanished, and she struck him backhanded across the table. Her metal-plated glove tore the flesh from his cheek-bones and broke teeth, sending him sprawling against the wall. 'You want payment for telling us what you did?' she snarled. 'You want payment because you arranged an assassination . . . well, then of course we'll arrange payment – in kind. Names!' she roared.

As Stinger struggled to his feet, his right hand found the stiletto hidden in his left sleeve. His fingers curled around the smooth bone handle; if he was going to die now he would at least take this ruthless . . .

Fodla's right hand moved – and a knife that was more like a short sword pinned the cloth of his sleeve to the table. The woman's face was set into hard cruel lines, and when she smiled, it was nothing more than the drawing back of her lips over her teeth, much as an animal does before it feeds. 'I know why you're called Stinger, but you won't use your little toy on me. Now I asked you a question. Answer me!'

'You can rot!' Stinger spluttered, blood dripping down his chin.

'You're going to tell me . . . sooner or later you're going to tell me. But do you think those you've been defending will appreciate what you've done for them, eh? All you'll have done is to buy them time – time to make good their escape, and continue on with their plans, with another messenger boy, another Stinger, or perhaps you'll have bought them time to arrange an assassination, eh? After all, they can't afford to allow you to live, can they?'

Stinger turned away and looked out through the shattered window. What the woman said was true: he owed his employers no loyalty, and they would have no hesitation about ordering his death, they had too much to lose . . . something on a nearby roof caught his attention, distracting him, but his vision was still blurred from where the woman had hit him, and he couldn't focus properly on it . . .

So he never saw the crossbow bolt that took him through the eye, killing him instantly!

Fodla tossed the stained crossbow bolt onto the polished table later that afternoon. 'We scoured the area as thoroughly as we could, but you know the Lower City: it's a warren. An army could hide out there . . .' she began and then, realising what she was saying, shut up and sat down.

'So you discovered nothing,' Kutor said softly. The late afternoon sunlight slanting in through the window washed around him in a dusky halo, lending him a slightly mystical air. This was the chamber formerly used by Geillard, where he had held all his conferences with his most trusted advisors. The new Emperor had continued to use it for that function, enjoying its warm, wood-panelled silence.

Kutor, Fodla, Keshian and Owen were seated around the circular table, while Tien tZo stood perfectly at ease beside the door, the fingers of his left hand resting lightly on the wood, reading the activity in the corridor outside by the vibrations.

'I don't think we've learned *nothing*,' Owen said quietly, rubbing his hands through his thinning hair. 'We know there is a definite conspiracy to oust you, probably headed by one or all of the Twelve Families, we know that Stinger knew the identity of one of the organisers, who was obviously someone of importance and probably someone close to you – otherwise why should this person bother to kill him? Now, what else do we know?' He touched the crossbow bolt with his forefinger. It was a black shaft of wood as long as a man's forearm, from elbow to little finger, and tipped with a broad-headed pyramid of metal. 'This is a handmade piece – no common or soldier's shaft; it's probably even grooved and fitted for a particular weapon.'

'An assassin's tool?' Fodla asked, reaching for the shaft and examining it again. The fletching was also black.

'Not especially, but a hunting tool, certainly. Now think, do you know of a lord here at court who uses black bolts, or has a black crossbow, or whose colours are black?'

'All of the nobility know how to use a crossbow of course . . .' Fodla said slowly.

'But with such skill?' Owen persisted. 'We're talking about a shot of about five hundred paces, with the target below the bowman, in shadow, and behind glass – albeit broken glass. A difficult – nay, an almost impossible – shot to achieve.'

'I know of no-one at court using that colour bow or shafts,' Keshian said, 'and while some of the younger people adopt black dress, it is not the official colours of any of the nobility.'

Owen gripped the bolt in his fist, his knuckles tightening around it. 'This is our only lead.'

'There must be an armourer in the city,' Tien tZo suggested softly, 'someone who deals with the nobility.'

Owen grinned triumphantly. 'Of course, of course! Someone who specialises . . .'

'I have just remembered something,' Fodla said. 'As Commander of the Imperial Army, I recently signed an order for several hundred thousand crossbow bolts and arrows to be made by various armourers across the city, and it occurs to me that each of these must have a distinctive style all of their own. Surely all we have to do is to bring the bolt to one of these armourers – and I think there is one in the palace at the moment – and ask them who they think made it?'

'The other thing we might do,' Keshian, the Chief Counsellor, added with a grin, 'is to put out the rumour that Stinger spoke before he was killed and that even now, we're putting together a case against his employers . . . It might be interesting to see who panics.'

'You'd probably find yourself without a court in the morning,' Fodla smiled.

Kutor raised his hand. 'I think both ideas have merit. However, let us try and identify the bolt first, and then we'll think about Keshian's suggestion. I'm not sure anyone will fall for it, however,' he added. 'They know that if we had a name we would act immediately.' He shrugged and looked at Fodla. 'But try to get me a name. I want to know for whom that bolt was made.' He stood up, abruptly ending the meeting. 'Until later, then . . .'

Night had fallen before the huge Commander returned. Messengers brought Owen and Tien tZo and Keshian to Kutor's official bedchamber, where they found the Emperor, leaning against the window, looking out across the city. Fodla was standing to attention at the side of the huge bed, her strong face grim, but her green eyes sparkling with triumph. Tien closed the door and stood against it, and Kutor turned. His face was stone and there were shadows under his eyes. In his hand he held the crossbow bolt. He tossed the bolt onto the floor between Owen and Keshian, where it rolled around in a circle, its metal head clicking on the polished stones.

'Pick it up,' Kutor said quietly, his voice unnaturally calm. 'Hold it to the light, and look at the underside of the head.'

Owen stopped, caught the bolt and brought it over to a smoking oil-lamp, where he and Keshian leaned over the light, turning the bolt to catch the light. There was a shape cut into the underside of the head . . . the familiar shape of a half moon . . .

Fodla looked straight ahead. 'I was told that the bolt had been made for the one-handed storyteller, Paedur the Bard!'

4   The Survivor

North of the River Mion is an icy wasteland, inhabited by beasts and bandits. The next town of any note is Thusal, an important, but lawless trading town. Once one ventures onto the north side of the river one is beyond the law, beyond all retribution except that of the gods . . .

Lilis' Geographica

The creature was squatting on top of a tall pillar of stone on the hill above Castle Nevin on the wrong side – the northern side – of the Mion River.

Paedur had crossed the river with first light, walking across the frozen surface of the Mion's black water. When he reached the bank, he had turned and raised his hook to Nevin and Aeal, who were standing watching him, while behind them smoke from the great funeral pyre of the slain Chopts hung almost completely motionless in the still early morning air. Burning the corpses had been the bard's idea; the beast-folk believed that a Chopt whose corpse was consumed by the flame and not by the members of his own clan would never reach his gods to find immortality. The pyre would have the effect not only of enraging the creatures but would also make them realise what would happen to their bodies if they were slain fighting along the Mion. The bard had also showed Nevin how the attack might be used to his advantage – and to all the Bastions along the river. This was the first time the beasts had actually attacked one of the ancient forts, and if reports of the numbers of beasts were exaggerated, it would almost certainly bring Imperial troops, and that would allow Nevin to place the district under the Rule of War. The Rules, which had been drawn up nearly two centuries previously, placed the control of the entire region in the hands of the most senior or experienced noble actually present. Amongst its many powers, it enabled this noble (in otherwords Nevin) to conscript every able-bodied man between the ages of fifteen and fifty summers, and call in all available food and weapons. As the bard had walked away, his footsteps barely creaking on the ice, Nevin had promised to call the Lords of the Seven Bastions together, and between them, they would raise the largest army the Northlands had ever seen to guard the Mion.

The bard walked up the hill, a tall shapeless figure, enveloped in a hooded travelling cloak, noiseless after the recent light snowfall, making for a pillar he remembered from the previous occasion he had been here. When he crested the hill, he spotted the creature crouched atop it. It swivelled its horned head to look at him, the lacquered plates on its arms and legs rasping slightly.

'I'm freezing up here!'

'How did you find me?' he asked, his voice neutral.

'I am Katan.' The voice, although distorted, was recognisably female; she unfolded her legs and dropped lightly to the ground. She then bent her head and twisted off the hideous helmet to reveal a broad square face, pleasant but not pretty, and a pair of hard amber-coloured eyes. Her hair was the colour of snow. She smiled humourlessly. 'You don't seem overjoyed to see me.'

'It concerns me that if you could find me then so could others . . .'

'I shouldn't think so.'

'Then how did you know where I was?' Paedur demanded.

The woman didn't answer immediately, but hooked her helmet to her belt and settled the two swords she carried on either side of her waist. She glanced sidelong at the bard, but he was still looking at her, awaiting an answer. She sighed, knowing she couldn't try his patience; his appreciation of time differed to most other humans'. 'I had help,' she confessed eventually.

'Churon?'

'How did you know?'

Paedur shrugged and walked past the standing stone and the woman. Without looking over his shoulder, he said, 'Only he knew where I was going. Did he tell you why?'

'He only told me I would find you at Castle Nevin,' she said, hurrying to catch up with him. 'My relationship with Death is still a little strained,' she added with a wry smile.

The bard nodded, but said nothing.

The woman was Katani, a warrior-maid of the fabled female warriors, the Katan. Betrayed and murdered, she had spent many years in Death's Domain before finally encountering the bard on his travels through the Silent Wood. She had travelled with him through Death's Domain, and had helped him bring down Mannam, the renegade god. Partially as a gift for this service, and also through the bard's assistance, she had been able to return to the World of Men. But there was little love lost between her and Churon, the man who had originally killed her, and who now held the position as Deathgod of the Faith.

'How long have you been waiting?' Paedur asked abruptly.

'I saw you battle – or should I say butcher? – the Chopts yesterday morn. I was on the wall directly behind and to your left; I'm surprised you didn't sense me,' she added.

'So am I,' Paedur murmured. 'Perhaps in the heat of battle . . .'

'So you were never in any great danger,' she continued.

'That's comforting,' he said, his voice and face neutral.

They continued on, comfortable enough in each other's company to walk in silence. The sky, which had been threatening all morning, grew darker around noon and it began to snow, great soft, silent flakes that quickly blanketed the ground, obscuring even the vaguest traces of a path.

Katani pulled on her horned helmet and unrolled a thick travelling cloak from her pack and swung it around her shoulders. She pulled up the deep hood and shivered in her fleece-lined, leather and metal armour. She was bitterly cold; she glanced sidelong at the bard, but as usual he seemed unaffected by the elements, and not for the first time she found herself undecided as to whether he was still of humankind or not.

She touched the bard's arm, and then drew her gauntleted fingers back with a yelp; something had stung, and when she looked at the fingertips of her gauntlets, she found they were scorched and blackened. 'We had better seek shelter; it looks like it's down for the rest of the day.'

Paedur nodded, the movement dislodging some of the heavy

covering of snow that clung to the fine hairs of his cloak. He pointed with his hook. 'Beyond the rise there is a fishing village and a Monastery of Ectoraige; we're sure to find shelter there.'

Katani nodded gratefully; her teeth were chattering together so loudly she couldn't talk. Paedur suddenly reached out and wrapped the curve of his hook around her armoured shoulder, the metal scraping on the lacquer. Katani watched the runes which were incised into the hook sparkle with a vague blue light and then warmth flowed through her shoulder and down into her body. This was no brief warming spell; this was a deep satisfying heat that seemed to come from within. Not for the first time, the Katan wondered what powers the bard possessed – and then she wondered did he even know the half of them himself? Without saying a word, the bard turned away.

As they crested the hill, Katani realised that they had now reached the coast, and the breeze coming in off the stone-coloured sea was laced with sleet and ice, and drove the snow in almost horizontally. Even with the bard's warming strength within her, Katani knew they couldn't survive a night in this weather. 'How much further to this village?' she called.

'It should be down . . .' Paedur began, then stopped suddenly, and even though the temperature was freezing, Katani felt the sudden chill that wafted from him. A tiny thread of blue fire crackled along the coarse hairs of his cloak.

Katani's hand immediately moved to her sword. 'What's wrong?'

Paedur shook his head quickly, silencing her. The snow was blizzarding, and visibility was almost down to nil. The only discernible features were the grey-black body of the ocean in the distance, and the indeterminate bulk of a building stuck high on the cliffs to her right.

'What's wrong?' she demanded, drawing her short sword.

'The village . . . the Monastery . . .'

'What about them?'

'They're dead!'

The Monastery of Ectoraige was ancient. It perched atop the

cliffs like a hulking beast left over from the dawn of the Planes of Existence. It was Culai built, and while its original purpose was obscure, it seemed more than likely that it had served wilder gods and demons than either the Faith or Religion, before the blue-robed followers of Ectoraige, the God of Learning and Knowledge, had converted the desolated building. It was of typical Culai construction, massively hewn stones that were not native to this plain, set one atop the other, perfectly joined without the aid of mortar. The gates were solid brukwood, the usually unworkable wood, smoothed and shaped by a craft or magic that had died with the Culai, and were bolted through with fist-sized squareheaded rivets. There was a school at the foot of the cliffs, build around the crudely cut staircase that was the only entrance to the Monastery. The building had commenced nearly two hundred years previously and successive generations had added to it as occasion and opportunity demanded. The school was constructed simply but solidly of cordwood which had been coated in what the fishermen called boat-paint, a distillation of various seaweeds which produced a thick, greenish tar which prevented boards from warping. During the summer months it stank, and even in the depths of the Cold Months it remained tacky. Young men interested in a life in the Brotherhood usually spent anything from three to five years in the school before climbing the thousand steps to the Monastery. But only a tiny proportion climbed the steps. The Monastery itself never held more than a hundred monks at any one time, but the School would usually have had up to five hundred young men studying in its long halls.

They had both been decimated.

Paedur and Katani moved swiftly and silently through the rambling school. It had obviously been attacked by what must have been a sizeable army of Chopts; their prints and their animal stench remained, their odours strong enough to overlay the marine smell of the tar paint and the sickly-sweetness of blood. The building had been surrounded by a palisade wall of sharpened stakes, more to keep marauding beasts out and wayward pupils in, than to repel a determined assault. The palisade had literally been torn apart in several places and the poles then used as a ram to shatter the main doors. Every door in the school had been shattered, the windows of horn and parchment paper torn or pulled out and the white-sanded floors scored with the marks of claws and bloody feet.

There was blood everywhere.

The sleeping chambers looked like an abattoir. Every bed was splashed with thick rust-brown stains and there was blood spattered all across the floor and in long speckled tracks up along the whitewashed walls; even the low beamed ceiling hadn't escaped the spurting blood. Both Paedur and Katani knew the signs; the sleepers had had their throats cut, hence the spattered blood, which indicated a huge force, working together and in absolute silence. And that was most unusual, for the beasts, although clannish by nature, preferred to kill in private, and even then they usually proclaimed the deathblow with a triumphant warcry.

The bard and the warrior made their way to the heart of the school – the chapel. The long chapel to the Faith had been desecrated. Every statue had been destroyed, and the pews crushed and splintered. The holy books had been torn apart, their gilded leaves scattered across the room; the scrolls had been piled in the centre of the floor and fired; the prayer rugs had been rent in pieces and befouled. Someone had even pounded upon the marble floor in a score of places, sending a spider-web of cracks across the white stone.

Paedur spoke for the first time since entering the school. 'This is not true Chopt work – they kill for flesh and sport, not for religion, and they care nothing for objects. They wouldn't have caused such wanton destruction.'

'Unless they had been incited,' Katani added quietly, glancing up at him. His sharp face was set in hard lines, and his eyes had taken the whiteness of the marble floor, turning them to stone.

'You can wait here while I go up,' he said suddenly, startling her. He raised his head slightly, and she knew he meant the Monastery on the cliffs above.

'I think I'd rather go with you,' the Katan said without hesitation.

Paedur nodded and abruptly turned away; Katani took one last look around and hurried after him, shaking her head, wondering what they were going to find in the building above.

The bard and the warrior-maid climbed the long flight of stone steps that led up to the Monastery. It was long slow work, even for the bard; the steps were piled deep with snow above a sheathing of ice, each one having to be cleared before a foothold could be found, and with every step the icy wind threatened to hurl them down to the school building below. It was exhausting, both physically and mentally, and Katani found the very presence of the sheer drop on her right-hand side an additional drain on her energy. Before they were half way up, the bard was half-carrying an exhausted Katani, dragging her from step to step, his voice knifing deep into the lethal doze she had slipped into, dragging her back to consciousness, urging her on. By the time they reached the top of the steps he was bearing all the weight of her body clad in its ornate and heavy armour with no apparent effort. He put her down in the lee of a large standing stone incised with the glyphs 'Learning leads to Knowledge, Knowledge leads to Power –' and allowed a trickle of his own strength to flow through his hook into her exhausted body.

The solid brukwood gates of the Monastery were still closed and for a moment the bard allowed himself the brief fantasy that the blue-robed monks were still alive and safe behind the walls, even though his enhanced senses told him otherwise. But if the gates were closed, then how had the creatures got inside?

He found the breach in the wall less than a hundred paces from the gates; there was a huge gaping hole in the stone wall, and the ground around the hole was littered with chunks of rock. It looked as if a levin bolt had struck the stone, destroying it. Paedur knelt and touched the wall with his hook, but the metal remained cold, the runes dull, giving him no indication how the hole had been made. But if it was magic – and it surely looked that way – then it was fire-magic of sorts ... and the Chopts abhorred fire. It was beginning to look as if more than just the beasts had been in on the attack.

Paedur crawled through the opening, which sliced right

through the massive wall as thick as he was tall, and found himself in a tiny courtyard which, although he had never seen one before, he immediately realised was the brothers' cemetery. The bodies of the monks were usually burned and their ashes stored in tiny philtres of glass in niches in the walls. If a monk had achieved special greatness or advanced either the cause of Learning or the Old Faith in general, then the philtre might be made of crystal or even precious stone. A simple plaque on the wall gave the Brother's name and age; if he had been martyred then that was noted by the single word. But here the small plaques had been ripped from the walls, the ground was littered with shards of blue glass and the ground was covered in a layer of a fine grey-brown dust.

Paedur muttered a benediction as he stepped across the ashes of generations of monks, and experienced a sudden burst of an emotion – the first real emotion he had felt in a long time – an emotion which approached anger. This needless, senseless destruction appalled him; there was no reason for this, no excuse, and again it was completely out of character for the creatures. There was something more to this, something sinister.

Beyond the tiny courtyard lay a long high hall, the intricate stonework and corbelling the hallmarks of the Culai master-builders. The windows, set high in the walls to admit the wan northern light, had once been glazed with delicate coloured glass depicting the Gods of the Pantheon, but each one had been systematically broken, which, the bard noted, had taken both time and effort. All the doors had been shattered, hacked with axes or swords, and the older doors, where the hinges had been of leather, had been completely removed.

This had all been done to a deliberate cold-blooded plan; only its purpose eluded him.

When Paedur flung open the Monastery's great brukwood gates, Katani immediately stepped back, both swords coming almost naturally to her hands. With the light behind him, and his eyes reflecting the snow, the bard was a black demon-shape with glowing silver eyes. He turned away without a word, and crossed the courtyard into the huge church building.

Katani hurried through the gates, suddenly reluctant to be alone on the wind-swept ledge before the gates. She slid her swords back into their sheaths, and put her back to one of the doors, unsurprised when it closed easily and noiselessly. Closing the second gate, she lifted the bar and dropped it into place, and then cranked the chains that locked the enormous metal hinges into position, rendering them immovable. The gates were locked for the night. She turned and hurried after the bard, feeling foolishly like a child, conscious of the creeping shadows around her.

Paedur was standing just inside the chapel doors, unmoving. His very stillness warned Katani and she slid her shortsword free and immediately moved to the right hand side of the door, stepping quickly inside, her back to the cold stone. Without looking at her, the bard pointed upwards with his fore and little fingers. She squinted up into the dimness, but could see nothing except the barest outline of the time-darkened rafter beams.

Paedur moved his right arm, urging her out into the aisle, towards the simple stone altar-piece which now lay shattered across the cracked marbled steps. He pointed to her sword and then to her belt, his instructions plain. Reluctantly, Katani sheathed her sword and, with a steadying breath, walked slowly and steadily out into the open . . . and immediately heard the sound. There was someone – or something – in the rafters. Her fingers touched the throwing spikes in her sleeves, and curled around the deadly slivers of metal. She needed another sound – another sound to identify the location of the creature – and then she would drop to the ground, roll and throw . . .

'*NOOOoooo . . .!*'

The bard's command was ice-cold fire in her brain, stopping her in her tracks, almost sending her to her knees with its power. She half-turned – but found the bard had vanished. Throwing caution aside, she drew her swords and launched herself forward, moving across to a small side altar, and rolling through the arched entrance. Here at least she couldn't be seen from above. Crouching, she peered out into the chapel, looking for the bard; she eventually spotted him crawling up the wall like some hugely deformed spider, moving swiftly, scuttling sideways, then throwing himself away from the wall to catch his hook on a beam, and finally swinging himself around and up onto the beam, to stand unmoving on it. She became aware of other sounds on the beam, a squeal of – terror? – followed by the patter of feet across the wood. Speckles of dust drifted down from the rafters onto her face, making her blink, and turn away.

There was a sudden rasp of steel, and then she saw something small and pale move towards the still figure of the bard. The creature was carrying a long curved sabre that seemed far too large for it. The scream began then, a high-pitched wail of absolute terror and rage, coupled with a deep and terrible anger. The sabre fell, the bard's hook catching and entangling the blade, turning, twisting it, wrenching it from the creature's grasp, sending it whirling out off the beam. It plunged point first into a wooden pew and remained there, thrumming.

Katani stepped from the side chapel, a throwing spike aligned along her index finger . . . and then something launched itself at the bard, something small and white and blue.

Abruptly all sound ceased.

Paedur stepped off the rafter . . . to land lightly on his feet before the startled woman. In his arms was a pale bundle.

Katani approached, trying to make sense of the white cloth-wrapped shape. 'What is it?' she asked quietly, pointing with her sword.

Paedur gently lifted a long strip of dirty blue cloth, revealing a boy's filthy face. 'It's a survivor,' he said, with a humourless smile.

They were to camp that night in the ruins of the church, sheltering in one of the small side chapels. While Katani tended to the boy, Paedur dragged in some of the broken pews chopping them up for firewood with his hook, using his hook again to strike sparks from the stones. When the wood was burning strongly, he went in search of water, returning a few moments late with a much-dented altar vessel piled high with crushed snow.

He crouched down beside Katani and looked at the still figure of the boy, now sleeping peacefully beneath the warrior-maid's heavy furred cloak.

'I can find no injuries,' Katani said, glancing at the bard; in the firelight her amber-coloured eyes burned a deep red and her ice-white hair was burnished copper. 'He is remarkably well, with the exception of some cuts, bruises and scrapes, and from the condition of his fingers and toes, some mild frostbite. He hasn't eaten for a time, and I dare say hasn't slept well either.'

Paedur nodded. He lifted the ragged blue robe which Katani had cut off the boy, turning it in his hand. 'An acolyte of the Order; I wonder how he escaped.' He stood up – and Katani abruptly noticed he cast no dancing shadow on the wall. 'He will not awake until close to midnight. If you remain with him, I'll go and find you something to eat.'

The warrior-maid sat back against the cold stone wall, her longsword unsheathed and lying across her knees; her shortsword by her side. Her armour, which had been crafted from the cast-off skin of the extinct ice-serpents of Thusal, protected her somewhat from the bitter cold, but she was still chilled, a deep internal feeling she hadn't been able to shake off since she had left Death's Domain. She reached out and touched the boy; he seemed surprisingly warm, and she wondered if the bard had any hand in that.

She looked at the boy, surprised by her own mixed emotions and the depth of her feelings of pity and sorrow at his plight and suffering. She had never felt the slightest maternal urge during her previous brief life in the World of Men, and she had died before she had gifted her clan with a child. The Katan were warriors; they fought and died without time for husband or family, without ties that might lessen their effectiveness as warriors. However, each woman was expected to bear at least one child for the Katan tribe. Usually the most auspicious time for conception was chosen by one of the Craft Women, which almost always ensured that the child was a girl, and the fathers were usually taken from the freelance male warriors who often accompanied the Katan. For the Katan walked with War, as the saying went, and a mercenary – male or female – might become wealthy fighting with the Katan allies. But Katani had never contributed her child to the warriors; she had never felt the urge, nor found a male warrior she respected enough. It had never bothered her before. She had never even thought about it until now . . .

When she had accompanied the bard from the Silent Wood back into the Planes of Existence she had resolved to do all the things she hadn't done in her previous life, to live her life to the full, to broaden her interests, and even to give up the sword. And of course she had done none of them. She had fallen all so easily back into the life of a warrior; killing was her only trade – and it was something at which she was a perfectionist. She knew a thousand ways to take a life . . . She looked down at the sleeping boy and wondered what it would be like to create a life.

She reached out, brushing a length of cobweb from his face, wondering about him. Who was he and where had he come from and, more importantly, how had he escaped the slaughter? He was small and slender, with fine smooth skin, which was a light tan colour beneath the dirt and bruises. His face was small, almost round, and although his head had been shaved bald recently, a thin black fuzz had appeared. She found it difficult to guess his age, but his face was smooth, and there was no evidence that he shaved.

She moved his top lip slightly; his teeth were all intact, and reasonably clean. She then lifted his hand, looking at it. The skin was soft, the nails, although broken and cracked now, had once been smooth and even, and there was no evidence of welts or callouses either on his palms or fingers. He was from a family of wealth, and had obviously only lately come to the order. She knew it was customary for third or later sons of a lesser noble to be sent to the school for an education, but this boy had obviously been intended for the brotherhood – otherwise why had he been in the Monastery?

When she looked up, she found the boy had opened his eyes and was looking at her. His eyes were a deep, almost chestnut brown, and looked huge in the gauntness of his face. She gently laid his hand down, and then patted it, smiling in what she hoped was an encouraging manner, careful not to expose her pointed incisor teeth.

'I am Katani,' she said slowly and clearly.

The boy nodded, attempting a smile. He opened his mouth – and screamed, his eyes wide with terror!

Katani whirled, her sword moving up and back in a back-handed slash, her left hand drawing her shortsword as she was coming to her feet.

Her sword struck metal and then the long blade was caught in a metallic half circle and twisted from her grasp. 'Paedur,' she breathed, and then realised what had frightened the boy: the figure standing in the doorway looked the very essence of evil, a shadowless black shape, eyes blazing red fire.

She sheathed her swords and knelt by the boy's side and wrapped her arms around him. He was gasping for breath, shivering uncontrollably. 'SSShhh, ssshh now. It's all right. He's a friend. He will not harm you.' His face was a rigid mask, his eyes squeezed shut, and she wasn't even sure if the boy could hear her. She looked up at the bard. 'Help him, please.'

Paedur stepped into the tiny chamber, the light flowing from his cloak like oil off water, and suddenly – swiftly – reached out and touched the boy lightly in the centre of the chest. He immediately slumped in Katani's arms, his features lax and at peace. He was breathing deeply, evenly. Katani then settled him back beneath the covers, and wiped the long trails of spittle from his chin and the tears from his cheeks.

Paedur tossed a pair of small birds into the corner beside the woman. 'Will you prepare these?' he asked abruptly.

Katani nodded.

'The boy hungers; it would be better to have food prepared for him; it will help ease his fear. In the meantime, perhaps I can ease his troubled mind.'

'How?'

The bard turned to look at the boy; he was sleeping easily now, his thin chest rising and falling beneath Katani's cloak, his features smooth and untroubled. Paedur reached out and, with the point of his hook, carefully pulled back the cloak from the boy's chest. He was naked beneath, the Katan having removed his soiled and damp clothing earlier; then the bard laid the flat of his hook across the boy's body. The metal glowed warmly red in the firelight, the twisting runes coming to a brief sparkling life, and the boy twisted his head, mumbling in his sleep. Beneath his closed eyelids his eyes darted.

'Who are you?' Paedur asked suddenly.

The boy's lips moved, moved again before they formed the single word, 'Gire,' he said, pronouncing it to rhyme with 'fire'.

'That's a Talarian name,' Katani said quickly. 'In my day there was a warrior in the Katan who bore the feminine version, Gireer.'

Paedur lifted his hand, silencing her. 'Where are you from?' he asked, his voice soft and gentle . . . and insistent.

'Talaria,' the boy said quietly. His voice had grown stronger, and he now lay still and restful; only his eyes, behind his closed eyelids, were active.

'And what are you doing here?

'I am to be a monk in the Order of Ectoraige.'

'And you are long here?'

'Less than one moon.'

Katani, who had begun to pluck the two small birds the bard had brought, looked up and grunted. 'Welcome to the Northlands.'

'Gire, listen to me very carefully. I want you to open your eyes and look around you. You will see two people: a man and a woman. They are your friends: they mean you no harm. Now open your eyes, and look to our right . . .

Gire's deep brown eyes snapped open, and settled on the woman. 'This is Katani, a warrior of the fabled Katan. You have nothing to fear from her; she is a friend to the Faith. Now, look at me . . .'

Even in his enchanted state the boy's dulled eyes widened in shock . . . horror . . . recognition?

'Do you know me?' Paedur asked curiously. 'Have we met?'

'I have never met you before.'

'But you know me?' Paedur persisted.

'I have heard tell of a man with a hook in place of his left hand.'

'And who is that?'

'He is legend; he is the Bard Paedur.'

'I am the Bard Paedur.' He pulled back his cloak to reveal the bardic sigil high on his left shoulder. 'Now, when I touch you, this enchantment will end, and you will awaken fully, and you will remember everything that has gone before. You will know us, and you will know you have nothing to fear.' He lifted his hook off the boy's chest and touched him lightly with the fingers of his right hand.

Gire's eyes cleared, and it was as if life had flowed back into his face, animating it, bringing it alive. He sat up suddenly and looked from the bard to Katani and then back to the tall shadowed figure. 'You really are the bard,' he breathed. It was more a statement than a question.

Paedur nodded silently, his face expressionless.

'I know all about you; even in Talaria, you are legend – of course they don't believe you are real. But the monks taught us about you. I've always wanted to meet you ...' The words tumbled over themselves in his excitement.

Paedur raised his hand, shaking his head to stop the flow of questions. 'Later, all this can come later,' he said softly. 'Now you must rest and eat. Later, we will talk and decide your future.'

'I'm going with you,' the boy said impulsively.

Paedur shook his head. 'You cannot go where I'm going.'

'Is it true you're immortal, that you were gifted by C'lte, the Lord of Life, with Life Immortal?'

'I am long-lived,' Paedur murmured.

'You cannot die?' the boy whispered in amazement.

'Oh, I can die,' Paedur's lips curled in a smile, 'but it seems I cannot stay dead. Now rest,' he commanded. 'We will talk later.' His index finger touched the boy's forehead; the deep brown eyes immediately rolled upwards and the boy dropped back onto the makeshift pillow, asleep.

'What are we going to do with him?' Katani asked. She had plucked the birds and was now cleaning them out with a tiny knife.

'He cannot come with us.' Paedur settled back against the cold stones, stretching out his long legs. He adjusted his cloak about his body and tilted his head back, closing his eyes. With the light gone from his eyes, and his pale expressionless face reflecting the flickering reddish-yellow light, he looked as if he had been carved from stone.

'What are we going to do with him?' Katani repeated.

'We will leave him in Thusal – there is a bardhouse there.'

'Thusal is hardly the safest of places now, is it?'

'Safer than travelling on the road with us,' the bard said quietly.

Katani contented herself with wrapping the birds into a ball of soft clay and then pushing them deep into the fire with the point of her knife.

She looked up at the bard, and it took an almost deliberate effort of will to separate him from the shadows flickering across the wall. 'Leaving the problem of the boy aside for the moment, have you decided what we are going to do?'

He shook his head briefly.

'Do you know where we're going, then?'

'Thusal,' he said shortly.

'And then?'

'In search of Geillard if he is here in the Northlands, and in search of the intelligence behind these Chopt raids.'

'And?'

'Kill them both.'

Katani looked at him. 'Why?'

'Because . . .' he began.

'Because the Pantheon, through Churon, ordered you,' the woman interrupted.

Paedur nodded. 'Perhaps not in so many words . . '

'And you're not going to question that?'

The bard's eyes opened, the firelight blazing in them, reflecting back at Katani. She looked away quickly and concentrated on the fire, rolling the hardened balls of mud around with a twig. Without looking up, she said. 'They've made you into their creature . . .'

'I know that. They paid me well for it, though,' the bard said quickly, almost defensively.

'Did you ever have a choice? While I was in Karfondal, I heard the story of how you became the Champion of the Gods. They tricked you, and then used you, first to save themselves from the Religion and the Sealed Vessel of the Chrystallis and then they used you to put Kutor on the throne and further the cause of the Faith, and now they're using you again. You've killed for them in the past and now you're planning to kill again – and all without question. You've become a quai!'

From the corner of her eye, Katani saw the bard's head coming up. 'Even the Katan,' she hurried on, 'the finest killers on all the Planes of Existence, never killed without reason or just cause; it is the *reason* which differentiates simple murder from killing.'

'Warrior,' Paedur said, his voice almost cold, 'I am a follower of the Old Faith. It is the One True Belief, and I am honoured to be its Champion. I will die – and kill – in its defence.'

'Without question?'

The bard didn't reply.

'If you kill without question, you become little better than those you are killing.'

Paedur closed his eyes without replying and bent his head, effectively ending the conversation.

Katani woke Gire a little later. She fed him water in sips, and then rolled one of the balls of fire-hardened mud from the fire. With the metal sleeve on her forearm she cracked it open and the delicious aroma of roasted fowl wafted around the tiny broken chapel. Gire's stomach rumbled loudly. Katani peeled off the solid mud covering, the bird's wrinkled skin pulling away with it, and she passed the bird to Gire on the end of one of her knives. 'Carefully, now; it's hot. Take small bits and chew thoroughly, otherwise you'll end up with a stomach-ache that not even the bard can cure.' She cracked open the second bird for herself, impaling it on two knives.

Gire, his mouth bright with grease, looked at the apparently sleeping bard. 'What about Paedur?'

Katani grunted around a mouthful of hot flesh. 'Paedur does

not eat, he does not drink and, despite appearances, he does not sleep.'

The boy nodded, seemingly unsurprised. 'Have you known him long?'

'Long enough,' Katani grinned. 'We spent some time dead together.' She laughed at Gire's expression. 'Eat your food. I'll explain later.'

They continued eating in silence, Katani watching in amusement as he picked the bones clean. When he was finished, she passed him the remnants of the water the bard had brought earlier and a rag to clean his face and hands. He sat back, his spine against the stone and rested both hands on his stomach. 'I feel human again.'

Katani couldn't resist a smile. 'Well, you're probably the only one of this company who is.'

'I haven't eaten so well for . . . well . . . not since . . .' his eyes clouded.

'Do you want to tell me what happened?' Katani asked.

The boy shook his head slightly.

'It would help – both you and us,' she said. 'In my land there was a saying, "Telling eases the trouble." '

Gire looked at Paedur. 'He can hear us,' Katani assured him. 'We need to know who attacked you, how many, what they were like . . .'

Gire nodded. He shivered suddenly and drew Katani's cloak tighter around his body, and then he looked into the fire, his eyes sparkling brilliantly with unshed tears. He took a deep sobbing breath and began . . .

'They came five – no six – nights ago. Hundreds of them.

'The evening meal was long over, and the mid-evening bell had rung, so it would have been sometime before the midnight bell, and most of the brothers by that time would have gone to their beds. The brothers disdain the use of artificial light, for they say it destroys the eyes and that knowledge should only be sought and absorbed in the pure light of day. So most retire to bed early, rising again just before the dawn.

'I was not abed, however, for I had received a summons earlier that day to attend the Master directly after the evening meal. I had been expecting the call for days, for I was new to the Order and had not yet had the opportunity to discuss my future with him, and it was said that he prided himself that he knew every man and boy's name, his family, country and ambitions.

'But when I climbed the steps and was admitted into the Monastery I learned that the Master and the Teachers were all in conference together, and would in all likelihood be there for some portion of the evening.

'I didn't know what to do. Should I wait, or would it be better if I were to return on the morrow? But there was no-one to advise me, and then I suddenly thought that this might be one of those tests the Teachers sometimes set a pupil: setting him a strange or difficult task, and then judging his performance. I decided to stay – at least for a little time. So, I sat down in the shadow of a statue of the Lord Ectoraige in the main hall, where I could see the conference room – and there I promptly fell asleep.

'I don't know how long I slept – not long I think, but I awoke suddenly, bitterly cold, and feeling strangely numb. I recall rubbing my eyes, which felt sore and gritty, and watching, almost stupidly, as a fog – a pale yellowish dirty fog – rolled down the corridor. It piled up around the doors to the conference room, like waves washing around a stone, until it had almost reached the handles – and then it was as if it had been suddenly sucked in under the door.

'I tried to move, but I couldn't; I couldn't even shout.

'I heard screams from within, deep, racking coughs, furniture falling – and then there was nothing, no sound, no sound at all.

'And then the beasts came.

'They were Chopts. I had never seen one before, but they had been described to me often. They walked like men, and they were filthy, their long hair matted to their bodies. Their speech was like the sound of animals. Their weapons were new – I remember that clearly – they were bright and sparkling, clean almost.

'There were others with them, and these were men. They were

wild folk, tall, with dark weathered skins, and beards and hair that looked as if they were wet, and the beards divided down the middle and were plaited. They carried swords that were almost as tall as themselves. They looked like warriors.

'They walked past me, and although they were no further away from me than I am from you, they didn't seem to see me, but perhaps that was because they were intent on the conference room. They opened the doors and went inside, and I caught a brief glimpse of the Master and Teachers slumped, some over the table, others on the floor, their skins the same yellowish colour as the fog.

'And then . . . and then . . . and then the beasts and the men killed them . . .

'And then they fed . . .

'Later, much later, I don't know how long, but it was long enough for them to have fed well, another man appeared. He was alone, and although he was smaller and thinner than any of the others, they all bowed to him, and seemed almost terrified of him.

'And I'll tell you true, when I first saw the bard, I thought it was him again. But I think he was smaller, but that might have been the only difference; he wore a dark cloak in the same fashion as the bard and moved just as smoothly and swiftly. I didn't see his face, but as he passed me, I caught a glimpse of one of his hands, and it looked like a twisted piece of rotten wood. There were two guards with him, and they were like nothing I have ever seen before: they were neither man nor beast. They weren't tall, but they were broad and looked incredibly powerful; they had two long tusks curling up from their lower lips, and these looked as if they had been painted in a twisting curling design, and their bodies were covered in short bristling hair.

'The small man stood in the doorway of the conference room and then I clearly heard him say, "Excellent. This will bring him like a moth to a flame, and like the flame to the moth, it will destroy him!"'

5 Sacrifice

What evil is committed and condoned in the name of religion?
from . . . The Warrior, the Life of Owen, Weapon Master

Owen stepped into the shop and immediately stood to one side
and paused, allowing his eyes to adjust to the relative dimness of
the interior before moving. It smelled of leather and metal, of
polish and grit, a smell which the Weapon Master over his long
years of campaigning had come to associate with death.

The shop was an Armoury, the finest in the Nations.

The shop was situated in a side street just off the quays, a tall,
thin, high building, that contained some of the most lethal
weaponery the Weapon Master had ever seen. Most were im-
ports, strange creations from each of the Seven Nations, others
from the outlying provinces, and even some from the Island
Kingdoms. The majority of them he knew and had used; of the
few he didn't, he could at least guess at their function, but that
still left one or two that were a complete mystery to him.

The proprietor of the Armoury looked very much like his shop
and its lethal contents; he was tall and thin, sharp-featured, with
perhaps a touch of Shemmatae blood in him, lending him a
curiously sinister appearance. He was wearing a long, loose-
sleeved merchant's robe of the newly-fashionable metallic cloth,
and his hands were buried in the drooping sleeves. He bowed
deeply.

'I am honoured, sir.'

Owen nodded slightly, his eyes moving, his senses alert, absorbing his surroundings. There was a third person in the shop, he
was sure of it: the small hairs on the back of his neck had risen, a
primitive warning signal that he had learned never to ignore.

'It is a pleasure to be in the company of a professional,' the
merchant continued, the smile on his face fixed and unmoving,

his black eyes expressionless. 'I am the Warlord . . .' his smile deepened at Owen's change of expression. 'You will pardon my little joke, but my name was – is – Wasloden, and its singularity and my singular occupation have encouraged the populace to address me by the title, "Warlord". I adhere to it out of a sense of amusement.'

'It is apt,' Owen said softly, his eyes moving over the man, probing the dimness behind him. There! He fixed the position of the third man behind and to the left of the Warlord, in the shadows behind a display of chain and linked mail shirts.

'And you are Owen, the Weapon Master of course,' the Warlord said, his smile deepening even further at Owen's obvious surprise. 'Oh, please do not look so alarmed; modesty would be false and unbecoming. I am aware – as I am sure is everyone in Karfondal – of your identity, and those of us with sources of information are also aware just who was the engineer of our present Emperor's sudden elevation to the throne.'

Owen silently worked out the details of the Warlord's sentence, and when he had finally got it right, he said, 'I am but a mercenary . . .'

'Nay, nay, more than a mercenary. The Defender of Car'-an'tual, the Weapon Master, the Killer, Wandering Death, and now Kingmaker.'

'You seem remarkably well informed,' Owen said; and then added dryly, 'If you have any affection for the person lurking in the shadows, you will tell them to go, lest I am forced to kill them – merely for my continued peace of mind, of course.'

The Warlord bowed again, the smile tightening on his thin lips, and then, without turning around he said, 'Go, go.' There was a movement behind him and a broad, stocky young man carrying a cocked and loaded crossbow moved from the shadows and hurried back down the shop. 'He is there for *my* continued peace of mind,' the Warlord said. 'And now, you will join me in a cup before we conduct some business?'

Owen nodded, and followed the Warlord back through the long dark shop and out into a surprisingly large courtyard. The courtyard was closed in by a high spike-topped wall on two sides, and although the third side was open to the river, it was protected by a deep ditch which was lined with spikes whose barbs were suspiciously discoloured. To one side of the courtyard was a series of man-tall straw poles. There was a simple red and white patch about chest height on each.

As they came out into the courtyard, the young man Owen had seen earlier was firing, reloading and firing his crossbow with surprising swiftness and equally surprising accuracy.

The Warlord stopped behind the young man and Owen, watching him, and seeing them together, noticed the resemblance between the two men.

'This is my son,' the Warlord said, deliberately not naming the boy.

The boy turned to the Weapon Master and bowed deeply, his eyes chill and sullen.

'Your speed and accuracy with that weapon are extraordinary,' Owen said, bowing slightly.

The boy bowed again, his expression unchanged.

The Warlord's face creased into the first genuine smile Owen had seen on it. 'My son has mastered the various types of crossbows, both hunting and target, and has even designed two versions of his own, which we should be marketing shortly. Perhaps they might interest you, Weapon Master; one is a bow shooting multiple bolts – a dozen would seem to be the best figure – and the other is a completely silent weapon, no noise, no snap of prod or twang of cord; it would be suitable for . . . night work . . .'

'An assassin's tool,' Owen said flatly.

'Ah well, yes, yes, of course it could be used for that, I suppose,' the Warlord said softly, as if the idea had only just occurred to him. He turned away from his son and crossed the courtyard to a tall slender doorway that was cut flush into the wall and without surround, lintel or step; it was so smooth and featureless that it might easily be passed over – especially in the dark. As Owen followed the man through the door, he noticed the heavy iron grill that was now fixed open against the wall directly behind the door. At night it would be locked in place, making access through the door – which was a handspan thick – almost certainly impossible. He suddenly wondered why the Warlord was allowing him to see all this.

As if reading his thoughts the Warlord said, 'My security must be tight.' 'There have been several attempted break-ins, all of which have, of course, failed. Men seeking weapons either for themselves or resale, I suppose. This is the finest collection in the Nations,' he added proudly.

'I've heard you also deal in precious metals,' Owen said quietly, following the man up a flight of narrow, uneven stairs.

The Warlord paused with his hand on the handle of a solid-looking brukwood door. He glanced back over his shoulder and smiled thinly at the hard-faced man. 'And who would have told you that, eh?'

'I've heard that because your security is so good various merchants have asked you to hold their metal, jewels or coin in safe-keeping for them. I've also heard that you're prepared to finance certain individuals or projects – for a consideration, of course.'

The Warlord turned away, his face a stone mask, and threw open the door and walked into a long white room. It was tall and thin, more like a hallway than a room, and barely wide enough to accommodate the two chairs positioned on opposite sides of a square table at the far end of the long room. Light, streaming in through the rectangular window above the table, burned off the white walls, ceilings and floor, giving the room a vaguely threatening oppressive atmosphere.

The Warlord strode to the end of the room and sank down into the padded seat of the tall-backed wooden chair and rested both arms on the table.

And the Weapon Master suddenly realised that the man had no hands. Two spikes of metal protruded from the stumps of his wrists.

Owen sat down opposite him, and immediately checked the window, but it was canted in such a way that although he could see out and the slightly stale breeze off the river wafted in, the room wasn't overlooked by any other building. He turned back to the man, his features assuming their usual impassive mask, carefully avoiding looking at the spiked arms. But the Warlord deliberately raised his hands. 'You may have heard about these – I can tell you the tale that I lost them experimenting with explosive powders, or I can tell you how they were severed in an accident aboard ship where they were caught in the ropes, or I can even tell you the tale how they were badly mangled as I fought off some wild animal. But the truth is they were chopped off by order of a court in Lostrice when I was a boy as punishment for stealing.'

'A barbarous thing . . .' Owen remarked, looking at the spikes, considering them as weapons, although the body of the spike was round, the tips had been flattened slightly to give them a pyramidal shape and then sharpened to give four – albeit small – obviously razor-sharp edges and a point. 'Why did you tell me?' he suddenly asked. 'Why didn't you tell me one of your stories?'

The Warlord smiled, and perhaps there was some genuine emotion in it now. 'Because you must have done some research before you came to me – and if you've come to me you must want something, something important, I'll wager, to bring you here yourself rather than sending a servant to summon me to the palace. Suffice it to say that I don't want to risk lying to you at this early stage in our relationship.'

'I admire honesty in a man.'

'Perhaps you would care to reciprocate,' the Warlord suggested.

The Weapon Master smiled thinly and, pulling out a black crossbow bolt, laid it carefully on the table between them. For a moment, it rocked back and forth on its black feathers, the tiny ticking noise loud in the warm silence of the room.

'I won't ask if it is yours,' Owen said watching the Warlord's eyes. 'The workmanship speaks for that, but let me tell you something of its recent history. It was pulled out of the eye socket of a man named Stinger this morning. He had been shot from quite a distance by someone of great skill. Stinger was a link in a chain which leads back to the conspirators who are plotting against the throne, and the Imperials are actively pursuing that link at the moment; indeed they are currently looking for the maker of this bolt . . .'

They have already been here,' the Warlord interrupted, 'and I told them it had been made for a one-handed bard . . .'

'. . . named Paedur, I know. I also happen to know that that isn't true. Which immediately made me wonder why you should lie, and there is no reason for you to lie – unless of course you had something to hide. I think you have, and that makes me think you might be the next link in the chain.'

'I don't think . . .' the Warlord began, beginning to rise to his feet.

Owen raised his hand. 'Listen. This is not perhaps what you think. If need be I could have come here with a full squadron of the Emperor Legion and have them beat down the door and tear this place apart, and then think of the fun Fodla would have had extracting information from you and your son . . .' He shook his head, smiling slightly at the thought. 'No, I came to you because I want you to put me in touch with the opposition leaders.'

'And why should I want to do that . . . assuming I could of course?' the Warlord asked curiously.

'I have a proposition for them.'

'What sort of proposition?'

'I made this Emperor – I can break him also, and just as easily.'

'And why would you want to do that?' the Warlord asked very softly, leaning across the table.

'For several reasons . . .'

'Such as?'

'Because although I am first and foremost a mercenary, I do have principles – principles which are very important to me. I defended Car'an'tual because of those principles. I made Kutor Emperor because I believed his claim to the throne to be a just one and also because I believed that Geillard's reign had degenerated into a useless mockery.'

'And now?' the Warlord asked, when Owen paused.

'And now I believe I was wrong. Kutor is no better than Geillard; perhaps he'll be even worse. Already he has diverted vital funds from the army to aid the refugees coming in from the devastated coastal regions. I learned this morning that there are reports of more coming up from the Southlands which have been hit by drought, and still more coming down from the north where the weather has turned unseasonally cold. Karfondal cannot cope with this sudden influx of people; it has neither the resources nor the space to contain them. Kutor, however, is planning new towns, new roads, and he intends to pay for them with a major reorganisation of the taxes. One of the more interesting bits of this new legislation will be to levy a substantially heavier tax on items which he will deem to be not of an essential nature – and you will find weapons amongst that class.'

'That is madness!'

'His long-term plan is to take the weapons away from the common people, but leave them in the hands of his chosen few, his army, his militia – therefore making it all the easier to control the people.'

'I've heard nothing about this,' the Warlord said quietly, turning to stare at the pale blue sky through the window.

'It is hardly the sort of thing he will announce in a proclamation, now is it?' Owen asked dryly. 'But there will be an announcement about the refugee aid programme soon, I should imagine. You can judge the truth of what I am saying then.'

The Warlord waved an arm, his spike glittering in the light. 'Oh, I have no reason to doubt you . . .'

'But this could be a devious ploy . . .' Owen suggested, with a wry smile.

The Warlord smiled thinly. 'I don't think so. It is too cumbersome and crudely contrived to be a ploy. I'm sure Kutor and his cronies could have thought up something more interesting, something original. And of course, I am a very good judge of men,' he added, 'I believe you.'

Owen looked at him without saying anything.

'Would you be prepared to kill Kutor?'

'I am a mercenary, not an assassin,' the Weapon Master said immediately.

'A mercenary is a paid warrior, an assassin is a paid killer – the roles are not so different,' the Warlord said. 'If the price was right, would you kill him?'

'No.' And before the Warlord could say anything, Owen continued, 'However, I would deliver him into the hands of . . . well, shall we say of those who have Karfondal's best interests at heart.'

'With what preconditions?'

'The only precondition would be the price, and that it would be paid in full up front.'

'That is unusual,' the Warlord said, looking at the table, touching the tips of his spikes together. 'The usual agreement is for half on agreement, half on completion.'

'But I am a man of principle; I would not attempt to cheat you.'

The Warlord bowed. 'I know that, but I cannot say yea or nay on this; I have not the authority. I will need to bring it before my principals. Come to my shop three days hence. I will know then.'

Owen nodded. 'Good enough.' He stood up, looking at the thin man expectantly.

The Warlord rapped one of his metal spikes against the wooden table, making the metal sing. The door immediately opened and the armourer's son stepped into the room. He was still carrying the cocked and loaded crossbow. 'Our visitor is leaving; please take him down.' He looked up at the Weapon Master. 'In three days.'

Owen nodded and stepped away from the table; then he stopped and looked back. 'Tell me, why did you tell the Imperials that the black crossbow bolt had been made for the bard?'

'Imagine the consternation it must have caused at court!' The Warlord grinned.

Owen shook his head slightly and walked away without another word.

The Warlord waited until he heard the door below shut solidly, and then he stretched to his full height and looked through the window, watching his son lead the Weapon Master across the courtyard towards the shop, and only when he was satisfied that the warrior was gone, did he turn back to the room. 'Well, lady?'

A section of the bone-white wall swung open and a tiny, old woman stepped into the room. Although she had always been

65

small in stature, the years had withered her even further, twisting her frail body into a mockery of its former shape. Her features were seamed with age, giving her an almost simian or mummified appearance, but her eyes were sharp. as hard as glass and the colour of a winter's sky.

She was the Lady Esse, a sorceress of almost legendary power, once Geillard's teacher, but long since gone into retirement to pursue her occult studies. When Geillard had been dethroned, she had immediately returned to the capital to organise the resistance against the usurper, and she was using the Warlord's armoury as her base.

'Is he genuine?' the Warlord asked, deferentially.

The tiny woman limped down the length of the room and sank into the chair the Weapon Master had vacated. 'What do you think?' she asked venomously. 'This is the man who fought with the Band of Kloor, and then forsook it – the only man ever to do so – with the assistance of the cursed bard. This is the man the bard sent to the Outlands to aid the outlaw chief; this is the man who organised Kutor's army; this is the man who came to the city during the height of the battle with the intention of assassinating the Emperor; this is the man who is responsible for the death of Salier. Because of this man, a usurper sits upon the throne of the Seven Nations while the rightful Emperor lurks in the Choptlands. And you ask me if he is genuine?' she spat.

'Then it is a ploy to discover the identities of those plotting against Kutor?' the Warlord suggested, but here the old woman didn't look quite so certain.

'Possibly, possibly. But I feel sure that the usurper knows, or at the very least has a very good idea of those who are against him. Indeed, this may be nothing more than a crude ploy to establish the names of the individuals or families who are actively plotting against him, rather than those who merely oppose him on principle. However, the man, this Owen, is interesting.' Her pale eyes closed into slits, 'I sense confusion within him, almost as if he himself were experiencing doubts about the new ruler – and these are doubts that might be capitalised upon later. This is no crude brigand, no simple mercenary. This is a man with principles, a proud man, a man of honour. And they are often the easiest to bend and use.'

'We could kill him,' the Warlord suggested.

'Aye – and bring the wrath of Kutor and his army down upon us, and if they don't get you, then that savage Shemmat servant of his will.' Her eyes snapped open, catching and holding the armourer's black eyes. 'At the moment, you are the link, Warlord; you are the only clue they have . . .' Her voice fell, and the Warlord felt something cold and chill walk up his spine. 'Remove you and we remove the link,' she said speculatively.

'Lady, you cannot . . .'

The Lady Esse shook her head slightly. 'I was merely thinking aloud. You may rest easy for the moment – you are truly useful to me and Geillard's cause.'

'There is no stauncher supporter,' the Warlord said fervently, realising how close to death he had come. He had seen the old woman kill without a second thought or qualm, merely because she had assumed there might be a threat in the future or because someone's present use was limited or finished. Working with the Lady Esse was a gamble. If her plans succeeded and Geillard returned to the throne, then those who had helped her would be placed in positions of extraordinary power. But there were risks, and besides the risks of failure, there was the prime risk of either her anger or her disinterest. Both were lethal. 'What should I do regarding the Weapon Master, Lady?' he asked diffidently.

'Bring him back. Tell him you need proof of his support for your cause, and in return give him . . . give him de Courtney's name . . .'

'But, Lady, he is one of us . . .'

'If the Weapon Master is on our side, then de Courtney will be safe, but if not . . . de Courtney's services are dispensable. His support is not perhaps as staunch as it should be, and those not fully with us are against us. He has contributed nothing in the past few moons, and he will run at the first sign of trouble. He will be no loss. There is also the problem that they suspect him because of his closeness to Geillard, so his name will be neither a surprise nor a revelation. And by giving it, we lose nothing.'

'But if he should talk?'

Lady Esse grinned mirthlessly. 'He will not talk!'

The Warlord closed up shop late in the afternoon, just as the sun was beginning to dip below the city walls, lengthening the shadows, allowing the first chill of evening to settle in. He had pulled on a travelling cloak over his merchant's robe and pulled up the hood, perhaps against the chill, but more likely to conceal his features.

Tien tZo waited until he was sure the Warlord was on the move before stepping out of the shadows and hurrying after him. The small Shemmat had once again donned the guise of a holy man, an Andam, one of those blessed – or cursed – with the wasting sickness associated with their faith. Completely swathed in the torn grey robes, with only his eyes uncovered, Tien had no difficulty in following the Warlord, his great height alone making him stand out from the crowd, and most of these people parted for the diseased holy man following behind.

The arms merchant took a circuituous route through the Lower City and then moved on through the banking district into the more prosperous trading section.

The perfumery was an ornately decorated establishment backing onto the main thoroughfare, a small shop rich in odours and essences which contrasted sharply with the distinctive sweet-sour scent of the city in general. Tien tZo watched from across the street while the Warlord spoke briefly to the short foppish owner who accompanied him to the door. The perfumery owner allowed the tall angular figure to continue his route up the street, before checking the street in both directions and then closing the door and pulling down the embroidered blind to indicate that the shop was closed. The Warlord stopped again, this time at a shop that was decorated in beaten brass and metal, and with a sign that proclaimed him a blacksmith. The Shemmat squatted in the street opposite the shop, his head bent, his eyes lost in the shadow of his cowl. He immediately decided that this was no common blacksmith, this was no maker of shoes, no hammerer of bars; this man created tiny, delicate artifacts from glowing metal, turning a simple torch or even a doorhandle into something of beauty. Again, the Warlord spoke to him briefly and hurried on, and when he had gone the blacksmith too closed up shop.

In all the Warlord spoke to a dozen merchants, all of them wealthy men, with fine addresses in the best districts. Tien tZo had the distinct impression that he was arranging a meeting or gathering of some sort.

Hurrying now – as if he had lingered too long – the Warlord made his way to the Cathedral of the Religion which stood in the main square, and which had once been dedicated to the Old Faith. When Kutor had taken power – and against the bard's wishes – the new Emperor had refused to rededicate the old temple to the Faith, and had merely had it closed and sealed, banning all worship in it. He had sworn that as a token of his thanks to the Gods of the Pantheon, he would build the finest cathedral in all the Planes of Existence to the Faith. But that had been before the realities of the situation had sunk in – and Karfondal had been flooded with refugees. Now only the promise remained.

When he had turned into the main square, Tien tZo immediately thought that the Warlord was going to pray before the sealed and chained doors of the cathedral, but the merchant had hurried on up the rose-coloured marble steps and, ignoring the main doors, slipped in behind one of the supporting pillars – and didn't reappear. It took Tien a few moments to realise that the man must have gone inside somehow. From his position in the shadow of an alley, the Shemmat studied the occupants of the square – and immediately spotted three watchers, or guards. Although they were dressed as common fruitsellers, Tien recognised by the way they walked and moved that they were armed and alert.

But he needed to get inside . . .

And then he remembered the last time he had visited the cathedral. It had been in the last days of the battle, before Kutor had ascended the throne, when he and Owen had come to Karfondal in an attempt to kill Geillard and as many of his advisers as possible. That had been the first time he had worn the Andam disguise; he had sat on those rose marbled steps and prayed to

69

his ancestor and the Cathedral Guards had come and taken him around the side of the cathedral into a tiny side street . . . The Shemmat's dour face broke into a rare smile: he had his way in.

The smell hit him as soon as he forced open the lock. The Shemmat had lived with the smell of death for almost all his life, and he knew the stink of it, and its attendant odours of blood and faeces, sweat and urine. Something – no, many things – had died here!

Tien waited until his eyes adjusted to the gloom and then slowly and quietly stripped off the Andam robes; beneath he was wearing a simple cotton shirt over cotton breeks tucked into his old boots. In his belt were two hand axes and there was a long, slim-bladed knife in a sheath sewn into his right boot. Drawing the knife, he padded softly down the corridor, following the death-smell.

In a tiny room at the end of the corridor he found seven dead bodies. They were all female, all young – the eldest around seventeen or so – and in every case their chest had been opened and their hearts torn out. They had been sacrificed!

The Shemmat closed the door and had begun to silently retrace his steps when another door opened and a short, stout young man wearing a heavy black robe stepped out into the corridor. The hood of his robe was thrown back on his bald head and his pale face was glistening with sweat. His eyes were glazed and there was a curiously vacant smile fixed to his lips. He was carrying another corpse over his shoulder, the dead girl's blood seeping into his heavy robe.

The young man stopped, his eyes beginning to blink rapidly. In the single moment it took him to come out of his trance Tien tZo killed him with a single blow above the lip that drove slivers of shattered bone into the brain. He was dead before he hit the ground.

Quietly, furiously angry with himself, Tien tZo dragged the two bodies to the small reeking room and tossed them in on top of the piled corpses.

He had reacted instinctively, killing the man – and now those who congregated here would know that their sanctuary had been discovered. So he had but one chance to find out as much as he could . . .

Settling his weapons, Tien stripped off the dead youth's heavy black cloak and pulled it over his own head. Moving quietly to the door the youth had come through, Tien pulled up the hood – and stepped out into the cathedral. He was standing behind and to the left of the altar, facing a surprisingly large congregation of a little more than a hundred people, and even as he was walking up to stand behind the altar-stone, his hands buried in his sleeves, copying a similarly dressed man opposite him, two things were immediately apparent: the congregation were all male, and all from the nobility or wealthy merchant classes.

The Cathedral of the New Religion – because of its original use as a temple of the Old Faith – was a curious mixture of styles. There were empty spaces where statuary of the Pantheon had stood, and blank – scrubbed or painted-over – inscriptions on the walls. The new statues of the Religion's gods were crude and looked almost unfinished, while the invocations to the gods of the Religion looked like graffiti on the elegant walls.

And the congregation was lost within the vastness of the building. They were gathered in the long pews directly before the altar, serious men, for the most part soberly dressed, but it was their expressions that interested Tien. He had seen that look before, the glazed, fixed stare, the mouth slightly open, tongues moving frequently across dry lips. It was the same expression he had seen in the arena or on those ghouls who wandered a battlefield following an engagement. It was the blood-look. They had come to see a sacrifice.

Tien had discovered seven bodies in the room below, and then there was the one the smiling thug had brought down, which made eight, and there were four girls sitting on a bench before him – four to be butchered. Twelve young women, and he had no doubt that they were virgins. What he did find surprising, however, was that the four remaining girls were sitting quite still, unshackled and unbound. Tien looked at their eyes for signs of drugging, but they were bright and alert; which meant that they were giving themselves freely for sacrifice. He looked at the congregation again, concentrating now on the first two rows, and immediately spotted the likenesses between at least two of the girls and two of the men there.

71

There was movement and a small wizened woman limped down from the altar throne. In her brown seamed face only her eyes – which were a pale watery blue – seemed alive. She didn't have to speak: without a word the next girl stood up and shrugged off her simple robe, and then, naked, she climbed the steps to the altar, bowed to the old woman, climbed up onto the blood-stained stone and closed her eyes.

The old woman reached out and touched her lightly on the face, and the girl's whole body twitched. 'Fear not,' the woman hissed, 'your gift to your god will be rewarded a thousandfold.'

The girl nodded jerkily. 'Forgive my transgressions,' she said quickly.

'Your presence here forgives them.' The old woman reached down by her side and lifted a slightly curved butchering knife. Although it had been plated in silver and the hilt inset with gemstones, Tien tZo still recognised the basic shape – it was designed to cut flesh and bone with the least resistance.

'Lord Trialos,' the old woman said suddenly, 'we call upon you again in the name of these here present to accept this virgin bride as a token of our allegiance and devotion to you. And if you find this body acceptable, then take it as your own and walk amongst us. But thy will be done, and we dedicate the body's essence to your cause to use as you so wish.'

And she plunged the knife down, driving it in below the young woman's breast.

Tien tZo heard bone pop and crack, and the woman convulsed once and died. The old woman turned the knife, cutting through flesh and bone, opening the chest, and then she reached into the bloody mess and pulled out something which filled her hand, something darkly reddish-purple, veined – and pulsating!

'Accept this body, accept this escaping life essence, accept this death,' the old woman screamed. And then she tossed the heart into a burning brazier. It spat and hissed and added its own horrible odour to the many others in the room. 'Her heart is yours . . .'

And the corpse, its chest torn open, its heart consumed by the flames, sat up!

6 Gire

And he was the Champion of the Old Faith, and his enemies were many
. . .

Life of Paedur, the Bard

'Mannam!' Paedur breathed. 'It can only be Mannam.'

'The once-lord of the Dead? But he is human now and lost on
the Planes of Existence,' Katani said quickly, feeling something
cold settle against her spine.

'Not lost, merely missing. Until now. It can only be Mannam,'
Paedur insisted. 'He swore vengeance when the Pantheon strip-
ped him of his godhood, not only on me but on them also.
Obviously, he is exacting that vengeance now through the
Chopts.'

'And his guards?.

'The Torc Allta, the Boar-Folk,' Paedur sid quickly.

'And the sword-bearers are Gallowglas, professional mercenaries . . .'

The bard nodded. 'Aye, and related to the Chopt tribes. Interesting that they are all – Chopt, Torc Allta and Gallowglas –
cannibal and flesh-eaters.' He stopped suddenly, realising the
boy was still there, staring open-mouthed at him. 'Is that all they
said; nothing more?' he asked gently.

Gire shook his head. 'Nothing else. The small dark man turned
away, followed by his two beast-guards . . . the . . . the Torc
Allta?'

Paedur nodded absently. 'Why werent you killed?' he asked
suddenly.

Gure shook his head, looking quickly from the bard to Katani,
his eyes sparkling with moisture. This was the first real emotion
he had shown during the telling of his tale and Katani couldn't
help but wonder if the bard had somehow dulled his senses a

little to allow him to relate the events with no outburst of emotion. 'I don't know why I wasn't killed. I've gone back to the spot again and again. I can only think that I was sitting in the shadow of the God of Learning, and behind the statue is a small ventilation grille – perhaps that prevented the yellow gas from taking hold of me. But I still don't know why they passed me over.'

The warrior nodded. 'But where are the bodies of the slain? There must have been hundreds of bodies?'

'They took them away with them!' He saw Katani's startled look and nodded quickly. 'The beasts came back with carts – large-wheeled wooden carts – and piled them high with bodies and parts of bodies and took them away with them. When I wandered the Monastery halls and down through the School later, I found no bodies at all. All that remained were the deep track marks in the snow, all heading back into the Northlands. They had taken away all the bodies!'

'Why?' Katani whispered, aghast.

'Food,' Paedur said shortly. 'It's a hard winter in the Northlands; they're bringing food home to their families, much as any human hunter would.'

Gire drew up his knees and leaned forwards, wrapping his arms around them. 'But why did they do it; why did they attack the Monastery and school? Why did they deliberately destroy all the holy relics and books? Why? And what did the little man mean when he said that it would "bring him." Bring whom?'

The bard's lips curled into something like a smile. 'You belong in the Order of Ectoraige if you question everything like that,' he said. 'And you probably deserve answers,' he added. 'The small dark man was undoubtedly Mannam, once the God of Death, the Lord of the Silent Wood. But god no longer. He was tried by his peers – the Pantheon of the Old Faith – found guilty of crimes against the dead, stripped of his godhood and returned to the World of Men as his punishment. He blames me for that. The creatures with him, the beasts with tusks, were the Torc Allta. When I walked the Silent Wood, I killed several of their number and they swore an oath to slay me; obviously they have joined forces with Mannam.

'And this was a trap, a lure as it were, to draw me. By killing the followers of the Old Faith in this bloody fashion – sacrificing them almost – the Gods of the Religion grow stronger, and a welcome bonus of course is that by doing this terrible deed, they knew I would come to investigate.'

'All the Brothers, the monks, the students . . . they were all killed just to draw you here?' Gire whispered, his eyes, which had been wide and round, now settling into slits. His face tightened into a mask of contempt. 'You are responsible for their deaths – all their deaths!'

'Stop that!' Katani snapped. 'The bard was no more responsible than you were. If there is any blame, then let it lie with the Gods of the Old Faith, who didn't warn their followers that death in this terrible fashion was stalking them.'

'Perhaps they did,' Paedur said quietly. 'Remember the Brothers were meeting in conclave when death struck.'

'A late warning is no warning,' Katani muttered. 'But what do we do now?'

'This place is undoubtedly watched – although whether by magical wards or by distant watchers, I'm not sure. However, I've felt no presences, either occult or human,' he added, by way of reassurance.

Katani leaned forward. 'Bard, hundreds of men and boys – all staunch followers of the Faith – were butchered here in the name of the New Religion; the very stones have been bathed in their blood. The gods and followers of the Religion will need no watchers to know that one of the Faith is here.'

'You're right, of course.' Paedur stood up, flowing silently to his feet, his cloak settling around him like a shadow. 'Get dressed, boy. You're coming with us.'

'Where are we going?' Gire asked, something of the bard's seeming nervousness conducting itself to him.

'Out of this place first; we'll decide our destination later.' The bard pulled his hood around his head and then, having become one with the night, slipped out into the ruins of the chapel. He allowed his enhanced senses to flare and immediately the pitch-black night flared to light as the bard became aware of the aura of life that every living creature exuded. He was surrounded in a shifting mass of colour, and he stood still for a moment, absorbing the colours, identifying and sorting them. Katani was behind him, vibrant colours surrounding her stark whiteness – the aura of one dead – obviously the legacy of time in the Silent Wood. Beside her the boy radiated fear and exhaustion, and his aura was curiously overlain with a pale blue tinge the bard had never encountered before. Paedur blanked these from his consciousness and concentrated on the area within the chapel, and found it deserted save for the usual night creatures. Expanding his consciousness he quested beyond the Monastery walls, slowly and methodically blanking out the life-auras of the myriad creatures that inhabited the secret places of any ancient building, gradually turning the night to black once again.

He found them on the steps beyond the gate.

The colours were strange, they were mixed and distorted and tainted with a gritty greyness. It took him a moment to resolve the coloured shapes into – Torc Allta! The auras were alien to this Plane of Existence, and the greyness was the grey of the Ghost Worlds between the planes, through which the Boar-Folk had the ability to travel at will.

He sorted through the auras, counting. There were certainly four, and possibly one other, but the colours were so broken and distorted that he was unable to tell. Two were on either side of the gate, and the other two – or three – were grouped on the steps. He – and Katani and the boy – were trapped, then. There was no way past them – the steps were the only entrance to the Monastery of Ectoraige. In the past this had proved the monks' salvation, for a single man could easily hold the steps against an army. They were now likely to prove his bane.

There was movement behind him and the bard spun around; Katani and Gire had emerged from the small chapel. Behind them a curl of grey smoke twisted in the darkness, and the odour of doused wood was bitter on the air. The warrior was in her full armour, with both swords in her hands. Gire was wearing his tattered blue robe, and had Katani's travelling cloak tied around him. He was carrying one of the Katan's throwing knives.

'There are Torc Allta beyond the gates and on the steps,' Paedur said shortly.

'Is there any other way out?' Katani asked.

'None that I know of.' He stooped down and looked into Gire's eyes. 'Do you know of any other way out of this building?'

Gire shook his almost bald head. 'None.'

'So we fight,' Katani said, almost tiredly. She had had one lifetime of killing, and had endured countless years in the timeless world of the Silent Wood, slaying – butchering – the dead, and now, back again in the World of Men, she was once again killing.

'We fight on our terms,' Paedur said quickly.

The Torc Allta waited with all the patience of beasts. Their prey was close now, very close. They had tracked him from the Mire that bordered Death's Kingdom, across the myriad Planes of Existence to this place, seeking vengeance on the brothers he had so foully killed and mutilated.

And if they took the Katan warrior, then that would be a bonus. Her flesh they would feast upon immediately – soft, succulent, woman-flesh. The bard they must deliver alive to the rest of their company, so he could be ritually slain and his flesh distributed in the proper fashion.

With the bard dead and their mission complete, they could plan their future, and those plans did not include returning to their own desolate plane.

They had fed well since they had come through to this Plane of Existence. They had slain many and eaten well, and if their companions, the Chopts, had too much beast blood in them for their liking, and if the Gallowglas were too human for them to be truly comfortable with, then when the time came, they too would feed the Torc Allta . . .

The two guards at the gate stiffened, and the three lurking on the steps heard the sudden sound also – it was the chink of metal, brittle and sharp on the chill air. Then their sensitive sense of smell caught the odours of burning wood and turf. Fire had been lit inside the Monastery – which probably meant that the bard was going to stay the night. The guards on either side of the gate looked back down the steps for directions, but their instructions had been clear: under no circumstances were they to enter the Monastery. Although the butchery they had wrought in the hallowed halls would have washed the Old Faith Magic from the stones and coated the whole building in a miasma of blood and death, there was still every chance that the bard, the Champion of the Old Faith, would be instantly aware of their presence. They were counting on the fact that exposure to the atmosphere of the Monastery would dull his senses, and render him vulnerable, so that when he left the Monastery they would be able to take him.

The fire inside the Monastery had obviously been fuelled: sparks and large black cinders began spiralling to the heavens and a pale glow suffused the night sky. The Torc Allta were both puzzled and alarmed now. Surely these were not the actions of a nervous man, nor those of someone who wished to travel quietly?

One of the Torc Allta darted out of the shadow of the door and crouched on the top step, looking down at his three companions 'Let us leave now; this noise, this display, bodes ill for us . . .'

'We wait – he must leave eventually,' a voice snarled from below him. 'Return to your post.'

The first guard nodded and walked slowly back to the huge locked doors, rubbing his curling tusks in frustration. His every sense told him something was wrong, that they should leave now . . .

Something cold and wet moved across his chest. His hand came up, expecting to find water, rain . . . but came away warmly sticky. He lifted his hand and held it to his snout, and then his tongue darted out, tasting it – blood. The noises in his head increased, and as he opened his mouth to shout a warning, the noise overwhelmed him.

The second guard saw the first fall to the ground, a vague shape in the dimness. He stepped away from the door, wondering if he had tripped and fallen, when he was abruptly deluged in liquid. It was bitterly cold and the sudden chill drove the air from his lungs. He opened his mouth to scream – when the smell hit him. It was fish oil. There was a shape in front of him; tall, black, with a silver hook where his left hand should have been. The hook darted out, and the guard reacted, bringing up his short-hafted jabbing spear; the hook slid down along the haft, striking sparks from the metal hand-guard . . .

The explosion lifted the Torc Allta off his feet and threw him against the wall. Completely wrapped in flame, he staggered to his feet and wove his unsteady way past the still, silent shape of the bard, instinct alone guiding him towards the steps and his own kind. He teetered on the top step, and then staggered forward – straight into the arms of his companions. In a screaming, bellowing, squealing heap, the four bodies, one aflame, tumbled down the hundreds of steps to the School below. All noise had ceased long before they hit the bottom.

Paedur turned his head to look up to where Katani and Gire were standing on the battlements above the door. 'We fight on our terms.'

In the icy fastness of a buried cave in the heart of the Northlands, beyond Thusal, a tall, twisted creature watched the bard in a block of smoothly polished ice, which he had turned into a scrying stone with the assistance of Hirwas, God of Far Seeing, one of the twelve Trialdone of the New Religion.

He watched impassively as the bard and his two companions climbed down the uncounted steps from the Monastery to the School below. Even without his powers of godhood, and even from this distance, he could feel the approach of the bard, feel the power he radiated . . . and once again experienced the fear. He had some protection though; in return for his allegiance to the New Religion, he had extracated several promises from the new gods, and they included both patronage and protection. There was something else in his favour at the moment – the bard was unaware of the mutated nature of his own powers since he had returned from the Silent Wood. It might be possible to use that ignorance for his destruction.

79

The bard would be destroyed, and without him the Old Faith would wither and die and its Pantheon of Gods with it, and then he would have his vengeance, sweet, sweet vengeance.

And Mannam, once-lord of the Silent Wood, the abode of the Dead, smiled involuntarily, his seamed face cracking, tiny runnels of clear fluid running from the wounds, like sap leaking from a wounded bark.

'Thusal is the next town,' Gire said, as they climbed the score of steps that led off the side road onto the impressive width of the King Road.

Paedur nodded impassively.

'And Thusal has been cut off; there has been no word out of it for the past several moons. The Brothers thought it might be besieged by the Chopts and their allies, or perhaps that it had already fallen,' Gire continued, looking at Katani.

'Perhaps the road is blocked,' she said, her voice sounding faintly muffled inside her horned, demon-mask helmet. She was wearing her full armour, more for protection from the elements than any attacker. It was bitterly cold, and there were banks of hard-packed snow on either side of the road, although the centre of the road was still relatively clear. Thus far in the season, there had been no heavy snowfalls.

'In the olden days,' the boy continued eagerly, his nervousness making him talk, 'there were pipes running under the King Road, which carried water from the hot springs of the Northlands, and which served to keep the road free of ice and snow.'

Paedur glanced at the boy. 'And who told you that?'

'I read it in a book in the library at Ectoraige.'

'You read?'

Gire nodded proudly. 'Four languages, and I can read Culai script.'

The bard turned to look at the boy, his reflective eyes taking the white of the snow, making him look blind. 'You didn't learn that from the Brothers.' There was a note of genuine respect in his voice.

'My mother taught me.'

'A learned woman.'

'It was said she knew everything,' Gire said simply. 'She was the Lady Sophia . . .'

'The Teacher?' Paedur said abruptly.

Gire nodded. 'She was called that.'

'A tall, elegant woman, with deeply black hair, and deep chestnut-coloured eyes?'

Gire nodded.

The bard smiled, one of his rare genuine smiles, which lit up his face, lending it a human cast once again. 'I studied under the Lady Sophia at Baddalaur, the College of Bards. She was an almost legendary figure when I was there as a young man. And truly, I've heard it said that she knew everything. There were stories that she had done a deal with one of the Duaite or Auithe for a perfect memory, but whatever, it is true that she had only to look at a scroll, or a page of manuscript once to have it word for word. She was a very fine lady,' he added fondly, shaking his head, 'and I've often wondered what had happened to her. When I went back to Baddalaur some time ago, I asked after her, but she had left then, and no-one knew where she had gone.' He suddenly reached out his hand and the boy tentatively took it, and Katani, walking behind them allowed herself a smile; it was difficult to reconcile the often terrifying, sometimes god-like bard with the occasional human touches which showed through the armour. And she wondered what he had been like before he had become the Champion of the Old Faith.

'My mother delighted in telling me that she created the single greatest scandal at Baddalaur since Arin the Bard Master was stabbed by one of his pupils because of an affair of the heart . . .' Gire said quickly, and added, 'but she never told me what the first scandal was . . .'

Paedur smiled, remembering. 'It was before my time, but it was the talk of the college for seasons afterwards; Arin was a man of strange tastes, and he developed an affection for a young boy from one of the western families. When he made his advances – at the dead of night too – the boy was so angered that he picked up a stool and cracked Arin over the head with it. In a rage, Arin pulled a knife, which the boy – who stood taller than the Bard Master, and was broad on proportion – promptly took away from him and stabbed him in . . . stabbed him with it. The man conducted his classes for the rest of that season standing up.'

Gire laughed, his laughter ringing flatly across the ice-locked landscape. As far as the eye could see, there was nothing but the blasted whiteness of a snowscape, unrelieved by any vegetation or habitation.

'I often wondered,' Gire said, 'but Mama would never tell me.'

'And what was her scandal?' Paedur wondered.

'She married one of her students!'

The bard blinked, but said nothing.

Gire grinned. 'And to make matters worse, he was much younger than she.'

'What is so strange about that?' Katani asked. 'In my time, it was accepted that the wife should be older than the man; experience being necessary to curb the impetuousness of youth.'

'Times and mores change, Katani,' Paedur said, 'but in the Outland tribes that custom persists. Here, however, the wife is usually of an age, if not younger than the husband.'

'Foolishness,' Katani grunted, turning her attention back to the landscape. Although it looked deserted, she couldn't shake the feeling that they were being watched.

Paedur looked down at Gire. 'And your mother left Baddalaur?'

'She never spoke about her reasons for leaving, but I suspect that she was forced to leave. And I know that when she returned to Talaria with her new husband – my father – she was not well received by my father's family. Apparently, they were in the process of arranging a suitable marriage for him – something political, no doubt. But my mother vindicated herself when she designed a drainage system that ensured that the borderlands would never again suffer drought and when the Taourg Pirates raided the coastal villages, my mother designed the ballista which sank four of the pirate ships the first time it was used and ensured that they never again raided Talaria's coasts. In my land she is worshipped almost as a goddess.'

'Did she decide to send you to the College of Ectoraige?'

'I am the youngest,' Gire answered, 'and my two brothers and two sisters all have their appointed careers. My mother prevailed upon my father to send me to college; she said I would find my destiny there.'

Paedur looked at him curiously, but said nothing. The Lady Sophia's precognitive talent was well-known, and there was a single volume devoted to her successful predictions in the College Library. The bard wondered what destiny she had seen for her son.

7 Andam

I often knew fear before I encountered the bard, but after him, and the events he set in motion, I learned the true meaning of terror . . .

Tien tZo, biographer of Owen, the Weapon Master

'There was panic when the corpse sat up,' Tien tZo said quietly, his voice even, his hands still on the table before him, and yet everyone present could sense the tension within him. 'They were hoping for it, perhaps some of them were even expecting it, but when it happened, they ran terrified. And I ran with them.'

'You're sure the body was dead?' Keshian asked quietly. 'I've seen too many men with fatal wounds, killing wounds, death wounds, continue to fight on long after they should have died, the physical body moving even though the essence had left it. I once saw a man with an arrow in his heart fight on to kill the archer who had "killed" him.'

'I know, I know,' Tien tZo said quickly. 'I've seen that happen, but this was not like that. The woman was dead: the old woman had cut her open like any other butchered beast, a long cut beneath the breast, and then up along the breastbone, opening the chest like the door to a cage. I saw her tear out the heart, rip it, tubes and veins, from the chest, saw her hold it aloft while it still pulsed and trembled, before finally throwing it into the fire. The heart was consumed – I almost threw up when the stink hit me.'

Owen reached over and placed his hand on his friend's shoulder in a rare gesture of physical affection. 'Gently, gently, now.' He looked around at the three people in the room, Kutor, Keshian and Fodla, and shook his head slightly. 'If Tien says the corpse rose up, then it rose, and we must consider the possibility that the body has been inhabited by something from the void or the Ghost Lands.'

'So it is a quai?' Fodla said.

The Weapon Master shook his head. 'More than a quai, I think. A quai is a dead body controlled by someone living, but what we have here is a dead body occupied by something which was deliberately called down. This girl was sacrificed with the sole intention of providing a habitable shell for her god.'

'They were calling down Trialos,' Tien reminded them. 'Could not the god have heeded that call?'

'I hope not,' Fodla said, feelingly.

Owen turned back to Tien. 'What happened when the corpse rose?'

'There was panic . . .'

'I know there was panic,' Owen said gently, 'but what did the thing – this corpse – do? Did it speak, did it raise a hand, turn . . .? I want to know what it did.'

The Shemmat shrugged. 'It did . . . nothing. It merely sat up on the bloody table and looked around, its head moving, slowly, its eyes wide and unblinking – like a serpent,' he said suddenly. 'That's what it brought to mind – a serpent.'

'In the panic that followed, did anyone remain behind?' Keshian asked.

'The woman, the old woman, the one who killed the girls and called down the god, she remained, and so did the Warlord,' he added quickly. 'He was at the back of the cathedral as I passed him, but he had stepped out of the milling throng, and seemed to be waiting.'

'How did he look?' Keshian asked.

'I didn't stop to find out,' Tien snapped. 'I was too busy getting out.'

'You did well,' the Emperor said quietly. 'Thanks to you we now have some indication of the old royalists' plans. We know the Warlord is involved, and this withered old woman should be easily identifiable . . .'

'She is the Lady Esse,' Fodla said, the surprise in her voice evident. 'I thought you knew.'

'I am a bandit from the Outlands; my friends are mercenaries, thieves and brigands; I'm afraid I am not well-used to who's who in the old Imperial Court,' Kutor said sarcastically.

Fodla grinned good-humouredly. 'You'll find there's little difference – they're barbarians all. The woman Tien described could only be the Lady Esse. When I first came to court many years ago, she was the real power behind Geillard's father, and even when Geillard, the deposed Emperor, took the throne, she was still active, her hand evident in every major policy decision. Salier, Geillard's late unlamented chief counsellor, magician, and personal attendant, was her student and some said, her son, but I personally think that is unlikely.'

'And what was this woman, this Lady Esse?' Kutor asked.

'She was a sorceress, a sorceress of incredible power, who had once staunchly upheld the Old Faith, but for some reason which no-one knows, changed her allegiance to the New Religion. She is an evil woman – and I use the term very carefully – embittered by her stature and her looks, detesting the Faith and everything connected with it, and loyal to only one thing, and that is Geillard and the power he wields – or perhaps it is just the power.'

'And she is a follower of the Religion?' Owen asked.

'Personally, I always believed that she followed older, wilder gods, for her power was phenomenal. But yes, she professes to adhere to the Religion and from what Tien has just described, she obviously has been working on its behalf.'

'Could she be working with them solely to oust me?' Kutor asked.

'Very possibly.'

Tien tZo coughed softly. 'If I may be allowed to say something . . .' he said diffidently. When he had their attention he continued, choosing his words carefully: 'We really need the bard now; his knowledge of these people, the gods they worship, and the powers they wield would be invaluable, but we don't have the bard, and we're the poorer for it. Since none of us here has that knowledge – that specialised lore – may I suggest that we find someone who has?'

'It is an excellent idea,' Kutor said eventually, when the Shemmat's words had sunk in. He looked at the faces around him. 'Another bard, perhaps?'

'I was thinking of someone else,' Tien continued.

'Who?'
'The Andam!'

Deep in the heart of the Southern Marshes was a temple, a simple honeycombed artificial mountain that had been old when the Culai had first walked the World of Men. Its builders had not been of human kind, and the building was constructed with curiously shaped windows, strangely low doors, and no stairs; low, gently sloping ramps curved up to the topmost floors. There was nothing else like it in all the Planes of Existence.

It had lain neglected and forgotten for many generations until a warrior, the last of a massacred unit, wandering lost in the treacherous marshes, discovered the ruin. Seeking shelter in the building, he had undergone a terrifying visionary experience wherein he had travelled back through the lines of time to the First Age of Man, when the gods walked the World of Men and it was during this vision – and because of it – that he formulated the *Epistles of the Andam*. This was the Old Faith in its purest form, a stark, harsh belief, adhering strictly to the principles laid down by the First Gods, but believing only in a single supreme deity rather than a pantheon of gods. And although the belief differed from the Old Faith in several other major respects, its priests and followers were regarded with a certain amount of awe by the believers of the Faith.

The wandering priests were a familiar and generally welcome sight on the roads of the Nations. They were gifted with the power of healing, and exercised their powers without regard for a patient's religion or belief. It was also said that they were powerful magicians.

But the Andam had paid a price for their belief and their gifts; four out of five of the priests who went to study in the temple in the Southern Marshes where the Andam belief had originated, contracted a terrifying wasting disease, which ate into the flesh and drew the skin so taut on the bones that it eventually cracked and split, leaving long open gashes on the flesh. To hide the shocking effects of the disease, the Andam priests wrapped themselves in robes of grey, usually leaving only their eyes free.

When Tien tZo had entered Karfondal before the fall of Geillard, he had come disguised as one of the Andam. While queuing for admittance to the city he had been drawn into conversation with another of the Andam. Although the man had seen through the Shemmat's disguise, he had nevertheless vouched for him with the city guards, allowing him access to the city. Once through the gates, the Andam had blessed him and gone on his way, and Tien had never seen him again.

Tien made his way down to the older part of the city. Karfondal, like most cities, had grown up on the ruins of an earlier settlement, and time and growing prosperity had moved the grander houses away from the stink of the quayside. And the waterfront – like the waterfronts of so many cities – quickly gained an infamous reputation.

In the past few moons, following the Cataclysm when the very fabric of the Planes of Existence had been rent, Karfondal had been flooded with refugees. And the vast majority of them had settled in rough shanty towns on the banks of the River Dal. Some of the dwellings – which were little more than scraps of cloth and baked mud tied onto a wooden framework – were actually built on the foul ooze of the Dal. There was no water, no sanitation, and the stench was incredible. The dwellings – if they could be called that – were built one on top of the other, and the partition between them was sometimes nothing more than a scrap of cloth. Whole families occupied a room no bigger than a large box. A thin passageway separated one side of the 'street' from the other; it was nothing more than a stinking quagmire of ankle-deep filth at the best of times, which occasionally dipped into a shallow basin that could swallow a child.

For once, the Shemmat didn't feel out of place. There were representatives of nearly every nation in the known world; from Thusal at the top of the world, to the Dark Continent at the bottom, and all the Island Kingdoms, City States and Nations in between.

The smell of death overlay the expected smells of humanity, with its cooking and excrement, and the ever-present stench of the river. This was the perfect breeding ground for revolution.

This hadn't existed before Kutor came to power – and although he was not the cause of it, people had short memories: the city dwellers would only remember that the refugees had come in with the bandit-chief, and the refugees would only remember that they had a better life before Kutor had taken the throne. Either way he would lose – and the Religion would be quick to step in and capitalise on that loss.

Tien found the Andam shelter deep in the heart of the shanty-town, in the centre of a dingy square that opened out onto the docks. It consisted of a score of tents made of grubby grey canvas that had been stitched together and then pegged out on a wooden platform. A long line of refugees ran from the tent's opening, across the square and back through the dingy streets; there were men with slumped shoulders, women with babes in arms and dull-eyed children standing patiently for the loaf of hard bread and the satchel of sour wine or milk that the priests distributed without asking for payment. Tien wondered briefly where they got the food and wine.

The Shemmat walked across the street, bypassing the silent line of people, and hopped up onto the wooden platform. Immediately the crowd came to dull, angry life, a buzz rippling down the line like a swarm of approaching insects. There was movement in the mouth of the tent and four of the Andam appeared. They were unlike any of the other priests Tien had seen in the past; these were tall, broad men, their grey robes doing little to disguise their muscular build. They were carrying metal-tipped staffs and the look in their eyes and the hard set to their faces was anything but priestly.

The priest nearest Tien lifted his staff, holding it in both hands and spun it once, the movement smooth and practised; then he pointed to the throng. 'Join the queue, brother, there is food and drink enough for all,' he said pleasantly. Again, unlike any of the Andam the Shemmat had seen, this man had the hood of his robes thrown back, revealing a broad, slightly flat-featured face – which showed no signs of the Andam disease. Tien tZo wondered if the four men were merely hired muscle brought in to ensure order.

The four were now crowding around him, and Tien knew if it came to a fight, their own positioning would hinder them, preventing them from using their staffs effectively, and he had no doubts that he could dispose of them easily enough. However, what about the crowd – how would they react? They had fallen silent now with the appearance of the Andam, watching, enjoying the entertainment, wondering what was going to happen, but Tien didn't want to think what might occur if he tossed the four priests into the mud at their feet.

'I have not come seeking alms,' he said slowly, keeping his voice measured and reasoned, looking at each in turn, trying to decide which was the leader, and who would make the first move.

'I thought you looked a little too plump, a little too well-dressed to seek alms at our shelter,' the first man spoke again. 'But we'll feed all, irrespective of appearances.' He looked at Tien again, noting the axes in the small yellow-skinned man's belt. 'What do you want, brother?

'I wish to speak to one of the Andam.'

'We are Andam,' the man said.

Tien said nothing, but the slight shifting of his expression betrayed his suspicions.

'Truly we are; not all of us contract the holy sickness.'

'My business is . . . is not to be discussed in the open,' Tien said. He made to take a step forward – and the four staves came down, barring his path. 'My business concerns a certain hook-handed bard,' he said softly.

Suddenly indecisive at the mention of the bard's name, the four men looked at one another, and then one slipped away and ducked back into the grey tent. He appeared a moment later, and nodded, and the three remaining guards stepped aside, allowing Tien to enter.

The interior of the tent was dim and dusky, with the only illumination coming from a brazier on a tall stand in the centre of the surprisingly large open space. The flame was guttering, dancing blue-green across curling pieces of wood, emitting a pale white smoke, and the tent was heavy with a sharp, slightly acrid odour of herbs and spices which served to disguise the smells of the people, the river and the city. Otherwise the tent was bare except for half a dozen huge baskets and a simple wooden bench.

There were four more Andam in the tent. One was tall and broad, like the brothers outside, two were typical Andam priests, small and frail, completely swathed in their robes and heavy grey bandages. The fourth man was also robed in the Andam fashion, but he was tall and thin, towering over the two smaller men. He was sitting behind the wooden bench, his bandaged hands wrapped around a much-travelled staff.

'So we meet again, Tien tZo, of the Shemmatae,' the Andam said, coming slowly to his feet, leaning heavily on his staff.

Tien was completely taken by surprise. 'My lord . . .'

The Andam smiled, his teeth white and strong in the shadow of his cowl. 'There are no lords here, only brothers of the One.'

'You're the Andam I met . . .' Tien said suddenly.

The priest nodded. 'We have met before.'

'I came looking for you – but if the truth be told, I never expected to find you.'

'But you did. And what brings you in search of the Andam? Salvation, perhaps?' Again the quick smile.

'I fear I am past salvation,' Tien said with a wry smile, 'but I am in need of help.'

'How may I help, brother?'

Tien looked around the tent, at the other Andam and the guards who were within earshot. 'Can we talk elsewhere. I have no wish to cast doubts on your brothers' honour or trustworthiness, but I fear we may be overheard by those not of the Faith, and what I have to say to you is too sensitive to be lost to the enemy yet. And if we talk elsewhere,' he added, 'then the people outside will not have to wait.'

The Andam nodded. 'Of course. We will walk.' He glanced down at the two seated priests. 'I will return shortly; continue feeding the people.' He looked at Tien again. 'This way, please; we will go out the back way.'

As Tien hurried past the table, he glanced down into the baskets that surrounded it and found them to be full of bread – long dark loaves – small caskets of milk or wine, and one was filled with fruit. 'Tell me,' he said, when they stepped off the wooden platform into the muddy ground, 'how do you manage to feed so many, with never a shortage, nor any turned away empty-handed? Is your supply so inexhaustible?'

'It is a simple spell – well, perhaps not so simple,' the Andam amended, 'but it is nothing more than a spell of multiplication, creating two from one, and then four from two, and so on. As long as we retain the original object, we can create as many as we need.'

'What do I call you?' Tien said, glancing up at the tall priest.

'How many Andam do you know?'

'Just you,' Tien said with a smile.

'Then call me Andam,' the priest said. 'It will suffice.' He jerked his head back in the direction of the tent and the long line of silent people. 'If you or the bard have any influence at court, then you might use it to see if you can do something to alleviate this situation. There is genuine suffering here: people are dying and diseased. It's only a matter of time before plague takes over, and when it does, then it will be something like Yellow Sickness or Water Fever, and it will not just be contained in the Lower City or on the docks, it will spread throughout the entire capital.'

'I was thinking much the same myself earlier as I was looking for you,' Tien said. 'I didn't realise things were so bad there, and I truly don't think Kutor knows either. He has allotted certain funds for the refugees but obviously not enough. Don't worry, I'll tell him – or perhaps you could even tell him yourself,' he said suddenly.

Andam glanced sidelong at him, but said nothing. He walked on and turned down a side street that led directly onto the wooden pilings of the docks, before asking, 'What do you mean?'

'I mean I could arrange for you to meet the Emperor.'

'Why would you want to do that? What would be the price?'

'There would be no price – except perhaps a little advice.'

The Andam smiled quickly again. 'Perhaps you should start at the beginning and tell your tale . . .' he suggested.

Kutor fixed the bolt in the door and then turned and leaned back against the polished wood to survey the small room that had become his prison; he might be Emperor of the Seven Nations, but everything he could call his own was in this room.

He stripped off his swordbelt and tossed it onto his bed, and then pulled his surcoat over his head to get at his link-mail shirt – nowadays he went nowhere without the metal shirt and without carrying arms of some description. At least when he'd been a bandit in the Outlands, he had been able to relax once in a while, and there he had been surrounded by his friends. It was something he had been thinking about a lot recently, turning it around in his head, trying to discover a solution, but all it did was to turn circle after circle and get him nowhere – he was stuck with it. He couldn't abdicate – not just yet in any case – and besides he owed it to those who had given so much to make him ruler, especially to the memory of those who had given their lives.

Keshian kept telling him everything would be fine when they broke the conspiracy, but Kutor knew that when – if – the conspiracy was broken, there would be something else that would keep him a prisoner in this tiny cell.

He had entertained the vague fantasy of just upping and leaving. He could slip out one night, take a horse from the stables and ride off with as much money as he could manage. He'd do it, too – except that he would probably have the cursed bard arrive after him – or more likely, have him there waiting for him when he arrived.

And where was the bard now? Where had he gone when they most needed him? North most likely, but what was north, except cold and Chopts, and both were deadly?

What was he to do? People were coming to him daily with questions, things to do, deeds to sign, decisions to be made, always decisions. When he'd been a bandit chief, things had been easier: he had been making decisions for only ten, fifteen, sometimes twenty people; now his decisions affected thousands if not tens of thousands of people.

And was he taking the right decision in agreeing to support the Old Faith? Could he in all honesty say he approved of the

Faith with its rigid insistences and observations upon law and devotion to a Pantheon that rarely – if ever – demonstrated its power. The Religion, on the other hand, was a modern, accessible belief, with a small but seemingly powerful pantheon of gods who almost daily appeared to demonstrate some aspect of their power.

If the truth be told, Kutor, Emperor of the Seven Nations, supported the New Religion. And perhaps the time was drawing near for him to admit it.

The old woman slumped in her chair. 'There, 'tis done. The room is warded, cleverly too, but not cleverly enough. The thought is planted . . .'

'And now what?' the Warlord asked eagerly.

'Now, we wait. On no account can this be hurried. He must think this is his own idea. The conclusion must be his and his alone.' She smiled, her face dissolving into a spiderweb of wrinkles. 'If we cannot break him, we will surely bend him . . .'

'It is not Trialos,' the Andam said quickly, when Tien tZo finished his tale.

'How can you be sure?'

'Because if Trialos walked this plane, then I – and every other sensitive or part-sensitive on this Plane of Existence – would know. I would imagine it's just a loose presence from the Ghost World, some cursed thing which heard the call and latched onto an empty body. It happens.'

'Are they dangerous?'

'They are savage creatures usually, some of them with a taste for human blood because it contains a part of the essence of life, and by drinking the blood they are taking that person's essence into themselves.'

'Vampir!' Tien breathed, suddenly chilled.

Andam shook his head slightly. 'Not exactly; the vampir sustains its life by drinking the blood of the living, while this is a dead creature seeking to restore itself to a semblance of life by drinking blood.'

'Vampir!' Tien stressed savagely. 'Can they be destroyed?'

'The host body must be completely consumed by fire.'

Tien grinned. 'That can be arranged.'

'Perhaps not,' Andam said. 'You don't know the identity of the creature that is now inhabiting that poor girl's body. It need not even be of human kind. But you can be sure that now it has got a foothold in the World of Men it is not going to relinquish it so easily. It will be strong, and it will also have access to some small magics – whatever lore it absorbed in the Ghost Worlds.'

'Can it be controlled?'

The Andam shrugged. He walked to the end of a rotten wooden pier and looked down into the scummed water. 'I certainly wouldn't like to try and control it. But this Lady Esse should have some measure of control over it – but for how long, I don't know.' He turned and looked at Tien, his metal-grey eyes glittering beneath his hood. 'You should also know that it will have the power to call others of its kind to this Plane of Existence, and you can be sure they will not side with the Old Faith!'

8   Conspiracy

Man is unique amongst the beasts in that he will betray his own kind
. . .

from . . . The Warrior, the Life of Owen, Weapon Master

The howl ripped through the Lower City, a terrifying, terrible cry of hunger.

The howl shattered the night silence again, rising now to an eerie wail that brought the shanty town to life – but no-one ventured out into the open. In the squalid tents children cried, but were swiftly quietened, and both men and women stifled their moans. The wealthier merchants checked the bars on their windows, called out tentatively for their guards, while the poorer shopkeepers checked weapons and the few people still unlucky to be on the streets – the late revellers and the women of the night – scurried for shelter.

The third cry was all the more horrific because the note of triumph in it was clearly audible!

And then there was silence.

The vampir had awoken at twilight. This was its first sign of 'life' since it had sat up in the girl's body on the bloody altar stone two days previously. Then it had merely looked around and after the panicked exit of the congregation, it had slumped into a deep, trance-like slumber. But in that time the huge wound in the body had healed, until all that remained was a thin white scar beneath her breast and up along her breastbone.

Just when the Warlord had thought the girl was dead – truly dead now – he had noticed the fluttering of her eyes beneath the closed eyelids; whatever had taken up residence in her torn corpse remained.

It was too late now, but he was bitterly regretting that he had allowed the Lady Esse to bring the creature to the Armoury. She had argued that the cells were the safest place for it; the three cells were buried deep beneath the building, the walls, floor and ceiling as thick as a man's body and sheathed in metal. The bars on the door were each the thickness of a man's arm; there were no windows. The cells were usually used for holding precious metal, script or coin, or sometimes special consignments of weapons, and were virtually impregnable.

On the Lady Esse's instructions, the Warlord had sent his son out earlier that evening to find one of the women of the night; with the huge increase in refugees in the city, the numbers of women walking the streets, trying to find the price of a meal for themselves or their families had increased dramatically, and the Warlord's son was careful to make his choice from this group. He had returned just before twilight, with a tall, blond-haired, pale-eyed woman from the Northlands. The woman had been given a heavily drugged wine and when she collapsed she had been dragged down the stairs to the cellar and thrown into the cell with the creature. The Warlord had then sent his son away, and he and the Lady Esse had remained behind to await the awakening of the creature.

This new presence in the cell seemed to stir the creature, and her muscles began to ripple and her fingers and toes to twitch and curl. In the world above as the light faded and the sun dipped below the horizon, the creature's eyes snapped open – and it was like looking into two pits. At a cursory glance she was a reasonably pretty young woman, newly come to womanhood, with pale close-cropped blond hair. But her eyes and her movements betrayed her – for both pupil and white were completely black, and seemed to have hardened, giving them a slightly metallic sheen, and she moved with all the fluidity of a hunting animal.

The Lady Esse sighed and nodded her head; it was as she suspected – it was a vampir, a presence from the Ghost World who had battened onto the newly-dead body.

'It is . . . is it the Lord Trialos?' the Warlord asked tentatively.

'Vampir,' the Lady Esse said.

'Ah,' he breathed.

'It is still useful,' the twisted old woman said. She nodded, murmuring softly to herself, 'Yes, the vampir have their uses . . .'

And then the creature howled!

Within the confines of the cell the noise was incredible. It sat forward, its head thrown back, its neck taut, mouth open, teeth bared, the sound issuing out from it in a single, breathless scream. The Warlord pressed his arms to his ears and staggered back, terrified that the sound would be heard in the streets above, and immediately realising that the scream could probably be heard all across the city.

The vampir came slowly, shakily to its feet – and screamed again.

The Warlord sank slowly to his knees at the incredible noise. He tasted salt and copper on his lips and realised that his nose was bleeding, there was a rushing roaring sound in his ears, and he was afraid lest his eardrums burst. Through a red haze he saw the creature – the vampir – take a step across the cell in the direction of the drugged woman, who was already stirring, the noise having penetrated to her subconscious. The vampir's head was thrust forward, its teeth bared, its hands stiff, the fingers hooked inwards like claws, and the Warlord had a brief momentary flash of a bear-like creature, and wondered if this was what now inhabited the woman's body. And then the vampir fell upon the stirring woman. Its teeth closed around the soft flesh of the neck, tearing into it – not the image the Warlord had of a vampir delicately sucking blood, this was a beast feeding.

And then the creature threw back its head and screamed again, screaming triumphantly, then bent its head and buried its face in the torn neck. The sounds of feeding disgusted even the hardened war-merchant.

The Warlord turned away from the cell door, pale-faced and sweating. He leaned back against the wall, and the two spikes that replaced his hands rattled slightly off the stone with the trembling of his body. Beside him the Lady Esse looked through the reinforced bars of the cell, watching impassively as the creature fed.

She turned to the Warlord, her eyes triumphant. 'Soon, we will have two . . .'

In the Andam mission deep in the shanty town on the banks of the Dal, the Andam priest sat up; he was shivering even though the night was muggy and close. He touched his face, feeling the bones through the parchment-like skin, and his fingers came away bloody. It could have been the sudden splitting of his skin which had awoken him, but he doubted it – he had lived with it for most of his adult life. There was movement at the far end of the tent, a hiss of cloth on cloth, and the Andam reached for his staff. Pointing it in the direction of the noise, the priest fired the staff, bringing it to a pale green light, but nothing was revealed in the trembling glow. However, his wounds were aching – a sure sign that something was amiss . . .

He was moving before he realised what was happening, throwing himself forward and down, hitting the wooden boards with a thump. Every joint in his body cracked and popped and scores of old wounds reopened as the skin was stretched by the sudden exertion. But Andam kept rolling, ignoring the flaring pain, rising to his feet, his staff coming around, swinging up and across his body, a hard emerald light streaming from it. Caught in the green light was a short, squat bald man, with a deeply curved scimitar held in both hands. The would-be assassin hesitated, trying to decide whether it was worth attacking the priest again. He decision made, he had actually started moving towards Andam when the tent flap was thrown back and four of the large undiseased brothers ran in, attracted by the green light that was flooding from the tent. The bald man spat something at Andam, then turned and fled through a slit in the tent. Two of the brothers followed him, while the other two remained with the priest.

'Holy Father, are you all right?'

'You're hurt . . .'

Andam raised both hands. 'I am unhurt; the blood you see is merely the result of old wounds reopening. Bring me some warm water if you will. I will bathe them.'

One of the men hurried away immediately. 'Did you recognise the man, Holy Father?' the remaining brother asked.

'No; I hadn't seen him before. He was an assassin of sorts, not a very good one, I should think.'

'But who would want to attack you, Holy Father?'

'I'm sure many people would, but you need not concern yourself with that at the moment. When I have bathed and rested a little, two of you may accompany me to the palace. I think it is time I spoke to the Emperor.'

'I heard there was trouble around here last night.' Owen had his back to the Warlord as he spoke, but he was watching the man's reflection in a highly-polished shield.

'Indeed, so my son told me this morning.' The man's thin face remained a mask, although Owen thought he saw something move behind his dark eyes.

'You heard nothing?' Owen turned around and deliberately walked past the war-merchant to examine a display of knives mounted on a board behind him.

'I sleep deeply,' he said suavely.

The Weapon Master laughed. 'You must sleep like one of the dead in that case – I heard the screams, and I was in my room in the palace. What is so special about this?' he asked, changing the subject, and pointing to one of the knives.

'Aaah,' the Warlord said, grateful for the change of subject, 'you have an eye for the unusual.' He skilfully lifted the knife from its pegs on the board, using his two spikes, and presented it to the Weapon Master. 'You will notice the rigid spine of the blade, and its thickness too – that is to lend it strength – and you will also notice the one-piece construction. Blade and handle are both of one piece, with the handle wrapped around with strips of leather and cloth. But the unusual feature of this blade is the way the underside of the blade curves gently away from the point.'

The Weapon Master balanced the knife in his hand. 'It's unwieldy and point heavy . . .'

'It will also pierce chain mail and some plate armour!'

Owen looked at the blade more appreciatively. Armour-piercing knives were not unknown, but they were usually huge, bulky things, more akin to swords than knives. 'Where did you get it?'

'There are a lot of fine weapons coming out of the north these days,' the Warlord said quickly, and then turned away, abruptly finishing the conversation: 'I have discussed your offer with my principals and they have accepted ... tentatively. You will of course understand their reluctance to accept this about-face by one of the chief architects in the removal of Geillard from the throne?'

Owen nodded. He continued turning the blade over and over in his hands, but his eyes were on the merchant's sallow face.

'You will go to the Duke de Courtney where you will receive your instructions, and he will make the necessary arrangements.'

'Arrangements for what?'

'Why, for the removal of Kutor, of course!'

De Courtney was a small, slightly foppish young man, with a sharp, hard face, a too-quick smile and eyes that never looked a person in the face. Owen distrusted and disliked him on sight, and his instincts told him that whatever else this young man was, he was no conspirator. He also realised that this man was expendable – which was why he had been given his name.

'I understand you are with us,' de Courtney said, immediately the servant had closed the doors on the large glass-roofed chamber.

Owen looked around the room before replying. The glass roof made it surprisingly bright, and the lightness was accentuated by the white marble walls and pale blue marble floor. An ornately carved and decorated white crystal fountain spat scented water in the centre of the room, the effect spoiled slightly because the water pressure was low and the water came in spurts rather than a smooth arc. Otherwise the room was bare, devoid of all furniture, pictures, tapestries, or ornaments. And against it the Duke de Courtney was a gaudy splash of colour, wines, reds and purples, robes in the latest fashions, matching the paint on his lips and cheeks, high-lighting his rather pale complexion. The Weapon Master walked around the edge of the chamber, while the gaudy young man stood in the centre of the room, nervously watching him.

'You are with us?' de Courtney asked again, and this time the doubt was clear in his voice.

'It depends what I'm supposed to be with you in,' Owen said

101

quietly. The room made him feel dirty, unwashed and unkempt – although in the last few moons he had never dressed so well, washed so often, nor ate so frequently.

'We are to topple the renegade.' The young man smiled delightedly.

'And who are we?' Owen asked suddenly.

'The Twelve . . .' de Courtney began and then smiled self-consciously. 'Aaah, I'm not supposed to tell you that until you have proved yourself.'

In the huge cellars beneath the Warlord's Armoury, representatives of the Twelve Families, Karfondal's ruling clans, were gathering, summoned by the Lady Esse. They had come, some reluctantly, others eagerly, but they had all come; they knew how destructively virulent the woman's wrath could be. They had come to see the creatures they had all heard about, the creatures that would aid them in their struggle against the renegade. They had come to see the vampir.

Owen had refused an offer of drink, and watched in silence while the young man nervously swallowed his own drink and then immediately started in on the second. 'I understand there is some difficulty in you actually killing the usurper yourself,' de Courtney asked, his eyes dancing across the Weapon Master's face.

'I am no assassin,' Owen stated flatly.

De Courtney said nothing, but his eyes betrayed him.

'Disbelieve me you may,' Owen said softly, 'but call me a liar and I'll butcher you here and now in your pristine hall, and stain these white walls red with your blood.'

'I didn't . . . I never . . .'

'You doubted my word!' Owen snapped.

De Courtney swallowed hard. Unconsciously, his hand drifted down to his belt, close to the ivory-hilted dagger.

'And so much as touch that knife and I'll take off your hand!' The duke's hand moved away from the dagger as if it were red hot. 'Now, tell me what you want of me?' Owen snarled, deliberately adopting the guise of the savage bloody-handed killer. De

Courtney was so obviously not a conspirator that Owen wondered what game the Warlord was playing in using the young man. He had half-expected to be attacked once he was in the duke's presence, but whatever he had been expecting it was not to be met by this frightened creature.

'Kutor has announced that he intends to visit each of the Seven Nations very shortly, survey the damage caused by the Cataclysm, and meet with the Viceroys. We need an itinerary of the usurper's travels over the next moon; we need to know where he's going and when, how many men he'll be taking with him, and where they're passing the night.'

'Is that all?' Owen asked sarcastically, but it was a wasted effort, the duke was too frightened to recognise sarcasm.

De Courtney suddenly shook his head. 'No, not quite. If it's at all possible, we would like to know the actual room he'll be sleeping in.' He paused and added. 'Can you do it?'

Owen nodded. 'Some of it I can get immediately, the rest will come a little later, but yes, you'll get your information.'

De Courtney rubbed his hands together. 'With it we can kill the usurper . . .'

'With these we can kill the usurper,' the Lady Esse said proudly, twitching back the curtain the Warlord had drawn across the cell doors.

'What are they?' a woman breathed, the loathing in her voice belying the fascination in her face.

'They are vampir: dead bodies inhabited by creatures from the Ghost World . . .'

The two vampir had come close to the cell's bars. On the surface, they were two naked young women, one bearing a slight scar beneath her breasts and in the centre of her chest, the other with heavy bruising around her throat. Only the metallic coal-black spaces where their eyes should have been betrayed their inhuman occupants.

'I thought the Lord Trialos had come . . .' the young woman continued, and then fell abruptly silent under the Lady Esse's grim stare.

'These are his gifts,' the ancient sorceress snarled. 'They have been sent to us by the Lord Trialos to further his – and our – ends.'

A white-haired man, with the pale blue eyes of an innocent, touched the young woman who had spoken, drawing her back from the Lady Esse's wrath. 'And how can we achieve this end?' he asked quietly, respectfully. 'How can we best use these creatures? What is your advice?'

The Lord Rocque was the last representative of one of the most ancient ruling families in the Seven Nations. The Rocques had seen Emperors come and go, and yet, surprisingly, they had never attempted to take the crown for themselves. The Rocques were administrators always, but yet wielding as much power as any King or Emperor. Lord Rocque had been treasurer to both Geillard XI and his son, and he had continued in the position when the renegade Kutor came to power solely because there was no-one to replace him.

The Lady Esse walked away from the cells and limped down the corridor into one of the Warlord's huge storerooms. The centre of the floor had been cleared, and a single ornately carved onyx chair placed on a beautiful Talarian rug. The sorceress sank down onto the cushioned seat of the chair and the Warlord immediately draped a heavy woollen blanket around her legs. The nobles found themselves seats on wooden boxes or remained standing, facing the old woman. The Warlord stood behind the Lady Esse.

From down the hallway came the muffled whimper of one of the vampir.

The Warlord looked around the room. The representatives of the Twelve Families had been meeting here since the usurper first seized power, and it amused him slightly to see how they resumed the seats and positions they had taken up on the first time they had met here. However, of the twelve present, only four were of any consequence, and their decisions would decide the other eight.

There was the Lord Rocque, now Kutor's treasurer, a man of extraordinary cunning and with a fortune that was reputed to rival Geillard's during the height of his power. He was an indifferent devotee of the New Religion, but recognised it as an interesting and successful way of gaining and wielding power. He was also aware, however, that Kutor would not – could not – afford to leave him in his position much longer, and that alone provided enough of a spur to encourage him to remove the usurper.

Standing to one side, his arms folded across an enormous stomach was the Lord Bleau. A great personal friend of the deposed Emperor, his vast estates and holdings bordered and surrounded Karfondal and the approaches to the capital. The Bleau family had built up their huge fortune from the slave trade, and the present holder of the title had supplemented it with the production of exotics: highly-trained, single-skilled slaves who performed but one function – and performed it to perfection. A man of immense wealth, he had a nightmare vision of his lands being forfeited and his private wealth confiscated . . . and Kutor's feelings about slavery were well-known. A deeply-religious man, however, he had been a long-time follower of the Religion, and had provided a major portion of the funds and nearly all the slaves and craftsmen which had gone into the building of the cathedral in the centre of the city. The fat man seemed unusually nervous tonight, the Warlord thought, but that might have been just from his proximity to the vampir.

The woman sitting in front of him, however, showed no signs of nervousness. Rumour had it that the Lady d'Homana had a heart of stone, and in truth, in all the years the Warlord had known her, he had never once seen the slightest trace of anything that even vaguely resembled the gentler emotions cross her hatchet face. Her age was indeterminate, although the merchant would have placed it somewhere around his own for she still dressed in a style that had been fashionable for young women at the time of his youth, a fashion which left her shoulders, upper arms, and most of her breasts bare. Despite her age, her skin was still flawless, and the Warlord wondered if there was any truth in the rumour that she bathed in fresh blood every day to keep it that way. He could well believe it. She derived much of her wealth from the Northlands, since her estates bordered the mineral-rich ice-fields, and she took a bounty on every animal trapped within her domain. She also kept a Gallowglas mercenary as a bodyguard and the rumour was that he was more than just a mere bodyguard; those who crossed her were apt to come to particularly bloody ends. Her attraction to the Religion – like Rocque's – was mainly the power and the opportunities for power which it offered.

As the Lady Esse looked up, preparing to speak, the Warlord glanced over at the fourth influential member of the twelve, Boazio, Master of the Fleet.

For generations, the Boazios had captained the Imperial Fleet, ruling the sea as others had ruled the land. The Boazio fortune had been originally made by piracy and the present holder of the title was still not adverse to lowering the Imperial colours on occasion and running up his own. His reputation with his mariners was impeccable, and he treated them with the utmost respect and fairness; they in return adored him almost to the point of godhood, and yet the Warlord knew that the tall, blond, ruddy-faced man, now into middle-age, had killed at least a score of servants at his palace, and when in his cups – and he only drank on dry land – had an evil temper. Surprisingly, his devotion to the Religion seemed a genuine belief, and he was a staunch devotee of Aiaida, the Lord of the Sea Wind. He abhorred Kutor for no other reason than he had usurped the Imperial Throne and followed the Old Faith.

'There is a way for us to kill this usurper,' the Lady Esse said suddenly, her voice rasping. 'We can do it in such a way that no blame will fall to us, so that it will appear to have been an act of the gods – a sign of their displeasure, as it were. Already, I have put about the rumour that the gods – both Religion and Pantheon – are angry with Kutor for usurping the throne of his half-brother . . .'

'Should we highlight that?' Lord Rocque said suddenly.

The Lady Esse's eyes flashed angrily at the interruption. 'Every man fears having his inheritance snatched from him by a greedy relative; that is how I am portraying Kutor.'

The Lord Rocque bowed, a smile playing across his thin lips.

'Later, when our plans are at a more advanced stage, I will have it put abroad that the gods – of either belief, whichever suits our purpose – have decided that Kutor must pay the price for his greed. And then the vampir will slay him.' She paused, looking at the faces for reaction, reading the different expressions, and then using her occult skills to probe below the surface, reading their deeper thoughts. Their fear of her brought a ghost of a smile to her twisted lips.

'I thought there should be at least six vampir,' she added.

'Why so many?' the Lord Bleau asked quickly, mopping his brow; he thought two of the creatures were two too many. He had seen many creatures that were neither man nor beast, he had observed creatures from other Planes of Existence, and had once even seen one of the fabulous frai-forde, the Star Lorn, but never had he been so frightened as when he looked, first at the naked female bodies, seeing those only, and then into the depthless black pits that took the place of their eyes.

'There will be six,' the Lady Esse said firmly. 'One each for Keshian, Owen, his servant and Fodla, and two for Kutor – of his death we must be assured.'

The Lady d'Homana leaned forward. 'And the resurrected warrior-bitch?'

'The Katan warrior has followed her bard into the Northlands.' The Lady Esse's lips curled. 'Steps are being taken to ensure that neither of them return.'

'The bard is a dangerous and powerful enemy,' Boazio said suddenly from the corner of the room.

'But this time he doesn't know what he's up against!'

'When will we strike?' Boazio asked.

'Soon. Kutor plans to visit the capitals of the nations. He will be on the road for three or more moons; there will be plenty of opportunity then.'

The Lady d'Homana sat forward. 'Even with the vampir, we will still need additional information on the usurper's movements,' she said quickly. 'Obviously the information we supplied the last assassin was incorrect in some way. My informants in the place tell me she got nowhere near the bed chamber.'

107

'We have a new agent in the palace, someone close to the throne. We are testing his reliability at the moment, and I am somewhat encouraged. He will supply us with the usurper's itinerary.'

'There is also the matter of the Andam . . .' the Lord Rocque said. 'The High Priest must be removed from the picture before we act.'

'That should be taken care of this very night,' she snapped. She glared around the room, almost as if daring anyone to question her further. 'So, if there are no further questions and no objections to my plan . . .?'

There were none.

9   The God-Touched

Thusal is the northernmost town of the Seven Nations, a disreputable den of every vice imaginable . . .

Lilis' Geographica

Thusal is the northernmost town, and is a valuable link between the barbarian Northlands and the civilised Southern Nations. What little law there is in this otherwise lawless land is to be found in Thusal . . .

Lilis' Geographica (Revised Edition)

This day came to us a brother, by name Paedur, called the Hookhand, with two companions – a female warrior in the armour of a Katan and a boy, late of the Monastery of Ectoraige . . .

Register of the Thusal Bardhouse

'I don't know how you got through,' the man said bluntly, putting a platter of still smoking bread on to the white-sanded table. 'You're the first – the only – travellers to make it across the Wastelands this season. Of course,' he added, smiling a gap-toothed smile, 'I realise you're no ordinary traveller.'

Paedur turned from the fire and looked at the man wearing the brown and gold robes of a Bard-Master. 'You're suggesting we were let through?'

Eiron, Bard-Master of the Thusal Bardhouse, eased his tall, spare frame into a chair and broke the crumbling bread for the woman and boy, passing it to them on simple wooden plates. He glanced up at the bard – the 'infamous' Paedur Shanaqui – and grinned again. 'Bard, Thusal is surrounded – it may not be evident, but it is surrounded, and this place is doubly watched. You reached here because they wanted you to reach here.'

Paedur looked at the old man, and for a single moment, that tiny part of him which was still human felt a pang of envy; if things had been otherwise, he might have lived out the remainder of his days in peace and simplicity like Eiron, continuing his research, writing, teaching perhaps. He had never asked to be the Champion of the Old Gods – but he hadn't refused it, either. 'Perhaps you had better prepare for an attack, then,' he said finally.

But the Bard-Master shook his head. 'If they were going to attack you, they could have done so on the King Road, or at any other point on your journey. No,' he shook his balding head, 'it is my belief that you are being drawn deeper and deeper into the Northlands for some reason.' He sat back for a moment and watched the woman and the boy devouring the steaming herb-bread, and then he stood up, his eyes on the bard's sharp face. 'Perhaps we will leave your companions to eat in peace and we will walk awhile in the corridors; the air is cooler there – our thoughts will be clearer.'

Katani went to stand up but the bard, in a rare moment of physical contact, rested his hand on her shoulder. 'No, stay, please. Eat and rest. Only the Gods know when you will be able to do either again.' Surprised, the woman looked up, and found that his eyes had taken the warm white gold of the table, giving his face an almost human appearance.

Eiron and Paedur stepped silently into the corridor and immediately turned to the left, heading down into the courtyard. They were almost of a height, although the bard was perhaps fractionally taller, but the Bard Master's rather chubby, red-cheeked face and his almost perpetual smile made him something the bard could never be again – it made him human.

Now that they were alone, they automatically fell into the respective attitudes of master and pupil, even though Paedur had far surpassed Eiron, and both knew it, but old ingrained habits were difficult to break.

'How did you get past the guards on the city gates?' Eiron asked softly, stopping to look out through the open doorway into the enclosed courtyard beyond.

'A simple glamour,' Paedur replied, pulling up his hood as they stepped out into the uncovered courtyard, more by habit than from any feeling of chill. Since he had been gifted by the gods he had become inured to extremes of heat and cold.

Eiron frowned. 'But if you could do that, then so could the beasts . . .'

'With respect, Master, my powers are somewhat beyond theirs.'

Eiron pulled up his own hood and grinned hugely. 'So I've heard. Tell me, brother, are half the stories they tell about you true?'

Paedur's eyes, white and grey from the snow on the cobbled stones, crinkled in a brief smile. 'Half are.'

'You are aware that the Council of Bards are trying to decide whether to venerate you or to strip you of your rank?' the older man asked very softly.

The bard stopped in shock. Eiron walked on a few steps and then turned and said, 'You have broken the basic precepts of a bard; you have interfered in politics; you have used your tales for ends other than teaching and the furtherance of knowledge; you have consorted with magicians, and have taken to using their arts . . .' Eiron shrugged. 'The list of charges grows daily. It need not worry you at the moment, but there will come a time when it should. You made enemies at Baddalaur.'

'Tell me what bard has not used his tales to influence people and events? Surely that is the main function of a bard, and my use of the arts is not entirely of my doing . . .'

Eiron raised both hands. 'I know, I know. You need not argue with me; at the last Council meeting when it was put to the vote whether to recall you for trial, I voted in your favour, if that is any consolation.'

'Thank you . . .' Paedur murmured.

They walked around the statue of Ectoraige, the God of Learning and Knowledge, one of the gods the monks, scribes and bards had in common. 'You know how they fear change, and anything which threatens the old Order, and by association, their rule. I suppose they're frightened that if the old Emperor regains his throne, he will begin a campaign against the bards solely because of you . . .'

'If Geillard regains the throne, he will begin a programme against all the followers of the Old Faith, not just the bards. This time they mean to destroy the Faith completely.'

'And that is why you are in the north?' Eiron asked shrewdly. They had crossed the courtyard and were standing before a tall arched door. There was no lock, but the Bard-Master touched four of the decorative studs in a certain order and then pushed the door open.

The library of the Thusal Bardhouse was small – and the shelves were completely bare.

'What happened?'

'When I learned what had happened at the Monastery of Ectoraige, I had the library stripped, the books, manuscripts, scrolls and charts sealed in waxed containers and then buried.'

'Why?' Paedur walked into the centre of the room, the empty shelves echoing slightly as Eiron moved to join him.

'It is my belief that the beasts – or whoever controls them now, for they have never been like this before – seem intent on destroying all knowledge. In the last few moons, whenever the farmhouses or isolated crofts or keeps were raided, the Chopts have ensured that signs of learning, the books, the scrolls, the maps, have been destroyed. They have never done that before – for what interest have they in books and lore? And then when I learned what they had done to the Ectoraige library, I knew what their plan was.' He looked up at the bard but in the dimness of the small room, his features were almost unreadable. 'They have set out to destroy all knowledge . . . or more likely they have been instructed to do this. Without knowledge there is no progress – only ignorance and regression. And an ignorant people are ripe for the wiles of priests and gods. Unlearned folk believe with a far stronger will than educated people.'

The bard was nodding slowly. 'You are close enough to the truth. I think they have been instructed to destroy all the evidence of the Old Faith, wiping this plane free of everything pertaining to the Pantheon and the Old Gods. Without knowledge, there will be no belief, and without belief, there will be no gods.' Paedur looked around the empty shelves again, deciding that there was no lonelier sight than bare library shelves. 'Have you advised Baddalaur of your suspicions?'

'I sent a messenger bird, but I've received no reply. They'll probably dismiss it as just another stupid idea.'

The bard grimaced; the Council's stupidity would prove their downfall.

They left the bare library and returned to the courtyard. Eiron led Paedur to a stairway that was almost hidden behind a species of wild northern creeper, and together they climbed the worn stone steps to stand on the top of the open watch-tower, looking down over the town of Thusal. Although it was still early forenoon, the lights were burning brightly in the town, and the sounds of early revelry were brittle and sharply distinct on the bitter air.

'Thusal, the last bastion of civilisation . . .' Eiron sounded almost disgusted.

'Compared to what lurks in the snow-fields, it is,' Paedur remarked.

Surprisingly, Eiron shook his head in disagreement. 'The beasts have a code of sorts – a savage, brutal code admittedly – but they live by it. Here in this supposedly civilised town there is no law but the blade and cunning.' He shook his head savagely. 'Aaah, but I'm getting too old for this. The Cold Months make me morbid. It's not a bad place really, once you get to know the rules. But the hard part is just learning those rules.'

'And what are the rules?' Paedur asked, leaning forward, his eyes sparkling with the glow of the distant lights.

'To mind your own business.' The Bard-Master looked at the bard. 'And speaking of business, what brings you to the Northlands,' he asked quietly.

'I thought I came looking for Geillard, but now I find I'm chasing Mannam, once-lord of the Dead.'

'I heard a tale that you were personally responsible for his demise as the Lord of the Dead . . .'

'How did you know?' Paedur asked quickly.

'I too am a follower of the Faith, remember. I have walked the myriad Planes of Existence. I have contact with the Ghost World . . .'

'It is true,' Paedur nodded, and turned back to the town.

'And when you find Geillard and Mannam – what then?'

113

'I'd like to tell you I'd kill them – but somehow I'm not sure any more. I'll certainly try to stop them if I can – and without bloodshed if that's possible. Although,' he added very quietly, 'I'm not sure that that is possible.'

Eiron nodded. 'It would be preferable; there is already too much blood on your head and hands. They are with the Chopts, you think?' he asked, continuing on in a brisker tone.

'I can only assume so.'

'Then you'll need someone who can lead you to the Chopt encampments and caves.'

'Is there such a guide?' Paedur asked, surprised. 'I didn't think there was any dealing with the beasts.'

Eiron grinned hugely. 'Of course there are dealings. The beasts bring furs and precious stones and herbs from the Northlands; in return they get blankets and food and unofficially, of course, weapons. However the trade in weapons seems to have died down – recently they've been carrying new weapons of their own, fine workmanship too. Perhaps they've finally trained a proper weapon-smith.'

'And where would I find such a guide?' Paedur asked patiently, aware that Eiron would receive few visitors in the course of the seasons, and therefore could be excused if he tended to ramble from the point.

'You'll find him at the Tavern of the Blasted Tree. His name is Bastion . . . he is called the Marked Man!'

The Tavern of the Blasted Tree had once been a church to one of the wilder northern gods and was so ancient that even its name and the name of its deity had been forgotten now. When its followers had died out, then so too had the god. The gods thrive on the faith of Man and without faith there is no substance.

Paedur pushed open the tall double doors of the church and stepped into the murky interior. The air was foetid, rank with odours, mainly human, and principally those of excrement and sour wine, tainted with the sharp stench of urine. Little of the church's earlier decorations remained, with the exception of a series of particularly well-done frescoes high on the walls, but

114

these were so begrimed now that only small portions gave a hint of their former excellence. The tall-sided, almost box-like pews remained, still in their original positions, and the bar was now where the altar had once been. Paedur found the whole arrangement vaguely obscene.

He walked down the centre aisle, aware of the stares he was attracting, although no-one made a move to challenge him. Thusal, like many towns on the outskirts of civilisation, had its share of drifters, and questions could often be answered with a knife or sword in the belly. Nevertheless, Paedur's height and bearing marked him apart from ordinary men, and even though he had kept his hood pulled forward over his face, his eyes had taken the light from the smoky torches and occasionally glinted gold or bronze from beneath his cowl.

The bar keeper didn't even look up at the new arrival, merely set up a glass of murky rofion and pushed it towards him. 'I'll take whatever coin you got.'

'I'm looking for Bastion.'

'Don't serve that here,' the bar keeper began with a gap-toothed smile, looking into the bard's shadowed cowl. But his eyes remained pitiless, and his left hand moved down to the edge of the bar.

Paedur tilted his head back and allowed the light from the trio of torches behind the bar to turn his eyes to brass. 'Touch the club under the bar and I'll take your hand off at the wrist,' he hissed. He moved his left arm, allowing the curve of his etched hook to appear from beneath his cloak.

Colour drained from the bar keeper's face. 'You're Paedur the Bard!'

'Bastion!'

The man started to shake his head, but Paedur moved his own head slightly. 'Tell me,' he mouthed, 'which do you fear more, Bastion or me?'

The man's bloodless lips formed the single word, 'Bastion.'

The bard smiled, his face stone, and the bar keeper thought it was the most terrifying thing he had ever seen. 'A pity. You should fear me. Bastion can only kill you, but I ... well, you

115

don't know what I can do to you, now do you? Bastion?' he asked again, beginning to lift his hook, blue-green fire writhing across the etched blade.

And this time the man's eyes flickered across the bard's left shoulder into a corner.

Paedur turned, slowly and casually, allowing his eyes to adjust to the dimness and then allowing his enhanced senses to flare as he probed the darkness. There was a figure sitting in the furthest corner of a pew, in the shadow of a pillar. The bard glanced back at the bar keeper, his eyebrows raised in a question. The man's head moved fractionally.

Paedur took the drink and walked across to the darkened corner, sitting down directly opposite the still-shadowed figure. He pushed the drink across the scarred wood. 'You're Bastion?'

The figure didn't reply, but something hard and metallic clicked twice in the dimness.

'I don't recognise the weapon,' Paedur said casually.

'You wouldn't, but does a man need to know what kills him?' The voice was soft, very soft and yet slightly rasping, as if the speaker's throat had once been damaged.

Paedur allowed his enchanced sight to come to the fore as he looked at the figure – and was shocked when he found it had no effect. He turned his head slightly, looking at the other patrons of the bar, seeing them as splashes of colour, mainly muted and dulled now with drunkenness and livid with disease. But turning back to the mysterious Bastion he found he could still see nothing except the vaguest outline.

'You are not of humankind,' Paedur said.

'Nor you, it seems,' the man hissed.

'Bard-Master Eiron sent me here to look for Bastion.'

'And you have found me.'

Again Paedur attempted to detect either an accent or inflection in the soft voice, but found it strangely neutral.

'Why?' the man asked simply.

'I need a guide into the Northlands. I need to find the Chopt encampments.'

'Why?'

116

'There is a war brewing – and the beasts are being used as pieces in the game. I must speak to them, try to stop this war, before they are butchered,' the bard said carefully, unsure where this strange man's loyalties lay.

There was a long silence, and then came the same metallic double click the bard had heard before. 'We will talk, then. Upstairs. You first.'

Paedur looked for the stairs and found them behind and to his right. Coming slowly to his feet, he deliberately turned his back on the man and took the curving wooden steps up to the balcony that ran round the building. He stood with his hand and hook curving around the rail, looking down over the crowd, deliberately shutting off his sense of smell, and dulling his senses back to normal.

Bastion joined him at the rail. 'Look at them – animals, stinking animals! And they hunt the Chopts as beasts.'

Paedur turned to look at Bastion, and only his bard's training kept his face expressionless. Bastion was diseased. Great weeping sores had turned his face into an open wound, and his eyes, tiny behind swollen cheekbones were hard and small and black. He was tall, almost as tall as the bard, but broad where the bard was thin. He was completely hairless and the bard no longer wondered at his hoarse voice.

'I am Bastion.' He said it proudly, almost defying reaction.

He was wearing a simple merchant's robe of a dark, intermediate colour, belted around the middle with a broad sword belt, on which hung a short cutlass, a broad-bladed Chopt knife and a long rectangular-shaped pouch.

'Who are you?' Bastion asked softly.

'I am Paedur . . .'

'. . . the Bard,' Bastion finished, nodding. 'Yes, I have heard of you.'

Paedur, anticipating his next question, lifted his left arm, showing his hook. Bastion examined it closely, turning his head to study it from all angles, but not touching the blade. 'Toriocht's work,' he said eventually.

Surprised, Paedur nodded. 'So I believe.'

'It is,' Bastion said assuredly. 'I've viewed his work before.' He looked up at Paedur, his lips drawing back from his teeth in a smile. 'Tell me about this forthcoming war.'

'There is little enough to tell. I believe that the Chopts are being used by Geillard, once-Emperor, aided by Mannam, once-God, to mount an attack on the Southlands in an attempt to overthrow Kutor, the new Emperor, and to destroy the Old Faith in the process. And who knows, perhaps Geillard and his followers will be successful – but the Chopts will suffer the heaviest casualties.'

'Promises have been made to the Chops,' Bastion said, turning away, leaning his broad arms across the balcony rail and looking down onto what would have been the central aisle of the old church. Paedur noted that he wore black gloves, and that his bare forearms were also scarred with the open sores.

'Promises that will not be kept. Neither Geillard's nor Mannam's words can be counted on.'

'The Chopts have eaten well these last moons. And that is a persuasive argument.'

'Human flesh, killed in the name of the New Religion!' Paedur said savagely.

'The Chopts have their own gods. And if they pay lip service to other gods then that is all it is.'

'But the deaths are perceived and accepted as sacrifices to the Religion', the bard argued.

Bastion nodded. 'I accept your point.' He grunted in amusement as two men below started an argument over a slattern. While they were fighting, she wandered off with another man. Then he turned to look at the bard, his scarred face expressionless. 'What you've told me bears out certain rumours that have come down from the north in the past few moons. There is war brewing, the clans are gathering and weapons are plentiful, and, for all the beast-folk's reputation, they are not usually wanton killers.' He nodded, as if coming to a decision. 'I'll take you into the Northlands if you give me your word not to harm any of the beast-folk.'

'I cannot do that. I can only swear not to attack them, but if I am attacked, then I will defend myself.'

Bastion nodded. 'That is good enough. Know this, bard: I am risking much by taking you north with me. The Chopts know me, trust me, and in their own fashion they are an honest race, loyal and true. They make good friends, but cross one and you are a dead man. Cross me, bard – betray me – and, for all your god-given powers, I will kill you.'

Paedur nodded. 'What are you, Bastion?'

The man grinned. 'I am nothing, bard.' He turned away and moved silently to the stairs but stopped on the top step. 'Meet me at the north gate at dawn.'

'I'll be there.'

'You know nothing about this man,' Katani argued, stamping her feet against the bitter cold. It was the still silent hour before dawn and it was bitterly cold. 'By your own admission, he is not of humankind, and you cannot read him.'

'I trust him. Eiron trusts him.'

'And if he is of the Religion?'

'I would know . . .'

'I am not of the Religion. Nor am I of the Faith.' The wheezing, gasping voice was so close that it startled them both. Katani's swords whispered from their scabbards as she spun towards the speaker.

'What are your gods, then?' Paedur asked, without turning, aware only that he hadn't sensed the approach of the man, aware of the pounding of his heart, suddenly feeling terribly vulnerable, feeling, for a single moment, human again.

'My gods are . . . my gods,' Bastion said, 'and my own affair.' He deliberately turned to look at the woman warrior in the early morning light, pushing the furred hood of his bulky white and grey quilted jacket off his head and in the grey light of dawn his ruptured skin looked even more hideous. Perhaps he intended it to shock, but Katani had been trained to school her features to betray none of her feelings, and her face remained impassive. Bastion stared at her for a few moments before speaking. 'You are Katani of the Katan, companion of the bard. You came with him out of the Silent Wood. You also have with you a boy, by name Gire, a survivor of the Chopt attack on the Monastery and School of Ectoraige.'

The bard turned, his expression stone, his eyes reflecting the purple-grey light of the morning. 'And how do you know all this?'

'I have survived so long in this wild land because I make it my business to know. I have learned a lot about you bard since we last spoke.'

'And does it alter your decision to guide me?'

'On the contrary; you are a man of honour – rare in these times – and dedicated to your cause, which would seem to be the upholding of the Old Faith. And I have since discovered certain . . . information, shall we say, which bears out what you told me. I will guide you.'

'Paedur, I must accompany you . . .' Katani began, but the bard raised his hook, the metal glistening with the dawn chill.

'No. You will accompany Gire back to the capital, and wait for me there. Stay at Kutor's side at all times; an attack on him is inevitable . . .'

'There have been two assassination attempts on the new Emperor,' Bastion wheezed. 'Both have failed.'

'But the next may not.' The bard turned to the warrior. 'Kutor must be kept alive. He is the figurehead, the rallying point, the symbol of the Old Faith. Protect him.'

Katani nodded. 'And the boy?'

'Keep him in Karfondal for the moment. When this is over I will take him south to Talaria myself.'

'Dawn,' Bastion said. 'Time.'

Paedur reached out and touched Katani on the shoulder. 'If there is trouble, I will contact you.'

'How?'

But the bard only smiled and turned away. With Bastion by his side, he walked forward without once glancing back.

Katani turned away, slamming her swords into their sheaths and walked back through the north gate and into Thusal, heading back towards the bardhouse. The bard was dismissing her – Katani, one of the finest warriors from the greatest warrior class ever to walk this Plane of Existence – to the status of a simple bodyguard, first of a boy and then of a man. Well, she would do it this time, but when this was all over, she had plans of her own. A highly skilled mercenary could command quite respectable fees, and when she had enough money she could retire, head south into warmer climes, or perhaps open a school, a training school catering to the sons and daughters of the nobility . . .

She glanced back over her shoulder, but already Paedur and Bastion had disappeared from view in the dim grey early morning light. Well, they were welcome to one another; they were two of a kind . . .

'How far?' Paedur asked eventually when they had walked several thousand paces in silence.

'The nearest camp about a day's march; the nearest settlement, perhaps a day beyond that, and the capital – if you want to call it such – half a day beyond that.'

'Two and a half days' march, then,' Paedur murmured. 'And have you any word of the men I'm looking for?'

'There are said to be strangers in the capital,' Bastion whispered, 'some of humankind, others Chopt-kindred.'

'Gallowglas and Torc Allta,' Paedur said.

Bastion glanced sidelong at the bard but said nothing.

They continued on in silence, into a dreary and blasted landscape. Although every outline had been softened or obscured by the blanket of snow, the effect only served to highlight the absence of life. Every tree and bush was bare and in some cases the branches were snapped off neatly when the weight of the snow had crushed them. The rivers were frozen solid and once they passed close to a frozen waterfall, where the bard paused in wonder, looking at the wan sunlight reflecting through the frozen droplets.

Close to midmorning, Bastion turned off the barely perceptible track they had been following and found his way down to a small hollow in the centre of which was a frozen pool. Tucked away in one corner of the hollow were the remains of a single-roomed dwelling; snow and frost had conspired to reduce it to a pile of tumbled stones. 'We'll stop here awhile. Unlike you, I need to rest and I need food,' he whispered.

121

'You seem to know a lot about me,' Paedur murmured, walking around the pool to examine the remains of the building.

'I like to know with whom I'm travelling.'

'Your sources are what interest me.'

Bastion grinned. 'My sources are impeccable.' He sorted through the satchel he had been carrying on his back and produced a small metal pot. Walking over to the edge of the pool, he stamped through the ice with the heel of his boot, and then scooped chill water into the pot. With flint and tinder he fired a few dry twigs and scraps of fluffy cloth which he had also taken from his satchel and set the pot to boil. He then broke some bread that was so hard it snapped with a resounding crack like stone, and dropped it into the pot of water to soften.

'Why do you prefer the Chopts to humankind?' Paedur asked suddenly.

Bastion looked up from the pot. 'Because they are an honest folk; because they do not judge by appearance.' He smiled ruefully. 'Humankind are not well-disposed to those who have been god-touched.'

'God-touched?' Paedur whispered.

Bastion's blighted hands rose to briefly touch his face. 'This. In the Northlands, it is called god-touched.'

'It is like no other disease I've seen before.'

'It is not a disease, bard,' Bastion said, sounding surprised at the bard's ignorance. 'I angered the gods, and this was their punishment.'

'Which gods?' Paedur whispered.

Bastion shrugged. 'Does it matter? I broke the cardinal rule, the Death's Law – Men are but the playthings of the gods. I was a piece on their gameboard which refused to play. They could not slay me, but with this they gifted me.'

Paedur walked around the pool and sank to his knees beside Bastion, looking into his wounded face. 'The gods did this?'

The water began to bubble in the pot. 'Listen to me, then, bard, and I will tell you how I was god-touched . . .' He added a thick granulated powder to the water and began to stir, immediately forming a pale, watery soup.

'I was . . . a successful man. Not wealthy, but not poor. I dealt in furs, rare and otherwise, ice-spices, exotic stones and woods, all the produce of the Northlands.

'I was recently married, a northern girl naturally, a beauty who had, I am convinced, a touch of beast blood in her, for she was an exotic rare creature herself, passionate and exciting.

'I followed my gods, she followed hers, and if they were not the same, then there was no argument, no dissent, and it mattered little to us, for we were in love. I was active in my church and with every possibility of becoming an elder when the time was opportune.

'And then one day I received a visitor, an elder of the church, a man I respected. He suggested that I should bring my new wife to the church to bless our marriage vows – for we had been married in a private civil ceremony – and that perhaps she should be introduced into the congregation as a new member of the faith.

'I explained to him that she followed her own gods, and I would not interfere with them, but he insisted that it was my duty as a follower of the . . . of my belief that I should encourage her to shift her allegiance.

'I listened and, perhaps because I respected the man, or perhaps because I was in awe of him, I agreed. That night I spoke to my wife, and that night we had our first argument.

'It passed, as all such arguments do, but it was not forgotten. When I left for worship on the Sabbath, I could see the anger or resentment in her eyes, and when she disappeared every month when the moon was full, I was curious and perhaps slightly jealous, for I had heard tales of the wild Sabbaths to honour the hard northern gods.

'I was often away for long periods of time in those days; it was around the time I was beginning to trade with the Chopts. The risk was high, but so was the profit. It was nerve-wracking work. When I camped with them, I rarely slept, and expected to receive a knife in the back at any hour of the night or day. To bolster my courage I often spoke to my gods – and, do you know, in my arrogance I imagined they replied.

'And then one day a deal went wrong – I insulted a chief's daughter – I'm still not sure how, but I think I refused a piece of clothwork she had executed. The Chopts were enraged, and I was forced to flee, with the beasts howling behind me.

'I took shelter in a cave in the Thusal Mountains, a tiny opening in the sheer rockface where they could only come at me one at a time and I could defend myself relatively easily – until my strength and stamina gave out, that is.

'I prayed then – I prayed to my gods as I had never prayed before. And even as the Chopts were coming at me, even as I was defending myself from their blows, I prayed. I promised my gods anything; I promised them everything. I promised to serve them to the end of my days without hesitation, without question.

'And my prayers were answered.

'There was a low roll of thunder across the clear sky and then lightening cracked across the heavens. The levin bolt struck the rockface almost directly below me – and the whole cliff gave way, wiping out the beasts.

'And then deep, deep in my skull, I heard the voice, booming like the thunder, sharp, painful like the lightning: "You are ours; you are our servant, now in this and in all things."

'And I bowed my head and agreed. "I am your servant."

'When I returned to my town, there was another shock awaiting me: my wife had been taken for questioning by the Inquisition. She had been put to the Question and found to be an enemy of – of our belief. She had been tried and sentenced, and her sentence was death.

'I was enraged beyond belief. I railed against the inquisitors, the town fathers, the elders of . . . our belief, but all to no avail. I prayed to the gods – the gods who had so recently saved me – but they wouldn't answer me.

'So I resolved to free my wife. Indeed, what other choice had I?

'On the eve of her execution, I made ready to break her free, when once again the booming, ice-sharp voice spoke deep in my head. "You must not do this. She has been condemned to death. Leave her to die."

124

' "No," I screamed.

' "You must," the voice commanded. "You are our creature now; sworn and oath-bound to us. You must obey us."

'And I refused, laughing my defiance at the gods.

'Freeing my wife proved to be almost remarkably easy. I had come prepared to kill, but the guards were absent from their posts, and the keys to her cell were hung within easy reach. But all the time, I could hear the voice, muted now, but still present, commanding me not to do this, that I was the creature of the gods.

'I ignored it.

'I opened her cell and unchained her, and together we raced through the silent deserted corridors heading for the horses I had hidden beyond the postern gate. But as we ran the voice grew louder and louder, commanding and then threatening . . .

'And still I managed to ignore it, although it now threatened to burst my skull.

'As we slipped through the postern gate, there was the low booming of thunder, ominously familiar, and suddenly I could feel my heart beginning to pound as the thunder rumbled closer and closer. I knew something was terribly wrong, that something was going to happen.

'I got my wife into the saddle and slapped her mount into motion. I was just reaching for the bridle of my own mount when the voice in my ear erupted into laughter, sharp, piercing, hideous laughter – and the lightning bolt struck!

'I remember the pain. The intense, cold, sharp, piercing terrible pain . . .

'And the laughter, I remember the laughter.

'When I awoke I was in Thusal, with my wife and some of the healers of her people tending me. I had been burned, terribly burned, and it was not expected that I would live. But I lived, for the gods did not want me for themselves yet. My skin should have healed, scarred certainly, but healed. But it never healed; this is what you see.

'I had been god-touched. I am one of those who inhabit the Shadowland between the Kingdoms of Life and Death, belonging

125

to neither, part of neither. That is why your god-enhanced senses are blind to me bard. I am like you.'

Bastion turned away suddenly, abruptly finishing the conversation. Paedur watched him for a few moments and then he too turned away, walking back around the small frozen lake, sorting the man's tale into his ordered bardic lore.

What Bastion had said, though, was disturbing, incredibly disturbing, for it shed a new light on the Old Faith. Paedur had been aware that Bastion had been very careful to mention neither the Faith nor the Religion, but the bard knew the Old Faith had used the Inquisition in the past and that those who failed the Question were deemed to threaten the Faith and often executed. It was glossed over now, ignored in the modern history texts, but the Faith had once been as repressive as the New Religion.

But what disturbed the bard most of all was the Pantheon's treatment of the man Bastion. And Paedur couldn't help wondering what would happen to him if he ever refused to obey the Old Faith or decided that he no longer wished to be the Champion of the Old Faith.

Gire was finishing off a bowl of hot salted gruel when Katani returned to the Bardhouse. He looked up as she quietly entered the long dining hall. 'Where's Paedur?'

She placed her horned helmet on the smooth wooden boards and dropped her gauntlets on top of it. She pulled out a chair halfway down the table and sank into it, resting both hands flat on the table top. Finally, she looked up at Gire, and said, 'He's gone into the Northlands.'

The boy looked at her open-mouthed. 'Without us?'

Katani smiled. 'You didn't think he was going to take you with him, now did you?'

'But he has to!'

Katani smiled. 'The bard does only what he wants to . . .'

'He has to take me! He has to! He has to!' Gire's voice, which had grown shrill, suddenly cracked and broke, and Katani, who was watching the boy's face, saw his deep brown eyes turn small and hard and black, and then something flickered behind them, and he slowly closed his eyes. When he opened them again, his eyes were clear stone grey!

Katani's swords whispered from their scabbards. 'Who are you – what are you?' she demanded surging to her feet. Behind her the door clicked open and reflected in the shining length of her longsword she saw Eiron. 'Don't come any closer; something has taken possession of the boy.'

'I know,' Eiron said quietly, almost sadly.

Katani risked a quick glance over her shoulder. The Bard-Master closed the door without turning and walked down the room to stand directly across from Katani. 'You need not fear,' he said.

'Who is it? What spirit controls the boy?' she demanded, looking at Gire, noting how the planes of his face had almost imperceptibly shifted, becoming harder, sharper, lending his face a certain adult solidity.

The voice, when it came, was deep and resounding, the tones calm and measured, like those of an old man. But they issued from the boy's throat. 'I am Ectoraige of the Pantheon, the God of Learning and Knowledge!'

10   The Tempting of Kutor

I discovered more about myself in the first few moons of my rule than I had in all my years in the Outlands . . .

Kutor, Emperor of the Seven Nations

Kutor had discovered he was a gardener.

He had never had a garden, nor shown the slightest interest in gardening, yet when he had first come to the palace at Karfondal and Fodla had shown him around the grounds, he had immediately fallen in love with Geillard's private garden – a small square patch of cultivated ground, completely walled in and roofed with crystal to allow the sunlight in and to intensify the heat. It had been the deposed Emperor's private plot, and none of the royal gardeners were allowed admittance. Perhaps it was its very neglected appearance, while surrounded on all sides by perfectly cultivated lawns, that had attracted him to it. It reminded him a little of his present situation – a rough bandit surrounded by the fops and ceremony of the Imperial Court. He had started work in it almost immediately and hadn't missed a day since.

Another part of the garden's attraction, he suspected, was because he lost his guards when he was within the confines of the walled garden. With the exception of his tiny cell-like bedroom, it was the one place where he was truly alone. Although both Fodla and Owen had argued with him, he had insisted that the two guards who had been permanently assigned to him would remain outside the garden. The only concession he had made was that the garden would be searched every day before he entered, and he would only be allowed admittance when it had been pronounced safe.

But it still didn't stop him from feeling trapped . . . Trapped not only by those who followed Geillard and who were actively

128

plotting against him, even while they smiled and bowed in his court every day, but he was also trapped by his own people, by those who had followed him in from the Outlands, flocking to his banner. He found he owed so many people so much. They had made him Emperor – for their own ends, admittedly – but hadn't that been what he had wanted all along? He certainly hadn't resisted. And so now, here he was with the world at his feet – and no way out . . .

Suicide!

The idea came to him suddenly, and he straightened, pressing his hand to the small of his back. Suicide. He grinned. Now wouldn't that upset all their plans, friends and foes alike. He could come into the garden, sit over there by the fountain, pop his arm into the chill waters and slit his wrists – completely painless . . . indeed, almost a pleasant way to die.

He wondered what they would all do without him. Carry on as usual, he conceded bitterly. They didn't need him; he was a figurehead, a totem, nothing more. Why, he hadn't been seen by the public for . . . for how long now? He had his daily reports; he knew that Owen had contacted de Courtney and that that foolish young man had let slip that it was the Twelve Families who were arranged against him. He was also receiving reports of the situation in the north: along with the flood of refugees and a bitter spell of cold weather, there was increased Chopt activity, which could very easily escalate into a bloodbath if it wasn't stopped quickly. And there were the plans for him to tour the capitals of the Nations . . . and to marry – Keshian had been talking of a arranged marriage recently . . . and there were orders to be signed . . . and roads to be approved . . . and the refugee problem needed to be looked at closely . . . and . . . and . . . and . . .

So, suicide . . . it came back to suicide again.

The Emperor wandered down the gravel path to the plain fountain in the centre of the garden and sat down on the low wall surrounding it. He looked into the clear waters, dipping his fingers into the chill liquid, bringing them to his lips; they tasted tart and bitter. Well, suicide would solve all his problems; no

129

more worries, no more decisions, no more pain ... no more regrets. For Kutor bitterly regretted having accepted the bard's invitation to become Emperor, and Kutor was rapidly coming to hate the Bard Paedur and all he stood for. The bard had used him. And where was he now? Where was he when he was most needed? Where was he with his heroic tales that would inspire and uplift men's hearts? Where was he?

Wood snapped and Kutor looked up, his hand falling to his waist, but he wore no weapon now. There was a figure standing over against the wall, amongst the trailing vines. He opened his mouth to call out – a word would bring the guards running, but something stopped him.

He looked at the shape amongst the vines and trailing creepers again. It was tall, and vaguely manshaped, but the sunlight, already distorted by the crystal roof of the small garden, shining through the leaves, dappled across the figure in a camouflaged pattern, rendering it virtually impossible to distinguish any of its features.

'Who are you?' Kutor demanded quietly.

'You do not want to know.' The voice was soft, a whisper, a rasp like that of grasses blowing in the wind, of leaves hissing against bark.

'What do you want, then? Speak now, lest I call in the guards and have them butcher you where you stand.'

'I mean you no harm, *Emperor*.' The emphasis was placed on the last word, making it sound like an insult. 'If I wanted you dead, then you would be lying at my feet.'

'Brave words,' Kutor mocked.

The figure stepped away from the concealment of the vines, and the Emperor felt something cold and solid settle into the pit of his stomach. He was looking at Death. He was looking at Mannam of the Silent Wood.

The tall, twisted figure in the cloak of seared and withered leaves, stretched out a hand that was gnarled and twisted like the branch of a tree, and a twiglike finger hooked in Kutor's direction. 'Do you want me to call you to me now?' the voice hissed.

And Kutor, who had been contemplating suicide barely

moments before, shook his head. Faced with the immediate prospect of death, he found he wanted to live. 'What do you want of me?' he asked quietly.

'Your faith,' Mannam hissed, 'and the faith of your subjects.'

Kutor frowned and started to shake his head – and then he suddenly realised that the bard had been instrumental in having Mannam deposed. 'You're not Death,' he gasped.

Wood snapped with the sound of Mannam's anger. 'But I can still slay you. I was a god for generations – that cannot be taken away from me, nor the knowledge I gained in that time. I may have been stripped of my godhood, but my powers are of the most extraordinary kind.'

'And you want my . . . faith?' Kutor asked, intrigued now. He looked down into the waters of the fountain and found that Mannam cast no reflection.

'"Faith lends Substance,"' Mannam said, quoting the ancient proverb. 'I intend to retake my throne in the Silent Wood, but before I do that I need the belief of the people on this Plane of Existence. I want you to believe in me, and to promote the belief in me throughout the Seven Nations . . .' The creature stopped; Kutor was shaking his head and smiling. 'There is something wrong?'

'Tell me why I should do this?'

'In return for my help.'

'And how can a deposed god help me?' Kutor asked.

'There are formidable forces gathering against you, enemies both on this plane and in the Realm of the Gods. The Twelve Families stand ready to move; Karfondal is a thunderstorm ready to burst; there are vampir abroad with your destruction – your personal destruction – in their black hearts; there is an army growing in the north, an army of humankind, Torc Allta, Gallowglas and the Chopts have agreed to lend their weight to Geillard's army.'

'I know all this.'

. 'But I can remove some of these obstacles,' Mannam whispered. 'In return you will build a fane to Mannam, the Dark Lord, and make worship there mandatory.'

131

'But the bard . . .'

'The bard cannot help you now. Soon he will be unable to help anyone – even himself. He has overstepped himself this time.'

The Emperor moved his hand to and fro in the chill water, creating reflections which sparkled in rainbow colours against the stone. 'There is more to this, I fancy. Tell me why you haven't approached the Twelve Families, for example?'

Kutor felt Mannam's gaze bore into him for several long moments, before he finally said, 'The Religion has its Deathgod – or Goddess, rather. The bard slew Libellius, the Religion's Lord of the Dead, and to fill the void left by his departure, the Lady Asherat, the Taker of Souls, came to the fore. She is young and vicious, and she will not give up her post so easily.'

'And Churon is the Lord of the Dead of the Faith – what is to say that he will abdicate?' Kutor asked.

There was a hiss like that of a leaf being torn in two. 'I did not say that you would build a fane to the Faith, but only to me. Also, an important part of our bargain would be that you let the Old Faith die out, while encouraging devotion to me . . .'

'You would grow stronger while the rest of the gods of the Pantheon weaken,' Kutor said slowly, nodding. 'But it would mean betraying the Old Faith, the bard, and those who put me on this throne.'

'And have they not betrayed you?' Mannam snapped. 'Have they not used you, abandoned you, made you a prisoner here? You owe them nothing,' the creature insisted. 'Where is the bandit prince who ruled the Outlands with a hand of iron, beholden to no-one, answerable to no man?'

Leaves suddenly blew up all around Mannam and Kutor, hissing, sizzling, rattling and clacking in from all sides. When the dust had settled Mannam, once-god was gone.

The Lady Esse sat back from the ornately carved scrying mirror and watched its reflective surface turn to black. She was well pleased; a few more pushes and Kutor might very well be theirs – without actually knowing it.

And even if the ploy failed, well, then the vampir would feast.

Tien tZo introduced Owen to the Andam priest. They had met in the midst of the vast Market Square, close to the fountain of Geillard I, the Emperor who had helped unite the Seven Nations, taking over where Churon the Onelord had left off – or so history said. Perhaps it was significant that the fountain hadn't worked for many years and the statue was chipped and worn, stained white by the passage of many birds.

Both Owen and Tien had pulled long travelling cloaks over their usual clothes, and had ensured that they weren't being followed. In the past few days the Weapon Master had been shadowed by two disreputable characters he had picked up on his second visit to the Warlord's Armoury. He had no doubts but that they had been assigned by either the Warlord or his employers to keep track of his movements.

They had arrived at the fountain well before noon, wending their way through the crowds that thronged the square. Tien noticed that while the food stalls had proliferated, the quality of the food – baked breads, stuffed vegetables, sticky sweetmeats – seemed to have deteriorated, and once he passed a stall that was selling what it called slivers of bird's flesh cooked in herbs, but the Shemmat's sensitive nose recognised the meat as being nothing more than vermin.

There was no fruit on sale, and spices were fetching exorbitant prices since the Cataclysm had struck in the middle of the growing season, destroying much of the present season's crops, and had wiped out the trade routes and many of the trading ports.

They passed clothes stalls, where many of the articles offered were suspiciously patched and stained, and on the shoe and boot stands, even the best item on sale had seen much usage. Weapon stands were more numerous now, and they were offering a surprisingly large display of used weapons – most of it picked up off the battlefields after Kutor's rebel army had rolled over the Imperial forces. The Weapon Master picked through it with a professional interest, but there was nothing he hadn't already seen, and most of what was available hadn't been cleaned after its last usage and the blades were already beginning to rust.

Owen and Tien walked past the fountain twice; the first time there was no sign of the priest, but he was there the second time they came around. Even so, they continued on their way, and then separated, giving a final check that they weren't being observed before making their way back through the crowd to sit down on either side of the grey-clad priest.

'This is Owen, my Master,' Tien said softly, without moving his lips, his eyes on the crowd.

'I have heard of the Weapon Master,' Andam said quietly, glancing sidelong at Owen. 'Indeed, who has not?'

'We should be brief,' Owen warned quietly.

The Andam nodded. 'There was an attack on my life last night.'

Startled, Tien glanced around. 'You are unhurt?'

'By the grace of the One.'

'How many?' Owen asked, not looking at the priest, watching the crowds milling around, watching their faces, their eyes, their movements, looking for someone paying more than casual attention to the three men sitting on the low wall.

'There was one man.'

'Have you ever seen him before? Would you perhaps have encountered him in your congregation?' the Weapon Master continued.

'I did not know him then, but I have since discovered that he is in the employ of the Lady Esse.'

'Was this a Gallowglas?' Tien asked quickly.

'If it was I would be dead,' the Andam said, the amusement plain in his voice. 'I tried to contact you last night,' he said then, in a different tone of voice. Both Owen and Tien turned to look at him. 'I went to the palace immediately . . .'

'Why?' Owen interrupted.

'I decided I needed your protection . . .'

'You think they will try again?' Tien asked.

'I am sure of it. I am the only reasonably powerful representative of a branch of the Old Faith in Karfondal, even though I am of the Andam branch. But the Faith itself has no High Priest here at present, and although it has many adherents, the few priests here are weak, untried men – boys, some of them. I

134

think if the Religion suddenly wants me dead then there is indeed something powerful afoot. I think they intend to work some great magic, perhaps call something else from the Ghost Worlds, perhaps even Trialos himself. If that is so then I would be able to detect and – in some small way – combat it.'

Owen nodded. 'Of course. And you think they were attempting to put you out of the way before they worked this magic?'

'I think so.'

'We didn't know you had come to the palace,' Tien said.

'I was refused admission!'

'Impossible!' Tien snapped.

The Andam shook his head slightly. 'No, not impossible. I presented myself at the gate, and the guards, recognising my status, allowed me into the inner vestibule. I asked to see you, Tien, but I was told that you were not available, nor was the Weapon Master, when I asked for him . . .'

'We were patrolling the streets, hunting the vampir . . .' Tien murmured.

'I then requested to see the Emperor himself – a bold enough request as you might think, but nevertheless, I made it.'

'And what happened?' Owen asked automatically. He was watching a figure standing over by one of the weapons-stands, a tall, thin man, with a long travelling cloak on his shoulders, tied at the neck, with the hood back. The Weapon Master noted that the cloak's ties were undone and that the man's hands were nowhere to be seen. He could easily be nothing more than a thief, a common pick-pocket, but . . . the Weapon Master had learned never to ignore his hunches. He looked up and found Tien regarding him quizzically, the Shemmat sensing something amiss; Owen deliberately shifted his gaze until it rested on the figure he had been watching. Tien looked at the man for a moment and then nodded slightly.

'The Emperor refused to see me!'

'Why?' Owen demanded.

'I was given no reason. But his Counsellor Keshian came to me and apologised, saying that the Emperor had had a busy and troubled day and was receiving no more visitors. I explained that

I had something of importance to tell the Emperor and, although I think the man himself was troubled, he said that Kutor had refused to see me under any circumstances. Keshian did say that if I was to return today, he would do his utmost to ensure that the Emperor saw me.'

'I'll see that he does,' Owen muttered.

'I left the message with the guards at the gate that I would like to meet you here today, and I left.'

'Kutor has been somewhat distracted of late . . .' Owen began . . .

. . . And then he saw the thin man at the weapons-stand raise his hands from beneath his cloak . . . he was holding a cocked and loaded crossbow. He saw his knuckles whiten as they tightened on the trigger . . . saw the bow snap and the bolt leap from the bow . . .

. . . He was aware that Tien was reaching over for the Andam, saw his hands close over the grey robes, but realised that he would never pull him out of the way in time . . .

His shortsword cleared its sheath, coming up around and down – and cleaved the bolt in two! His sword continued moving, describing an almost complete circle, and when it had reached the horizontal, Owen released it. It took the assassin – who still hadn't moved – directly through the centre of the chest, punching him across a table of swords, knives, axes and maces, knocking out the stand's supports, pulling the awning in on top of him. Tearing off his cloak, and drawing his longsword, Owen darted after his weapon.

Tien grabbed Andam and turned – and found himself facing two black-clad figures, male and female. They were both unarmed but they moved like assassins. The male, tall, broad and battle-scarred, moved in on the Shemmat, while the masked female positioned herself before the priest.

The man moved, pulling a long thin chain from his sleeve and snapping it at Tien's face. Instinct dictated that he grab for the weighted end of the chain, but the Shemmat knew that that was all the assassin was waiting for – while he was distracted, another weapon, knife, shortsword, throwing spike, would take him in the throat. He shifted his weight slightly, allowing the metal to buzz past his ear – and then his own throwing axe snapped out on the end of its leather thong. It took the assassin high on the thigh, opening the major veins down the inside of the leg, bringing the man to his knees. He opened his mouth to scream – and Tien's second axe took his head off at the shoulders!

He spun around, his right arm already drawing back, ready to launch his remaining axe – and found the female assassin lying shivering at the Andam's feet.

Owen came running up. He had been recognised and his name was now buzzing around the gathering crowd.

'Weapon Master . . . Weapon Master . . . Master . . . Weapon Master . . .'

He hooked his foot in under the shivering woman and turned her over. Beneath her full face mask, her eyes were hard and staring. Owen knelt and pulled off her mask, and then passed his hand over her ashen face; there was no reaction, and her breathing was laboured. He placed his hand below her breast and felt her heart pounding rapidly. Owen looked up at Andam. 'What did you do to her?'

'Merely let her see her true self.'

'She must have seen something terrifying,' Tien murmured.

'Few men ever examine themselves – their true selves – closely. Instinctively, they know they will not like what they find.'

'Will she recover? Can you bring her back?' Owen demanded.

'Of course.'

'The Weapon Master looked at Tien. 'We'll take her with us; perhaps she might be persuaded to tell us who hired her.'

Tien nodded doubtfully. He bent and lifted the woman off the ground – and a crossbow bolt snatched her from his hands!

The bolt was completely black, from pyramidal head to ebon feathers.

Kutor listened to the story of events and then lightly touched the bloody crossbow bolt with the tips of his fingers. 'It matches the bolt that killed the man Stinger?'

Owen nodded. 'Exactly.'

'And they can only be manufactured by this man, this War-lord?'

Owen nodded again. 'And probably fired by his son who is a more than accomplished archer. The shot that killed the woman was fired from at least three hundred paces away, from the opposite side of the square.'

Kutor looked up at the Weapon Master. The Emperor's face was almost unreadable, and his eyes were distant, as if he wasn't truly concerned with what had occurred. 'Perhaps the archer was aiming at someone else?' He looked at the far end of the room where the Andam priest stood, still and silent.

'It took the woman through the throat,' the Weapon Master said. 'The first attack was against the Andam, but then, when the tide turned against the attackers, she was killed to ensure that she didn't talk.'

Kutor sighed deeply. 'So we are blocked again. At every turn there is an enemy, a knife in every shadow, poison in every cup. It was easier before; life was simpler then. We cannot win; we cannot hold this position. Geillard will return. He has too many people working for him – and, you know, I think I would welcome his return. If he were to walk in now I might just give him back his cursed throne! This is getting too . . . much.' He shook his head and turned his back on the warrior. 'Too much. Too much!'

'Kutor?' Owen asked, but the Emperor had already walked away and had climbed the steps to his huge throne and slumped down in it. His lips were moving and he was talking softly to himself. The Weapon Master turned, and was startled to find that the Andam had come up silently behind him. 'Something's wrong. He is unwell . . .'

'Leave us,' the Andam said very softly, his grey eyes concerned. 'Leave us be. I am a healer; I may be able to help.'

Owen looked at Kutor, but the Emperor was lost in his own world, and the Weapon Master doubted that he was even aware that there were people still in the room. He turned and nodded to Tien and then left the throne room, pulling the huge wooden doors shut behind them, joining Fodla and Keshian who were waiting in the hallway outside. Briefly Owen explained what had happened.

'Possession,' the huge Commander of the Legion hissed.

Keshian nodded slowly. 'It would seem so . . . but who?' he asked. 'Possession takes power.'

'The only person in Karfondal with that sort of power is the Lady Esse,' Fodla said softly.

The short stout man nodded. 'Then this changes everything. We should attack now – hard and fast. Destroy them now . . .' Both Fodla and Owen were nodding, when Tien said:

'It is too soon.'

'If we leave it any longer, Kutor will be their creature and we will have lost everything we fought to achieve,' Keshian protested.

'Let us wait and see what the Andam says,' the Shemmat insisted.

The Andam walked slowly around the base of the throne, looking at the Emperor. The Andam priests were reputed to possess certain magical powers, but in truth, with the exception of healing, the majority of them were unskilled. However, the higher echelons of the priesthood had access to extraordinary power, drawing it as needed from its source, deep in the Southern Marshes. Usually a long period of preparation and ritual was required to ensure that it was used for the good of the Andam and the existence of the Planes of Existence. But there were occasions when the merest shadow of the power could be called up at a moment's notice – as when the Andam had stopped the female assassin in her tracks. And the Andam called upon that power now, pouring strength into the Emperor, chipping away at the accumulated detritus the Lady Esse and Mannam had laid on him.

'There is a stink of Death about you,' the Andam said quietly, walking up the steps to stand before Kutor, 'a stink of old gods, of promises and self-pity.'

Kutor raised his head to look at him.

'Your aura has been muddled by power and minor magics. You have been troubled, set upon, attacked, if you will . . .' He pitched his voice carefully, using something similar to the Bardic Voice, attempting to break through the Emperor's daze. 'The followers of the Religion have been working on you. Doubts have been planted like evil seeds, to grow and seem insurmountable, while promises have been made to you, promises which seem to hold the answers to your problems.'

'Mannam,' Kutor mumbled, 'there was Mannam.'

'A deposed god, who has cast in his lot with the Religion solely to gain vengeance on the bard and the Pantheon of the Faith. You have been used, Emperor . . .'

'But by my own people!' Kutor suddenly protested, and the Andam suppressed a smile; it was the first sign of interest the Emperor had shown.

'You were perfectly willing to allow them to make the decisions for you!' Andam snapped. 'The bandit prince of the Outlands could have been Emperor long ago if he had merely chosen to pursue his claim to the throne through the legitimate means. But fear and laziness prevented him. And when his hand was forced, he sat back content and allowed others to carry him along, and when he was handed the Kingship of the Nations he continued to allow others to make the decisions and rule through him.' The Andam turned and walked down the steps, pausing on the bottom step to look up. 'And that weakness was spotted and preyed upon by the Religion.' The Andam walked down the long marbled floor towards the doors. 'You are a fool, Kutor, and worse, you are a weak fool. You are a coward, for all your vaunted bravery. If you wear a crown, then act the part of a king!' He walked out of the chamber and closed the door behind him.

When the power left him the Andam sagged against the doors and Tien hurried to catch him before he fell.

'Well?' Owen asked.

'I tried to shake him out of his lethargy, while pouring power into him, strengthening his will, his self-respect, stripping off the layers of the Religion's magic.'

'Did it work?'

The doors were suddenly flung open and Kutor strode out.

Physically, the man hadn't changed, but gone was the short, soft stocky man, running to fat, and now Kutor, bandit prince of the Outlands, was back. He looked around at the five anxious faces, and he smiled broadly.

'It is time to act!'

11 Ectoraige

Ectoraige is the God of Learning and Knowledge. He rarely appears but prefers to speak through the medium of his followers. Traditionally, his appearance is that of a man wise in years but still sturdy, and he affects the blue teaching robe of one of the ancient Lore Lords . . .

Pantheon of the Old Faith

Born of Ice and Snow in the Winter of the World . . .

Chopt Proverb

'He is Ectoraige, I can assure you,' Eiron said quietly.

The creature that was both Gire and Ectoraige looked at Katani and she felt a sudden chill run icy fingers down her spine as the clear grey eyes settled onto her face.

The voice was strong, powerful and assured. 'Without me the bard dies – a true and final death also – and without me the Seven Nations will go down in flames, and with them the believers of the Old Faith, and thus will die the gods of the Pantheon. And without the Pantheon to counter the excesses of the Religion, the balance will tip and the Planes of Existence will drift back into the void from whence they came.'

Katani sank back into her seat, her swords clattering onto the wooden table. The creature had made the statement clearly and simply and she found herself believing him.

'I am Ectoraige. This boy is my tool, receptive to my thoughts, strong in body and mind, courageous, with an enquiring curiosity and an excellent pedigree for learning. He will make a good monk.'

'Why have you taken over this boy's mind, turning him into a quai, a mindless thing?' Katani hissed. When she had guarded the approaches to the Silent Wood, she had known many of the quai – the mindless creatures – and had come to fear and loathe them.

'He is not quai – not permanently at any rate. He is merely useful at this time as a mouthpiece. Were another tool available, then I would use that.' Although the boy's face remained expressionless, his eyes were darting, flashing, conveying a wealth of nuance and energy.

Katani looked over at Eiron. The Bard-Master caught her despairing gaze and smiled reassuringly. 'Trust him; he is a God of the Faith.'

'Do you believe that? Truly believe that?' she asked.

'I do.'

'And it is by his faith, his belief that lends me the strength to be here,' Ectoraige said through Gire's mouth. 'And now, Katan warrior, you must listen to me, if not for your sake, then for the sake of the bard, and if not for his then for the continued existence of this entire plane of life.'

Katani dismissed him with a wave of her hand. 'Just tell me what needs to be done,' she snapped.

'Follow the bard into the Northlands. He will need your assistance, for he will be betrayed and will be in sore need . . .'

'I told him not to trust Bastion!'

'And take care lest you judge too quickly,' Ectoraige advised, and the woman warrior had a brief and momentary glimpse of an old man with snow-white hair and the faintest of beards smiling benignly at her. 'I must speak to the bard through the medium of this boy.'

'So I must take Gire with me?'

'I am afraid so. And you must ensure his safety at all costs. Without him, I might find it difficult to find another suitable mouthpiece in the Northlands.'

'I'll keep him alive,' Katani growled, her expression sour. 'But would it not be better for you to tell me what is so important now, lest anything happen to him?'

'But if you were taken and tortured . . .?' Ectoraige asked.

'I am Katan!' the warrior snarled, affronted.

'But you are also humankind.' Ectoraige shook his head. 'No, what I say is for the bard alone. Now I will rest this body, for it is debilitating both for me and the boy. Leave him, he will rest peacefully. But we will speak again, warrior.' The eyes closed and a shudder rippled through the boy's body. His eyes flickered open and they were deep chestnut brown. He looked confusedly at Katani and Eiron. 'I feel so tired . . .' and then he rested his head on his arms and immediately fell asleep.

Katani looked over at Eiron. She stood up and sheathed both swords. 'Let us talk, you and I, about this God of Learning and Knowledge.'

The Bard-Master of Thusal and the Katan Warrior walked the small enclosed courtyard beneath a leaden sky. The morning's snow had been brushed off the smooth rounded cobbles, and the statues dusted clean, leaving the place looking oddly out of place with the rest of the snow-covered building.

Eiron had pulled on his brown and gold cloak, dragged the hood up over his head, and tucked his hands into his deep sleeves. Katani was wearing her armour and gauntlets, but had left off her helmet, preferring a broad brimmed conical hat.

'What do you know of Ectoraige, the God of Learning and Knowledge?' Eiron asked.

'I know nothing. When I first left the World of Men, he was unknown.'

'And you left – you died – on the Sand Plain?'

Katani nodded.

Eiron's head moved slightly beneath the enveloping hood. 'The worship of Ectoraige was just beginning then. It started in the Northlands, but quickly spread south, aided, I should add, by your old employer, Churon the Onelord. He was a great believer in knowledge.'

Katani grunted at the mention of Churon's name. 'Tell me about Ectoraige.'

Eiron nodded. 'Listen then, and I will tell you how a man became a god . . .'

The old man stood on the banks of the rushing river measuring the depth of the water by gauging its height against the bank. He turned to the short stout man standing by his side. 'It has risen again. By sunrise, it will have reached the top of the banks, by mid-morning . . .' He left the sentence unfinished, but they both knew the consequences if the river overflowed.

Mansen, Burgomaster of the City of Palentian, the seat of Count Palent, rubbed his hands nervously together. 'It's too late now to evacuate the city . . .'

'You should have listened to me,' the old man snapped.

'I did, but the Count . . . well, you know what the Count is like.'

Ectoraige, the Lore Lord, nodded wearily and turned away from the River Seme, swollen now by the unseasonal snow high in the mountains behind them.

'Is there anything you can do?' Mansen asked.

Ectoraige turned to look back up into the snowcapped mountains. He shook his head, his eyes darkening. 'I'm not sure; I don't think so.'

'But you have to,' Mansen protested. 'The people are counting on you. You saved us from the wolves, defended us from the bandits, even defeated the plague. The people trust you. I asked my servants to flee, but they refused. They said, "The Lore Lord will save us."'

Ectoraige ran a long-fingered hand through his fine white hair. 'But not this time, I think,' he said softly.

'But you'll try?' the Burgomaster asked eagerly.

Ectoraige smiled. 'Of course, I'll try.' He turned away and walked back to his horse. 'Will Palent give me any men?' he called back.

'As many as you need.'

'Send me as many as he can spare – the more the better – to the Seme Falls, as quickly as possible. I'll need digging equipment and a reasonably competent magician with knowledge of fire.'

Mansen nodded and hurried off for his own horse, looking nervously into the lowering skies, with their promise of snow and rain. The gods were in cruel form these days. The war with the Demons was obviously not progressing well. And then he reflected that perhaps the recent harsh and unseasonal weather was precisely because the war with the Demon-kind was not progressing well. The gods needed their prayers – and so did Ectoraige.

The Lore Lord rode into the mountains feeling the chill bite into his bones; he was getting far too old for this foolishness. At his age he should be sitting by some king's side, dispensing wisdom and advice with certainly one and possibly more wives to tend to his needs.

Well, this would be the last time, he promised himself. His knowledge, his lore, had surely not been collected and garnered for every land in the known world and from several Planes of Existence only to be frittered away on stupid schemes.

And what else could he be using his knowledge for? he wondered. Telling tales like some itinerant bard at some king's court. What use was knowledge if it was not used, not shared? Surely he had a duty to put his knowledge to good use – and what better use for knowledge than for the saving of humankind?

He reined in his mount in sight of the Seme Falls. At this time of year – the season had turned towards high summer – they should have been little more than a trickle. But the falls were in full flood, the river arching far out over the lip about five hundred lengths over his head. Even from the distance the mist and spray dampened his face.

Ectoraige urged his mount forward and when the path forked, he took the right-hand path which led up along the edge of the falls, turning and switching back through a forest grown wild with the constant moisture. Eventually he had to dismount and lead his horse upwards because of the amount of moss and treacherous slime underfoot. When he reached the top of the falls he moved out to the edge of the foaming river and looked down – and then wished he hadn't. Shrugging his shoulders, he moved back from the water's edge and attempted to find a relatively sheltered and dry spot.

Count Palent's warrior's arrived later that afternoon; a century of men with three wagonloads of equipment. However, there was no mage with them, the Count preferring to keep his magician with him.

146

Masking his disgust and disappointment, the old Lore Lord mounted his horse again and rode slowly upriver, looking for a spot suitable for his purposes. Every hundred paces or so he would stop and consult his chart of the region.

Finally, as the dusk was rolling in and the first stars were beginning to glitter in the clear sky, he reined in his mount for a final time and dismounted. He waited until the Captain of the Guard rode up to join him, and then he pointed to the river. 'I'll want the bank built up on that side . . . the beginnings of a channel gouged out along here . . . and then I'll need the river dammed across there.'

The young captain, clearly in awe of the famous Lore Lord, had merely nodded. 'It will be done as you say. We will need your assistance.'

Ectoraige smiled at the young man's unquestioning obedience. 'Of course.'

'When do we start?' the captain had asked.

Ectoraige had grinned humourlessly. 'If it is not completed by morning, then Palentian will be flooded and the sown fields swept away. You remember the harshness of the last winter and the amount of stores of food and fuel and city used? You remember the rationing and the threat of famine? If the fields are destroyed now then that famine will become a reality this winter, and those who survive the flood will surely perish.'

Ectoraige divided the men up into two groups of fifty, one raising the bank on the right-hand side of the river, the other cutting away a track on the left-hand side, but keeping the bank intact for the moment. When the time was right, the bank would be knocked away and simultaneously the river would be dammed. In theory, the river should turn and flow down through the forest into the plain below, bypassing the city.

They worked on through the night, working in shifts, and when they slowed down, or slackened, Ectoraige would simply say to them, 'Think of your families in Palentian.'

And all the time the river rose.

As morning approached and the work neared completion, the captain approached Ectoraige, who was sitting slumped against a tree, his robes filthy, his clear grey eyes dulled.

147

'My lord, we have a problem.'

Ectoraige looked up and nodded. 'I know. How do we dam the river and how do we break down the bank on this side?'

The captain nodded wordlessly.

'I wanted a magician,' Ectoraige explained, 'someone who could destroy the bank and then shift that pile of rocks up there' – he pointed to the hillside up above the river – 'and bring it down to block the channel. A good magician could have done that – why, even a poor magician could have done that!' He shook his head bitterly. 'But I'm sorry, I can think of no way of doing both together. I've ransacked my lore, but I can think of nothing . . .'

The captain had smiled. He walked away and rummaged through the carts, returning moments later with a satchel filled with a coarse brownish powder. 'This explodes when set alight,' he said. 'Watch.' He took a fistful of powder and allowed some to trickle from his hand into a neat pile on the ground, and then he used the rest of the powder to draw a small trail away from the pile. With flint and tinder he dropped a spark onto the first of the brown grains. The powder fizzled, sparked and then erupted into a sputtering flame. The flame writhed along the ground and when it reached the pile it exploded in a shower of sparking cinders.

Ectoraige's face was like that of a child. 'How much do you have?'

The captain lifted the satchel.

'Leave me some – enough to tear a hole in that bank, and then you take the rest. Use it to bring down that rock pile.'

The captain poured enough of the brown powder to fill a flask and then saluted and hurried off, calling his men. Ectoraige watched them go, and then he looked back at the flask. When the captain had demonstrated the powder's capabilities, he had immediately grasped the single remaining practical problem of exploding the powder beside the river. The damp . . .

'. . . his body was never found,' Eiron finished. 'He knew he would never be able to light the powder in the damp air, so he apparently dug a hole in the bank, crouched down over it, shielding it with his body and set the fuse alight.' The Bard-Master shook his head. 'Such a loss.'

148

'And Palentian?'

'Saved, of course. That was when the devotion to him began. And almost immediately he began speaking through suitable mediums. It was assumed that he never appeared in any other way because his body had been completely destroyed, but I'm sure that's not the case. He laid down the rules for the foundation of his colleges and schools, and of course as soon as the young men and women began to learn in his schools, veneration to Ectoraige increased, very quickly turning him into a powerful god.'

'And is he still so powerful?'

'Not as powerful as he once was. Now men worship power not learning, but his time will come again; I've seen several such cycles swing from might to lore and back to might again. Usually in times of tribulation it swings to might.'

'Do you believe him when he says that only he can save the bard and the Nations?' Katani asked seriously.

The Bard-Master stopped and turned to look into the warrior's amber eyes. 'Without Ectoraige's help, I am convinced the bard will die.'

Bastion moved the snow-laden branch away from his face and pointed down into the hollow with a black-gloved hand. 'Chopt camp,' he said shortly.

Paedur, who had been standing with his back to the man, turned round, his thin face pinched in a frown, his eyes reflecting the silver-white of the snow and ice.

'Something troubles you?'

Paedur shook his head. 'Something . . . but I'm not sure what. I thought something was following us, but if there is anything it is well-shielded.' He shook his head abruptly. 'I don't know . . . it might be nothing . . .'

Bastion nodded. He reached into his loose coat and pulled out a short, stubby-handled tube. He pulled back an ornate spur on the back of the tube and the bard heard again the double click he had heard in the Tavern of the Blasted Tree. 'It is a projectile weapon,' Bastion explained, 'shooting a dart as far as a crossbow can fire a bolt.'

149

The bard nodded briefly and immediately lost interest. He looked down on the Chopt encampment. His knowledge of the beasts was surprisingly limited; most of what he knew was culled from the archives of the Bardic Library at Baddalaur, the repository of all the knowledge in the known world. That knowledge was being constantly updated, but even so, the most recent records of the Chopts had been nearly three generations old.

Well, if he survived this, he would be able to add to that knowledge.

The Chopt village was not dissimilar to the more primitive villages of humankind. Behind a sturdy palisade of sharpened stakes was a village of simple square wooden huts surrounding a longer, larger hut from which issued a thin stream of grey smoke. The ground between the huts and around the larger hut had been churned to mud, and in one corner of the village a score of hogs rooted noisily. Other than that, there was no visible sign of activity in the village.

'It looks like any other human village,' Paedur said without turning around.

'Why, what did you expect?' Bastion wheezed.

'I'm not sure,' Paedur said, turning, and suddenly stopping. Less than a hundred paces away, directly across the snow-covered clearing were two of the Torc Allta, the Boar-Folk. Their beast-like heads were raised to the heavens, wet snouts tasting the air, their upcurved tusks gleaming yellow in the light.

'I know,' Bastion said softly, his voice barely above a whisper.

'How did I not know they were there?' Paedur demanded in a harsh whisper.

'Like me they are not fully of this world, but rather inhabit the Shadowland between. You are blind to those too like yourself, bard.'

One of the Torc Allta pointed towards the trees where the bard and Bastion were standing, and the beasts shifted the long tridents in their hands and moved towards them.

Bastion lifted the small tubed weapon and rested it on a branch. He ducked his head and looked down the length of the barrel, and then he pressed on a stud set into the back of the handle.

The weapon clicked loudly, and they both clearly heard something ping off the nearest Torc Allta's breastplate. The creature stopped to look down at the long scratch mark across the metal. It turned to its companion . . . and Bastion's second shot hit it in the side of the throat. It fell as if it had been struck with an axe.

'Poisoned,' Bastion murmured, pulling back the lever and when the stud popped out of the handle, firing again. This time the second creature's paw went to its face and touched the long sliver of wood that protruded from its eye. It opened its mouth to scream and Bastion's next shot took it through the mouth, killing it instantly.

'An interesting weapon,' Paedur murmured.

Bastion smiled. 'A gift from . . . from a weaponmaker I did a favour for. It is the only one like it on this Plane of Existence.'

'The legends speak of similar weapons,' Paedur said, ducking beneath a branch and walking slowly towards the still bodies of the Torc Allta. 'Some were reputed to be capable of killing from over a thousand paces; others could destroy whole armies at a time.'

'Myth!' Bastion snorted.

The bard smiled coldly. 'You're holding a myth in your hand.' He knelt beside the body of the first of the Boar-Folk. He could smell the rank beast odour from the creature, but only with what would have been normal human senses; with his enhanced god-given senses the creature was invisible. He turned the beast's head, examining the curling caste marks cut into the yellow tusks that protruded from the bottom lip. 'Warrior-hunter class,' he murmured. 'I'm afraid I lack the knowledge to interpret the clan and familial marks.'

Bastion nudged the second beast with his foot. 'They're dead – that's all that's important.' He paused and added with a smile wide enough to open the wounds on his face. 'And more importantly, we have some gifts for our friends below.'

Paedur looked up quickly, his eyebrows raised in a question.

Bastion kicked the Torc Allta again. 'Food for our hosts. The Chopts like fresh meat.'

Paedur stood back and watched Bastion deal with the beasts. They obviously knew the man, but even without his enhanced senses Paedur could feel their mistrust. He was the object of much curiosity and from the shifting patterns of the beasts' auras, they obviously regarded him as something fearful.

He remained still and unmoving, his arms folded into his sleeves, his hood over his face, listening, trying to place the language. It was familiar, hauntingly so, but with nuances and sounds that were totally alien to his ears, sounds that could or should only have been made by beasts. But the Chopts were more than beasts, he reminded himself. Remove the over-abundance of hair and dress them in civilised clothes and most of them could have passed unnoticed in any of the cities of the Nations.

He sorted through his huge store of knowledge, slowly and meticulously matching the language – and came to a simple, startling conclusion. With very minor alterations, and some accentual differences, they were speaking almost pure Culai – a language dead to all but the most dedicated scholar.

Bastion's haggling with the Chopt leader was obviously drawing to a close, and two of the creatures came forward, took up the two bodies of the slain Boar-Folk and carried them on their shoulders into the Chopt encampment. Most of the onlookers immediately drifted away after them, leaving only Bastion, the Chopt leader and a single guard facing Paedur.

Bastion raised his arm and called the bard forward; his scarred face was tight and his small dark eyes were unreadable, but the bard could sense his tension. Paedur stopped a score of paces from the trio, and raised his head slightly, allowing the snow to turn his eyes white and blind-seeming. The two Chopts moved uneasily.

'This is Paedur, a bard. There is no harm in him. He is wise in lore and legends and he has taken the hard road into the Northlands to prepare the legends of the Chopt so that the humankind may know the greatness of the People of the Ice.' He turned from the bard to the older of the two Chopts. 'This is Icewalker, Datar of this clan,' he said, using the Chief's given-name rather than his personal name, and being careful not to name the clan. Paedur also noticed that he had called him, 'Datar', the ancient respectful term for father, usually applied to a holy man.

The Chopt, a huge creature a head and more taller than the bard, and broad in proportion, bowed slightly, his eyes never leaving the bard's face. The only obvious signs of his age were the streaks of white running through the hair on his face and body and that he was almost completely toothless.

'And this is Ironwinter.'

The second Chopt bowed quickly and briefly, his eyes on the bards, his right hand resting on the gleaming new hilt of a Chopt knife in his belt. He was smaller than the older beast, though still taller than the bard, and whereas the former Chopt was bulky, the younger Chopt was almost slender. His features were typically Chopt: flat, with a broad, receding forehead and a similarly receding jaw, leaving his long canine teeth protruding slightly over his lip. His eyes were small and black, sunk deep behind high cheek-bones. His hair was long, black and coarse, and kept away from his eyes with a leather thong, and from what the bard could see of his body, he was covered in short, bristling hair.

Both men were dressed alike in ancient worn leathers and scraps of furs. They were both barefoot, and both of them carried long broad-bladed knives, the traditional Chopt knife – and, curiously , the knives were new.

The two men were looking at the bard expectantly, and he glanced at Bastion for instruction, but the man remained unmoving. Finally, Paedur raised his right hand and pushed back his hood, revealing his face.

The elder Chopt, Icewalker, stepped forward to stare into the bard's eyes, and then grunted with fright as he saw himself reflected in the perfect mirrors. He reached out with his left hand, the fingers curved slightly, the nails long, slab-like and filthy. He was about to touch the bard in the centre of the chest when Paedur pulled back, his left arm came up, his hook encircling the Chopt's wrist.

Ironwinter hissed with shock and his knife came out of its sheath in one quick movement.

153

'The Law of the Bards does not allow them to be touched by any man, lest it . . . lest it taint their knowledge,' Bastion said quickly. 'That is why they enjoy the ancient King Privilege.'

Icewalker nodded, but Ironwinter was less easily convinced. The older beast withdrew his hand slowly from the sparkling half-circle of the bard's hook, and only when Paedur dropped his arm did the younger Chopt sheath his knife.

Icewalker grinned at the bard, revealing his discoloured gums, still studded with the remaining shards of teeth, and wafted fetid breath in his direction. 'You are fast, humankind, fast, as fast as I've seen.' His accent was thick and slurred, but completely distinguishable, and the bard immediately wrote off another myth about the beast folk – that they could not speak any of the tongues of humankind. 'You will share our table.'

Paedur saw Bastion nod quickly, and he immediately inclined his head 'I would be honoured,' he said slowly and clearly.

The Chopt grinned again, and turned away, his hand closing on his guard's shoulder, forcibly spinning him around, and almost pushing him ahead.

'Someone doesn't like us,' Paedur said, as Bastion joined him.

'Ironwinter's parents were slain by humankind; he has no cause to love them.'

'"Love them?"' Paedur asked. 'You speak of the humankind as if they were a race foreign to you. Do you no longer think of yourself as humankind, then?'

Bastion smiled tightly. 'Do you?'

The meal was a long, slow and tense affair, with the Chopts wary of the two strangers and both Bastion and Paedur as cautious of their hosts.

The whole Chopt tribe of about twenty adults and roughly the same number of children had gathered to enjoy the feast. The Torc Allta had been treated as any other animal, gutted, cleaned, and then stuffed before cooking on a spit over an open fire. All the major organs had been removed and these were cooked separately, with the choicest pieces saved for the Datar and the other elders of the tribe.

Icewalker sat at the head of the long table. On his right-hand side sat two other beasts, both of them showing similar signs of age, and opposite these sat Bastion and the bard. Behind them stood what were obviously guards, while behind the two elders crouched two plump females, their task to masticate the tough boar-flesh before passing it on for them to chew in their toothless mouths. Behind Icewalker stood Ironwinter.

The room was dark, illuminated only by wicks floating in bowls of stinking oil, but the main illumination came from the roaring fire at the end of the long room. Most of the tribe were crouched around it, both for heat and to watch the two Torc Allta roast. The stench in the room was incredible.

'The Marked Man says you want to be taken to the Source,' Icewalker said suddenly, turning to the bard, a large earthen goblet in his hand.

Paedur glanced quickly at Bastion, and the man nodded. 'I am the Marked Man; the Source is their capital.'

The bard turned back to the Chopt leader. 'That is correct.'

'Why?' Ironwinter suddenly snarled. 'There is a stink of Death about you, you are not of humankind, you carry the destruction of the People of the Ice within you.'

Paedur looked at the young Chopt with more interest. His diction was perfect and completely without accent; this was no ordinary beast, and he obviously had some degree of Sight. 'Every man dies, every man carries his destruction within him,' he said softly.

Ironwinter leaned across Icewalker and rammed his knife into the wooden table before the bard. 'I do not trust you. I think you should die, bard,' he spat.

Paedur looked at the knife vibrating in the table, and then he slowly reached out and encircled it within his hook. His lips moved slightly. The hook glowed with a cool pale blue light, and then the burnished metal of the knife began to run in sluggish liquid, pooling on the wooden table, scorching the wood, the stink of burning metal and wood overlain with the acrid odour of power.

Behind his covering of hair, Ironwinter had paled, and his small dark eyes were now clearly encircled with white.

155

'And will you kill me?' Paedur whispered, his voice cold, lifting his face so his eyes burned with the light from the fire, turning them gold and flickering bronze.

Icewalker deliberately poured his drink over the sizzling remains of the knife. 'The boy is headstrong, but means well. He has reason enough to hate the humankind. You will forgive him.'

Paedur was unsure whether the last had been a request or a statement, but he slowly nodded. 'There is nothing to forgive; words spoken in haste . . .'

'I meant them!' Ironwinter said defiantly.

Icewalker suddenly struck upwards with his goblet, the earthen bowl shattering against the Chopt's chest, sending him staggering back. Before he could recover, the old beast swept his legs from under him, sending him crashing to the ground, and his own knife was resting against the younger creature's throat. 'You insult my guest; you invite bloodshed; you summon death,' Icewalker snarled. 'This man, this bard, is not humankind. He will kill you without thinking, without trying and with no effort. So if you wish to die then at least let it be by my hand.' Although he had been speaking in the Chopt dialect, Paedur had caught most of it, but he still turned to Bastion for a translation, deciding not to betray his knowledge of the language just yet.

'Icewalker says you are not of humankind and could kill the boy,' the guide said shortly.

'Tell them if my presence here causes them upset, I will leave.'

'Don't be a fool,' Bastion said quickly. 'You're in the Northlands now – the customs are different, the manners changed. You have accepted Icewalker's hospitality for the night, and you must stay the night. To leave before the dawn is the action of a thief or an assassin, and is extremely discourteous – and dangerous. If you even suggest it, Icewalker himself will probably use that nice new knife on you.'

The bard nodded. 'I'll abide by what you say. But you might compliment him on the knife, you'll notice all the creatures are carrying new weapons.'

'I noticed.'

Icewalker had resumed his seat. He slapped both gnarled hands down on the table and glared at the bard. 'You have brought dissent to my table . . .'

Paedur looked at the creature and allowed a little of his trained Bardic Voice to project. 'I brought meat to your table; I brought respect. I was met with threats and insults. I came to honour the Chopt Lore, but perhaps the Chopt Lore is not worthy of saving.'

Icewalker's lips pulled back from his gums in a broad smile. 'A threat unworthy of one who wears the cloak and device of a bard.'

Paedur bowed slightly, acknowledging his mistake; he was beginning to realise that he had badly misjudged these people. They might look like beasts, they might live and eat and even smell like beasts, but these were no unthinking animals.

'If you have travelled this far for our lore then you are not going to be so easily turned back,' Icewalker continued, picking up a second goblet which one of the females had placed before him. 'Tell me first what you want to know.'

'I would like to travel to your capital – the Source – and learn from any records that have been kept.'

'The People of the Ice keep no records in script or stone.' He tapped his head with a blunt nail. 'Here is where we record the history of our race. There are few skills amongst us, but our memories are prodigious.'

'You have the skill of metal work,' Bastion remarked. 'The new knives are a marvel.'

Something shifted behind the beast's eyes, and he looked uncomfortable. 'The knives were . . . a gift from the Source.'

The guide grinned. 'I thought the People of the Ice accepted no gift save the gift of the gods.'

'The knives are a gift of the gods,' Icewalker said shortly.

Paedur, sensing the way the conversation had shifted, changed the subject quickly. 'Can you tell me then the History of the People of the Ice?' he asked.

The Chopt looked surprised. 'You would listen to it?'

'I am a bard – my first and last delight is in the telling and hearing of tales.'

157

'Datar!' Ironwinter said warningly, but Icewalker ignored him.

'Can you tell me how the People of the Ice came to the Northlands?' Paedur asked.

Surprisingly, Icewalker shook his head. 'That is not my tale. Each clan of the People has a tale to tell; some tell of the creation of the People, others of their coming to the Northlands, others of their growth to Empire, and still others – and this is my tale – tell of their fall from power. I will tell you, bard, how the Chopt race became little more than beasts.'

As he had been speaking, the rest of his clan had gathered around to listen, their faces and mouths slick with grease from the boar meat. Paedur closed his eyes and allowed his senses to expand, taking in the room, reading the coloured auras, most of them reflecting something close to contentment, a simple people satisfied with simple pleasures. Ironwinter was still seething with rage, his aura flickering red and white, and Icewalker to his right was glowing with a soft satisfaction; obviously he wasn't often asked to tell his clan's tale.

The bard then allowed his consciousness to move beyond the long hall and out into the camp beyond. He picked up the sentries patrolling the walls, and then beyond them the stillness of the forest. A pack of wolves slunk by beneath the trees, radiating animal rage and hunger; there was a snowbear hunting on the banks of a frozen river; and to the north a pack of ice-cats had killed and were eating, but then beyond them there was no living thing, no movement.

Reasonably satisfied, Paedur opened his eyes, and found both Bastion and Icewalker looking at him. He smiled an apology, and the Chopt began . . .

This was the last days of the Shining Folk, the First Race; this was the time when the worlds were in turmoil and the Planes of Existence seethed and shifted. This was the Time of Ending.

The Shining Folk were hunted then, hunted by their own creations, by those who had sworn to protect them, hunted by their children. They retreated to the Outlands, the hidden places, secret groves and concealed valleys wherein to continue their works and magics. And so they moved north, driven away from the civilised world by the newly civilised peoples, and eventually they settled in a secret hidden valley deep in the Land of Ice and Fire. But the borderland between the Northlands and the newly-established Southern Kingdoms was guarded, and often the southerners sent forays into the bitter Northlands seeking their old masters and, if they were found, subjecting them to the most barbaric tortures before putting them to death

So in their desperation the Shining Folk brought forth the People of the Ice, the Chopt. They were the last creations of the Shining Folk, and the First Race used the sum total of their knowledge and lore to create a people both beautiful, strong and wise. They created creatures that were in their own likeness, but stronger and with a warlike barbarity that was unknown to the Shining Folk.

But this is not my tale; others have the telling of it. My tale is later, when the seasons have passed, and the Shining Folk have left this world for ever, leaving their sons, the People of the Ice alone.

The Chopt race created an Empire in the Northlands for the Shining Ones, using the last of their magic, working with their tools, following their advice, but when the First Race went the Empire of Ice and Snow collapsed, crumbled in on itself, dissolved in turmoil, bickering and revolution. The Empire fell and the race of humankind added its weight to its dissolution, and attacked its borders.

The humankind moreover, retained a little of the Shining One's magic and used this against the People of the Ice, and death and disease walked amongst the clans of the Northlands. The peoples separated, seeking safety in solitude, and to this end sought the ice caves and secret places, much as their creators had done in previous generations.

And then it was as if the very elements conspired against the Chopt race. The seasons turned and although the Northlands had always been a land of ice and snow, in the Turnings of the Year it was as pleasant as any other southern land, but now this too changed, and the ice and snow closed in on it, sealing it in an iron claw, creating the harsh and bitter land it is today. And it was said at the time that the weather had been influenced by the magic of the humankind, but there is no-one alive now to say the truth in this.

However, the bitter weather proved to be both the blessing and the bane of the People of the Ice.

The humankind had their own problems; their gods warred both with others like themselves and with the demon-kind and their troubles were reflected on the World of Men. The humankind –excepting those living on the borders of the Northlands – soon forgot about the Chopts, for their own troubles were many and manifold.

But the bitter weather that sealed off the Northlands, enclosed the small scattered tribes within tiny encampments and caves. And you must remember that this was still in the days when the People of the Ice were akin to humankind, soft of skin, though strong of heart; this was the time before the People of the Ice learned to survive in the Northlands.

Trapped as they were, they broke the First Rule of the Shining Folk – they bred with themselves.

The Shining Folk had left their children the Rules, seven guides for the continuance of their existence. Some are meaningless now, their content lost with the passage of the Seasons; only two remain relevant, not to breed with one's own clan, and not to eat of the flesh of one's own race.

The First Rule was broken, the Second never so.

The first generation – the result of such inbreeding – was much as their parents, the only noticeable difference being the quality and quantity of their hair which, it is remembered, was strong and coarse and covered much of their bodies. And in the bitter Northlands, this was no small advantage. So the elders of the clan examined the children and found them to be strong and hale and pronounced it safe for the clan to breed within itself.

The next generation was also hale. They too were covered in hair and as they grew towards maturity it was found that they were stronger than the previous generation.

But their taste for blood was strong too.

The next generation saw the beginnings of the fall. Their children were ugly – not all of them, but enough for the chiefs to recognise that here was the result of breaking the First Rule. The children were not monsters: their limbs and senses were correct, but their features were mis-shapen, and they were no longer in the image of the Shining Ones. They too were strong, and their taste for blood and flesh equally so.

Successive generations produced children that were more and more unlike the Shining Ones, but although their appearance became more and more savage – almost beast-like – their intellect did not change at first; but later, as the old learning was no longer recited and remembered, the Chopt lost the last of their gifts from the Shining Ones, the gift of knowledge.

What remained were much as you see the People today, strong in body, hardy, but lacking in knowledge and hungry for flesh. How the People discovered the flesh of humankind is another tale, but that was the beginning of the war with the soft-skinned ones. These were the People of the Ice who first brought terror to the fields of Men and caused the building of the Seven Bastions of the North along the banks of the Seme.

The humankind warred with the People, and the Chopts gathered together the last army ever to be seen in the Northlands and moved south on the soft-skinned ones. And in a battle that lasted seven days and seven nights they were driven back at the Seme by the very things they had once cast aside – the knowledge of the Elder Race.

The humankind employed their magic and knowledge to break the Chopts for ever. No more would they be a force to threaten the Southern Nations; now they were only bands of savage marauders, attacking isolated villages and farms, taking human flesh where they could.

All that remained to them was the promise, the promise that they would one day arise again as a Nation and carry fire and destruction into the Southlands under the leadership of a mighty Datar.

The People of the Ice await that day.

And it nears . . .

12   Confrontation

The nobles were growing confident, and with that confidence came a certain amount of arrogance; Kutor realised he must act soon, lest the usurper be usurped!

The Turbulent Years: a History of the Seven Nations

There was revolution in the air.

In the Lower City there were riots as more and more refugees poured into the city, stretching the new Emperor's aid to the limits. Shops and warehouses were raided for food and clothing, and the larger public buildings – theatres, arenas, auction houses and even churches and temples – were taken over by the homeless. Whole sections of the Lower City became refugee enclaves, where the only law was that of might and the sword.

Death, both violent and bloody, was commonplace and there were fires in the ancient wooden buildings every day; it was only a matter of time before there was a major fire that would gut the Lower City.

And through it all wandered the priests of the Religion, spreading rumours, creating dissent – but it was a dangerous and foolish job, and several paid the price of that foolishness – the Religion claimed these as martyrs to their cause.

In the confusion, the vampir were born.

Under the Lady Esse's direction, the two vampir walked the streets at night – and fed, taking their victims in the darkness from amongst the women of the street. They took only females, and most of them were pretty and young. Three of these women – coal-eyed and already inhabited by the creatures from the Ghost World – that staggered back to the Warlord's dungeon were just that, but the fourth was a stout, ugly woman from the Northlands, her skin weathered and hard, her hair bleached brittle white. The Lady Esse immediately locked up the shambling crea-

162

ture and then had the Warlord's son go back into the streets to find one of the type of women she desired.

While she was waiting for the boy to return with a suitable woman, the sorceress had chained the ugly vampir to the floor and doused her in oil. When the boy returned with his unconscious victim, she was chained to the floor beside the creature and then the Lady Esse set the vampir alight. The creature's howls ripped through the night, and then one by one, the five other vampir joined in the chorus, until it seemed as if the very gods themselves cried in pain. When the body was completely wreathed in flame, the sorceress plunged her dagger into the body of the young woman on the floor. She bucked and heaved, her mouth opening in a scream that never materialised and suddenly she opened her eyes – and they were coal black. The Lady Esse had her sixth vampir.

The following morning, the Emperor Legion marched into the Lower City in a display of strength.

The Emperor Legion enjoyed a terrifying reputation. It was the creation of one woman, and was composed entirely of women, all of them hand-picked and trained to an extraordinary degree of weaponship by the Commander of the Legion, Fodla. Indeed, such was its association with her that the legion was sometimes called Fodla's Own.

The very presence of the Legion was enough to quell some of the rioting immediately, and streets that had been bloodied and violent grew deserted and silent as the Legion in the Imperial colours of blue and black marched through.

A fragile, brittle calm returned.

In the palace, Kutor sat opposite the Weapons Master, while Tien lurked in the shadows behind his master. The change that had come over the Emperor was extraordinary; his newfound energy was infectious and almost exhausting, and Owen privately wondered if he didn't prefer the old Kutor.

The table between them was strewn with maps of the city, which had been marked and coloured to show the disposition of the Imperial Legion and the trouble spots. They were receiving reports at regular intervals and – on the charts in any case – the

163

Imperial Legion had taken control of most of the Lower City. The gates to Karfondal had been locked, and the guards doubled and redoubled, and the Way Stations along the roads had been alerted to stop and hold any travellers.

Owen pushed the charts aside and looked at Kutor. 'So what do you want us to do?' he asked, although he already had a very good idea.

Kutor smiled, showing his teeth in a feral smile. 'All eyes are on Fodla now; they are expecting – perhaps they are even hoping for – a bloodbath in the Lower City. But she has her instructions and there will be no killing unless absolutely necessary. It is not the refugees' fault there is not enough food and blankets, no shelter and no water available. It is not their fault that they have been driven from their homes by the elements, and in many cases it is not their fault they have been stirred up into this frenzy. The Andam has told me that the Religion's priests are working against them, raising passions.' Kutor's fingers toyed with a piece of coloured wax with which he had been marking the charts. He looked at his hands and then deliberately placed the stick down. 'Did you know that the Andam Brothers working the mission on the docks were slaughtered?' he asked softly. 'No? It has been assumed that it was the mob, but Andam tells me that it was the work of a Gallowglas and a band of hired thugs who killed the Brothers in cold blood and then wrecked the mission to make it look as if a mob had stormed through.' The Emperor leaned forward. 'And that is your first mission. I want that Gallowglas – and the mercenaries who were with him, if possible.'

Owen nodded. 'That should be easy enough.'

'Perhaps not,' Kutor smiled grimly. 'The Gallowglas is in the employ of the Lady Esse – he is her personal guard. The same lady has just overseen the creation of four more vampir. They are being kept in the cellars beneath the Warlord's Armoury. And that is your second mission. I want those vampir dead or destroyed, or whatever it is you do with the creatures. Perhaps the Andam can help?'

'They will have to be taken during the day when they are sleeping,' Owen mused. 'But how do you know where they are?'

'Since his brothers were slain, the Andam has apparently been drawing on some sort of occult power – it's almost as if their deaths provided him with the power – which makes him even more powerful than the Lady Esse.'

'Then why doesn't he use his power against the sorceress?'

'To do so would be to taint it,' Kutor said, 'or so he told me. So I am afraid you will have to kill her yourselves without aid of any description.'

Owen looked uncomfortable; this sounded too close to assassination for his liking.

Kutor shuffled the maps together on the table. 'Now let us consider the Twelve Families. Of the twelve only four are of any consequence: the Lords Rocque and Bleau, Boazio, the Master of the Fleet, and the Lady d'Homana, who also has a Gallowglas bodyguard. I want them all removed.'

'I am not an assassin,' Owen said softly.

The Emperor looked surprised. 'You are . . . a warrior.'

'A warrior is not an assassin.'

'You are a mercenary in my employ,' Kutor reminded him coldly, 'and if I tell you to kill, then you will kill!'

'You forget yourself, Kutor,' Owen blazed. 'You forget who put you on this throne; you forget whose presence here keeps you on it. Who do you think would support you if I or even Fodla left you?'

'I the Emperor . . .'

'You are a bandit, a usurper, nothing more. Without me, without the bard, without our support you would still be a bandit.'

Kutor surged to his feet. 'And what am I now? I am a prisoner, a puppet to be moved to your will. And all of this is with your support – then perhaps I would be better off without it!'

The two men glared at one another and Tien, recognising the very real threat of violence, began to move towards the two men, when the Andam swept into the room. 'Enough! Enough of this squabbling. You remind me of children in the market, fighting over scraps.' He looked at the two men, noting Kutor's angry flush, and the Weapon Master's set expression. The Andam's harsh, whispering voice was almost raw with emotion. 'Save your anger for your enemies. Accept that you need one another;

165

Kutor would not have become Emperor without the Weapon Master's aid and experience, but Owen would still be nothing more than a penniless mercenary wandering the fringes of the Nations. Accept that. And also accept that the bard brought you together in the name of the Pantheon. Remember that. And when you speak of making and breaking, remember that the Gods of the Old Faith can make or break at will.'

'They are not your gods,' Kutor said sullenly.

'But they are yours,' the Andam hissed. 'And while you sit here squabbling together, your enemies conspire and act.' Within the grey cowl, the priest's head turned to Owen. 'Go, slay these vampir if you can – they present the greatest threat. Let the humankind wait for the present.'

Owen stood up, grateful to be doing something that didn't go against what little conscience he lived by. 'How may I destroy these creatures?' he asked.

'Fire,' the Andam hissed, 'only fire.'

When Owen, followed by Tien had left the room, the Andam priest turned back to Kutor. 'And now you must prepare yourself; a delegation from the Twelve Families awaits . . .' And Owen could have sworn the Andam was smiling.

The Warlord turned as the door to the Armoury opened and a small figure stepped in, and then stood there, fully illuminated by the light and outlined against the door. The Warlord grinned; this was no professional. Sliding the spikes that took the place of his hands into his sleeves, he hurried down the long shop, his face settling itself into its customary mask. His steps faltered but otherwise he showed no surprise when he saw the figure standing in the light; it was a Shemmat. He recognised the distinctive skin and eyes, but he couldn't remember when he had last had a Shemmat in the shop.

'You're looking for a weapon?' he inquired.

The man grunted.

He had the look of a warrior, the Warlord mused, but he might be nothing more than a servant – many of the Shemmat in the Nations were in service, a relic of the days when their an-

166

cestors had been defeated on the Sand Plain and the survivors sold into servitude. If he was a Shemmat servant – especially from a family of servants – then there was a possibility that he was tongueless, the custom persisting in some of the households which followed the traditional ways.

'Is this something for battle or for more personal protection?'

'To kill . . .' the Shemmat muttered indistinctly.

'A battlefield weapon, then,' the Warlord said, turning away. He suddenly felt uncomfortable. There was something about this man . . .

He had dealt with warriors of all types in his long career as armourer and weapons-merchant to the Imperial and mercenary armies. There had been men he had liked, others he had positively loathed; some had amused him, others had made him angry, but only a few – a very few – had actually made him nervous. He glanced around at the Shemmat again, and found the man staring at him, his green eyes glittering slightly in the light reflected from the piled weapons. His expression was like that of a serpent, poised about to strike.

The Warlord turned, and indicated a display of maces, war hammers, morningstars, clubs and short pikes. 'For someone of your stature, I would suggest something which would give you a little extra reach, but not a long pike or spear which would be too heavy, and too unwieldy for your size. A mace perhaps: either this type, which is nothing more than a spiked ball on a long shaft, or this type, where the spiked ball is attached to the shaft by a chain.' He looked back at the Shemmat, and once again found the small man staring intently at him. The Warlord was suddenly grateful for the knowledge that his son was at his back, hiding amongst the weapons and armour, his crossbow levelled at the customer's throat.

'Axe,' the Shemmat said.

The Warlord started to shake his head. 'An axe requires great skill and dexterity . . .'

'And there is no one with greater skill than my servant, Tien tZo,' Owen said very softly, coming out from behind the Warlord, a stiletto pressed to his son's throat.

167

Too late, the Warlord realised what it was about the Shemmat that had been bothering him; the way he moved, his stance, all indicated confidence, self-assurance, even arrogance – qualities few servants would have possessed. Also, he should have recognised the Shemmat as being the Weapon Master's servant – but who looked for servants? He turned back to Owen, his usually sallow complexion now ashen. 'What is wrong? I thought you were with us?'

'Vampir,' Owen breathed the word, 'Tell me where I will find vampir.'

'I don't know what . . .' the Warlord began.

'You son lives and breathes; the vampir are dead things.' Tien said suddenly, pitching his voice low, turning it into a menacing hiss. 'Is your son's life worth that of the dead things?'

'I cannot,' the Warlord said, shaking his head.

'Perhaps you should remove the boy's ear,' Tien suggested, glancing at Owen.

The Weapon Master nodded and raised his knife . . .

'In the cellar. They're in the cellar. Four of them; the Lady Esse has taken the other two away with her . . .'

Owen nodded and then looked at Tien, his mouth open to say something . . . when the Warlord moved! The spikes that took the place of his hands flashed out towards Owen's face. Owen reacted instinctively, jerking back, using the young man as a shield – and one of the spikes took the youth through the throat! The boy's eyes opened wide in surprise and he died without a sound.

Tien rapped the Warlord across the back of the head with the flat of an axe, and his senseless body dropped to the floor on top of his son's corpse. Tien looked across at Owen, but the Weapon Master's face was set in an expressionless mask, a mask Tien knew well; the body at his feet was already forgotten, and would never be mourned over. Now the Master was composing himself to kill – and to die too, if necessary.

They smelt the creatures and their lair long before they found them. There was the rank, foul odour of something long dead, mingled with the sharp, acrid, salty smell of fresh blood, overlain with other, less readily recognisable smells, not least of which was the odour of rotting flesh.

'I'm surprised the entire street doesn't smell this,' Tien said softly, as they stood on the top of the stairs looking down into the cellars.

'We're close to the docks,' Owen said shortly. Drawing his short sword, and pressing his back to the left-hand wall, he began to descend the steps. Tien waited until he was four steps down before drawing his left-hand axe and pressing himself to the right-hand wall, and then following the master, step for step down into the darkened cellars.

There was a door at the base of the stairs, a thick solid bruk-wood door, reinforced with strips of iron and studded with round-headed bolts. But any door is only as strong as its lock, and Tien had once served a brief apprenticeship to a locksmith. He worked on the lock with a pair of slender metal probes, and the lock clicked open almost immediately.

The cellars were vast, far bigger than the shop above, and consisted of scores of rooms on either side of a long, broad corridor. The storerooms were filled with weaponry from just about every Plane of Existence, each one wrapped and carefully oiled and neatly stacked; there were also stores of non-lethal military equipment from blankets to sandals. One of the largest rooms was almost empty, but it had obviously been used for meetings; all the boxes had been pushed to the walls, and there was a large ornate chair in the centre of the room.

And at the end of the long corridor they found the cells.

Four pretty young women slept naked in one cell. They were filthy, their hair matted and unkempt, their bodies smeared with feces and blood – and there was blood everywhere – splashed high on the walls, on the floor, even speckled across the ceiling.

Owen looked at Tien. 'Are these the vampir?'

The Shemmat nodded. 'The first vampir was called to the body of a young woman; this cursed sorceress has obviously continued to do that for some reason.'

'I find it difficult to accept,' Owen murmured, drawing right up to the thick cell bars, finding that they too were smeared with blood.

'Look at their wounds,' Tien hissed.

'I don't see any wounds.'

'Then look at their scars!'

The Weapon Master looked beneath the filth and dried blood, and found that two of the women were carrying terrible scars across their throats, as if they had once been torn out. There was another whose abdomen was streaked with what looked like claw marks, and a fourth, whose scars were still purpling across her chest. He shuddered and turned away in disgust. 'Find something that burns,' he hissed, swallowing hard.

'I saw some oil . . .' Tien said, and disappeared down the corridor.

'Owen?' The voice was soft and feminine – and familiar!

The Weapon Master froze, not truly believing what he had heard, unwilling to turn round.

'Owen, it is I.'

The Weapon Master started to shake his head, his mouth opening, silently forming the single word, 'N-n-n-o.'

'Owen, look at me?'

Owen brought his sword up before his eyes, and looked at the mirror-bright blade. In the reflection was the face of Lisse, his sister. His long-dead sister.

'Look at me, Owen. It is I, it is Lisse, your own baby sister.' And when Owen didn't turn, the voice changed, becoming harsh, 'The sister you killed!'

Owen turned – and found himself staring into the coal black eyes of one of the vampir. The black ovals expanded, swallowing him, drawing him forward, pulling him in, drowning him . . .

. . . There was a sound, the sound of his own heart pounding, pounding, pounding, his blood surging through his veins, the roaring of that blood in his ears, and running through it, keeping time with the pounding, his sister's vaguely mocking voice . . .

'Remember me, Owen? Remember little Lisse? Remember how you betrayed me, and not only me, but the whole family? Remember how you cursed us, condemning us all to death, calling on your new-found gods to bear witness to you . . .'

Owen staggered forward another step, the automatic step of a sleepwalker. His eyes were glazed and his face expressionless.

'And remember how we died, struck down by the plague you had conjured? Do you remember all that? And did you think we would forget? Did you think we would forgive? What you did was unforgettable, unforgiveable.

'And do you know what I want now?

'You took my life – as surely as if you had struck me down with your sword, so now I want you to give me yours. I want you to give me your blood . . .'

Owen stepped up to the bars, and filthy clawed hands reached for him, drawing him in closer. His head was turned, exposing his neck and the vampir bent her head down, her mouth open, exposing teeth, ready to rend and tear – and a thrown axe struck her high in the chest, lifting her clear off the floor, punching her back against the wall. She screamed, a screeching cry of rage and anger rather than pain, and one by one the vampir's eyes opened.

Tien grabbed Owen, dragging him away from the bars, spinning him across the room, and then he smashed a jar of oil across the bars of the cell. The rancid, slightly sour odour of fishoil filled the cells, and the stench seemed to send the vampir wild. They attacked the bars, arms and legs flailing, their blackened nails tearing at the thick metal, teeth rasping on the bars. Tien darted back to the door where he had dropped the box containing the jars of oil. He threw two more, smashing one to the floor around the vampir's feet, the second breaking high on the wall behind the creatures. He placed his next shots carefully, ensuring that each of the creatures was doused in the thick, foul-smelling oil.

The vampir who had enticed Owen staggered forward, pulling the axe from her pallid flesh. She swung it once and then launched it with savage fury through the bars of the cells. The leather thong on its handle caught in the bars, dropping it sharply to the ground. The metal head struck sparks off the stones . . .

The explosion lifted Tien clean off his feet, sending him tumbling down the corridor, a solid sheet of flame licking down along the walls, scorching the air, lapping against the door at the far end of the corridor.

The Shemmat staggered to his feet and dashed back into the room – and blundered into Owen who was staggering out. The Weapon Master was a ball of flame, having absorbed the full force of the blast, and it was nothing more than blind instinct that had brought him out.

Tien tripped him, bringing him to the floor, rolling him over, smothering the flames. He pulled off his own smouldering jacket and beat at the tiny blue flames licking at his master's clothing, dragging him away from the inferno that still raged in the cells.

Tien looked back into the room once – and froze in horror. It was sheathed in flame, and the four figures of the vampir writhed in their cells, one of them wrapped around the bars, arms outstretched. Their mouths were open as if they were screaming, but Tien heard nothing. He watched as the dead flesh blackened and then curled and crisped, exposing the muscles beneath, and then this too fell away, the fatty flesh boiling and hissing, spitting like cooking meat. Soon there was nothing left but the skeletons – and the eyes. The black eyes, deep as night, cold as ice, the eyes remained in the white skulls. The skeletons continued to flail against the flames, but they were weaker now, the bones themselves turning brown then black, then crumbling into filthy powder as the intense heat ate into them. Tien deliberately threw the remainder of the jars at the skeleton creatures, watching in satisfaction as the flames, renewed, ate into the remaining slivers of bone and scattered the dust.

The Shemmat turned back to his master. Owen was semiconscious, most of the skin on his face gone, all his hair burned away, his head almost seared to the skull. However, his leathers seemed to have taken most of the burns although it was burned through to the flesh in some places.

'It's over,' Tien whispered. 'It's over.' He dragged Owen to his feet and carried him down the corridor and up the steps leading off the burning cellar. The door at the top was hot to the touch – and it was locked!

Tien eased Owen gently to the steps and pushed against it, thinking that perhaps the heat had swelled it in its frame, but there was slight play at the top and bottom. Stooping, he put his eye to the large keyhole – just as a large spike punched its way through! Tien staggered backwards, almost tumbling down the steps, his right eye watering: the spike had brushed his eyelashes.

Keeping well back, he bent and looked through the keyhole again – and once again the spike was jabbed through the keyhole and immediately withdrawn. The Warlord was waiting . . .

Drawing his remaining battle-axe, Tien once again peered through the keyhole. The spike appeared immediately – and Tien hammered down on the projecting end of the spike with the blunt end of his axe, bending the metal at an acute angle. The spike was now trapped. But so were they – and the flames were spreading. When they reached the storerooms the whole building would go up; the Shemmat had seen enough explosives and oils to outfit the Imperial Army . . . and a smile touched his normally impassive features. Leaving the Weapon Master lying semi-conscious on the steps, he raced back down into the flames which had now found supplies of blankets and furs and were eating through them, belching acrid grey smoke into the cellars. If the fire didn't get them, the smoke would.

Tien found what he was looking for in the first storeroom. Luid-dust, named after Luid, the Fire Sprite, was a gritty, slightly pebbly brown powder which ignited with an impressive explosion. He grabbed the nearest bag and hauled it back up the steps to the door. Without even pausing to check on Owen, he tied the bag around the Warlord's hook which was still stuck through the keyhole. Moving quickly now, he dragged Owen back down the steps into the first storeroom and propped him up against a wall. Next, he punched a hole in a wooden box and snapped out a spar, and then he raced down the corridor to where the flames were licking around the entrance to the largest storeroom, the one in which the Lady Esse had plotted with the Twelve Families. Tien plunged the wood into the fire and held it there until it was burning furiously, the dry wood splintering and crackling. Turning, he ran back down the corridor to the foot of the steps. Judging the distance carefully, his eyes watering from the smoke, he swung the burning spar of wood underarm and then threw it towards the bag of Luid-dust . . .

The explosion blew out the door and most of the wall surrounding it, punching a hole clean through the opposite wall, and out onto the Armoury's rear courtyard.

No trace of the Warlord was ever discovered.

13 The Henge

And treat only with respect what the past yields, lest your disrespect destroy you . . .

> *Proverb, common to most of the Seven Nations*

Katani's amber eyes snapped open, and she remained still and unmoving, wondering what had awakened her. Around her the night was silent and chill, and her blanket was dusted with a light covering of snow. Above the trees she could see the Lady Lussa riding proud and full across a cloud-streaked sky, turning the snowscape into sharp bands of black and white.

She had dozed off, sitting up against a tree, and directly across from her, in the shadow of a bush, she could see the small bundle that was Gire, almost lost beneath the furs Eiron had forced on them when they had finally left the Bardhouse three days previously.

A clump of ice fell to the ground at her feet from the trees above.

The woman relaxed; her warrior senses were so finely attuned that she awoke for the slightest reason, and then was unable to return to sleep until she had discovered what had alerted her. It was not, however, a trait she regretted – it had saved her life on far too many occasions.

She settled back into her armour, shifting her spine away from the rough gnarled tree trunk and was about to close her eyes again when a second jagged piece of frozen snow fell to the ground. This piece was a little further away, closer to Gire.

Without moving her head, Katani looked up. The trees were coal-black shapes against the purple of the sky. With the light from the Lady Lussa slanting through them, distorting their shapes, adding depth to them, it was impossible to make out if anything was lurking up there. A bird probably, Katani thought, or a small rodent. Another clump of ice fell to the ground, almost at Gire's feet . . .

Katani was moving even as the creature dropped out of the branches, her sword whining in the chill air. The Chopt turned at the sound, his own knife coming up automatically. Katani's sword sheared through the metal, and continued on to take off the Chopt's head in one long smooth stroke.

Katani kicked the body aside, wrinkling her nose at the copper-tart stench of fresh blood on the sharp night air. She was about to shake Gire awake when the boy sat up. His eyes were stone grey. 'Look to yourself, warrior,' Ectoraige said crisply.

Katani whirled to find that four of the beasts had materialised out of the shadows of the trees. Two were armed with barbed tridents, one had a sword and the fourth was carrying two of the long Chopt knives. Their lips had drawn back from their teeth and saliva shone wetly on their receding chins. In the moonlight their eyes were tiny and black.

The two beasts with the tridents moved apart from the others and Katani realised that they were going to try and take her from all sides at once. The swordsman and the knifeman were directly in front of her, standing a little apart, watching her eagerly, hungrily.

Katani screamed! The keening death psalm rent the brittle night air, shocking the beasts. And the warrior moved, her second sword coming free as she launched herself forward, then down, rolling between the two beasts before her, her swords slashing out, taking the creatures behind the knee, crippling them both. Still moving, she rolled to her feet, turned, cut and cut again, her sword finding throat and face. Two were dead, and it had taken less than a handful of heartbeats to do it.

The two remaining Chopts charged, the short stabbing tridents held before them in both hands. The nearest one jabbed – and Katani's shortsword took the head off the weapon. Her long-sword sliced out, opening a long gash in the beast's chest sending him reeling back, both paws clutching the gaping wound.

The second beast attacked then, and Katani barely turned her body in time; the barbed prongs screamed off her armour, and the beast lunged forward off-balance. The warrior cracked downwards with her mailed fist and the knurled pommel of her shortsword snapped into his skull driving him to the ground. Spinning on her heel, Katani's longsword tore out the wounded beast's throat; continuing to spin, she came down on one knee, plunging her shortsword down through the other's throat as he attempted to rise.

'Truly you are Katan.' The boy stepped out from beneath the trees, and Katani had to wait for the light to fall on his face to see whether it was the boy or the god talking. His eyes were their usual warm chestnut brown once again.

Katani stooped down and methodically cleaned her weapons in the rags of the Chopts' clothing. 'Why, did you think I was otherwise?' she asked, looking up.

Gire shook his head, his expression serious. 'But the Katan are legend; my mother spoke to me of their exploits, and she also told me that the last of them died at the Battle of the Sand Plain, many generations ago.'

'The last of them did,' the warrior said quietly, coming to her feet, sheathing her swords. 'I was the last of the Katan Warriors to die on the Sand Plain.'

Gire's face twisted in puzzlement. 'I don't think I understand.'

Katani shook her head. 'Oh, the reasons are easy enough. I died, and walked the Silent Wood, guarding the approaches to Death's Kingdom for . . . for many seasons. And then Paedur the Bard appeared . . .'

'He was dead?' Gire asked, astonished.

'Not then,' Katani smiled, gathering up her blanket and retrieving their bags from a niche in the branches of the trees. 'No, he came to the Silent Wood in search of two companions who had given their lives in the service of the Pantheon. We . . . met and I travelled with him for a while, and then we did a service for the Gods of the Pantheon, and created a new Deathgod. In return, I was allowed to return to the World of Men once again. I am the last of the Katan Warriors.' She slung her bundle over her shoulder. 'We had better move; the blood will bring predators of all sorts and I don't want to be here when they arrive.'

The boy nodded. He was quiet and obedient, and although he was aware in a vague way that God Ectoraige was speaking through him, he accepted it without question or comment. He followed Katani, aware only that she was chasing the bard because of something which the God of Learning had passed on to her. He had no knowledge of what the god was saying, and he experienced the times of possession as a dream-like state. When he awoke, however, he found he had absorbed a little of the god's knowledge – odd, scattered fragments, which he carefully filed away for future use.

They had left Thusal three days previously, and had made surprisingly good time along the tracks that led into the north. The smooth width of the King Road officially ended in Thusal and beyond it there was nothing but a series of tracks worn by centuries of travellers, trappers and traders and they headed out into the ice-fields to ply their dangerous trade with the beasts. One in four never returned.

Three days out of Thusal and this had been the first attack. They had been lucky. Katani had been expecting one much sooner, and the previous day, when they had been trailed by a dozen huge ice wolves, she had been sure they were going to die beneath scores of finger-length claws and teeth that supposedly could shear through a solid slab of frozen meat. The wolves had been shadowing their trail since noon and as the evening had drawn in, she had begun to seek a defensible position. But in the undulating barren landscape there had been nothing. Abruptly, however, the wolves had vanished, and later that night she had heard them howling in the distance. She didn't know what had happened, but she suspected that Ectoraige had something to do with it – after all, it wouldn't do for his mouthpiece to get eaten, now, would it?

Morning found them close to the ruins of a fort, a simple beehive-shape construction of crude unpolished stone. There were gaping holes in the rounded roof and part of one wall had collapsed.

'Chopt handiwork?' Katani asked, slowing down, wondering what might dwell in the ruins.

'I think not,' Gire said, and Katani had to glance at him to make sure it was the boy and not the god talking. 'It's an old trading station – the round shape is traditional – but I fancy the elements have wrought this destruction.'

'Is that possible?' Katani asked.

'Bitter cold can snap metal,' the boy said, 'or so I was taught.'

Katani nodded. 'I believe you. Now, I wonder if yon ruin is occupied?'

'Why?' the boy asked, his voice suddenly deepening, becoming even more authoritative. 'There is distance to travel, and even the gods themselves hold no sway over time.' The boy turned to look at Katani and she found herself staring at the cold hard eyes of the god.

'The boy, or his body, at least – and I – need hot food,' Katani snapped. 'And you could have warned me last night,' she accused. 'The beasts could have slain us.'

'There were only four of them,' Ectoraige said mildly. 'And in any case I wanted you to fight and slay them!'

'Why? In the name of all the gods such a risk is uncalled for! We're running enough risks without you calling down others on us.'

'There were wolves on your trail,' Ectoraige said, as if that explained everything.

'So?' Katani demanded.

'So, had you not given them something to eat – then they would have eaten you. As it was they were satisfied with the slain Chopts.'

'You are a god,' Katani said, rounding on the slight figure of the boy, 'And a powerful one, I understand. Can you not render us some more substantial assistance? We are going to need all the help we can get if we're to complete this mission and reach the bard in time to warn him.'

'I don't have the power,' the god said simply. 'My followers, the monks, were butchered, their students, my future generation of believers, dead also. Without their worship, my power wanes daily. The few who still believe and still pray to me are not enough and are just not strong enough to enable me to do all you wish. I am dying, warrior, slowly but surely dying. Without faith there is no substance,' he quoted. 'Without the belief of Man, the gods have no power.'

Katani nodded. 'I see. I did not know.' She breathed deeply, abruptly conscious of how exposed they were out on this snow-covered plain. She looked at the ruin again. 'Can you tell me if anything lives within?'

The boy looked at the ruin of a trading station. 'It is empty now,' he said, 'but snow bears sometimes seek shelter within if the night is exceptionally bitter.' His voice changed and when he looked back at Katani, his eyes were brown. 'I'm cold and hungry.'

Katani put her arm around his thin shoulders. 'Come on, we'll shelter in the ruins and get something to eat . . .'

'Our companion here means to kill us.' Paedur's voice suddenly echoed ice-cold, knife-sharp within Bastion's head.

Without breaking stride, the guide nodded slightly.

Paedur continued looking at the Chopt, Ironwinter, who had been chosen to lead them to the Source, the Chopt capital. 'Could you find the Source without this creature?' the chilling voice continued.

Bastion shook his head almost imperceptibly.

'He will try to kill us, although whether he means to do it now or when we reach the Source is not entirely clear. At the moment he is radiating hate and rage.'

It had only been with the greatest reluctance that the elders of the Chopt clan had agreed to allow the two outsiders to be taken to the Source. However, under no circumstances would they provide directions or a map, not even to the Marked Man whom they trusted after a fashion. A guide would be provided – and Ironwinter had been chosen. The bard had been looking at the Chopt when Icewalker had called out his name, and even without his enhanced powers he had been able to read the satisfaction on the beast's face. Given the opportunity, Ironwinter would kill them, and feast on their flesh.

They had started the following morning, rising just before the night birds had winged their way home; in the northern climes time was measured by the passage of the creatures, since the elements were not to be trusted, and no satisfactory method of measuring time had yet been discovered that would survive the rigours of the bitter weather.

Although the beasts were up and about early, Paedur had been waiting for them in the long hall when they arrived to break their fast. Ironwinter arrived first; he was dressed as if for battle, with a sword slung over his back, two Chopt knives in his belt and he was carrying a trident. The bard noted that all the weapons seemed to be new and displayed a curiously fine degree of workmanship.

Bastion arrived a little later; there was a Chopt woman on his arm, the same woman he had left with the previous night, and the look of disgust on Ironwinter's face was almost palpable. The bard read his aura, and it was white and blank, the aura of a killer.

Breakfast was a gruel that looked surprisingly bloody and the bard didn't care to guess what had gone into its making, glad that he only had to make a show of eating to please his hosts. He noticed that the two dead Torc Allta whom the beasts had feasted off the previous night had disappeared from the cooking spits, although there had still been some flesh on their bones when the Chopts had retired for the night. Later, he would learn that they were used much as any other beasts the Chopts killed: the flesh eaten, the muscles used for thread, the skins tanned for clothing, the bones used to make pins, needles, trident heads.

They had left immediately after breakfast, following a silent Ironwinter who had set a stiff pace, obviously hoping to upset his unwanted charges. However, Bastion was an accomplished and experienced trapper and the pace presented him with no problems, and the bard felt neither exhaustion nor pain.

They walked on through the day, stopping for neither food nor rest. As the evening drew in and the wind changed direction for the night, Ironwinter abruptly diverged from the track he had been following – which was, in effect, nothing more than a long narrow depression in the snow – and headed down towards a clump of standing stones.

As soon as they had turned off the track and approached the stones, Paedur felt the immediate tingle of ancient power. The runes incised into his hook began to sparkle and glitter, and he thought he saw a similar glitter on the nearest stone.

'Ancient,' Bastion said shortly.

'And powerful,' Paedur added, 'but not harmful.'

'Not to our friend, in any case,' Bastion nodded at Ironwinter who had stepped into the centre of the standing stones and laid his two hands flat on what might have once been an altar stone.

A thin line of white fire crackled around the stones, sparking from one to another.

The stones had been arranged in a perfect triangle, three stones to a side, each stone taller than a tall man and broader than two men standing side by side. In the centre was another triangular-shaped piece of stone, but this was laid flat on the ground. This was the stone the Chopt had touched.

'I've never heard of this,' Bastion murmured, 'nor anything like it.'

Paedur stopped before stepping between the two stones. He lifted his left arm and brought it close to the stone; the hook blazed with a cold blue-white light. Paedur brought his hook closer to the stone before finally resting it against the gritty surface. When metal touched stone, the entire slab of stone pulsed with a chill white light, and then slowly and in sequence, each stone pulsed into a trembling light.

Smiling with a certain grim satisfaction Paedur stepped through the opening between the stones and the light died. Bastion followed him. 'What was that for?' he murmured.

Paedur nodded towards the Chopt; Ironwinter was staring at him, his eyes wide, his expression almost one of horror. 'Just a demonstration,' the bard whispered into Bastion's skull.

Later, much later, when the Lady Lussa rode high in the heavens, and the Sceptre and Orb had risen to join her, Ironwinter came to stand before the bard.

Paedur, who was sitting with his back to one of the stones, looked up at the Chopt, his eyes taking the sparkling brilliance of the night stars.

The Chopt radiated confusion and fear. 'Will you speak to me of these stones, Datar?' The term of respect did not come easily to him.

'Tell me what you know of them,' Paedur said softly.

Ironwinter squatted down before him. 'They are relics of the past, relics of the Shining Ones.'

'And?'

'We are taught that if we are ever forced to spend the night in the ice-fields, then we should always attempt to find one of the stone clusters to shelter within; no harm comes to those within the protection of the clusters.'

Paedur nodded. 'Beasts would be sensitive to the lingering aura of power resonating from the stones; they would be loath to approach. Can you not feel anything?'

'A tingling, a warm prickling sensation, not unpleasant.'

'Are there many such clusters in the Northlands?'

'I know of half a score intact, and perhaps the same number again which have tumbled and are reputed to be useless and worse than useless – they are reputed to be haunted.'

The bard nodded. 'That would be true after a fashion. Once the henges are disturbed, their energies are released into themselves, and yes, if you were to stand close enough to them, you would hear voices and see strange and wondrous things.'

Ironwinter nodded. 'I have seen and heard them. I fled lest my essence be stolen by the spirits of the stone.'

Paedur shook his head. 'There are no spirits within these stones.' He touched the stone behind him ringingly with his hook, and both stone and metal sparked. 'There are stones like these in the Southlands, they are called Henges there, and the ancients used them for several purposes, but principally as a means of travel.'

Bastion, who was sitting across from the bard, moved closer. 'I thought that was myth.'

'There is often more than a grain of truth in a myth. No, I assure you it is true. The Great Henges were linked, and a man might travel either from place to place upon his own plane or from plane to plane, instantaneously.'

The Chopt shook his head, his black eyes narrowed to slits. 'This is too much; explain.'

Paedur smiled. He briefly read the beast's aura, noting the murderous white blankness was gone and had been replaced by a genuine curiosity, interest and something else, something approaching awe.

'The Culai, the race you call the Shining Ones . . .'

Bastion interrupted. 'The Culai were the Shining Ones?'

The bard nodded.

'Then the Chopt race was created by the Culai?'

Paedur nodded again. 'Aye, much in the same way that they created some of the other races that walk this and the other Planes of Existence, much in the same way that they created the humankind and the beast-folk. Not all of their experiments were successful – consider the Chopt race for example. But unlike many of the other races which died out or reverted to their animal form, the Chopts reverted to a primitive form of the humankind – probably the same basic stock the Culai had used when they were working on the humankind. The Chopts have survived because successive generations adapted themselves to their environment.'

'And the stones?' Ironwinter persisted.

The bard turned back to the Chopt. 'In the ancient past, and up to relatively recently too, it was possible for a man to step through a similar arrangement of stones – except that it was a circle rather than a triangle – and then, by the process of a fixed spell emerge a league or a thousand leagues distant.'

Ironwinter nodded, his eyes wide.

'And some of these henges allowed travel between the planes . . .' He saw the Chopt's blank expression and looked at Bastion, who shook his head. 'The People of the Ice have no concept of the multiple worlds,' the Marked Man said quickly.

Paedur turned back to the beast. 'There is more than one world,' he explained simply. 'There are a myriad worlds, a myriad Planes of Existence. Some are like this place and others completely different, so strange that you would not recognise it as a place fit for life.' He raised his hand and pointed to a standing stone. 'Imagine that to be a world, and then that next stone to be another, and the next stone a third world. Don't look so doubtful, I have travelled between the Planes of Existence. Nowadays to pass from stone to stone, to cross that gap between the worlds, requires a magician or sorcerer of great power, but in times past, it was possible to cross by stepping through the stone Henges.'

'And has this cluster – this Henge – that power?' Bastion wondered softly, looking around.

'There is still power within it; every time a Chopt comes here and lays his hand on the centre stone he is imparting some of his nervous or psychic energy into it. You saw how the Henge glowed with power when I touched it. So, yes,' he nodded with a slight smile. 'If you're asking me can this Henge still be used then the answer is yes. The only question is: where does it lead?'

'There is a similar cluster in the Source,' Ironwinter said quietly.

'Aaah,' Paedur breathed.

'What are you thinking?' Bastion asked.

Paedur stood up suddenly. 'The shape of this Henge is wrong; only a circle can generate great amounts of power, so as these are different, I would imagine they are of limited power.' He glanced over at Ironwinter. 'What do the Chopt legends say of these stone clusters? Think . . . think carefully, now, the exact phrasing.'

'When in danger or lost seek the sanctuary of the stones; it will succour you,' the Chopt said slowly, mouthing the phrase carefully.

Paedur smiled, and it changed his features, making them softer, almost human. 'I think perhaps that in times past these Henges were automatically triggered if a Chopt was in danger – possibly it operated off the life-aura which changes in colour and intensity with emotion.' He shrugged. 'It's only a guess. But these are limited Henges – they have a single use only, and a very short range.' He turned to the Chopt again. 'How far are we from the Source now?'

'A day, a night and a day's travel.'

Paedur nodded. 'We will try it. Here; stand with your toes touching the centre stone.' He shoved Bastion up against the centre stone, moving the bulky man with ease. 'Now you, Ironwinter.' The Chopt took up position facing Bastion, and Paedur stood up against the third side of the triangular stone. The bard then stooped and struck his hook ringingly against the stone.

For a single moment the thin high note hung vibrating on the still night air, then it disappeared. And then Bastion swore softly, and Ironwinter whimpered deep in his throat like an animal. The stone at their feet was changing colour, the plain grey granite was suffused with a pale bluish colour. The lighter covering of snowflakes that had lain over it vanished in a hiss of steam, and the scattered few flakes that drifted onto it now hissed as they touched it. The blue light deepened, becoming stronger, more intense, and then suddenly a solid triangular shaft of light shot upwards into the night sky, blinding them.

And then it winked out.

Paedur bent his head and massaged the throbbing pupils with his single hand, blinking away the throbbing blue after-image. The chill within him told him that something had happened, although he wasn't sure what. He tilted his head back and opened his eyes – and discovered they were in a high-roofed cave, but the blue explosions on his retina prevented him from picking out details.

He heard Bastion on his left sit down suddenly. 'Curse you, bard, you've opened all my wounds.' The pain in the man's hoarse voice was clearly audible. And then on his right hand-side he heard Ironwinter's excited voice. 'You did it, bard, you've taken us to the Source!'

And then another voice spoke from behind the bard. It was soft and susurrant, chillingly, terrifyingly familiar. It sounded like the rasp of wind-blown leaves.

'Welcome to the Source, bard!'

Paedur whirled, falling into a fighting crouch. Beyond the triangular Henge stood a shape, a vaguely human shape but twisted, like a bent and withered tree. The figure shuffled forward, its every movement accompanied by a sound like leaves crisping underfoot – and Mannam, once-lord of the Dead stepped up to the Henge stones.

Branches snapped, and there was the obscene sound of the creature's laughter. 'Now, I will destroy you!' Mannam hissed.

Cold, blue-white light wound around the bard's hook and darted out towards the figure in the cloak of seared and withered leaves. But the levin bolt didn't pass out of the triangle of stones. It twisted visibly in mid-air and arced onto the nearest stone and then it flashed from stone to stone bringing them each to a brief incandescent life.

Paedur used his power again, drawing on a different source now, and the ball of sizzling energy that formed on the tip of his hook was a pale green colour, the essence of the warm earth. The bard tossed it, much as a man would toss a ball underhand, and it floated slowly – almost lazily – through the air towards the shadowy figure of the once-god.

And once again it shifted, moving in mid-air to fall onto the nearest stone, where it exploded in a wash of crackling, sparkling green light, which flowed down the stone like liquid.

And then from behind Paedur came a rapid clicking sound. Paedur clearly saw the poisoned slivers of wood from Bastion's weapon shoot past his face – and saw them shatter against the stones.

'You are trapped, bard,' Mannam hissed, 'trapped within the cluster of stones, trapped by your own stupidity, your own ignorance and your own arrogance.' Wood snapped as the once-god laughed again. 'You couldn't resist demonstrating your knowledge, your power, could you? And see where it has led you now. You are dead bard!'

'I have been dead before,' Paedur said coldly.

'I will destroy you!'

'If you had the power, you would have done so already,' Paedur said, glancing around at Bastion and Ironwinter. 'But in the same way that we cannot get out, I don't think you can get in.'

A second figure loomed up out of the shadows. 'You are correct of course, bard. But I think the advantage is ours.'

Paedur heard Ironwinter's sudden intake of breath as the figure stepped up to the edge of the triangle of stones. The creature rested a large, blunt-nailed paw on the stone and opened its mouth in what might have passed for a smile. Its features were flat and bestial, its eyes small and deepset above a rounded flaring snout. From its mouth two tusks jutted upwards, each one intricately decorated in clan and caste marks.

'I am Fenar na Torc Allta,' the huge beast said. 'I am the lord of the Torc Allta, the Boar-Folk.' Its huge head turned slightly, looking at each of the three figures in turn, before its gaze returned to settle on the bard. And then Paedur clearly saw the short coarse hair on the back of its hands rise. 'I have come for you, bard. I have tracked you across the Planes of Existence to avenge my people.'

'You seem to be a very popular person,' Bastion murmured from behind the bard. 'Two dangerous enemies.'

'I'm not sure which is the more dangerous,' Paedur admitted. 'The Torc Allta is a dangerous beast, strong and vicious in battle but he lacks magical power, while Mannam, for all his apparent frailty, is possibly even stronger and I'm unsure what power he still retains from his days of godhood – some certainly.'

'If we survive you can tell me how you managed to upset them both.'

Paedur smiled one of his rare smiles. 'They are only two of many, I'm afraid.' He looked out at the two figures standing beyond the stones. 'What happens now?'

'Now we kill you!' Mannam hissed gleefully.

Paedur nodded almost impatiently. 'Yes, yes, I know that. But I mean this instant. What do you plan to do with us now?'

The huge Torc Allta looked at Mannam, obviously at a loss. Whatever they had been expecting of the bard, it was obviously not this slightly impatient argumentative attitude.

There was movement in the shadows behind the pair and two more figures stepped into the cave, and although they were both humankind, the once-god and the Lord of the Torc Allta bowed to them. They stood beside the once-god and the beast looking only at the bard, looking almost surprised that he had been captured so easily.

'This is a day for reunions,' Paedur said softly. 'Geillard XII, deposed Emperor of the Seven Nations and Praetens, once Susuru warlock to Churon the Onelord.'

'A better class of enemy,' Bastion murmured.

'They are united in many things,' Paedur said quietly, 'but principally they all want my destruction, and with my death, they hope the destruction of the followers of the Old Faith will follow and without them the end of the Gods of the Pantheon.'

Praetens stepped up to the stones. The small frail-seeming white-haired old man smiled toothlessly. 'No, nothing so simple now, bard. We have concocted a much grander plan in which your death will be but a small and pleasant interlude.'

The bard walked forward to the edge of the stones and looked out at the old man. 'I see you still inhabit the body of a slopman; is your power so weakened now that the infamous Susuru warlock cannot perform a simple essence transference?'

Preatens face twisted in rage and his left hand moved, his fingers hooked. Thin streaks of intense red-black light lanced out from his fingernails like claws – only to be twisted onto the stones and broken.

The bard nodded and stepped back, satisfied. He had proven his point; although his power couldn't extend beyond the stones, neither could they be attacked from the other side. The triangle of stones attracted power to them, probably absorbing it for their own continuance. Many of the ancient objects were self-perpetuating in this manner.

Paedur turned back to the four figures beyond the stones. 'You have captured me, but you have no use for those who accompanied me: they were merely guides. Bastion is well known to the Chopts as the Marked Man; they will vouch for him. And Ironwinter is a clansman – you can have no use for them.'

Mannam shuffled forward, his cloak rasping against the stones. 'Bastion is known to me; he is remarkable because I once refused his essence. The Chopt is nothing. But, in any case, they are both tainted by your presence. They will die with you.'

Ironwinter suddenly moved, his knife coming up to slash at Mannam's hooded face – only to have his knife bounce off an invisible curtain between them. 'I am Chopt,' he growled. 'I demand to see Stonehand, Lord of the People of the Ice.'

Fenar's tusks clicked tightly shut. 'That is impossible.'

Ironwinter threw back his head and suddenly howled, the sound echoing and re-echoing off the cave walls, bouncing, magnifying until it had become a blood-curdling, ear-shattering wail. The bard, the once-god and the Torc Allta were unaffected but Geillard, Praetens and Bastion were forced to the ground, their heads buried in their hands, faces locked in pain. Bastion's facial wounds split and reopened until his features were a mass of blood and liquid.

Paedur touched Ironwinter on the shoulder and the beast reluctantly stopped. 'I imagine it is a wasted effort,' he said, his voice sounding unnaturally loud in the sudden silence. 'No-one can hear you. I think we are deep underground, in an unused part of the Source . . .?' he raised an eyebrow and looked at Fenar.

The Torc Allta nodded. 'This is the Closed City; the beasts imagine it to be inhabited only by dangerous and blood-thirsty spirits, and they never come here. This cave is one of several Henge-rooms which are in the very deepest sections, and there are a series of doors between here and the upper caves. These doors are soundproofed and incredibly solid in the manner of all Culai creations. Perhaps they had occasionally unwelcome visitors through the Henges from the outside world; perhaps that is why they turned their gates into prisons. And the gates are one-way bard, lest you get any ideas; if you try to go back there will be nothing but a huge surge of power that will leave you nothing but a husk.'

'What are you going to do with us?' Paedur asked reasonably.

The Torc Allta opened his mouth in a smile. 'Nothing has been decided yet; I admit that although your capture was carefully planned only Mannam was certain he could lure you here. I would imagine there will be a trial, but not for you – too many people want you dead – but a trial to decide who gets you. Your companions will be passed to either the Chopts or the Torc Allta for consumption. I would imagine they will be saved until the feast at which we will all gather to watch your destruction.' The

Torc Allta's mouth opened, displaying his sharpened teeth behind the two curved tusks. 'Not even your gods can help you now, bard; they hold no sway in this forsaken place. Soon we will destroy you!'

'Why is it called the Source?' Katani asked, lying flat and peering over the edge of the sunken valley, down onto the cluster of wood and stone buildings below.

'Because this is where the Culai created the Chopts, the People of the Ice.' Katani didn't even have to turn round to know that the God Ectoraige had taken possession of the boy again. 'When the First Race fled north in their final days on this plane, they sought shelter in those caves.' He pointed down to where the cliff face opposite was dotted with caves; the largest of them even had huge, typically Culai-wrought, doors. 'Deep in the mountains they worked their magics to create the Chopts, and later the Chopts ventured out of the caves and built their own dwellings, first in the valley and then on throughout the Northlands.' He indicated the primitive huts. 'These are their first buildings, this is the Source, the Chopt Capital.'

'And the bard is here?' Katani asked, glancing around at the god.

Ectoraige nodded. 'Deep within the old caves, in part of what is now known as the Closed City I can sense an aura of immense power. But it is muted, dulled, as if something is sapping that power, draining it.'

'But it is the bard?' Katani insisted.

Ectoraige nodded. 'I'm sure of it.'

'Well, what do we do now?'

'Now, we wait until nightfall; we can move freely then.'

Katani raised an eyebrow. 'How?'

'There is no moon this night, and the beasts are loath to walk the night when there is no Lady to light their way; they fear if they die they will not find their way to the Otherworld. And besides,' he added with a sly grin, 'the Chopts do not post guards here at the Source; no-one knows the location of this place.'

Katani sighed. 'So we wait.'

Behind her the boy's eyes changed colour, turning from stone grey to deep brown. And then he rested his head on his hands and immediately fell asleep.

The warrior shook her head and turned back to the valley below, wondering how they were going to get down to the caves on the far side of the cliffs. Directly below her the ground fell sharply away for about five hundred paces. At the bottom there was a patch of what she at first took to be shrub, but later realised must be small stunted trees. Running down the centre of the valley and bisecting the almost circular Chopt camp was a rapidly flowing river – and then she realised something else: there was no snow in the valley. Where she was lying was covered in a thick and permanent snowfall and although she could see the odd flake drifting down into the valley itself, there was no snow on the valley floor, and the river was unfrozen.

The Chopt camp was in the centre of the valley, a huge collection of wood and stone huts of various shapes and sizes, the method of construction obviously crude and primitive. There were signs of activity in the valley below and there were enough of the creatures moving in and around the caves for her to guess that at least some of the caves were still inhabited – and probably a damn sight warmer than the stone huts too!

She contented herself with plotting a course down the cliff face and across the Source and up into the caves on the far side where Ectoraige had determined the bard was being held. Once inside the caves her plans became somewhat hazy – free the bard certainly, kill anyone who got in her way, and then . . . well then the bard would know what to do. He knew everything.

'I don't know what to do,' Paedur said evenly, walking withershins around the triangle of stones. 'This device, this cluster, swallows my power and even now I can feel it drawing on my energy, draining me.'

Bastion dabbed at his bloody face with a cloth. 'My wounds have opened and remain open, and they only do that in the presence of power.'

'If Stonehand, my lord, were here, he would not allow me to be kept in this place,' Ironwinter growled.

Bastion grunted. 'Chopt, I doubt if your lord could do anything to get us out of here. If a Susuru magician, a deposed god, a dethroned emperor and a vengeful Torc Allta cannot get us out then no-one can.'

'But there has to be a way out,' Ironwinter protested.

Paedur nodded, agreeing. 'There has to be. I would imagine this trapping function was to allow either the Culai or the early Chopts to monitor who and what came through here. But there must be a key to this cell.'

Bastion stood up slowly and limped over to the edge of the stones, peering into the darkness beyond. 'Are we looking for a physical device, or would a spell have been used?'

'A physical device, I would imagine: something to shut off the power even momentarily.'

'But obviously not something immediately recognisable,' Bastion continued. 'Something in plain sight, but something which might easily have been passed over in time.'

And they both found they were looking at the ornate frieze of tiles that had been laid on the floor directly beyond the standing stones. Ironwinter followed their gaze.

'They tell the tale of the creation of the Chopt race,' he said slowly, 'but the order is wrong. See,' he pointed with a hairy paw, 'that scene should come first, and then that, rather than that scene . . .'

Paedur looked at Bastion and nodded. They had the key, all they needed now was to work out how to use it.

Katani's fears about descending the cliff face in the dark proved to be ill-founded. When night came on, the boy had awoken, but his eyes had been those of the gods. He stood up and without a word had led her off to the right to where a tiny staircase, each step barely as wide as her foot had been cut into the stone. Still without speaking, he led her down the countless hundred steps to the valley floor below. At the bottom of the stairs there was a tiny hut, a simple one-roomed round stone shape, almost lost against the cliff face. From inside they both clearly heard the rasping, buzzing snore of a beast asleep.

193

'Well-room,' Ectoraige said softly, 'one of a dozen in the valley, but with one distinct difference – its waters are hot!'

Katani nodded; she could feel the heat seeping up through the ground into her feet.

They entered a forest of small stunted, trees which she at first did not recognise but which she later realised were common toor trees, which had obviously been warped by the unnatural temperature of the place. And immediately beyond the forest the first of the buildings began. The huts were crude, far cruder than Katani had expected, and it was only as she neared them that she realised that they were, in fact, ancient. All of the buildings were dark, but there were sounds from some indicating that they were at least inhabited, but strangely there was no light seeping out into the night.

Ectoraige led her through the scattered buildings keeping to the shadows, moving so swiftly and silently that even Katani, who had been trained since birth to such skills, found herself losing sight of him occasionally.

The first obstacle they encountered was the bridge across the river that bisected the town. The bridge had been built in three sections, the two end pieces fixed and rooted solidly on dry land but the middle piece which joined the two halves was missing – obviously it was removed at night.

Ectoraige stopped in the shadow of a tumbled building and waited for Katani to join him. He pointed towards the bridge. 'The gap is approximately two man lengths – can you jump it?'

The woman-warrior squinted into the night. Two man lengths, six double-steps carrying weapons and wearing full armour and all of this over a rushing river! 'What's the alternative if I can't?'

'You stay here and I'll go on alone, and rejoin you later if I can.'

'I'll jump.'

'If you fall you're dead.'

'I'll jump,' she said decisively.

Ectoraige nodded. And then he moved, running lightly across the ground. His feet made no sound on the bridge's wooden spars; he leapt at the very edge of the bridge, his legs bunching, pushing him up and over – and Katani could have sworn that he hung in the air a fraction longer than was natural. He landed lightly on the far side and immediately darted away into the shadows.

With a brief prayer for protection Katani settled her weapons around her and after a final look around, darted towards the bridge. She had paced it out mentally, attempting to gauge her steps, working out where exactly she would be when she hit the edge.

She had misjudged.

Katani knew at the final moment, just before she launched herself out across the void – which looked enormous now – that she was not going to make it. She had jumped high – too high – and slightly wide, which meant that even if she did come down within reach of the edge, she would only be able to grasp it with one hand.

'Paedur, help me now!' she gasped as she sailed through the air.

The gust of warm air from below struck her like a blow, spinning her around, pushing her forwards and over. It was enough. She hit the far side of the bridge in a clatter of armour and weapons. She was up and running before the first shaft of light darted out from the nearest Chopt dwelling. And then a small hand grabbed her, pulling her into the concealing shadows.

'Nicely done,' Ectoraige said evenly, and Katani was unable to work out whether he was being sarcastic or not.

Light was appearing from buildings all over the Source, and Katani was able to see that the interiors of the crude dwellings had been covered with beautifully woven rugs, piled one overlapping the other. Some were simple geometrical designs, others were ornate and intricate Chopt hunting scenes. That was why no light had seeped out, and within the buildings it looked warm and comfortable. She revised her opinion of the inhabitants.

'Will they investigate?' she hissed.

'They cannot. The middle section of the bridge is kept on this side.'

Behind them, some of the cave doors opened, sending long

shafts of light down onto the bridge. Armed shadows moved in the light.

Mannam had come to gloat. He shuffled around the triangle of stones, his cloak hissing, crackling together, the sound like that of swept leaves.

'You cannot know how long I have waited for this,' he clacked. 'You cannot know how many times I have dreamt of this scene. It has kept me from despair.'

'I am glad I did something to help you,' Paedur said evenly. He was sitting cross-legged in the centre of the stones, facing the apex of the triangle, sorting through his lore, checking the legends, seeking a way out of the trap.

'You present us with a problem, do you know that, bard?' Mannam continued. 'Because you are virtually immortal, we cannot just leave you to die here of hunger or thirst, so you must be slain. And you see, so many of us want you dead. Do you know the price the Gods of the New Religion have offered for you? Fenar of the Torc Allta wants you, Geillard wants you and even Praetens wants you – although his case is weakest of all, for he plans to occupy your body.

'No, I think we will end up flaying you – that is a spectacle we can all watch. We will give your skin to the Torc Allta – they can probably eat it or something. And then we will dismember you, but slowly . . . oh, so slowly. The Torc Allta and the Chopts who are masters of this torture have devised a plan that will keep you alive for many seasons – long enough for you to see the death of the Old Faith.'

'That is a song I have heard before,' Paedur said almost tiredly.

'But this time it is different; this time it is real; this time it will happen,' Mannam snarled. 'Even now the Gods of the New Religion are gathering to plan the destruction of the Pantheon of the Old Faith. And, bard, because of all the pain you have caused them, they will ensure that you remain alive to witness the destruction of everything you loved!'

14   The Gods of the New Religion

The Gods of the New Religion fear not these petty godlets and spirits of the Old Faith, for the Gods of the New Religion are strong . . .

Epistle of the Religion

The Gods of the New Religion were gathering.

In a vast empty cave deep in the heart of the series of caves called the Closed City, Mannam, once-lord of the Dead, presided over the Calling of the Gods, a ritual older than the race of humankind.

The dark twisted figure stood in the centre of the dusty floor and raised his arms high; his cloak slipping down his arms, revealing skin that resembled a dun gnarled bark, and hands that were little more than knots of twisted wood, his fingers curled twigs. He raised his head, and his eyes blazed red in the shadow of his cowl.

In the gloom in the furthest corner of the cave, Praetens stretched out his quavering left hand and pointed it towards the once-god, while Geillard and Fenar each placed their hands over the magician's upraised right hand. A tracery of red fire wound its way around their hands, tying them together, allowing the magician to suck strength from them and direct it towards Mannam.

'Come, Gods of Light and Dark, Gods of Night and Day, Gods of Fire and Ice . . .'

The cave took the once-god's voice and sent it trembling around the room, echoing and re-echoing, building in volume and power.

'Trialos, come to us. We call you in the name of belief, in the name of faith, in the name of trust . . .'

A pale mist gathered high in the cave, almost as if a cloud had formed and the dry, slightly musty air of the long-disused cave was suddenly tainted by something foul and rancid. The mist thickened and as it did the foul odours were almost lost beneath the suddenly cloying scent of flowers.

'Come to us now, lord,' Mannam commanded, the strain showing in his voice.

The mist thickened to an almost solid waxen ball close to the ceiling. It throbbed, slowly, with an almost heartbeat-like intensity, and its waxy pallor was shot through with tiny red tendrils that looked suspiciously like veins.

Mannam's whispering voice had risen to a shriek. 'Come to us, come to us now. Come – we so command it!'

And the ball suddenly fell.

It plummeted from the ceiling to stop, quivering, above the once-god's head. It was throbbing violently now, pulsing deeply, like a huge heart. And then a segment broke away, falling to the dirty floor to pulse and twitch like a giant slug. A second segment detached itself and fell to the ground, followed by a third. What was left of the cloud – a vague gaseous shape – seemed to draw in on itself and then it flowed down into Mannam's outstretched hands. The once-god stiffened, and then fell, shuddering to his knees.

The three slugs thrashed around on the ground, lengthening as they moved, their waxy, greasy covering sloughing off, like a serpent's skin. Patches of what looked like pale flesh appeared.

Praetens had broken contact with Geillard and Fenar when the last of the cloud had been absorbed into Mannam. He darted forward and knelt by the shuddering figure. And both Geillard and the Torc Allta heard the magician's sudden sharp intake of breath. Mannam had raised both arms and held his hands out-stretched before him – and what had once been a twisted knot of twigs was coated in a thin covering of pale flesh, and now recognisable fingers and hands had appeared, thick veins visible beneath waxen flesh.

'The Gods of the New Religion have gifted you,' Praetens said. 'Another gift like this and your features will be of flesh and blood again.'

The Torc Allta suddenly spat an oath as one of the writhing slugs split from top to bottom, and out from the sticky white mass appeared a human arm. A second arm appeared and then a body rose up out of the fluid, a tall, dark, naked figure that was unmistakably female. Her hair was long and a deep lustrous black, but was plastered to her back with the liquid, and her features, though of humankind, seemed slightly distorted, although not in any immediately recognisable way.

She looked over to the second shell, which had also cracked, and the figure that sat up from the milky fluid was male, and like his female counterpart, dark complexioned and of humankind – although there was certainly beast blood in him. The third slug cracked open and the figure that rose smoothly to his feet was taller than the once-god, and yet as broad as the Torc Allta. He ran his hands through his wet hair, brushing the white fluid away from his face and then abruptly opened his eyes. They were the colour of blood.

He looked at the four figures and smiled hugely. 'The Lords of the New Religion thank you. You shall be rewarded to your heart's desire, as has the once-god.' His huge head moved slowly, his blood-red eyes lingering on each face in turn, and each of them – even the fearless Torc Allta, even the once-god – shivered for what looked at them was powerful even beyond imagining.

'I am Sheesarak, the Destroyer.' His voice had a slightly echoing quality to it which was amplified by the cave.

The female had stepped out of the remains of the slug and glutinous white fluid dripped from her body. She brought her hands together and her dark skin suddenly glowed with an intense white light, which vaporised the fluids, leaving her dark skin glowing softly in the dim light. Her mane of hair crackled with power, flowing around her like a cloak.

Her voice was soft, slightly sibilant, and she spoke slowly and distinctly, as if the language of humankind was alien to her. 'I am the Lady Asherat. I am the Taker of Souls.'

The third creature came to his feet; his resemblance to the Lady Asherat was marked, but his features were distinctively marked with traces of beast blood, especially around the eyes which were slit-pupilled, like a cat's. 'I am Ghede, Lord of the Beasts.' His voice was a deep growl, like a mountain-cat's snarl.

199

Sheesarak looked around, his blood-red eyes blinking slowly, and then he was joined by the Lady Asherat and Ghede. He stretched out both hands and they placed both their hands in his and bowed their heads in respect. The gods' lips moved and the trio were abruptly clothed in simple robes of a metallic red-black cloth.

Sheesarak looked up and his eyes found Mannam. 'We have been sent by the Lord Trialos to prepare the way for him. We are of the Trialdone, the Companions of the Lord.'

Mannam bowed slightly. 'We have heard of the Twelve Trialdone.'

'The Lord Trialos decided that our respective and combined talents should be sufficient to destroy the Old Faith. Now we must prepare.'

Mannam bowed again. 'There is a room set aside for your use.'

The Lady Asherat spoke. 'And when we have planned the destruction of the Faith, let us amuse ourselves with their creature, the Bard Paedur.'

Fenar, the Torc Allta, laughed. 'I doubt if there's enough of him to go around.'

'We shall each have a piece,' the Lady Asherat said without humour.

'Bard, if you do not get us out of here we are dead.' Ironwinter crouched before the bard, staring into his face, seeing himself reflected in the mirror eyes.

Paedur nodded abstractedly. He was kneeling on the floor, scratching on the stones with the point of his hook, while Bastion stood behind him, looking over his shoulder.

'We will get out,' the Marked Man said to the Chopt. 'The bard has a plan.'

Although Ironwinter said nothing and his expression didn't change, he still managed to look unconvinced. Bastion motioned him to his feet and then led him over to the edge of the standing stones. He pointed to the decorative tiles that ran around the outer rim of the cluster. 'As you said, they tell of the creation of the Chopt race . . .'

'But they're in the wrong order,' Ironwinter protested.

Bastion nodded impatiently. 'We know, we know. But we think – we are convinced – that if the tiles are touched in the correct order then the stones' power will die, allowing us to escape.'

The Chopt considered this and then he finally nodded. 'That may be so, but there is a slight problem . . .'

Bastion smiled tightly, careful not to split any further the already open wounds on his face. 'I know – how do we touch the tiles?' He looked back at the bard. 'That is what Paedur is working on now.'

The bard came smoothly to his feet, a rare smile on his face. 'I think I have it – I hope so, because we will only get one chance . . .'

'This way – quickly!' Katani shoved the boy in through an opening, her sensitive battle-trained hearing catching the almost silent pad of bare feet closing in on them. She was still unsure whether the beasts had actually caught sight of them on the bridge, but, although there had been no outcry, scores of the creatures were still roaming around, the only sound the pad of their feet and the occasional clink of metal on stone.

Katani followed the boy, still possessed by the essence of Ectoraige, down through what was obviously nothing more than an air duct or chimney in the cave system. The interior was coated in a vaguely luminescent fungus, which, while not lighting the tunnel, meant that they were not moving in total darkness. The tunnel was surprisingly smooth and regular, although in her bulky armour it was more than a tight fit for Katani, and on two occasions, Ectoraige had to return to unbuckle greaves or breastplate to allow her to squeeze through.

Light appeared, a vague, slightly sulphurous glow far ahead of them. Katani looked at Ectoraige, the boy's face a vaguely pale glow in the wan light, and he nodded without hesitation and set off towards it. Shaking her heard, Katani followed. If only the bard knew what she was doing for him.

As they neared the light, they heard the voices – a group of people chatting together, differing accents, differing sounds, and one more powerful than the rest booming out regularly.

The light was coming through a grille set high in the wall of what was obviously a long disused cave. Even the burnt herbs and the odours of food couldn't dispel the rank cloying odour of mildew and decay, and the air-duct was clogged with dirt and thick trailing webs.

Katani and Ectoraige lay flat in the tunnel and peered through the filthy grille. The cave beyond had once been a grand hall – a king's throne-room perhaps, a ballroom – but the ornate wood – panelling on the walls had rotted away and now hung in tattered strips from the original stone. If there had been curtains, and the metal hangers seemed to indicate that there had been, they had long since disintegrated and whatever colours the room had been decorated in had been long hidden beneath a thick layer of grime.

Only the table in the centre of the room and the eight chairs positioned round it were new.

But neither Katani nor Ectoraige had time to study the cave; all they could see were the eight creatures – humankind and otherwise – that sat around the highly-polished table.

The table was circular and in its centre was an ancient but beautifully wrought candelabra, holding the traditional twelve candles. Ectoraige slid across to Katani and named the eight sitters. 'The three to the side, in the metallic robes are Trialdone, Trialos's creatures, Gods of the New Religion.' He sounded slightly awed at the sight. 'Sheesarak the Destroyer sits in the centre, with the Lady Asherat on his left hand side, and Ghede, Lord of the Beasts, on his right. Asherat was a very minor spirit until the bard killed Libellius, the Death Lord of the Religion. She is now the closest the Religion has to a Deathgod.' Ectoraige shifted slightly, 'The creature in black . . .' he began.

'. . . is Mannam,' Katani spat. 'I know him, and I know Geillard, once Emperor of the Nations, and the old man there is Praetens, the Susuru magician. Who are the beasts?' she hissed.

'The Chopt is Stonehand, Lord of the People of the Ice, but he is thoroughly under Praetens' control; he is – in every sense of the word – a puppet. The Torc Allta is Fenar, the Lord of the Boar-Folk. He has come to avenge his brethren's death in the Mire.'

'As evil a gathering as you're ever likely to find,' Katani murmured.

'And they all want the bard dead,' Ectoraige reminded her.

'We all want the bard dead,' Mannam said suddenly. 'All that remains to be decided is how he should die.'

'His death will be a symbol of the fall of the Old Faith,' Ghede said suddenly, his voice harsh, his lips drawing back from his flat, slab-like teeth.

'His death is secondary,' Sheesarak said slowly, his booming voice echoing in the confines of the cave. 'Let us first decide upon the complete and absolute destruction of the Faith. You –' he pointed a long-nailed finger at Geillard, 'do you support the cause of the Religion without question, without hesitation?'

The tall, thin man nodded quickly. The harsh conditions and long moons of travel had taken their toll and his usually thin features were now skeletal. 'I support the Religion. It was on account of the Faith and the bard that I was deposed.'

'Do you have support still?'

Geillard nodded. 'My following in Karfondal is still strong amongst the nobility. They fear this new Emperor, this Kutor, they fear what he is, what he has done and they fear what he might do in the future. They will have no hesitation in rallying their forces and rising up against him.'

The god smiled, displaying teeth that matched his eyes and fingernails – they were blood red. He shifted his massive head and looked at Mannam. 'And you?'

'I was a god before the bard took that away from me. My vengeance is on him. I was a god before my brothers and sisters cast me out into the World of Men. My vengeance is on them also. You need neither fear nor doubt my loyalty.'

Sheesarak nodded and then turned to look at Praetens. 'You are known to us. 'What is the price for your support?'

'A body,' the magician said without hesitation. 'A young body, strong and male. That is all I ask.'

'And you, Torc Allta, where do your loyalties lie?'

Fenar grinned, displaying his sharpened teeth. 'My loyalty is with the Boar-Folk; I care nothing for your squabble. I have travelled across the Planes of Existence in search of this bard. And I will have his flesh,' he added ominously. 'Deny me that and you will have cause to regret it.'

The Lady Asherat hissed and turned to look at Fenar, her dark eyes clouding with blood, turning them a deep baleful red.

'There are many here with a claim on the bard. But you shall have a part of him,' Sheesarak promised. 'What is the price of your support?'

'We are not mercenaries – we are not Chopts!'

'You would be honoured supporters. Name your price,' the god insisted.

'Flesh without question – you would allow us to kill and eat and never question the why or where of it?'

Sheesarak nodded.

'And a place in this world.'

'Explain.'

'My people – the Boar-Folk – are now few in numbers, and there has not been a birthing in the Mire for nigh on two generations. We are a dying breed. I am looking for a nation, a land, an island kingdom particularly, where the Torc Allta could live without hindrance or let, and be allowed to pursue their own culture.'

'And if we gave you this we would have your support in return?'

'Our absolute and unquestioning support.'

'I give to you – on behalf of the God Trialos, and in the name of the Twelve Trialdone, of which we are a part – any of the outlying provinces or island kingdoms that you find suited to your needs.'

'Then you have our support.'

Sheesarak finally turned to the still silent figure of Stonehand, the Chopt King. 'And what of him?'

'He is under my thrall,' Praetens said. 'He will do what I command him to do, say what I tell him to say.'

'And what promises have you – through him – made to the People of the Ice?'

The old man laughed breathlessly. 'I have promised them land and flesh – humankind flesh. It will fulfil an ancient prophecy, and they found it to their liking. The Chopts will follow Stonehand's words without question. So, they are mine, and through me, they are yours to use as you will.'

Sheesarak threw back his head and laughed and the walls took the sound and threw it back until it was a cacophony, hideous and wailing. 'Then there is no way that victory can elude us. This, then, is the plan devised by the Lord Trialos for the destruction of the Faith . . .'

Paedur stood with his hook pointing towards the stones. He was still and his face was expressionless.

Ironwinter lay on the ground with his head at the edge of the stones, as close as he could possibly get to the invisible line of power that surrounded the Henge; his task was to watch the ornate tiles.

Bastion stood behind the bard. He was holding the short-barrelled tubed weapon in both hands, holding it as steadily as possible, pointing it at a spot the bard had shown him on the ceiling high above. In the hollow handle of the weapon there were eight of the poison-tipped slivers of wood.

'Ironwinter?' Paedur asked. The beast grunted without looking up. 'Bastion?' His reply was the double click of the weapon being readied.

Paedur breathed a sigh and then suddenly unleashed a thin intense stream of white fire towards the nearest stone. All the stones lit up with power as they drank in the raw energy, and the air was abruptly filled with the harsh metallic stink of power.

Bastion breathed a sigh also and pressed the stud on the handle of the weapon. There was a click and a sliver of wood snapped through the thinned shell of power surrounding the cluster of stones, ricocheted off the stone ceiling and snapped onto the ground, just clipping the edge of a tile.

'Too low,' Ironwinter growled.

Bastion fired again. Again the sliver broke through the thinned barrier and bounced off the ceiling – and this time it struck the tile dead centre. With the faintest of clicks, the tile sank into the ground.

'That's it, that's it,' the Chopt said excitedly. 'But hurry, hurry, the bard cannot last.' Paedur was sagging visibly, his usually pale features now ashen, and the reflective glow gone from his eyes, leaving them like soiled and spotted mirrors.

Bastion fired again – and missed. His fourth shot struck the low ceiling at the correct angle and cracked perfectly into the tile. Again it sank slightly.

The bard's stream of power was weakening now; the light was no longer so intense, and whereas before the light had been without heat, now the temperature had risen dramatically.

'Again, again!'

The Marked Man fired again – and missed. He corrected the angle and fired again – and missed.

'Bastion . . .' Ironwinter warned.

Bastion fired just as the bard's power died and he crumpled. The Chopt rolled over and caught him as he fell – and didn't even see the sliver strike the third tile dead centre. It sank with the faintest of clicks.

Abruptly the cluster of stones turned black.

Bastion looked at Ironwinter in astonishment, and then they both grabbed the bard and dragged him out of the triangle of standing stones. They had barely passed over the ornate tiles when the three key tiles rose again with a series of laboured clicks, and the stones resumed their usual granite appearance.

'Now what?' Ironwinter asked with a smile.

Bastion grinned. His face was a mass of blood since his concentration had opened the wounds on his face. 'Now we get out of here!'

Sheesarak the Destroyer concluded, '. . . And so we have decided that since the Old Faith can only be rekindled by the existence of some sort of records of the observances and teachings, every teacher, every priest, every scribe, every monk and every bard should be put to death as a first priority. The Lady Asharet will see to that.

'But first we must destroy the source of all this knowledge about the Faith. We must destroy the great Bardic Library at Badaalaur. Without it, the Faith dies!'

'I think he's dead,' Ironwinter gasped.

'He's immortal, he cannot die – I think,' Bastion grunted.

They were standing in the corridor outside the cave which held the cluster of stones, wondering which direction to take. The Chopt was carrying the bard slung over one shoulder, while the Marked Man paced ahead, his cutlass and almost empty weapon in his hands.

'I cannot hear a lifebeat,' Ironwinter hissed, turning his head slightly to press his ear to the bard's chest.

'He's immortal – he doesn't have one.'

'Only the dead don't have one.'

'I don't have one,' Bastion grinned. 'Now, which way?'

The Chopt shook his head. 'I don't know. This is the Closed City; no-one has ventured here in a thousand seasons.'

Bastion shook his head in frustration. He expected Mannam and his unlovely companions to appear at any moment; the bard's use of power wouldn't – couldn't – have gone unnoticed. But which way? The walls of the tunnel had been painted in a thick luminescent paint – an old Culai trick – made from a natural phosphorescent fungi that grew in most cave systems. They had refined it to provide a solid, if dim, source of light. The tunnel stretched in a straight line in both directions until it faded into shadows. It was lined with dark openings, which obviously led into other caves, but these were all dark, and looked likely to be disused. Finally, the Marked Man dropped to his hands and knees, examining the lie of the ground – and immediately discovered that the floor to the left-hand side of the tunnel was coated in a fine layer of dust – undisturbed dust. He stood up and set off in the opposite direction without a word.

With a grunt, Ironwinter settled the unconscious bard onto his shoulder and set off after him, hoping the Marked Man knew what he was doing.

* * *

'We've got to warn the bard,' Katani hissed desperately.

Ectoraige shook his head. 'I know. Be still, they're leaving . . .'

In the room there was movement as the gods, beasts and men abruptly came to their feet, with Praetens pulling the enchanted Stonehand up with him. They moved away towards the door, chatting quietly together, small, inconsequential things, like a merchants' guild meeting discussing the price of grain and carriage and the weather. When the room was empty, Ectoraige suddenly gripped Katani's arm, making her jump.

'We must hurry.'

'The bard, where's the bard?'

'Come on. We've got to get away from here.' The god in the body of the boy brushed past the warrior and raced back down the tunnel, and his sudden sense of urgency touched Katani with a strange fear. Something was wrong, desperately wrong. Whatever the god had come to the Source for, whatever information he had possessed, had been changed or altered in some way by the gathering they had just witnessed. He had brought her to the Source to free the bard – or so she thought – but now here he was fleeing the Source and without even looking for Paedur.

Katani caught up with him as he was preparing to crawl through a low archway. Her longsword whispered from its sheath to touch his throat, just beneath his left ear. 'Wait . . . wait a moment, now. Where is the bard? I'm not leaving here without him.'

The god's stone-grey eyes blazed and Katani clearly saw the hardened features of the man through the softer flesh of the boys' face. 'I am Learning and Knowledge. I know where the bard is. I am going to him now.'

'Something you learned in the cave disturbed you . . .'

'Foolish child! The Pantheon was aware that the Religion was planning something like this. That is why the bard was sent here; that is why I was sent here. My chief concern now is the bard; he is in mortal danger, and needs our help – that is the cause of my haste.'

Katani reluctantly sheathed her sword. 'I thought . . .'

'What you thought is of no consequence at the moment. The

bard needs us now.' He dropped to the ground and wriggled through the archway.

'You sound as if he might actually die,' Katani called after him.

'The bard is immortal,' Ectoraige's hollow voice echoed back. 'He cannot die, but in his present weakened state he is susceptible.'

'Susceptible to what?'

'Possession!'

The old man walked into the chill night air and breathed deeply, sucking the raw chill into his lungs and then abruptly doubling as a coughing fit wracked his body. For the thousandth-thousandth time since he had occupied this aged and enfeebled body, Praetens, once of the Susuru and then magician to the Onelord, cursed his blighted luck that day of the Battle of the Sand Plain. He had died that day, died as the Shemmatae magicians attacked, and only a last desperate effort of his will had sent his essence into the nearest weakened body – that of a nameless slopman, the lowest and foulest of occupations.

He had worn that body of the slopman for so long now that the had almost forgotten what it was like to be strong again, what it was like to be able to run, to lift weights, to see and hear clearly, but most of all what it was like to eat. He was toothless now – having removed the slopman's few remaining original teeth to prevent poisoning himself – and he was forced to take his food like a child, mashed into a paste. For a while he had experimented with providing himself with a set of teeth, but his heritage and magic was Susuru, and the Susuru were not of humankind, so the few teeth that had grown had been exercises in agony, as fangs that the Torc Allta would have been proud of filled his small human mouth.

But soon . . . soon he would take on a new body. He had no real hope of taking the bard's body – too many others had claims on it. But there would be a body – humankind certainly, a man, young, tall, and broad, handsome, hopefully, and when the magician inhabited the body, it would remain in that state for ever, never aging, never dying. But he only had one chance, and that was why he had to make his choice carefully. A man could shift his essence only twice; the first and second time weakened the body's essence to a certain extent, but the third ruptured it entirely, and what took up residence in the host body was never sane, and sometimes, as the weakened essence passed through the Shadowland, it picked up an unwelcome passenger or two.

But in the coming war there were sure to be hundreds, thousands, of suitable candidates. And now that the Gods of the Religion had manifested themselves and the Torc Allta had thrown in their lot with them, was there any way they could lose?

He stretched, looking up into the night sky, his dimmed eyes seeking the brighter stars, gauging the time by their position – and then he smelt it, the tell-tale stink of power, raw, magical power! But here – in the Closed City!

Praetens turned – in time to spot the two figures stagger out from a cave mouth lower down. He looked again, and immediately realised that what he had taken for a large second figure was actually a Chopt carrying a body – and then he recognised the Marked Man, and Ironwinter . . . carrying what could only be the bard.

He had actually turned to sound the alarm when a sudden thought struck him, and he turned back to look at the escaping prisoners, a smile twisting his thin lips.

The bard was unconscious – obviously drained by his use of power, and that power must have been incredible to escape the pull of the cluster. That was of no importance. They had escaped; it was enough. The magician's weak eyes narrowed. Was there a better host, a more fitting host than the body of the creature that had caused so much sorrow to the Religion? What a huge joke it would be on the Gods of the Pantheon to see their creature now serving the Religion. And in that single moment, he decided that the bard would be his new body!

The ritual was surprisingly easy, requiring no preparation and no special invocations. Taking his knife from his belt and holding it in his left hand he pointed the blade downwards, and placed his right hand across his heart. Then he began the ritual known as Casting the Net. In his mind's eye he visualised a net in the air above the bard, a thin, silver spider's web creation floating on an ethereal breeze, rippling slightly. When he could clearly visualise the web, he coloured it red and black, the colours swallowing the silver like fire.

And then within the net he set the beast.

The beast was a product of his own imagination, and every magician used his own particular version of the beast. Praetens' image was squat and foul, with too many legs, a head that had too many eyes and a body that was bloated and obscene. When his visualisation of the beast was complete he allowed himself a brief smile of satisfaction – rarely had the ritual of visualisation come so easily and never with such spectacularly clear results. Why, he could almost reach out and touch . . .

He allowed the web to drift lower, until it was moving above the head of the Chopt carrying the unconscious bard. Praetens brought the beast out from the centre of the web to crouch at the spot where he would touch the bard – and then he allowed the web to drop!

It wrapped itself around the Chopt, bringing him crashing to the ground – and although he couldn't see it, Ironwinter could clearly feel the metal-strong strands of the web – and then he felt something warm and loathsome brush past his fingertips.

And only Praetens saw the beast crouch over the sprawled body of the bard, and only Praetens saw that a vaguely milky substance had begun to gather in the beast's jaws . . . but Praetens never even heard the whistling longsword that took his head off at the shoulders!

Bastion whirled at the sound, and spotted the round white object bouncing down the stones to come to a stop at his feet. He turned it with his foot, and found himself looking down on the staring eyes of Praetens, with more life and humanity in them now than they ever had while he breathed. There was a smile frozen on the magician's lips.

Ironwinter came surging to his feet, slapping at the invisible bonds that had only moments before bound him. At his feet the bard groaned, and shifted in his sleep.

Bastion raised his weapon as two figures appeared like smoke out of the night, and lowered it again when he recognised the ornate Katan armour of the bard's companion. The longsword in her hand was still thick with gore. She passed by him without a word and knelt by the bard's side.

'Does he live?' She looked up, looking beyond Bastion to the slight figure of a boy who stood still in shadow, but although the silhouette was that of a boy, the voice's cadence was that of an aged man.

'He lives.'

And then from the caves in the cliffs behind them, echoed and magnified to a terrible crescendo, came a scream of absolute rage.

Bastion smiled tightly. 'I think they know we have gone.'

Sheesarak's rage was awesome to behold – and almost comical in its childishness. Along with Mannam, Fenar and Geillard, he had come down to the cave in the Closed City to see for himself this terrifying creature, the bard Paedur. Both Ghede and the Lady Asherat had declined the invitation – they were taking to their chambers to enjoy the sensations of possessing a physical body once again.

As they walked down the long corridor that led to the cave, Mannam had suggested to Sheesarak that perhaps it would be possible for him to use his power to destroy the stones and allow them access to the bard and his companions.

Fenar na Torc Allta had been looking at the god when Mannan had put the suggestion. Sheesarak had nodded his broad head, but a little doubtfully, Fenar thought. Privately the Torc Allta thought that if the bard had not been able to break out, then neither would this New Religion usurper be able to break in. Becoming tired of the once-god's prattle, he had gone on ahead of the other three and so was the first to spot the empty triangle of stones – and somehow he wasn't entirely surprised.

Mannam stopped and began to choke, and then Sheesarak screamed. The sound started low, but grew from a bass rumble to a shrill piercing sound, and the cave took it and amplified it, sending it pounding, throbbing, shrieking out into the chill night air. Walls cracked, floors split, and blocks that had stood for centuries tumbled from the ceilings.

Fenar turned and calmly walked from the chamber, followed a moment later by Geillard. Behind them, Mannam and Sheesarak were beginning to argue while the cave tumbled in around them, seemingly unconcerned – perhaps even unaware – of what was happening.

'I sometimes think,' Geillard said tiredly, 'that I may be worshipping the wrong gods.'

Sheesarak's howl had ripped through the Source, blasting houses, tumbling fences, barns, totems, even uprooting small trees. The Chopts, terrified by the sudden signs of life from the haunted Closed City, turned and fled to the concealed entrances that led to the underground caves, and later when Katani and Ectoraige, with Bastion in the lead and Ironwinter still carrying the bard, marched through the devastated Chopt capital they found nothing moving, nothing stirring in the ruins.

15   The Armourer

The Armourer is the Maker of Weapons, a mythical figure who brought
the killing tools to the World of Men . . .

Tales of the Bard

The three Trialdone, the Gods of Trialos, called upon their
brother, Kishar Stormbrother, the God of Storms, to find and
take the escaped prisoners. Gone were the plans for lingering
torture – all they wanted now were the deaths of the bard and his
companions. And just as Bastion and Katani, Ectoraige and
Ironwinter were beginning to think that they had made their
escape, the storm came rolling in over the flat undulating ice-
fields . . .

Later the Chopts would come to call that particular storm the
Taker of Souls. It scoured through the Northlands like Death
incarnate, and whole villages, Chopt and humankind, were lost
beneath its howling fury. The King Road – which had remained
clear since it had first been laid down generations past – was lost
beneath a blanket of snow as high as a tall man's head; bridges
cracked and snapped beneath the weight of snow and ice; rivers
turned into solid sheets of ice; every living tree and bush was
flattened by the weight of snow or ripped up by the wind's fury.
The creatures – whether they walked on two legs or four – that
didn't find shelter immediately were buried, and perished in the
bitter conditions; their carcasses – whole and frozen solid – were
to surface over the next three generations of the Chopt, their
flesh still edible.

Ironwinter had sensed the coming of the storm first. He had
stopped, his broad flat head turned towards the heavens, his
beast's snout damp and trembling. Bastion felt it next: the sudden
stinging in his wounds, the touch of fluid as the old scars cracked,
warned of the foul weather coming. And then Ectoraige, who

had been watching the movements of the clouds above the mountains and the sudden shifting of the wind, knew what the signs heralded. Katani only realised that something was amiss when Bastion, who was in the lead, suddenly left the road and began to run towards a nearby outcropping of rock.

'What's wrong?'

'Rockscourer coming!' he whispered hoarsely, dabbing at a cut above his eye.

'What's a rockscourer?' Katani demanded, imagining a serpent or northern ice-beast, but the Marked Man had hurried on towards the rocks. She looked down at the boy, who was still inhabited by the spirit of the god.

'A rockscourer is a particular type of northern storm, with high winds, heavy snowfall and a sharp drop in temperature. The Chopt call it a rockscourer because it cleans the rocks and stones of lichens and mosses, scouring them of all signs of growth,' he said seriously, and then he added with a slight smile. 'And if it catches us in the open we're dead!'

'There are times when I think I was better off dead,' Katani murmured.

'You probably were,' Ectoraige grinned, and set off at a run for the rocks. Katani sighed and followed him.

As they neared the stones, Katani realised that they had once formed the walls of a building, probably a Way Station, but the weather, combined with the local Chopts' depredation of the stones for their own dwellings had reduced it to a heap of rubble, the remaining walls moulded together by the elements into a solid lump. Bastion, who disappeared into the midst of the stones, appeared as the remainder of the group hurried up. The Marked Man's face was covered in blood and his expression was that of pure disgust. 'Nothing, there's no shelter, we'll have to go on.' He looked at Ironwinter. 'This is your land – where's the nearest shelter?'

Ironwinter suddenly looked evasive. He shrugged his broad shoulders, almost dropping the bard to the ground. 'There's nothing really . . .' he began.

'There must be something,' Bastion snapped. He glanced up

into the lowering skies. Clouds were visibly scudding across the heavens, and the clouds themselves were the colour of metal, dark and brilliant.

'The Armoury,' Ectoraige said softly. 'Are you not forgetting the Armoury?'

The Chopt snarled, his lips drawing back from his tusks in a savage grimace. 'What do you know of that?'

'The body may be that of a boy, but I am Ectoraige, the God of Learning and Knowledge. Nothing of your lore is hidden from me. Now, I suggest you take us to the Armoury lest we are caught by the rockscourer.'

'But the geasa . . .' Ironwinter mumbled.

'Does the geasa – the forbidding spell – call for you to lay down your life for the People of the Ice and their secret? Does it call for you to die for a king who is under the thrall of the Chopts' enemies?'

Bastion climbed up out of the stones. 'But the Armoury is a myth,' he said, 'and the Armourer nothing but legend.'

Ectoraige grinned. 'Well, this legend, this myth, might just save your life.' He turned back to Ironwinter. 'Will you lead them or shall I?'

'I'll take them.' The Chopt whirled away, doubling back on the path and striking out across the flat plain. Flurries of snow whirled around their heads, slivers of ice in their midst, and the Chopt suddenly increased his pace. Less than a thousand paces from the tumbled stones he suddenly took a path that led down into a hollow. Running through the hollow was a thin rushing stream, crossed at its narrowest point by a simple stone bridge. But instead of taking the worn track to the bridge, Ironwinter led them down towards the river. At the water's edge he turned and followed a thread of a path under the bridge. The noise under the arch of the bridge was incredible, the rushing water foaming and booming, echoing and re-echoing off the stones.

And then Ironwinter, who was in the lead, vanished.

Katani, who was walking behind him, was looking at him one moment, and then she turned to check on the boy behind her and when she looked back he was gone. She stopped in shock;

from the rear, she heard Bastion swear, his hoarse voice echoing slightly.

Allowing her short sword to come to her hand she moved forward, her right hand pressed against the slimy stones – and suddenly she was touching nothing. She turned and found she was looking into a tall, slim opening – a doorway – in the stones. There was movement within the opening and her sword came up, and then light sparked and flared and a torch flickered into life. 'This way,' Ironwinter grunted and turned away, taking the light with him. There was nothing left to do but to follow him.

The Chopt led them down a long almost perfectly straight tunnel that was obviously ancient, and almost certainly created by some magical power. It was as if a levin bolt had sliced through the earth, fusing the stones into polished, molten slag, leaving the tunnel walls, ceiling and floor with a black, mirror-like coating. Ironwinter's torch danced and flickered along the polished surfaces, illuminating it in places to an almost painful brilliance. After the noise beneath the bridge, it was surprisingly quiet within the tunnel, the rocks seeming to absorb sound, but nevertheless, they all clearly heard the sounds of the storm breaking outside, an ominous rumbling, like the growl of a hungry beast.

At the bottom of the tunnel was a gate of iron bars, and beyond that a second door that looked to be made of stone.

Ironwinter stopped before the gate and rattled the huge chain that held it closed. He stuck his torch in a bracket on the wall, bent over and laid the bard on the ground and then settled himself on the floor beside the unconscious figure.

'What now?' Bastion demanded, his whisper hissing around the corridor.

'Now we wait.'

'For how long?'

'As long as it takes. If the Armourer is occupied then it could take some time, a day, two days, perhaps longer, but if not – well, we might get in soon.'

'It had better be very soon,' Ectoraige murmured, 'otherwise we might just freeze to death down here.'

'Are we not safe?' Katani asked.

The boy shook his head. 'The tunnel is straight, the wind and cold will just roll straight in. If the tunnel had been curved or twisting we might have stood a chance.'

Even as he was speaking, they could feel the chill creep in, and now that they had finally stopped moving, the cold began to seep through their clothing into their bones.

'That is no natural storm,' Ironwinter grunted.

Ectoraige nodded. 'Aye, a product of Kishar Stormbrother, I shouldn't wonder.'

'They must want you badly,' the beast said.

'They want us all badly,' Ectoraige said. 'No matter where your loyalties once lay, you are associated with us now – if they catch you, they will kill you, make no mistake about that.'

Ironwinter nodded. 'I know.' He was about to say more when the stone door suddenly rumbled open, flooding the tunnel with warm golden light and the combined heat and smell of burning metal.

One of the People of the Ice stood in the doorway. He was old and stooped and certainly one of the oldest Chopts Bastion had ever seen, since the beasts did not tend to live much beyond their middle years, but this man had all the appearance of being a century or more. He shuffled up to the metal gate and stared out through the bars. His eyes lingered on the comatose figure of the bard and then turned to the boy, and surprisingly he bowed. 'We welcome one of the Pantheon.'

Ectoraige bowed in turn. 'I give you thanks on behalf of my companions and myself. We seek shelter from the wrath of the followers of the New Religion and the evil weather wrought by Kishar Stormbrother.'

The ancient Chopt touched the chain, and the bar, as thick as a man's thumb, slid back of its own accord. 'You are freely welcomed.' He raised his arm and pointed through the stone door. 'Enter, you are expected.'

Ironwinter picked up the bard and was the first through the door, followed by Bastion, then Katani, both swords in her hands now, and finally Ectoraige. He paused and spoke briefly to the Chopt, chatting as if they were old friends, before moving inside.

The inner room was an armoury.

The cave was huge, stretching perhaps a thousand paces in every direction. Against the nearest wall was a monstrous forge, while all around, strewn over every available space were weapons, some finished, others in various degrees of completion. They hung on the walls, were piled in corners, spilled from chests and a few – a very few – lay neatly shelved and catalogued. Every available weapon seemed to be represented, from every time and nation, from the crudest club to the most fabulous crossbow. There were even examples of Bastion's dart-thrower. But mostly there were the Chopt knives, the broad-bladed, drop-pointed knives that were the favoured weapon of the People of the Ice, and the weapon which most of humankind had come to associate with them. There were thousands of them, hundreds of thousands, some larger than usual, others slightly smaller, some drop-pointed, others spear-pointed, single and double-edged, some curved, others straight-bladed.

And all of them sparkling new.

The light from countless candles spilled across the metal, burnishing it to bronze, sparkling, glittering, glinting, turning the cave into a constellaton of golden light. A figure stepped out from the midst of the weaponry and the light, a tall, slightly stout woman. She was naked except for a long blacksmith's leather apron and a pair of high leather gauntlets and she was completely hairless. She made straight for Ectoraige and stopped before him. She was holding a long-handled blacksmith's hammer in her left hand and she kept patting it into the palm of her right hand. Although she was naked and unarmed save for the hammer, there was something so threatening about her that Katani moved around behind the woman, ready to strike. The woman stood as tall and as broad as Bastion, her muscles rigid and defined clearly beneath deep bronze skin. Her features, while those of humankind, were slightly mis-matched; her eyes were bright, bright blue and set wide apart, giving her a vaguely guileless expression; her nose was small and slightly off-centre; and her mouth was a thin narrow line set above a strong jaw.

The woman bowed quickly, jerkily, before Ectoraige, and her

mouth moved several times before she actually spoke, as if speech were something she was unused to.

'Is it time?' Her voice was surprisingly soft for so large a woman.

Ectoraige shook his head almost sadly. 'Not yet, lady, not yet.'

'But soon. It will be soon,' she said, a statement rather than a question. 'I have awoken. There will be war.'

'Soon,' Ectoraige agreed.

'Tell the woman warrior to put away her toys lest I shatter them and her,' the huge blacksmith said suddenly.

Ectoraige looked at Katani and shook his small head slightly. The warrior stepped back and sheathed her swords. 'This is the Armourer,' he said, introducing the woman. 'She is legend.' He then introduced his companions one by one to the Armourer.

'Bastion, the Marked Man.'

The Armourer nodded. 'He is known to me.'

'Ironwinter.'

'He too is known to me.'

'Katani, once of the Katan, now the last of their number, the sole survivor of the Battle of the Sand Plain.'

The Armourer smiled, her face shifting, giving it a somewhat distorted cast. 'I made weapons for that war.'

'And the one on the floor is the bard, Paedur. He is the Champion of the Old Faith.'

The woman grunted in surprise and knelt beside Paedur; she lifted his left arm, examining his hook. Then she touched it and the runes incised into the metal came to a sparkling, glittering life. 'Toriocht's work?' she asked, looking up at Ectoraige.

The boy's face shadowed briefly. 'Aye, the Smith made it.'

'I know his work.'

'What are you?' Katani suddenly asked. 'And where are we?'

'This is the Armourer,' Ectoraige said quietly, 'and this is the Armoury where the Chopt weapons are made.'

'But tell them the why of it,' Paedur said abruptly, coming smoothly and silently to his feet. His usually thin features were now gaunt and he was ashen-faced, his eyes nothing more than black stones in his head – even the reflective glare had gone from them.

The Armourer stood up and walked away, muttering distractedly to herself, heading back towards her forge. Moments later the air was split by the clanging of metal on metal.

'Aaah, you are with us once again, bard,' Ectoraige said smoothly. 'Come, let us find a place to sit and warm ourselves. Are you aware of what has happened?'

Surprisingly, Paedur nodded. 'I was aware; it was only my physical body that was exhausted. My spirit rested in the Ghost Worlds.' He nodded at the Armourer, now bathed in the ruddy glow of the fire. 'But I'll admit, I thought that woman legend.'

'She is, but she exists,' Ectoraige said. 'And her function remains the same. She is cursed to follow her old traits.'

Bastion cleared a table of short throwing darts and heaved his bulk up onto it. 'And what were her traits?'

'She brought the gift of weapons to the humankind.'

'She is not of this plane, then?' Paedur asked.

'She is not, but she is trapped here now for an eternity. There is a geasa on her chaining her to this Plane of Existence until a Belief – a Faith – dies. When a system of belief dies, she will be free again, and so, when there is a war brewing, involving deities, she awakes from her slumbers and sets about forging her weapons of destruction. She takes no sides; she merely wishes to be free of her curse. She has slept these five hundred years, and she awoke but recently.'

'That is why the People of the Ice are all carrying new knives,' Bastion said suddenly.

'So there is a full-scale war between the Faith and the Religion coming?' Paedur said, looking directly at the god.

'There is. The Gods of Faith and Religion go to war once again – and for the last time, I think.'

'They intend to destroy the Library at Baddalaur,' Katani broke in.

Paedur turned to look at her in disbelief, and the woman clearly saw his eyes turn to mirrors once again.

Ectoraige nodded. 'I think this will be the Last Battle. The Armourer is awake and working, and already in some of the outlying reaches of this place the borders between this world and

221

the next are breaking down. A combined army of the Chopts, assisted by the Torc Allta and the humankind who accompanied Geillard, will sweep down out of the Ice-fields taking all before it, heading for Karfondal. Supposedly the army is under Geillard's command, but we know he is but the puppet of the Religion. Three of the Trialdone now accompany the deposed Emperor, as well as Mannam the once-god. They are throwing everything into this effort. We overheard them planning, and as Katani said, they intend to destroy the Library of Baddalaur on the grounds that if all knowledge of the rituals and observances of the Old Faith are destroyed, it can never be recreated, and thus the Gods of the Faith die.'

'Will that happen?'

Ectoraige shrugged. 'It could. And they have forgotten the Magician's Law, the Force of Equals. Because the Faith and Religion exist, a balance of sorts is maintained; but take away one of those and the balance tips. Without the Faith, the Religion will continue unchecked, sliding this Plane of Existence into Chaos. Unable to maintain control, the borders between this and the Shadowlands will crumble and this plane will be overwhelmed and eventually destroyed: and with its destruction, then the other Planes of Existence will decay into a collapse.'

Paedur nodded wearily. It all sounded so familiar.

'You must stop them, bard,' Ectoraige said softly.

'And what about the Gods?' Paedur demanded.

'Even now the Gods prepare to do battle on the chequered fields of Ab-Apsalom. You cannot count on them for help.'

'When will the army march?' He looked at Ectoraige and then turned to Ironwinter.

The Chopt shrugged. 'Soon, soon, I think. Preparations are almost complete.'

'What do you know?' Paedur snapped.

'Only that we are to carry a war into the Southlands, taking advantage of the recent turmoil, both political and geographical. We are to march on the capital, destroying everything in our paths. Thusal will fall first and then Baddalaur – or so I have been told,' he added quickly.

Paedur shook his head slightly, and he looked over at Katani. 'Perhaps you should have stayed dead,' he smiled.

She nodded. 'I know. And what now?'

He settled his cloak over his shoulders and shrugged. 'The only route to Karfondal is through Badaur, the town surrounding Baddalaur, the Bardic College. That is where we shall stop them – or die in the attempt.'

'I think you'll probably die,' Ironwinter said softly.

So do I, Katani silently agreed.

16   Desertion

We fought for many causes – most of them were lost!
Tien tZo, Shemmat servant of Owen, Weapon Master

The explosion ripped out almost an entire section of the quayside, devastating the Lower City and killing more than a hundred men, women and children. But it did have one positive effect: it immediately quelled the riots that had raged through the Lower City, and every able-bodied person was pressed into service to prevent the fire from sweeping throughout the slum and tenement quarters, much of which was constructed from wood.

Tien dragged Owen out of the burning building, across the filthy, foul-smelling square and into the large tenement opposite. He kicked open the first door he came to and found himself facing a startled couple who were finishing a meagre meal. The man opened his mouth to protest, but the look on Tien's face and the sight of Owen's tattered and bloody flesh silenced him.

'You,' Tien glanced at the man, 'find Fodla, the Commander of the Emperor Legion. Tell her the Weapon Master is hurt, and bring her here. Hurry!' The man took a quick look at Owen and then hurried out into the street which was already beginning to fill with smoke and foul-smelling fumes. 'And you,' he turned to look at the woman, 'can bring me some hot water.'

'I've no hot . . .'

'Then boil some!' the Shemmat snapped. 'I'm sorry,' he immediately apologised, 'but my master is hurt . . .'

The woman pushed a blackened kettle over a small bed of glowing coals and then knelt beside the two men, touching small fingers to Owen's blistered cheeks. 'Burnt?' she whispered, and looking questioningly at Tien.

Then the building across the street exploded. The fire had finally reached the Warlord's supplies of Luid-dust, fire-works, marker flares, cinder-blocks, and fire-wood. Streamers of fire erupted high into the sky, some falling to splash onto the surrounding buildings, starting more fires.

The woman fell onto the floor with a startled cry. She was about to turn and crawl under the table when Tien touched her arm, gently, his calloused fingers like harsh sand. 'There is no danger, I think. But you must help my master. The water?'

'Your master?' the woman asked, frightened eyes going from Tien to Owen.

'I've told you; he is Owen, the Weapon Master,' Tien said proudly.

Realisation dawned in the woman's eyes. She stood quickly and looked through the shattered window at the building opposite. 'The Warlord!' she gasped.

'Is dead. And the water is boiled.'

While the woman brought the water, Tien carefully peeled off Owen's scorched leathers, cutting away the skin where it had become fused with the cloth. With the hot water he gently sponged the wounds clear.

'Will he live?' the woman asked.

Tien placed his hand flat against his master's chest. 'He is strong,' he said confidently, although his eyes betrayed his concern. 'He has survived worse wounds.' He looked up. 'Why hasn't Fodla come?' he demanded.

'Here I am.'

The Commander of the Legion strode into the small room, immediately seeming to fill it, followed by the Andam priest; in the background the woman's husband lurked, still bemused by the speed at which events had occurred.

Fodla knelt by Owen, her broad face creasing in concern, her fingers seeking a pulse at his throat. 'How?' she asked.

'He destroyed four of the vampir – and the Warlord,' Tien said softly.

'And most of the Lower City too, if we're not lucky,' Fodla said sourly.

'It very nearly cost him his life!' Tien blazed.

The huge woman nodded. 'I know, I know,' she said gently.

Her experienced eyes took in the Shemmat, noting his single battle-axe and the scorchmarks on his sleeves and boots, and she fancied he had played more of a part in the vampir's destruction than he was telling. 'I'll get some transport, and in the meantime if you would see what you can do,' she said, looking up at the Andam.

The grey-robed priest nodded. 'Go, then, try to contain the fire,' he said, his voice a strained whisper. Fodla stood and hurried from the room without another word. The Andam turned to look at Tien. 'And now you must trust me – as you did once before, if I recall. I want you to leave us – assist Fodla if you will – but leave us alone for some time.'

'But Owen . . .'

'I will not harm him,' the Andam said.

Tien looked at the priest, seeing only his eyes in his enveloping robes, and those eyes burned with something which the Shemmat decided could only be raw power. He nodded once and then walked from the room.

The Andam turned to look at the young woman who was standing still and silent in a corner. 'If you too could leave us for a little while . . .?' he said gently.

She nodded, and scurried around the priest, her eyes never leaving him, regarding him with a superstitious awe, her fingers automatically making the Sign of Protection.

Alone now with the unconscious man, the Andam sank down onto his knees and stared at the Weapon Master's bloodied and blackened face. The burns were serious enough, and would leave his face a mass of scar tissue unless . . . unless he drew upon his power to heal him. Since his brothers had been slain, the Andam had communed with the Andam Source, made himself one with the ancient power that was at the heart of the Andam belief. All those who followed the Andam way used the power of their Source at some time during their lives, but only a few ever took the path of communion, becoming part of it, submerging themselves in the raw power. The Andam Source consumed, consumed utterly and completely, and so to become one with the Source was to die.

But the Andam priesthood had some measure of the Sight, especially those touched with the disease that destroyed the flesh, and on the night that his brothers had been taken, Andam had looked into the probable future – and found it terrifying. There had been images, many terrifying and bloody images, there had been death and torture, war, beasts and destruction. On the chequered fields of Ab-Apsalom he had seen the Gods of the Pantheon sorely pressed by the combined forces of the Demons and the Gods of the New Religion. Every shred of his power, his magic, would be needed then. So should he, could he afford to use it – to waste it? – now on the Weapon Master?

But had he the right to make that decision? Surely the decision had already been made for him; he had been with Fodla when the man had come to the Commander of the Legion with the tale of the wounded warrior . . . and he alone had the power to heal.

Sighing slightly, the Andam reached out and touched the Weapon Master's face . . .

. . . There was pain and there were memories, and perhaps that had been another reason why he had been reluctant to heal Owen, for to heal meant he had to touch, and the Andam priesthood was particularly receptive to the emotions and thoughts of others. And before he could begin the healing process the emotional turmoil would have to be soothed, the thoughts settled so that they did not intrude.

The Weapon Master's memories were of the events in the Warlord's cellars. There was a face, a girl's face, his sister's face, drawing him, pulling him, trapping him, and the Andam's eyes hardened, recognising what had happened. The vampir deceived by illusion, fastening on memories, using them to create an image and then using that image to lure its victim within striking distance. Through Owen's eyes the Andam saw the creature who wore two faces, the dead face of the vampir and the heart-shaped face of his long-dead sister. He saw it lure Owen, saw the hands reach out . . . And then he saw the creature struck down with the thrown axe, saw the oil and the flames – and the Andam realised then who had destroyed the vampir.

There was pain and confusion, and in the confusion there were disjointed images from the Weapon Master's life, most of them from the past, some from the possible future. There was death – death always – past and future, and there was fear. Beneath the seemingly imperturbable killer lurked a deeply fearful man, a coward almost.

But the Andam was no judge. When Alile the Judge Impartial eventually came to weigh Owen's fate, he would consider the deeds as well as the intent.

Closing his eyes, the Andam reached out his hands and touched the burnt body . . . and called upon his Source . . then the priest stiffened as the power – white-hot, ice-cold – lanced through his body, opening every wound on his flesh, turning his body into a mass of agony. The skin split on his fingertips and where he touched the Weapon Master, he left trails of blood. And there was life in the blood. He moved his hands across the wounds, touching the scorched and blackened skin, brushing over the blisters – and leaving in his wake, clear, clean skin . . .

Moving from head to foot, the Andam covered Owen with his blood, and as the blood seeped out of the Andam, life flowed into the warrior . . .

The Andam slumped exhausted, and Owen sat up. He was aware, on a deep almost unconscious level, of what had occurred, but like a dream the events were rapidly fading. He stood stiffly, his joints popping and cracking, and looked at himself in the bowl of water Tien had used earlier for cleaning his wounds. His face was a bloody mask, but beneath the blood, which was drying to a crusty flake, he was healed and whole again. He plunged his face into the tepid water, washing away the blood and the memories. He knelt beside the slumped Andam and touched him gently on the shoulder.

'Datar?' he whispered, using the ancient term for father, for holy man. 'Datar?'

The Andam reached out and Owen caught his arm, lifting him gently to his feet. The renewed contact sparked the dregs of power within the priest which sent echoes deep into Owen's brain, bringing with them the vaguest of memories. 'Datar, what have you done?'

'I've done what is necessary; what I feel to be necessary,' he corrected weakly.

'And how long have you left on this Plane of Existence?'

The Andam shrugged, and then winced as torn and aching muscles protested. 'Only the God knows. But long enough, I suspect.' The priest turned to look at Owen and his usually sharp grey eyes were dulled and pained. 'Time is running out for Kutor and his followers and with their destruction will come the destruction of the Old Faith. It is time to act!'

The guard turned as the door opened, tensing, and then relaxing as the young woman walked boldly down the centre of the corridor, a large tray in her hands balanced precariously before her. The tray was easily one of the largest the guard had ever seen, and she noted the five crystal goblets and the ancient stone crock of what must surely be a fine vintage. She experienced a brief twinge of envy, but decided that after today's events, she'd rather be a simple guard in the Emperor Legion, than one of the five people in the room behind her.

She looked at the servant, wondering just who she was, but her face was concealed behind the glasses and the stone crock. She allowed her eyes to wander down the girl's body, almost completely visible beneath the light robes. There was a scar running down between her breasts . . .

The guard swung her short stabbing spear around – just as the sharpened edge of the tray sliced through her throat!

The Andam was moving and Owen's sword was in his hand even before the sound of breaking glass beyond the locked door had settled. Tien and Fodla bustled Kutor over to the far side of the room and positioned themselves before him.

'Unhuman . . .' The word formed on the Andam's lips – and then the door was struck a blow that actually ripped the lock from the wood, and the vampir strode in. It might have looked incongruous, one nearly naked young woman facing six people, all of them, with one exception, armed, but no-one was laughing. The vampir's eyes were blank, empty, cold and lifeless. It turned its head, almost as if it were an animal seeking a scent; perhaps the number of warm bodies in the room confused it, Owen thought, abruptly chilled with the memory of what a creature like this had done to him.

'It will concentrate on Kutor,' the Andam said softly, and the creature's head snapped in his direction, 'but it will destroy anything that comes in its way.'

'Divide,' Owen said, drawing its attention to him.

Tien tZo moved, and the vampir edged closer to him.

Then a thrown knife bit deeply into the creature's throat. It didn't even flinch, perhaps it didn't even notice. Fodla pulled a second knife from her sleeve and snapped it towards the creature's face. It sliced through the flesh, just below the eye, but it drew no blood, and didn't even slow the vampir's slow, tentative steps towards Kutor.

'On my command,' Owen whispered, readying his sword and knife. Tien settled his remaining axe in his hand, and slipped a long slim knife from his right boot, while Fodla moved her matching swords before her in tight circles.

They all clearly saw the muscles in the vampir's thighs tense and stiffen as she prepared to jump – and then the creature burst into flame! The intense cold-white light ate through the body, turning it into an almost solid pile of filthy grey ash. It crumpled to the ground, Fodla's knife in its midst.

'She would have slain you all,' the Andam said weakly, turning away.

The Lady Esse stared deeply into the coal black eyes of the vampir, her gnarled hands resting lightly on its shoulders. Looking into the eyes of this vampir, she saw through the eyes of its unholy sister.

She saw the female guard standing outside the door, saw the way her eyes moved speculatively up and down the vampir's body, saw the sharpened edge of the metal tray bite deeply into the woman's throat, nearly severing the head from the body. She saw a foot rise, snapping its heel into the wood of the door just above the lock, breaking the doors open, and then she found the vampir facing the usurper and his minions.

230

The ancient sorceress' lips tightened as the vampir looked from face to face. She saw their mouths working as they talked, and then she saw the large woman – Fodla – throw a knife. Slowly ... slowly, infinitely slowly, the throwing dagger arched through the air, and the Lady Esse blinked as it thudded home below her range of vision. There was movement – the Weapon Master and his servant preparing weapons – and then a second thrown dagger moved slowly through the air, and even the hardened sorceress flinched as the dagger touched the vampir's face. Well, no matter, the vampir were impervious to pain, and Fodla would pay, as they all would pay ...

And then there was fire!

The vampir before her – through whose eyes she was seeing the events – staggered back, her mouth open, and the scream which bubbled through her lips was that of pure and absolute agony. The sorceress's hands tightened on the vampir's shoulders, but the creature fell away, her wails increasing in intensity as her eyes – no longer black now, but red and flame – reflected the fire that was consuming her sister on the other side of the city. The Lady Esse broke the contact between the two creatures and then dropped the last remaining vampir into a trance-like state. One left, just one and this one would not – could not – fail.

The small stunted woman walked slowly across the room and tugged on the slender bell rope; a servant immediately appeared at the door. 'We are moving. Is all in order?' she snapped.

'Everything is packed and awaiting your order and directions,' the servant bowed.

'Send the wagons out, then – send them north to Baddalaur. They will be met on the road by one of my agents.'

'My lady.' The man bowed, and backed from the room.

'Rom!' the Lady Esse called.

The door opened and a hugely tall man stepped into the room, his features and colouring typical of the Gallowglas tribe.

'We are for the north,' the woman snapped. 'Baddalaur first and then Thusal if necessary. The creature failed,' she added, more quietly now, 'and now the usurper and his people will move against us. They have no other alternative. Send the knife to the Twelve.'

And that night, the heads of the Twelve Families of Karfondal each received a tiny ornate dagger.

The raids came in the still silent hour before the dawn. The raiding parties were composed principally of the Emperor Legion, backed up by the troops hand-picked by Fodla and Keshian, all seasoned and experienced warriors – and all of them unquestionably loyal to either Kutor or Fodla. They raided the palaces and town houses of the heads of the Twelve Families, with orders, signed by Kutor and bearing the Imperial Seal, to arrest them for treason.

But the raiding parties found nothing. The heads of the households, along with their wives and children, mistresses, lovers, personal servants and guards, were gone, leaving only the regular servants behind to tend hastily vacated houses. They all told stories of a rider coming late in the night, speaking briefly with the master of the house and then moving on. As preparations for an immediate departure had already begun, by the time Kutor's troops arrived the Twelve Families were long gone.

The dawn brought with it several other surprises. There had been desertions from the Imperial Army – and on an unprecedented scale. Several thousand men had vanished overnight – in some cases whole battalions, from cooks to captains' had disappeared, taking with them not only their kit, including weapons and rations, but also wagons filled with supplies of food, clothing, blankets and weapons.

'We've lost just over one-third of the army,' Keshian said sombrely.

'And these would have been men loyal to Geillard?' Kutor asked, his longer stride easily outpacing the smaller, stouter man as they strode down the corridor towards the Lord Rocque's suite in the palace.

'Not necessarily,' Keshian panted. 'It's difficult at the moment, with so many men missing, to form any sort of picture about those who've gone, and the remaining troops are understandably reticent. They would certainly seem to have been men who were traditionalists, loyal to the old ways, perhaps even followers of the Religion, rather than the Faith, and some of course were troops who were loyal to the Twelve Families and went with them.'

They turned left down a brightly-lit corridor where Owen and Fodla could be seen deep in conversation outside the Treasurer's door. They both turned as Kutor, with Keshian in tow, came hurrying up.

'Later,' Kutor snapped as they both opened their mouths to speak. He pushed his way into the room – and found himself standing in the midst of chaos. The usually pristine chambers of the Lord Rocque were covered with papers, parchments, charts and rolls. Every drawer had been emptied and the enormous fireplace at the far end of the room was piled high with smouldering ashes. The Andam was on his knees before the fire, sifting through the ashes with a poker.

'What happened?' Kutor asked in astonishment.

The Andam gestured with a cloth-wrapped hand. 'Every record had been destroyed: every note, every tally book, every tax account burnt. The fifedom records, tax districts, genealogies, even the charts and maps which were redrawn after the Cataclysm have all been destroyed. It seems the Lord Rocque was determined to leave nothing useful behind.' The Andam looked up at the Emperor, his grey eyes piercing. 'You know what this means, don't you?'

'I'm not sure . . .' Kutor said hesitantly.

'They do not intend to return – or if they do return,' he amended, 'They will not be re-establishing the old Order. They're wiping the slate clear, preparing to start afresh.'

'Andam's right,' Owen said softly. 'Those troops who deserted could have simply risen against you; an uprising would have drawn many to its banner, and there are enough disaffected parties in the city at the moment to lend them support, or who would simply have joined in for the booty.'

'What are they doing, then?'

'It is my guess that they're heading north to join forces with Geillard's troops, and then the combined forces will deal us a solid, crushing blow.'

'Geillard hasn't the forces,' Kutor protested.

'You've seen the reports,' Keshian interrupted. 'We're talking about a combined army of Chopts, Gallowglas and humankind, which will at least equal our numbers, if not surpass it.'

'It will also have the advantage of fighting for a cause it believes in,' Owen said quietly. 'Much as our army did when it took Karfondal.'

'The deserters can't have gone too far; we could follow and attack them.'

Fodla shook her massive head. 'It wouldn't work; our troops would be fighting men they know, men they would have drunk with, gambled with, sung with perhaps only the previous night. They would have no heart for it.'

'We could use some of the mercenary forces to harry them,' Kutor suggested.

'No! How do you think the men will feel if they see the mercenary forces attacking their old friends? We've worked too long and too hard to have them fight as a unit and consider themselves one unit – Kutor's army – rather than the Imperial forces and the mercenaries. Something like this could wipe out all that work. No,' she shook her head, 'far better for us to allow them to join up with the northern army and be absorbed into it. At that stage, the deserters will have visibly aligned themselves with the enemy; we can fight them then.'

'All we have from the north are rumours,' Kutor said quickly, looking around at the faces.

'The reports . . .' Keshian began.

'There are no rumours,' the Andam said quickly. He touched the fire and immediately the ashes flared into incandescent light. 'Look.' For a moment they saw nothing, and then, within the flames, images formed, tiny pictures of a huge seething shape crawling across something white, like a mass of insects across a blanket. But then the image changed, becoming larger, clearer, and the mass resolved itself into an army, a Chopt army, and moving through the army were the Gallowglas, cousins to the Chopts, professional mercenaries, and alongside them were creatures only the Andam recognised. 'Torc Allta,' he whispered, and they all knew the name. The pictures changed, now showing a huge human army that was part and yet separate from the Chopts and the beasts. The humans were a mixture, some of them soldiers, others obviously mercenaries, others who looked as if they might be trappers, hunters or farmers, and then the image changed, the swirling flames seeming to pick out a face, a single human face, a face they all recognised: 'Geillard!'

The flames died, leaving only ashes in their wake, but a picture remained in those ashes, a picture of a devastated landscape, whole villages wiped out, towns decimated, the land laid waste. The Andam looked up, his eyes cold and dead in his head. 'They intend to destroy this world, Kutor; they intend to destroy it and then have their gods recreate it afresh.'

'Can they do that?' Kutor asked, wrenching his gaze away from the ashes.

The Andam stood. 'No,' he said, his voice wooden. 'There is a balance that must be maintained, both on the spiritual and physical plane. Disturb that balance and Chaos reigns. They intend to destroy the Old Faith totally; they intend to ensure that it will never revive. They are killing every follower of the Faith they can find: every priest, every teacher, every monk, scribe and bard. The churches and fanes are being torn down stone by stone, the statues pulverised. The College of Ectoraige has been decimated, the monks and students massacred. They intend to destroy the Library and College of Baddalaur. If that happens, then the Old Faith will have been dealt a mortal blow. And when the Old Faith dies – as it surely will if the College is destroyed – then the balance will tip and this plane and every other Plane of Existence will be annihilated.'

'So what do we do?' Kutor asked, looking at the Andam, but it was Owen who answered.

'We make our stand at Baddalaur!'

Three days later, the remnants of the Imperial Army set out on the long road for the College of Bards.

17   The Return to Baddalaur

*This day returned to us a brother, by name Paedur, called the
Hookhand, who has achieved certain fame and notoriety and some say
has brought the brotherhood into disrepute . . .*
Register of Baddalaur, the College of Bards

Five travellers made their way into Badaur, the town that lay at
the base of Baddalaur, the College of Bards.

The town had grown up around the College and had only one
function – to service the largest college of learning and the finest
library in all the Planes of Existence. Students from every nation
came to study in Baddalaur's Culai-built halls, and Badaur provided them with lodgings, food and entertainment. At any season
it might be expected to be full, but now, with the land locked in a
bitter chill, the town was filled to overflowing, with few of the
students or scholars willing to venture out onto the roads. Daily,
stragglers were trickling in from the Outlands or the Northlands
and no-one paid them any attention – except the guards on the
gates who were running a lucrative little operation on the side
. . .

Neer was on duty when he spotted the five figures out in the
snow-fields, and he immediately began assessing their worth. His
experience as a professional soldier had given him an excellent
eye for the relative values of things, and over the past couple of
moons he had been practising – daily. No-one entered Badaur
without first having to pay a fee – a Chill Fee, Neer jokingly
called it, and the name had stuck. The fee varied according to the
wealth of those seeking admittance, and the last couple of moons
had made him and the others guards very wealthy men indeed.

The grizzled veteran squinted out into the ice-fields. The five
figures were coming in along the barely outlined track that had
once been the King Road, coming from the north – which could

only mean Thusal. Trappers almost certainly – most of those who lived in the northern town trapped the ice-beasts for a living, but they could also be farmers, fishers, miners ... anyway, they were sure to have wealth, either in the form of script money, metal coinage or plates, furs or weapons. There were some nice weapons coming out of the north these days; he absently patted the new Chopt knife that hung on his belt.

Four adults and a child, which probably meant that one of the adults was a woman, but nevertheless that still left five separate payments. He stepped out of his shelter beside the gate and raised a gloved hand. 'Halt.'

Three of the adults and the child stopped, but one, tall and thin, kept moving as if he hadn't heard the guard. Neer dropped his spear across the man's path. 'Halt, I said. Where are you coming from? Where are you going?'

The man Neer had stopped didn't move or speak, but a bulky man in a furred cloak, stepped forward and whispered, his voice obviously raw with the intense chill, 'We've walked from Thusal, fleeing the weather. We seek shelter in Badaur.'

'Many people seek shelter in Badaur at the moment; why should you be admitted?' Neer said, lowering his voice. It was subtle enough and yet most people got the hint, but this crowd were obviously too numbed by the cold to even think – or else they were incredibly stupid.

'We seek admittance,' the bulky man whispered again. 'Let us through.'

Neer shook his head slowly, his eyes small and dark and amused. He took a certain pleasure in toying with the travellers, exercising what little power he imagined he possessed. 'There are certain formalities to be ...'

'Let us through!' The voice was as chill as the ice, and Neer jumped with fright. He stepped away from the man who had spoken and brought up his spear, levelling it at the man's shadowed face.

'I think the town is full,' he said venomously. 'There is no admittance.'

Metal winked on the chill air, and suddenly a curved hook

wrapped itself around the barbed head of his spear. With a twist and wrench, the spearhead was sheared clean off. The cowled man raised his hand, pushing back his hood: and even before the eyes – mirrored, reflective eyes, now the colour of snow – turned on him, Neer knew the identity of the traveller.

'I am Paedur, the Bard.'

In a town where hierarchy and power were measured by knowledge, and knowledge was a closely-guarded secret available only for a price, news of the bard's arrival travelled through the streets with extraordinary speed.

The bard's reputation had preceded him; in parts of the Nations he was already considered as a legend, and stories of sightings of him were universal. So as he walked through Badaur, heading up the Avenue of a Thousand Steps to the College of Bards, a still, silent crowd gathered. They lined the Avenue, watching, looking only at him, almost completely ignoring the four figures that walked behind him. They had come expecting to see someone – something – remarkable. Most of them were disappointed. His legendary hook was hidden beneath his snow-covered cloak, and he stared straight ahead, looking neither right nor left, denying them the opportunity to see his mirror-bright eyes.

When he had passed by, most people turned away, some of them embarrassed or even annoyed that they had left what they had been doing to see . . . well . . . to see a man.

One of the watchers, however, didn't turn away. He kept pace with the small group and only when the College's Culai-built gates swung open and the bard and his companions disappeared inside, did he turn back, heading for the outskirts of the town. Moments later, a snow-eagle lifted to the iron-grey skies; it immediately winged its way northwards.

The bard had come home.

By the time the afternoon had faded into evening, Mannam and the Trialdone were aware of the fact.

The guest chambers in the College of Bards were spectacular, more like a royal bedchamber than a guestroom in a school. The rooms – a connecting suite comprising of bedchambers, a deep-sunk ornate marbled bath and a large central conference room complete with long table and a dozen chairs – were luxurious. The floors were covered in beautifully worked carpets, deep-piled and warm to the touch where they covered the hot-water pipes sunk into the floor. The bare stone walls had been covered with tapestries and decorative furs, and one wall of the conference chamber was covered in books, all bound in warm reds and browns, golds and bronzes which immediately lent warmth to the large circular room. Gire – abruptly abandoned now by the god – walked around the rooms, touching the furnishings and finally ending up in the bath chamber. His cry of delight brought Katani and Bastion running.

'Not even in Talaria do we have this.'

Bastion smiled. 'In very few courts would you find this, I'll wager.' He touched a spigot and steaming hot water hissed out. 'It might be nice to try . . .' he said longingly.

There was a shadow in the doorway. 'Try it, we'll be here for a while.' Paedur stepped into the room. 'I have to see the Council of Bards and . . .' he shrugged, 'well, there are certain formalities to be observed. We'll certainly be here for two, possibly three days.'

Bastion looked at Katani; they both knew the bard didn't intend to leave Baddalaur.

Katani, who was slowly removing her armour a piece at a time, piling them up on a broad bench beside the bath, looked up. 'What is this council for?'

'I will warn them of the approaching army, and the Religion's threat. They can decide what to do,' Paedur said, not answering her question.

'Can the Library be moved?'

He shook his head. 'Impossible.'

Bastion looked around. 'What about the important pieces?'

Paedur smiled wistfully. 'There are just too many of them. Now, bathe and eat, drink, sleep, enjoy all the comforts of this place – they'll be the last you'll have for a long time, I'll wager.'

Paedur turned and walked back into the conference chamber.
Ironwinter was sitting in the centre of the floor, rubbing his long-
nailed paws against a snowcat's spotted pelt.

'What of me, bard?' he asked, without looking up. 'What will
happen to me?'

'You are under my protection,' Paedur said quietly, pulling
the door to the bath chamber closed behind him. 'Nothing will
happen to you.'

The beast shook his head. 'That is not what I meant. I am
Chopt first and last. I belong in the ice-fields with my people.'

'Your people have been tricked. They are being led by a king
who is in thrall to the Religion. They are being led to their destruction.'

'Are they, bard? Are they? How can you be so sure?' Ironwinter
surged to his feet, facing the bard. He was taller than Paedur,
and although slender by Chopt standards, was still far more
powerful than the bard. 'The prophecy is being fulfilled: "When
the Weapon Maker wakes, and the gods war, then will come the
time of the Chopt." The Armourer has awoken. There is war
coming. And how can you be so sure your gods and your people
will triumph? Times change, bard. The seasons turn. Perhaps the
Season of Humankind is drawing to a close and the Season of
the People of the Ice is dawning.'

'If it is then it is a blighted season,' Paedur said, and made to
walk past the beast, but Ironwinter stretched out his arm, almost
– but not quite – touching the bard.

'I would rather die with my people, then.'

Paedur shook his head. 'The Gods – all of them – move and
weave us at their will and whim. Do you know the Death's Law:
"Men are but the playthings of the Gods?" The Gods, yours and
mine, placed us together at a certain place in a certain time. Your
destiny is now irrevocably woven with mine. For better or ill,
you are seen by your people as having chosen to accompany me;
they see you as a traitor. If you return they will kill you.'

'What am I to do?' Ironwinter asked, the anguish plain in his
voice.

Gently, very gently, Paedur reached out and touched the

beast's bare arm with his fingertips. 'I have no Sight. I cannot see into the future. But I think it is inconceivable that the Gods – yours and mine – would have thrown us together for no purpose. All we have to do is to divine that purpose.' He was about to turn away, when he added: 'I think the People of the Ice will be in need of a king when this is ended.'

'This is not a trial,' the voice from the shadows said as soon as the bard had closed the door behind him.

'A trial presupposes a crime,' Paedur said, turning and walking forward into the circle of light in the centre of the floor. There was a low three-legged stool in the centre of the circle, but the bard ignored it, preferring to stand.

This was the council chamber of the College of Bards, and Paedur knew that in the darkness beyond the light there sat three hundred bards, all of them full professed, many of them Bard Masters, but no apprentices. Immediately before him, almost visible in the light, sat Seon, Master Bard of Baddalaur, whose word was absolute and who had ruled the College and dictated the Bardic Law as he saw it for well on three generations. There was unhuman blood in him, and it was even rumoured that he was alien to this Plane of Existence. Immediately to Paedur's left and right sat two Bard Masters, and if the trial – and he had no illusions that that was what it was – were to follow the traditional cause, one would speak in his defence, the other speak against him, with the Master Bard having the deciding vote.

Paedur, who had been deliberately suppressing his enhanced senses since he had entered the College, now allowed them to come to the fore – and immediately the huge chamber burst into incandescent light. The bard rapidly sorted through the myriad auras, reading the colours, and was surprised to find that most of these were various hues of red – the predominant mood of the assembled bards was anger! On his right-hand side – as his advocate – he was surprised to find his old companion Gwion. Although he would have been of an age with Paedur, he had grown old in the service of the College and his hair and beard were now streaked with grey, and the lines around his eyes and forehead told of weakening eyes. His aura spoke of confusion, frustration and something else, something the bard couldn't quite define, but something that looked suspiciously like fear.

To his left sat a surprising figure, another figure from the bard's past, and someone with no love for Paedur. As the bard stripped away his aura – which was one of anger and self satisfaction – Paedur realised that time had done little to change him. Urien's thin features had been handsome in his youth, but now that age had touched him, they were merely cruel.

Theirs had been an inexplicable rivalry; they had taken an instant dislike to one another, and on several occasions it had come to blows. Once Paedur had cut the young Urien quite badly with his hook and whatever chance there had been of the rift mending had been forever lost, for what had been a simple dislike had then turned to hatred. Gwion had once said that he thought it was because they were so alike, so chill, so aloof, so confident.

'This has all the trappings of a trial,' Paedur said loudly, addressing the Master.

'We are here to judge a bard,' Seon said coldly, his usually clipped accent now sounding almost staccato. But the bard's sensitive hearing caught the nervousness in the man's voice.

'And what has this bard done to deserve being tried before the Council of Bards?'

Urien spoke suddenly, and the harsh, slightly mocking tones he had often adopted deliberately in his youth, had remained with him, making him sound sour and bitter. 'The Bard Paedur is charged with having brought the bardic vocation into disrepute, with deliberate and exaggerated misuse of his lore and with having taken a prominent part in politics.'

'These are serious charges,' Seon snapped. 'How do you answer them?'

'I thought this was no trial?' Paedur smiled.

'Answer the charges and state your case. Later there will be a trial – if it is deemed necessary.'

The bard's expression hardened. 'You are playing with words. This is a trial. But I will play along with your game. With the

242

exception of bringing the bardic vocation into disrepute I accept that the charges levelled at me are true . . .' He paused while the assembly murmured amongst themselves, and then added. 'But I was acting under instructions, and cannot be held accountable for my acts.'

Gwion spoke quickly. 'There are tales that the Bard Paedur has been chosen as the Champion of the Faith . . .'

'Tales . . . gossip!' Urien spat.

'I am the Champion of the Old Faith,' Paedur said loudly, and then he slipped into the bardic Voice, a method of voice projection, coupled with a touch of the Old Magic that resulted in catching and holding the listener's attention – sometimes against his will.

'I am the Champion of the Old Faith; I am the God-Sought, God-Taught; I am the Teller of Tales, the Weaver of Lies, the Bringer of Faith.

'I have walked C'lte's Kingdom of Life; I have sailed the Sea of Galae, the Haunted Sea; I have walked the Culai Isle, and seen the last of the First Race go down in destruction that threatened the fabric of the Planes of Existence; I have walked Mannam's Silent Woods; I have deposed a god and put a new god in his place.

'I am Paedur the Bard.'

The echoes rolled round and around the huge hall and when they had died, there was complete and utter silence.

Paedur raised his left arm and allowed the light to sparkle off his hook, and then, calling upon the Fire Sprite to help him, he fired it, calling up an intense blue-white flame. Moving his wrist slightly, he spun the flame into a ball, which he then tossed up towards the ceiling. When it had almost reached the blackened spars it burst, flooding the chamber in a warm blue light.

'You have interfered in politics,' Urien said into the absolute silence.

'I have told my tales to renew belief in the Old Faith,' he said simply. 'I put Kutor on the throne at Karfondal only because the Pantheon instructed me to do so. I travelled north to Thusal and the Ice-fields beyond because the Pantheon – the same Pantheon you all worship – instructed me.'

243

He turned his head to look at Urien and the man recoiled at the bard's expression, for it was as cold and as lifeless as a statue. 'And I deny I brought the bardic vocation into disrepute – if anything I have demonstrated the power of the bard and what we can achieve when we set our minds to it.' He turned back to Seon, the Master. 'For too long the bards have stagnated and merely contented themselves with being collectors and tellers of tales; we have squandered our talents. Our forefathers – the same bards who first set up the Bardic College here – were always a force to be reckoned with. They sat with kings and princes. They walked with gods and demons. They helped shape the world – all we shape now are seats.'

'Bard, you go too far,' Seon warned.

'No, I don't think I go far enough! But what matter? Soon, it will be too late . . .'

'What do you mean?' Gwion asked quietly.

'There is a war brewing in the Northlands, a war organised by Geillard and the remnants of his followers, supported by the Chopts and some of the Torc Allta. Three of the Trialdone have taken corporal form, Sheesarak the Destroyer, the Lady Asherat, the Taker of Souls, and Ghede, the Lord of Beasts; and Mannam, once-god of the Faith sides with them. Even the Armourer has awoken.'

'They will be defeated,' Urien said shakily. 'We have nothing to fear.'

'No, no,' Paedur hissed, 'not this time. This time the first target of this huge cannibal army will be the literature and learning of the Old Faith. Every book, every scroll, tablet, chart, page and parchment will be destroyed. Without the observances of the Law, the Faith will die – or so they believe. They intend to butcher – and probably eat – every monk, scribe and bard they find. They have destroyed the Monastery of Ectoraige – and they intend to raze Baddalaur to the ground!'

Paedur waited until the tumult had subsided. 'And they are already moving against us. And since we cannot move the Library before they arrive, that leaves us but one course of action. We fight!'

'We'll die,' Urien said savagely, his voice close to hysterical. 'This is madness.'

'And if we die, we will die fighting for what we believe in!'

'So they called you to trial, and you turned the tables on them?' Katani raised her glass of clear northern wine and toasted the bard.

'He was magnificent,' Gwion said, lifting his glass also. They had all gathered in the conference chamber of the large suite, Katani and Bastion, Gire, Ironwinter and Gwion. The meal had been magnificent, although Paedur had eaten nothing and Ironwinter had taken the tiny slivers of spiced meat, carried them to the fire and scorched them thoroughly until they were to his liking.

'Will they fight?' Bastion asked. Now that he was relaxed and away from the bitter cold, the wounds on his face had healed and only in a certain light did the scars show.

'Bards – with the possible exception of Paedur, here – don't fight,' Gwion said with a grin. He was a short stout man, of the bard's age, although he looked much older, and with a tiny spill of jet black hair across the top of his head and large round eyes that seemed to be of deepest black. He obviously enjoyed his food and drink.

'They'll fight to protect the lore,' Paedur said. 'Even now, they are shifting the more valuable materials into the vaults buried deep, deep underground. Even if the entire building is razed to the ground, they will survive.'

'Except that they will be underground, buried beneath a pile of stone,' Katani observed with a wry smile.

'And even if we could clear the Library, where would we take it? In this weather the roads are barely passable,' Gwion continued. 'And people make the mistake of thinking that the Library is just one building, while in effect it is over a hundred buildings, not counting the single rooms, the vaults, the cellars, the attics, and the outhouses, all of which are full of material. Even the entire College of Bards, with all its apprentices, couldn't clear the place in a season.'

'You could if you decided what was junk and could therefore be disposed of,' Paedur grunted.

'Yes, like the *Tales of the Shanaqui*,' Gwion said innocently.

Paedur threw back his head and laughed, the first time any of the company had ever seen him do it. 'Yes, yes, exactly,' he said, and then, seeing Katani's puzzled frown, he added, 'My tales are recorded here under the sigil of the hook, the Shanaqui.'

Ironwinter grunted to attract their attention. He was squatting before the open fire, tearing at his strips of meat with drooling fangs. 'And what now, bard?'

'Now we wait.'

'For what?'

'There has been a revolt of some sort in the capital – the reports are sketchy and incomplete, but it seems that a major portion of the army has deserted to Geillard's cause. They were last seen heading north, followed a few days later by the Imperial Army under Kutor himself. Nothing has been heard from Thusal for the past few days, no report from Eiron, and the assumption here is that Thusal has fallen . . .'

Katani bowed her head and muttered a brief prayer for the Bard Master of Thusal, who had remained even though he knew what might be the eventual consequences.

'You could go,' Paedur suggested, looking at each one in turn. 'Head east or west, wait until the fighting has died down . . .'

One by one, they all shook their heads, and Bastion spoke for all of them. 'Sure, where would we go?'

'So, here we stay; we have nowhere else to go. There is a Chopt army and their allies coming down from the north, and reinforcements coming up from the south, with our own troops somewhere behind them.'

'Can we win?' Bastion asked.

Paedur smiled, a movement of his lips only, it never reached his eyes. 'We can fight!'

18　Death's Law

The dream ends at Baddalaur . . .

Paedur, the Bard

Men are but the playthings of the gods, pieces to be moved to their will; this is Death's Law . . .

Grimoire Magnum

The board was set, the pieces gathered and ready. The game was about to begin . . .

Tales of the Bard

The sun was still a vague glow below the horizon when the bard climbed to the top of Baddalaur's highest tower and looked to the north. The battlements were coated in a thin layer of ice, and the breeze coming in from the north was bitter. Here, above the College and the town, there was no sound, and in the silence, the shrill voice of a solitary bird sounded very loud and lost. And suddenly for some unknown reason – and for the first time in as long as he could remember – Paedur felt very lonely indeed.

There were those whom he could call friends, but how much of their purported friendship was made up of fear or loathing? How easy was it to befriend one of the unhumans? That was another 'gift' he owed the Gods of the Pantheon; when they had made him Champion of the Old Faith, they had neglected to inform him that it would cost him everything, from his friends to his humanity.

But too late now . . . far too late . . .

He looked back into the north. As far as the eye could see the landscape was blanketed in white, nothing moving, nothing disturbing the pristine cover, the unseasonal weather having closed in – permanently it seemed – turning the fields into a close approximation of the Northlands. Paedur smiled thinly, Mannam's and the Trialdone's work, but while the bitter weather worked to the Chopts' advantage, he couldn't help wondering how the rest of the beasts' allies were faring in the intense chill – especially the Torc Allta, whose homeland was warm and moist.

He wondered if the snowscape before him was as empty as it seemed. Allowing his enhanced senses to come to the fore, he quested out into the wasteland, and was immediately struck by its emptiness – there were no birds, no beasts, either large or small, roaming around. Obviously the sudden cold weather had caught them by surprise and unprepared. He moved further out into the snow-fields – and discovered three Chopts lurking in the snow, watching the College, their auras dirty splashes of colour on the whiteness of the snow. These were mature, seasoned warriors, their auras tainted by the colour of the New Religion, radiating distrust for the huge stone buildings and simple blood-lust, mingled with a little hunger. The beasts had not eaten for some time and they hungered for the flesh of humankind. They were scouts for the army, and that meant that the army itself was no more than two or three days behind.

They would have to be killed eventually, Paedur decided, if for no other reason than to cause confusion or delay reports to the Chopt camp. At the moment any delay – no matter how small or insigificant – was welcome, since it allowed the Imperial troops under Kutor to draw nearer. He toyed with the idea of slaying the beasts himself – but then realised that it would expose his position to the Trialdone and weaken him fractionally. Far better to allow Katani to slay them.

Reverting to his normal human senses, he leaned his arms on the cold stone wall and stared vacantly into the north, his reflective eyes half-closed against the wind, reviewing the events of the last few days.

The numbers of refugees flooding into Badaur had increased, and the town which usually held around three hundred souls, now hosted close to two thousand. Every spare room, cellar and attic in the town were being used, and already food and fuel were running short, and all attempts at rationing had failed. Badaur was nothing more than a town servicing a college – it had no need for troops or officials necessary to enforce such regulations. Some of the Bard Masters had attempted to enforce some authority – but authority tends to wither in the face of fear – and they had either been ignored or mocked.

The town was rife with rumours, and stories about the size and ferocity of the Chopt army grew daily, until it had assumed gigantic proportions. There had been calls for the women and children to be sent to the south, but these had ceased swiftly when the College had announced that there was a renegade army already on the King Road, fleeing Karfondal, hoping to meet up with the Chopts around Badaur. They were trapped.

Fear walked the narrow streets and winding lanes, keeping many indoors, huddled behind barred doors – as if that would do them any good. But in the Wall Streets – those abutting onto the town's high walls, containing the bars and brothels – an almost carnival air prevailed. Here, the priests, the bars and the whores were doing an excellent trade, but the atmosphere was brittle, close to hysteria, and the bard knew it would take very little to send it over the edge.

He was familiar with the reports that were coming in regularly from the Seven Bastions. The main body of the Chopt army had bypassed the Seven Bastions, leaving only small contingents – each one heavily armed and battle-trained – to besiege the castles. Their purpose was obviously not to attack, merely to keep the garrisons inside. All sorties from the Bastions had been beaten back with heavy losses, but the Chopts had been careful not to engage in any protracted fight. Paedur assumed that later, when Baddalaur had fallen, the Chopts would either fall back and destroy the Bastions or simply starve them out; either way, they couldn't afford to have them at their backs while they pressed on towards the capital.

And what if Baddalaur fell? What if the bards were butchered and all the knowledge held within these hallowed halls was destroyed – what would happen to the World of Men then? Would it go down in flames as Ectoraige claimed?

And if Baddalaur was destroyed in the name of the Religion and the power generated by that destruction transferred to its gods, how powerful would that make the Gods of the New Religion? Strong enough to defeat the Pantheon of the Old Faith?

The bard had tried contacting his own gods, but with no response; they, too, were preparing for war.

And if the gods were unable or unwilling to assist him, then he would have to fight the approaching army some other way – or at least hold them until Kutor and his army arrived, but that was still some four days away. And what hope had a single man against an army of thousands?

Katani's plan was simple and direct. 'The town is indefensible; its walls are too low, its gates too many and too flimsy – it is wide open. But Baddalaur itself is a different matter. It is Culai-built; its walls are thicker than a tall man, and it has but one gate, and that is solid teel-wood.' She looked at the faces around the table, Bastion and Ectoraige on her left, Ironwinter on her right. Sitting directly across from her was Seon, Master Bard of Baddalaur, and standing behind him, looking deep into the blazing fire was Paedur the Bard.

She took a deep breath and continued slowly. 'I suggest we evacuate the town to the College and then booby-trap the empty buildings, the walls, the gates even the alley-ways. The Chopts will take Badaur – we know that – but at least we can make them pay dearly for it.'

'The College is already full . . .' Seon said stiffly.

'Nonsense,' Ectoraige said. 'You could easily double or treble the numbers here without too much trouble. I think the plan has merit. Paedur?' he asked.

'I think it is an excellent suggestion,' he said, and then paused. 'There are two possible problems, however,' he said slowly, glancing sidelong at the group around the table. Firelight and shadow took his face, painting it red and black. 'You must first convince the townspeople to move – and secondly, I think we are forgetting the Trialdone.'

Ectoraige smiled, his boyish smile completely in contrast with his deep voice. 'This is a college of storytellers and myth-makers, surely some of these professional storytellers could go down into

the town and frighten the people up here.' The smile faded and
the god's stone-grey eyes looked directly into the bard's reflective
gaze. 'But you must face the Trialdone yourself. If the People of
the Ice were to lose the Trialdone, then it would be a bitter blow
to them. The seasons would immediately begin to return to
normal and without the Trialdone, the killings committed in the
Religion's name would take longer to be absorbed by the new
gods. Their deaths would not only weaken the Chopts, but also
all the gods of the Religion. But only you can face the Trialdone,
bard, and you must do it in the Ghost World.'

'They are gods and I am but a man,' Paedur said into the
deathly silence.

'They are not gods, bard, and you are more than a man!'

'Could we turn the Chopts back?' Seon asked, fear making his
clipped accent sound harsh.

'No.' All heads turned to Ironwinter. The beast shook his
head. 'Not now; it is too late and they are too far down this road
to be turned aside now.'

'Who commands them?' Seon demanded. 'Could he not be
prevailed upon . . .?'

'They follow Stonehand, Lord of the People of the Ice; his
word is law.'

'But you said he was in thrall to Praetens,' Seon said, turning
to Ectoraige.

'He was,' the god said, 'but Praetens is dead now, and
Mannam, the once-god had taken over the spell.'

Bastion cleared his throat. 'What would it take to lift that spell?'

'The death of Mannam,' Ectoraige said. 'Or if not his death,
then he would have to be wounded, hurt or threatened – something that would call upon all his power. At the moment, a tiny
fraction of power is all that holds the king in thrall.'

'And if the spell was lifted or broken,' Bastion asked hoarsely,
'how do you think Stonehand would react? Would he be aware
of what had been happening? Would he know he had been used?'

Ectoraige nodded. 'I'm sure of it.'

'Then let me slay this Mannam,' Ironwinter said quickly. 'I am
Chopt. I can pass through their ranks . . .'

251

'It would need two,' Paedur said quietly. 'One to distract or wound Mannam – and I would suggest fire as the most likely method – the other to assist Stonehand. When the spell is broken he will be disorientated and confused, but susceptible. If someone was to suggest to him that the Chopts were to retreat, there is every possibility that he would agree to it.'

'I will go with Ironwinter,' Bastion said.

'So it is settled . . .' Ectoraige coughed, and the cough broke, changing in timbre to become high-pitched and shrill. 'I must leave you now,' the God of Learning and Knowledge said quickly. 'I can do no more. I have lingered too long in this body as it is. I go now to fight with my brothers on the chequered fields of Ab-Apsalom.' He turned to look at Paedur, and even as he spoke, his eyes visibly changed from grey to brown. 'So it comes back down to you again, bard. Should you fail then we all go down with you. Look to your lore, bard, look to your lore . . .'

. . . Deep-brown eyes blinked around the room, and the boy Gire said simply, 'I feel so tired now.'

Paedur walked with Katani along one of the galleries that looked down into Baddalaur's main library. The huge three-storeyed building was deserted and completely silent, the huge walls and cushioned doors blocking out all sound, and the Katan found it difficult to believe that there were whole families sleeping in the corridors outside.

Badaur's inhabitants had moved up from the town with surprising speed and with very little reluctance; the threat of the Chopts was enough for them to leave their flimsy dwellings for the comparative safety of Baddalaur's Culai-built walls. Now, every room – with the exception of the main library – was occupied, from the attics to the cellars. All the old wells – and there were more than a score – were uncovered and cleaned, and after some threats, all the resources and supplies from the town had been pooled and passed onto the bards for eventual distribution in the coming siege. A few had resisted this sharing of wealth, but usually a visit from Paedur – or the threat of a visit – was enough to make them change their minds. When the town was completely emptied, Katani, Bastion and Ironwinter had moved in, and turned every street, door, window, cellar and well into a devastating booby-trap. The first wave of Chopts that swept through Badaur would be cut to pieces, but enough of the traps were within the buildings, and these would only be triggered at a later stage.

'Can we win this conflict?' Katani asked quietly, not looking at the bard, but concentrating on row upon row of polished brown, ochre, bronze and gold leather bindings, each one embossed with the eye and triangle sigil of the College.

'That depends how you define "win",' the bard murmured, not looking at her.

'Will we survive?'

'The beasts are many and we are few.'

'That is not an answer to my question.'

Paedur bowed his head slightly. 'It isn't, but I don't have an answer to your question. I do not know. All we can do is fight, but remembering that if we fail then this Plane of Existence and all the others go down into Chaos.'

'Truly?' she asked.

'Truly,' he nodded.

They continued on in silence, until eventually Katani asked, 'So what happens now?'

'Now we wait. The beasts approach from the north, the rebel army from the south. Our own army also approaches from the south, but it is too far away to help us. All we can do is to try and ensure that the Chopt numbers have been reduced considerably by the time they arrive.'

They had reached the end of the gallery. Above, around and below them lay the library. The cool, pale northern light lanced in through the tall, high windows, washing the books, scrolls, charts and maps in wan ghostly light. Dust motes swam in the slanting rays, giving the place an almost timeless character – as if this was how it had been since the dawn of the world, and this was how it would be when all the Planes of Existence aligned and the worlds collapsed onto one another and ended. Paedur gestured down with his hook to the main floor, with its long reading tables, some still piled high with books and charts. The walls were lined with books. 'With this I could create a world, give it a history, past and present, a geography, a pantheon of gods, a technology and a future. Knowledge is power – and this is the greatest collection of knowledge in any one place . . .'

'And yet it is all too vulnerable to destruction by beasts who can barely speak, let alone read,' the Katan murmured.

'Ignorance always tries to tear down knowledge.' His eyes blinked soft and golden in the light for a few moments, but then he turned back to Katani, and they took the whiteness of her hair, making him look blind. 'I go to fight the Trialdone this night . . .' He paused, and then reached beneath his cloak and handed Katani a short tube of time-yellowed ivory, stopped at both ends with gold. 'When all else seems lost, you may use this; open it and read the scroll within. Ectoraige told me to look to my lore as if an answer lay therein. I've looked, but I discovered nothing . . . however, I remembered this.' He tapped the tube with the flat of his hook, and Katani saw a blue spark wind around the tube and leap onto the metal.

'What is it?' she asked, turning it over in her hands.

'Something . . . Something I won a long time ago. It may even be the solution.' He shook his head. 'I don't know.'

'You sound as if you don't expect to return . . .' Katani said very softly.

The bard smiled slightly. 'I didn't say that.'

'I know you didn't.'

He turned away abruptly and strode down the gallery towards the stairs. Caught by surprise, Katani hurried to catch up with him. 'There are three Chopt scouts to the north of here. They are watching our every movement and reporting back to the army by means of messenger birds. I was unsure whether to kill them or not, but now with Bastion and Ironwinter about to set off for the Chopt camp, it becomes necessary.'

Katani smiled hugely. 'I will see to it personally.'

Mannam consulted his charts and then turned to Geillard. 'At this rate another two days travel should see us pounding on Baddalaur's gates.'

The deposed Emperor's long-fingered hands closed into fists. 'Then everything will be as it was,' he said softly.

Within his cowl of seared and withered leaves, Mannam, the once-god smiled deeply.

Owen the Weapon Master pushed away the charts and looked across the table at Fodla and Kutor. 'At this rate, we've another four days ahead of us at least.'

The Commander of the Legion shook her head. 'Geillard's forces will be there in two, and the deserted soldiers in or around the same time. We're going to arrive too late.'

'But a small party riding hard could be there in two days,' Tien tZo suggested quietly.

Kutor looked at him. 'What would that achieve?'

The Shemmat shrugged. 'Only the Gods know – but it might be enough to tilt the balance. Wars are not won by huge armies, but by the actions of single men.'

'How small a party?' Keshian asked.

'Three, possibly four men.'

'Make it three men and leave before sunset,' Kutor said tightly. He was all too aware that this campaign was balanced on a knife edge, on decisions made, on immediate action and incisive decisions. He didn't even want to stop to think whether those decisions were the right ones.

The Lady Esse took the deeply curved, black-handled knife and approached Rom, her Gallowglas bodyguard. The red-eyed creature that was the vampir followed her silently, like an obedient pet.

She looked up into the Gallowglas's impassive face. 'Stretch out your hand,' she commanded.

The huge warrior immediately stretched out his left hand.

The twisted old woman took the knife and quickly slashed open the man's palm. His face and eyes remained expressionless, betraying nothing. The Lady Esse then turned to the vampir and, wrapping her hand in the creature's greasy hair, shoved her face onto the man's bloody hand. The creature began to drink. 'Obey this man whose life's blood you have sipped,' she commanded, lifting the blood-smeared face off his hand and staring into its crimson eyes. 'Obey him!' And then she shoved the face back to the palm. 'She will follow you, do as you command,' the old woman said to Rom. 'But ensure that she is fed – otherwise her craving for blood will be such that she will feed off you.'

The Gallowglas bowed deeply.

The Lady Esse spread an ancient chart on the table before her. Her long-nailed finger tapped it. 'This is Baddalaur before the town grew up around it. These lines represent air ducts into the lower cellars and ventilation shafts to regulate the library rooms. Some of them must still exist.' She allowed the chart to snap closed. 'Find one and you have your way into the College. I want you both to leave now. I want you to reach Baddalaur before the army – and I want you to slay the bard. No-one else matters now. Just the bard. Paedur the Bard must die!'

The bard couldn't remember the last time he had slept. He wondered, as he lay down on the cold stones on the top floor of the tower, what it would be like to close his eyes and drift off into dreamless sleep. Since he had become one of the God-Sought, God-Taught, and the Champion of the Old Faith, he had lost much of the simple pleasures of humankind; he ate but rarely, drank only water, and never seemed to sleep. The closest he came to sleep was when he shut down all his senses one by one, cutting off the exterior world and retreating into himself – and even then he was still always aware of his surroundings.

Composing himself, he prepared to enter the Ghost World. Every human entered the Ghost World while they slept; while the physical body rested, the essence – the soul – wandered through the formless space of the Ghost World, the grey void between the Planes of Existence. Mystics claimed that dreams were a fragmentary remembrance of the soul's experiences within the Ghost World.

But the bard knew that the Ghost World was much more. To

those with power, it was a place where thought could become fact, a place where dreams and nightmares walked hand in hand, moving at the whim of their creator. It could be a place of great beauty – or one of absolute terror.

And the bard who went to do battle with the Trialdone had no doubt which it would be.

The Chopt stretched his stiffened legs and eased back his cramped shoulders. He had been lying in the snow for most of the day, watching the distant College of Bards, observing the movements in and out – and now, with the sun beginning to sink down in the west, he was as convinced as he had been at sunrise that it was all a total and absolute waste of time. The town around the College was sealed tighter than an ice-locked lake, and he and his two companions were too far away from the building to make out the numbers and disposition of the guards on the battlements. So far all he had to report was that no-one had entered or left the town all day, and that was poor return for a day spent freezing in the snow. Well, he'd wait until the sun sank and then he would join his brothers . . .

He closed his eyes and rolled over in the snow – and Katani's longsword removed his head from his shoulders!

The warrior had left the town through one of the postern gates as dusk was seeping in across the ice-fields. She had daubed her armour with whitewash, left off her helmet, and powdered her face to match her ice-white hair, so that even Bastion and Iron-winter, who were watching her as she moved through the banks of snow, could barely pick her out from her surroundings.

She had found the first beast by the simple expedient of following her nose. The creature might be perfectly disguised in the ice-fields, but he stank – a rich, musky animal odour, combined with the stench of raw flesh, that stood out like a beacon on the cold sharp air.

She found the second beast by the same method, and killed him while he still slept.

Night had fallen by the time she approached the third beast, but this time he was prepared. Something – perhaps the stench of blood on the air – had alerted him. He had turned in time to see the creature in white glide through the bushes towards him, and for a moment his heart almost stopped in his chest as he imagined that the Lady Lussa – the White Goddess – was coming for him. But then the fading light had glinted on the creature's sword and he realised that this was no Goddess or Duaiteoiri – this was a mere human, and the humankind were easy prey.

The beast lunged with a trident as soon as the creature came within reach – and Katani deftly sliced the head off the weapon, and then her second sword licked out and tore through the creature's throat. While he gagged in surprise, she removed his head.

By the time the Lady Lussa had risen much higher in the heavens, Katani had returned to the town and Bastion and Ironwinter had left by the same gate to set out on their own mission.

No-one, especially Bastion and Ironwinter, expected them to return.

The vampir suddenly picked up her head, her nostrils flaring like a hunting animal's having found the scent. The red-eyed creature in the body of the woman stopped and silently pointed out across the ice-fields, away from the town and College. Her pointing fingers moved twice more, and the Gallowglas by her side got the impression that she had scented three fresh corpses in the snow. He was tempted to investigate. What had died in this desolate landscape so close to Baddalaur?

The vampir made a sound deep in her throat – the vampir had not the power of speech – but the Gallowglas recognised the query in her voice. He shook his head and pointed towards the shadowed bulk of Badaur with Baddalaur rising massive and ominous above it. 'The Lady Esse would not permit it,' he said roughly. He was unsure how much the creature understood. Sometimes he imagined it was nothing more than an animal in a human body – an animal with a taste for human blood – but there were times when he looked at her and he thought he discerned a gleam of intelligence in her eyes. 'There will be blood within the College – including the ichor of the bard, and that should be a rich feast indeed.'

The Gallowglas settled his huge sword on his back and then continued his search through the gnarled clump of bushes that grew in the lee of an ancient outcropping of weathered stone. He was working mainly by touch, for although the Lady Lussa provided ample light, it still left the interior of the stone in deep shadow, and he was loath to strike a light which would only betray his position, but if needs be . . .

He discovered the grille close to the ground, a rusted rectangle set into the stone outcropping, completely concealed by the bush. He wrapped a large hand around the grille and pulled. Nothing happened. Gripping it in both hands he leaned back, exerting his full weight on the grille but it still didn't move. And then a small pale hand – its nails were long and filthy he suddenly noticed – wrapped itself around one of the rusted bars and ripped it clean out of the wall.

Rom lay on the snow-covered ground and peered into the darkness of the tunnel. He could see nothing, but musty, cold air wafted past his face. If it had originally been part of the air-shafts that honeycombed Baddalaur, then it ran directly into the lower cellars of the College.

The Gallowglas smiled grimly. He had his way into the College of Bards. He glanced at his pale-skinned, red-eyed companion – and had no doubt but that she could kill the bard.

Owen the Weapon Master reined his mount and pointed to the distant shape on the skyline. Behind him Tien tZo and Fodla halted their own labouring mounts. With the Lady Lussa rising almost directly overhead, it looked like an image – a faery image of a castle – towers and turrets spiking the night sky.

'Baddalaur,' Owen panted. 'We should be there by dawn.'

The grey void of the Ghost World was bright with shifting, twisting lights, tiny sparkling balls that spun and sizzled against the vaguely damp texture of the place between the planes.

The bard could taste the power, the raw energy that strode through the Ghost World. The expanse, which was usually inhabited by the shadowy essences of those who slept in the myriad

259

Worlds of Men, was empty, and the bard guessed that there would be many nightmares in the World of the Humankind that night.

He turned around and looked back, seeing his own body lying on the simple bed in the tower in the College of Bards. It was possible for him to bring his physical body through into the Ghost World, but it took energy and power, and Paedur knew he would need all his power to survive this encounter with the Trialdone.

If they attacked him, taking him by surprise, there was no way he could survive, so he would have to carry the fight to them. Willing himself higher, the bard moved straight up through the shifting grey mass, which allowed him an overview of the patterns of power and light that were forming and reforming in its misty heart.

The bard spotted several areas of power in the Ghost World below, but there were three distinct spots that were positioned close together, and all of them tinged with the vaguely reddish-black glow of the Religion.

The bard drifted lower . . .

The Trialdone had created a garden for themselves out of the stuff of the Ghost World. A simple garden of stunted trees and low shrubs, surrounding a green-scummed pond whose waters were solid with the detritus of the forest. Vaguely wondering why they had expended energy in the creation of the image, the bard stepped onto the rotten mulch. By accepting the creation and entering into it, he had also accepted its reality. Now the trees, the bushes, the foul weeds, the odours of wood and rot, the bitter-sweet smell of putrification were all real.

Paedur waited patiently, his senses alert, watching, listening.

There was no sound in this creation, no birds sang in the trees, nothing moved through the undergrowth. It might look like a forest dell, but it was still a dead place.

And then there was a scream.

High-pitched and agonised, it echoed through the creation. A cold knot settled in the bard's stomach, for the scream had been familiar, hauntingly familiar. Although he knew it was a trap, the sound drew him. Ducking beneath an overhanging branch, he set off through the trees towards the sound. The Gods alone

260

knew what the Trialdone had brought into the Ghost World, but whatever it was, it was obviously something the bard knew.

The trees ended abruptly and across a small almost circular clearing he spotted the cell, a simple construction of stone, daubed with mud, and then – suddenly, terrifyingly – he realised where he was. He was back in the Forest of Euarthe, back where it had all started, back where Mannam had first come for him.

The scream rent the fetid air once again – and then he knew why it had been so familiar. He was hearing his own voice.

His first thoughts were to blast the cell, call down his power and unleash it in a levin bolt that would rip through the stone cell and whatever – or whoever – lurked inside.

But his own voice? Why his own voice? And this was no magical imitation, he knew that much. This was the voice of Paedur the Bard.

Touching the knife in his boot, a weapon he had not used for a long time, he crossed the clearing in four quick strides. He called upon his enhanced senses just before he burst through the opening. There were three of power and one of humankind within . . .

In the still quiet hour before the dawn, Bastion and Ironwinter came upon the Chopt army. They immediately realised that their intelligence reports had been wrong on two accounts – it was far larger than they had suspected, and it was also far closer to Baddalaur!

The Chopt and the Marked Man lay in the snow and looked down over the edge of the bluff onto an army that stretched almost as far as the eye could see. It was a huge chaotic mess, with absolutely no order or pattern to it – but this, combined with its size, only rendered it more intimidating. Abruptly, both Bastion and Ironwinter had absolutely no doubts that this army could indeed take and destroy Baddalaur.

'Where would you expect to find Stonehand's camp?' Bastion hissed.

The Chopt shrugged. 'It could be anywhere.'

Bastion ground his teeth in frustration. Time was against them; they needed to find the king's tent now.

Ironwinter suddenly pointed. 'There; that tent is not unlike the king's tent, and it is alongside other tents of quality. That one is certainly of Torc Allta design, and that one off to the left is Gallowglas, I'm sure of it.'

Bastion followed the Chopt's pointing arm, and slowly nodded in agreement – but the king's tent was on the other side of the camp. To reach it they would have to walk right through the huge army.

But moving through the army proved to be surprisingly easy. There was such a racial mixture of humankind, the various Chopt tribes, as well as Torc Allta and Gallowglas, that no-one paid any attention to the cowled man and the Chopt as they made their way through the churned mud and slush towards the tents of the leaders.

As they drew near the tents, they separated. Their plan was simple; Ironwinter would walk past the guards and into the tent while Bastion would attempt to gain entry through the rear. They would take Mannam first; both man and beast were carrying small pots of Luid-dust and oil. They would break the pots on Mannam and then push him into the fire . . . after that their plan got hazy.

'You! You're Ironwinter!' One of the Chopts standing guard before the tent suddenly shouted, fumbling with his trident.

Ironwinter hit the beast just below the snout, shattering the jaw bone, teeth and neck in one blow. Continuing to move, he smashed the hilt of his knife up between the second guard's eyes, sending him crashing back into the tent . . .

Time slowed . . .

Ironwinter raced into the tent, and found himself facing a huge Torc Allta. His knife lifted, slashed, slashed again and the Torc Allta was down, his throat open from ear to ear. Behind him, but seated at a table was another of the Boar-Folk, the one called Fenar, and beside him sat Stonehand and Geillard. Mannam stood behind the Chopt king.

Ignoring the others, Ironwinter grabbed the pot of Luid-dust and oil from his belt and threw it left-handed at the once-god. It fell short and shattered on the ground, soaking his feet. The

Chopt smelt the sweet sharp scent of the oil and then the Torc Allta was before him, his left arm extended – and Ironwinter felt the pain in his chest then . . .

Time slowed . . .

Dimly he saw the back of the tent split apart and Bastion's scarred face appear behind Mannam. He saw the man's arm go up and fall . . . dimly heard the breaking of the pot, distantly smelt the oil . . .

The pain became agony as the Torc Allta ripped the sword from his chest and turned, and in the last few heartbeats of clarity that remained to him, he saw the spark – and felt the heat and clearly heard the explosion. His eyes fluttered, and his last image was of the once-god burning in a solid pillar of flame.

Time stopped.

The pillar of flame sliced through the night sky, a roaring crackling, thunderous column that looked curiously like a huge tree. And Katani, standing alone in the tower in Baddalaur, bent her head and wept for the first time ever. Her wish was that her companions' passing had been swift and painless.

The blast that destroyed Mannam, badly burned Stonehand and Geillard, but curiously both Bastion and Fenar were barely scorched. Both man and beast had been thrown clear by the explosion, and later, when Bastion was brought before the Torc Allta, their conversation had been brief and civilised.

'I admire bravery,' Fenar na Torc Allta said, blinking at the Marked Man through singed eyes, his hands rubbing at flame-yellowed tusks. 'But I deplore stupidity.'

'The line between the two is very fine,' Bastion said very softly. All his wounds had opened and he was in great pain.

'What did you hope to gain?'

Bastion shrugged and then winced as torn flesh and muscles protested. 'Ultimately a little time, I think. We had some plan about releasing Stonehand from Mannam's spell, but it was a vague, formless plan. We knew if we slew Mannam, we would have struck a great blow for our cause.'

'You have seen the size of our army; how can you doubt that we will succeed?' Fenar asked.

'But you have seen what two determined men can do. And you are facing a host of determined men.'

'I still think you will lose.'

'So do I,' Bastion agreed, very quietly.

Fenar stood. 'Because you are a brave man, I will do you the honour of killing you myself, and your meat will honour my table.'

Bastion bowed to hide his smile – and Fenar na Torc Allta took off his head with a single blow of his sword.

Later, the leaders of the Torc Allta were joined by the Gallowglas leaders as well as some of the elders of the Chopts, to enjoy the flesh of the would-be assassin. The meat – served raw or cooked according to taste – was consumed with all the ceremony and respect due to a brave man.

Later still, the guards standing outside the tent would investigate the curious silence within. They would find the diners dead – all dead; they had been poisoned by the meat. Bastion had been a walking dead man for far too long; his flesh had been rotten.

Within the stone cell, the Trialdone were torturing the figure of a man. Ghede had wrapped his beast-like arms around his body, while the Lady Asherat held the figure's left arm out from his body. Her eyes were bright, even in the darkness, and her tongue was like a serpent's, flicking wetly across her lips. Sheesarak the Destroyer stood before the figure, both his hands closed tightly around the man's wrist. He twisted – and the man threw back his head and screamed again . . .

. . . And the face and body were those of Paedur the bard . . .

There was a sickening crack and blood splashed across the trio. Sheesarak lifted his hands; he was holding a curved runeetched silver hook, tendrils of flesh and muscle still attached to the end.

Even as he attacked, Paedur knew what they were doing. He could feel the agony already beginning low in his left arm, just above where his hook joined the bone of his wrist. They had created a simulacrum – a likeness – and by destroying it, they were hoping to destroy him. Indeed, they would destroy him unless . . .

His hook opened the copper-colour flesh of Sheesarak's back from shoulder to base of spine, and as the god spun around, the bard's hook cut at his face, opening a second wound from jaw to eye, sending him reeling away, his face a mask of reddish-blue blood.

Paedur continued moving, his hook punching into Ghede's shoulder, sinking into the flesh, twisting, tearing away a huge chunk of muscle . . .

And then the Lady Asherat was behind him. Her hair wrapped itself around him like coiled ropes, sliding off his cloak, the fur sizzling. It touched his flesh – and burned red weals into the skin. He felt her long nails sinking to her fingertips into the flesh of his back, and knew if she closed her hands, she would literally tear away gobbets of flesh. He reversed the knife in his right hand, striking backwards blindly, feeling the blade meet brief resistance and then sink home. Her grip on his flesh loosened. He turned the knife in the wound, wrenching it upwards . . . and then dropped to the floor as Ghede lurched for him. He slashed at the creature's face as he went down, sending him stumbling into the Lady Asherat. Her hair – like a nest of serpents – coiled around the Trialdone's bare flesh, hissing, sizzling, burning through to the bone. Strands touched his eyes, his mouth . . . panicking, the huge beast struck at her, its great claws battering the fine features, cracking her skull. Her blade-like fingernails sank into his chest just below his heart . . .

The bard used the opportunity to open both their throats with his hook.

Now only the Destroyer remained.

Tien spotted the disturbance in the snow in the pale dawn light. 'This way. Here!' He reined in his mount and dropped from the saddle, examining the marks around the opening in the outcropping of stone. Owen and Fodla remained on their mounts, watching him, not wishing to disturb the ground with their own tracks.

265

'A man, tall, heavy, armoured ... and a woman, small light, bare-footed. Together they pulled this grille from the wall and went inside ...' He stood and looked towards the College. 'It leads to Baddalaur.'

Owen and Fodla both dropped from their saddles. Without a word, they followed Tien into the tunnel.

There were people everywhere.

It took the Gallowglas a few moments to realise what had happened; the townspeople had been taken into the College, which meant that there were several floors and the Gods alone knew how many people between him and the bard.

Rom stepped back into the cellar and pulled the door closed, wedging it shut with a length of wood. The vampir stood on the stairs behind him, her pale face and red eyes masklike in the vague light that filtered down to the disused cellar. He was unsure how much the vampir understood, so he kept his commands simple and direct. 'There are people outside. Many people. Too many to kill. We must have a distraction – something that will draw the people away from here. Do you know where the bard is now?'

The creature's face remained expressionless but she nodded once.

'Are you sure?'

Again the single nod. And then the vampir pointed, her arm raising up, her fingers curling, pointing with index and little finger.

Rom nodded. He lifted his long two-handed sword which was as tall as he, and pulled it slowly and lovingly from its leather sheath. He dropped the sheath – he wouldn't be needing it again – and pulled off his cloak so as to leave his arms unencumbered. He was going out to die – but he would take many of the enemy with him. Death held no fears for him – the Lady Esse had promised to return him to this world when the Religion's Gods had triumphed. And what honour would be his then? He would have been instrumental in the destruction of the ultimate symbol of the Faith – the cursed bard, Paedur.

He looked at the vampir for a final time. 'I will draw the enemy away from here. You must kill the bard. Do not fail us now!'

And the Gallowglas stepped out into the crowded hall . . .

Three bards were standing directly in front of the door, talking to a baker from the town. They had almost convinced the man to assist in the College kitchens when his eyes suddenly widened in shock as he looked past them. They turned slowly, curiously – and the Gallowglas's huge blade scythed through the three of them. The Gallowglas allowed the terrified man to scream once before he killed him also.

There was a single shocked moment of silence and immobility, and then everyone turned and fled down the corridor, while the Gallowglas stood and laughed.

Rom strode down the hall, using his huge sword selectively, killing some, wounding others. He favoured those wearing the colours of the College. He always allowed them to scream before killing them, smiling as their cries brought others to the corridor, to his sword.

He glanced behind only once, and that was to see the vampir dart out of the dark cellar opening and move swiftly and silently in the opposite direction.

Time, all he needed now was time. Time to allow the vampir to slay the bard.

'Vampir,' Tien breathed, throwing back his head and breathing in the dry atmosphere of the tunnel.

'What?' Fodla demanded.

'I can smell vampir on the air; can you not smell it?'

The Commander of the Legion breathed deeply, and then nodded. 'Blood and dead meat.'

'The bard!' Owen snapped. 'It must be after the bard.'

'But who is with the creature?' Fodla asked. 'You said there were two . . .'

'A large, heavy man . . .' Tien mused.

'Gallowglas – the Lady Esse's guard,' Owen said quickly. 'We've got to get to the bard.'

Katani was standing in the tower, looking out over the walls, watching the line of the Chopt army march across the snow-fields when she heard the screams from below. She looked down in time to see a huge warrior, wielding a sword as tall as himself, come marching out into the courtyard, wreaking slaughter. She saw guards running at him – only to be cut down by the fearsome sword.

She turned and looked into the room behind her where the bard still slept, wondering what to do. He had left instructions that on no account – no matter what happened – was he to be disturbed. His breathing was rapid, his long thin hair was plastered to his head and his pale face was sheened in sweat. Beneath his closed eyelids, his eyes were darting.

Another chorus of screams brought her back to the parapet, but still she lingered a moment longer, loath to leave the bard's side. Was this just a single warrior on a suicide mission, or had more of the Gallowglas managed to breach the College's defences? But if there were more, well, then, where were they? Convinced that this was a single warrior, she turned and raced down the stairs to do battle with it – and ran headlong into the vampir!

The vampir screamed – a blood-chilling sound that was designed to freeze its victims immobile – but the sound was cut short as Katani's gauntleted fists closed around its throat. Off-balance, the vampir staggered backwards and then fell, dragging the warrior down the stairs with her. Even as they were falling, bouncing off the stone steps, crashing into the walls, the vampir's fangs were slashing at Katani, rasping along her link-mail and her fists were hammering at the Katan's body armour. All Katani could do was to hold on, her hands locked around the creature's throat, blanking her mind to the agony of snapping bones and torn flesh, concentrating on the creature in her hands, forcing the head back, her thumbs in the soft flesh of the jaw, pressing . . .

It was two hundred and twenty steps to the bottom of the tower . . .

They burst out of the tunnel following the screams. In the corridor they found the first of the bodies and it was then a simple matter of following the trail of death and destruction.

They found the Gallowglas standing in the centre of the courtyard, surrounded by the dead and dying. The huge warrior was splashed with blood, but none of it seemed to be his. He turned slowly towards the three – now the only people moving in the courtyard – and his eyes brightened.

'The Weapon Master and Kutor's Commander. I am pleased that I warrant such attention. Will you come at me together, or will you do me honour in single combat?'

'Kill him now,' Tien advised, 'a thrown knife . . .'

Owen stepped forward. 'Single combat.' He glanced back over his shoulder at Tien and Fodla. 'Find the bard,' he said, 'I'll take care of this.' He was slowly walking across the courtyard to the Gallowglas when the huge warrior attacked. For all his size, and the weight of his sword he moved surprisingly swiftly, using the longsword as if it weighed no more than a knife.

Even though he was unprepared for the sudden assault, Owen was already moving as the sword came whistling in, but the blade still caught him low on the side, the blow cracking his armour, but not cutting through to the skin, spinning him away, half a dozen ribs cracked or broken. Ignoring the wounded man, the Gallowglas advanced on Fodla, his sword scything from side to side, its length giving him a decided advantage.

Fodla attacked with two swords, wielding them in a blinding intricate pattern, a move designed to confuse – but the Gallowglas's longsword simply swept through them both, shattering one and spinning the second from her grasp, snapping her wrist in the process.

Tien's thrown axe took the creature through the throat, stopping it in its tracks, and then the small Shemmat was alongside it, his knife licking out, slicing tendons and muscles, bringing the creature to its knees. In a last desperate movement Rom struck out blindly, the flat of his sword striking Fodla across her left knee, shattering it. And then Tien killed him.

A rib had punctured Owen's lung and he was spitting blood. 'Find the bard,' he hissed desperately.

And then from beyond the walls came the distant, but distinct savage howling of the Chopt army.

Tien found Katani first. She was lying at the bottom of the stairs that led to the highest tower in the College; she was unmoving and her legs were twisted at awkward angles. And it was only when he knelt beside her that he discovered that she was lying on top of a bloody rag that had once been a woman . . . a vampir, he corrected himself, seeing the creature's teeth. The Katan's hands were still locked around the creature's throat, but the top of its head was missing, where it had repeatedly struck the stones on the way down.

Tien gently touched Katani, brushing strands of her white hair from her face – and her amber eyes snapped open!

'Vampir,' her mouth formed the word.

'I know.' Tien nodded. 'The bard?'

Katani's eyes moved upwards. 'He . . . he does battle with the Trialdone . . . he cannot be woken . . .'

'The Chopts are close.'

Katani's mouth worked, and blood began to trickle from her lips. 'My belt pouch . . .'

Tien carefully, gently, lifted the woman's broken body and pulled off her belt pouch. Inside he found an ivory tube. It was cracked now and inside he could see a sheaf of ancient parchment.

Katani nodded when he showed it to her. 'The bard gave it to me. Carry me to the battlements . . .' She saw the hesitation in his eyes. 'Do it!'

Tien nodded and began to unbuckle Katani's weapons and heavier armour. It looked as if she had broken every bone in her body; there was surprisingly little blood, but she would be bleeding inside, he knew. She was surprisingly light when he lifted her and she made no sound, although he knew she must be in agony. 'The bard?' he asked.

'The bard fights his own battle. He is beyond our help, and we beyond his.'

Sheesarak the Destroyer touched his face with his right hand, his fingers coming away sticky with his own blood. The bard's hook had opened a wound from the point of his jaw to just below his left eye. A fraction to the right and he would have lost the eye. He could also feel his blood trickling down his back where the bard had first slashed him. 'You have wounded me,' he said, his voice astonished.

'Have you never been cut before?' Paedur asked, concentrating intently on the god, unwilling even to devote a fraction of his power to heal the wounds in his back from the Lady Asherat's claws. He remembered then that when she had walked the World of Men, she had slain women – always young, always virginal – using her nails, and then had bathed in their blood in an attempt to retain her youth. He wondered vaguely if her nails had been poisoned.

'I will cut you, bard,' Sheesarak lifted the simulacrum's hook in his right hand. It was identical to the bard's, even down to the runes etched in the metal; in every respect it was the bard's hook. The Trialdone had obviously prepared their creature very carefully indeed; the closer it resembled its victim the more effective the magic – and this one looked identical! 'What will happen if I cut you with your own hook, eh?'

'It is not my hook,' Paedur said, glancing into the shadows behind the god to where the figure of the simulacrum sat rocking slowly to and fro, cradling its wrist.

The god smiled, exposing his long red teeth, and his voice regained some of its echoing quality. 'Oh, but it is, bard. This is no simulacrum ... this is no mud doll, no golem, no magical construct. This is Paedur the Bard!' The god stepped back and sank his long fingers into the creature's hair and pulled him to his feet, dragging him forward.

'Look – judge for yourself!'

And the bard found himself looking into his own long, thin face. There were differences of course. The simulacrum's face was slightly plumper, the eyes were dark, the mouth not so cruel, but it was still unmistakably his face.

'This is how you might have been, bard. This is you had you not accepted Mannam's quest. We plucked this bard from one of

271

the closer Planes of Existence, indeed, one so close that it almost mirrors this one, but with minor – very minor – differences, of course. On that other plane, the bard Paedur didn't accept Mannam's quest, and the train of events that were set in motion then which lead up to this present situation, never occurred. On that neighbouring Plane of Existence, this creature, this shadow-you, is aware of your activities only as nightmares.' Blood trickled into the god's mouth, making him grimace. 'But do you know, bard, he is inextricably linked to you . . .' Slowly, the god drew the hook in his hand up along the man's back, opening the flesh in a huge wound . . .

And both the bard and the man screamed!

'You see, bard, you are linked. And if he dies, then so do you.'

Paedur rubbed a shaking hand across his face. He tasted salt. 'But you removed the hook, and I felt only the vaguest discomfort.'

Sheesarak shrugged, and then winced as the pain of his back wound bit through him. 'The hook is a magical construct, and not truly part of you.' He cut the man again and again, and each time Paedur felt the wounds. He moved his right hand around and felt the blood on his back.

'Oh, yes,' the Trialdone continued, 'you will bleed. And you will die.' The god laughed, the sound rising to boom around the small stone cell. 'Do you know what is happening on the World of Men, bard? Even now the Chopt are preparing to attack the College of Bards; your servants are all wounded or dying. We have won, bard.' He raised the hook high, and then brought it down and around, resting it against the man's throat. 'It is time to die . . .'

Paedur moved. Calling down his power, he lunged forward, his left arm extended, his hook punching through the man in the god's arms, sundering the heart, bursting through his back – and then plunging into Sheesarak's heart! The god's howl sundered the fabric of the Ghost World, catapulting the three figures into the grey void. The hook in the god's hand rose and fell spasmodically – striking Paedur at the base of the skull, plunging deep into the spine! With his strength flowing out of him, Paedur drifted away from the god, one arm locked around the man Paedur, the other still buried in his chest . . .

The Chopts flowed across the plain in a vast undulating wave, the howls and cries suddenly joined by the throbbing of giant war drums from the south; the Lady Esse and her forces had arrived.

Luid-dust destroyed the gates of Badaur, and then the army – of humankind, Gallowglas, Torc Allta and Chopts – swarmed through the town. Many died in the traps that Katani, Bastion and Ironwinter had laid, plunging into cellars set with spikes, opening booby-trapped doors, dying beneath hails of poisoned darts, setting off explosions. But the booby traps were finite in number, whereas the army seemed infinite.

Baddalaur's defenders – and they seemed pitifully few – lined the walls and attempted to keep the attackers away from the gates. The Chopts launched attack after attack, firing casks and satchels of Luid-dust against the huge iron-studded doors. Many fell short, but enough struck home or fell close enough to coat the base of the door and the ground around it in a fine layer of brown dust.

Now it was only a matter of time – a very short time – before it was set alight and the doors were breached. And when that happened it would all be over.

Katani appeared on the battlements directly above the gates. Tien stood behind her, physically holding her upright. With numb and broken fingers she pulled the single sheet of parchment from the ivory tube and unfolded it.

The words swam before her eyes, moving, twisting, changing symbols – until suddenly they were in a language she understood – Ko-eche, the dead language of the Katan Warriors. As she looked down the words, she felt a slow strength burn into her fingers and down through her body, and Tien suddenly felt the woman straighten and stand tall and erect – although both her legs were broken.

And Katani began to recite the Lament of Lugas.

Her first words were lost in the roar of battle – and then her voice suddenly gained in power – until it was booming across the

273

ice-fields. The noise, the roars, cries and screams all died, as everyone – man and beast – stopped, somehow compelled to listen to the ancient magical Lament.

But the Lament of Lugas had been created by the Old High Magic, and that magic drew its energy directly from its user. The flames began. Tiny at first, they lapped blue-white around Katani's feet, like miniature waves. But the heat was intense, strong enough to drive Tien back.

The Katan's voice thundered out, the sound high and eerie, the magical symbols woven into the words soothing, calming, dulling battle-incensed men and beasts. Weapons dropped from numbed fingers as, enwrapped in the spell, they all watched the slight figure on the battlements, seeing the blue flames wrap themselves around her and grow higher.

The Katan was burning, the intense heat melting away her mail shirt, turning the metal to liquid. The pain ate through the euphoria that had taken her and her voice faltered . . .

. . . And the Lament was taken up by a second voice, a strong, powerful trained voice.

Paedur the Bard gently lifted Katani out of the flames and handed her to Tien, and he took the scroll of parchment into his right hand. His eyes – no longer reflective now, merely dark and pained – looked across the courtyard and lingered briefly on Fodla and Owen, and then he turned back to the confused army. He took up the Lament again, reciting it without looking at the scroll, and the flames of the Old High Magic rose higher, consuming him, drawing its energy from him, sending it out into the massed armies below.

And the army turned away, single men at first, and then in greater and greater numbers, the men and beasts wandered away, each one wrapped up within his own thoughts, their task forgotten, hatred and enmities wiped clean by the Lament of Lugas.

The blue flames flared higher into a magnificent leaf shape – and then vanished. There was no sign of Paedur the Bard.

It was later, much, much later, that Tien tZo remembered that the man who had lifted Katani out of the flames and continued the Lament of Lugas had no hook . . .

Epilogue

So the wheel turned.

The Lament of Lugas, the Dove's Cry, that had set the bard out on his quest, now finished it. Lugas the Bard had invested the Lament with the last of the Old High Magic, imbuing it with the power to quieten even the most maddened of warriors. Even as the last words were hanging on the air, the army was disbanding, all thoughts of battle forgotten. And those who heard the Lament were never the same again.

When Kutor and his army rode into Baddalaur two days later, they found the fields deserted, the bodies of the dead smouldering on a huge funeral pyre. The dead included the remains of an old woman who had been found in one of the deserted wagons of the renegade army. Her corpse had been in an advanced state of decay and identification was impossible, but it was speculated that she had been the Lady Esse, perhaps slain by the power of the High Magic.

With the sudden loss of their followers, the Gods of the New Religion suffered a crushing defeat on the chequered fields of Ab-Apsalom, and when Kutor instituted the Faith as the official religion of his Empire, he effectively ended any real threat by the Religion. His reign was long and remarkably peaceful. Many said he had the blessing of the Gods.

Fodla and Owen recovered from their wounds and were eventually wed – much to everyone's surprise, even their own.

Tien requested and was given his freedom by Owen and joined the Order of Bards. He created a huge body of work, including the definitive biographies of both the Bard and the Weapon Master.

Gire went on to re-establish the Order of Ectoraige. He dedicated it not only to teaching but also to medicine and healing. Geillard, who never recovered from the burns he received when Mannam was destroyed, was one of his long-term patients.

Towards the end of his life the old man embraced the Faith, and he is buried in the grounds of the Monastery.

The Katan Warrior never fully recovered from her wounds. Her broken bones never set properly and her mind had been disturbed by the Old High Magic that fed off her essence. She never fought again, and one night she simply walked out of Karfondal and disappeared.

Katani was never seen again, although rumour and later legend placed her in the Northlands in the company of a tall dark-eyed man with one hand . . .

Life of Paedur, the Bard